# Beyond Scandal

"I must have been crazy to stay away for four years," he muttered. "What the hell was wrong with me?"

She was frozen as Dom kneaded her arms, pulling her even closer. Her breasts brushed against his chest. "I promised myself something," he said, his eyes glittering, "but I cannot keep it. I would be truly mad to."

"No." Anne found her voice. "What are you doing?"

"Kissing you," he said flatly. His arms went around her. His mouth covered hers.

Anne's pulse rioted. Her mind went blank. It had been so long. The desire that crested in her so suddenly, so uncontrollably, became explosive. Hot, liquid, fiery. She moaned against his lips.

# BRENDA JOYCE

# Beyond Scandal

**AVON BOOKS**
*An Imprint of HarperCollinsPublishers*

This is a work of fiction. Names, characters, places, and incidents are products of the author's imagination or are used fictitiously and are not to be construed as real. Any resemblance to actual events, locales, organizations, or persons, living or dead, is entirely coincidental.

AVON BOOKS
*An Imprint of* HarperCollins*Publishers*
10 East 53rd Street
New York, New York 10022-5299

Copyright © 1995 by Brenda Joyce
ISBN-13: 978-0-06-123524-5
ISBN-10: 0-06-123524-5
**www.avonbooks.com**

First Avon Books special printing: August 2006
First Avon Books paperback printing: October 1995

Avon Trademark Reg. U.S. Pat. Off. and in Other Countries, Marca Registrada, Hecho en U.S.A.
HarperCollins® is a registered trademark of HarperCollins Publishers Inc.

Printed in the U.S.A.

10 9 8 7 6 5 4 3 2 1

*This book is dedicated to Roberta Stalberg and Judy O'Brien, two new and very special friends who have enriched my life immeasurably—things just wouldn't be the same without you both. I treasure your friendship. Thank you.*

*Also a very special thank you to my new editor, Carrie Feron, for everything.*

# Prologue

*Essex, England—1852*

$\mathcal{T}$his, surely, must be the most miserable day of her life. Anne tried to shut out the sounds of her cousin's happy chattering as Felicity dressed for her engagement party. Although her betrothal to the Viscount Lyons would only be announced that night, the whole county and half of London already knew about the news. Anne wished she didn't know and that she were anywhere but in her cousin's bedroom. She had asked to go to her own chamber, a small, dark room which she hated, but her aunt had refused, insisting that they needed Anne's help to prepare Felicity for the second most important evening of *her* life.

But they had not needed Anne's help yet, because Edna's French maid was handling everything. Anne watched as Felicity's waist was cinched so tightly that she lost two inches. She had never been envious of Felicity before, but now she stared at her full breasts and round hips and almost hated her for being so utterly feminine and so utterly beautiful. Anne had felt small and dark and plain before, but today she felt ugly, unloved, and terribly alone.

Anne squeezed her eyes shut. Felicity didn't guess that her every happy word was like a blade to Anne's

1

heart. Anne had loved Dominick St. Georges for more years than she could count. She had never tried to hide her feelings from anyone, but her aunt, uncle, and cousins all had been tolerantly amused or openly skeptical of Anne's certainty that one day Dom would not only notice her, but marry her as well. But she could fall off her horse at his feet, she thought in anguish, as Felicity had done, and he would not even notice her then.

Anne's heart felt as if it might burst. If only Felicity would stop going on and on about how handsome and rich Dom St. Georges was. "Oh, Mama," Felicity gushed for the hundredth time, "I am so incredibly happy and so very excited!"

"As you should be, catching such a man," Edna Collins said bluntly. "Thank God the duke and the marquis summoned him home and ordered him to marry. To think that, had another day gone by, you might have already been plighted to Lord Harold Reed."

Felicity was the youngest of Edna's five children and her only daughter. She had come out four years ago, and since then had a dozen offers of marriage. She had rejected them all. Anne had listened to numerous family debates about whom Felicity should choose and one and all had agreed that she must wed this year. Everyone had decided that she should accept Lord Reed, an older but very wealthy baron. Then Dom had come courting, and all other prospects had immediately been forgotten.

Anne swallowed, hard. She had not come out, not because she was only seventeen, and not because her aunt and uncle would never lavish the money necessary for a come-out, but because Anne loved Dom far too much to ever seek to marry anyone else.

She would remain a spinster for the rest of her days. Oh, God. And would she continue to love Dom, forever, even though he was her cousin's husband? Anne quickly wiped away seeping tears, before Edna or Felicity might see.

The French maid gave Anne a small, sympathetic glance.

But Edna did not notice, involved as she was now with her daughter. "You behave yourself and be a good wife to him and you won't lack for a thing. You put up with all of his ways, be they good or bad," she warned.

But Felicity, blond, beautiful, and blue-eyed, laughed almost slyly. "I know all about Dom St. Georges's reputation, Mama. I know he has the most beautiful women in the world, and that he loves his racehorses far more than them, too. Do you think me a fool? I know how to be a lady, Mama. But surely I shouldn't be too ladylike. I won't have Dom running off to his mistress right after our wedding night! Nor will I have him fonder of a horse than me!"

Edna made a rough sound that might have been approval. "But if he does keep his mistress, or prefer his horses, you just ignore it."

"I am up to the task of taming the reclusive and coldhearted Viscount Lyons," Felicity laughed. Then her blue eyes gleamed. "I most certainly will not lose sight of the fact that one day I will be the marchioness of Waverly, and later the duchess of Rutherford!"

Anne could take it no more. In her mind's eye she saw Dom, golden-haired and bronzed, smiling warmly at Felicity, his single dimple digging deep in his right cheek. She leapt to her feet, rushing across the length of soft blue Persian rug and past the frothy white bed to the oak door.

"Anne! Just where do you think you are going?" Edna called sharply. "Come back here right now, young lady."

But for the first time in her life, Anne ignored her

formidable aunt. She rushed from the room, holding on
to her last bit of pride.

Anne stood alone by the wall in the ballroom of
Waverly Hall, the primary residence of Dom's father,
the marquis of Waverly, Philip St. Georges. She stared
across the crowd to where the St. Georges family stood
with her aunt and uncle and her cousins on the threshold of the ballroom. Her gaze remained helplessly riveted on Dom St. Georges.

Clad in a black tailcoat and black trousers with a
satin seam, the sapphire studs on his snowy white shirt
catching the light from the five huge chandeliers overhead, he was a magnificent sight. He was the most
beautiful man she had ever seen, his features straight
and even and almost too perfect, but it was his incredible St. Georges coloring which so arrested everyone:
the golden skin, the topaz eyes, the thick, gold-streaked
brown hair. Anne, however, had always been overwhelm-
ingly drawn to his eyes. Golden, mesmerizing, and hinting
at secrets and, perhaps, tragedy, his eyes called to her
the way a siren did to lost sailors at sea. They were
the eyes of a lonely man.

Now he stood beside Felicity, who was ravishing and
voluptuous in a pale blue evening gown. She glowed,
but he merely nodded or gave a polite smile to the
constant stream of guests who paused to congratulate
him and his bride. But then he was not a demonstrative man.

Felicity, however, was beaming, laughing, and clinging to him. Anne had never seen her behave so shame-
lessly before. Dom remained attentive, yet somehow,
he also seemed bored.

Their gazes suddenly met from opposite points across
the room. Dom quickly looked away, but Anne did not.

This was not the first time that night that their
glances had connected so precipitously and inexplica-

bly. Tonight he had finally noticed her. Yet she could not think why. Her cheeks were pale, her expression lifeless, but her eyes were pink and swollen, the tip of her nose red. And she wore a plain and childish gown, one of Felicity's hand-me-downs. It was navy blue, but that was not dark enough for Anne—she wished it were black.

He turned his head again and looked right past the vicar and his wife, across the entire length of the parquet floored ballroom, directly at Anne.

Anne did not look away. She lifted her chin. Dom broke eye contact and put his arm around Felicity while speaking with the vicar.

Anne stared. It was a strange moment, but one that meant nothing. The engagement had been announced. Dom had placed a magnificent eight-carat sapphire surrounded by rows and rows of diamonds on Felicity's finger. The crowd had applauded, and when Dom had kissed her cheek, they had cheered as well.

Felicity was whispering in Dom's ear. He had to bend slightly in order for her to do so. Her very bare bosom pressed against his arm. Dom made no effort to move away; his other arm was still around her waist. They were a stunning, ideal couple. Anne turned away abruptly—and crashed into a tall man.

"Whoa," the duke of Rutherford said, reaching out to restrain her. The Rutherford ruby signet ring gleamed on his right hand. "Hello, Anne. Why are you not with your family and mine, receiving the guests?"

She stared up at the duke, a man who had always intimidated her, though he had never been anything other than kind to Anne. But he was one of the wealthiest, most noble and powerful men in the kingdom. Anne swallowed dryly. "I . . ." she thought frantically. "I do not feel very well."

"I see." His golden eyes were kind. "Is there anything I can do?"

Anne's gaze had drifted back to where Dom and Felicity stood, Dom silent, Felicity chatting with some of the local gentry. "No."

The duke followed her gaze. "They make an attractive couple. A pity that they do not suit."

Anne blinked. Surely she had misheard him. "You— do not approve?"

"I am lucky my grandson is finally marrying. And, as he has pointed out, the Collinses are a fine family, their blood is actually bluer than ours, and they are not half as impoverished as the rest of our class. How can I disapprove? Dom is stubborn. He ignored me when I tried to tell him that she could not make him happy."

Anne looked at him closely. How astute the duke was. "But . . . she is so very beautiful."

"Beauty is in the eye of the beholder, my dear. Anne, you are far too pale. Perhaps you need a bit of air?" It was a mild command.

"Yes," Anne gasped gratefully. "That is exactly what I need! Excuse me, Your Grace." She turned away.

As Anne crossed the crowded ballroom, avoiding the guests, she thought she felt Dom's eyes upon her back. She told herself she was imagining it.

Anne had just reached the open French doors which led to the terrace and gardens when a serving maid ran up to her and pressed something into her hand. Anne faltered as the maid fled, realizing she held a folded piece of parchment.

Curious, she moved to the threshold of the terrace and opened it. Her heart slammed to a stop.

The note was from Dom. He wanted her to meet him in the garden.

Anne was shocked, disbelieving. Was this a joke?

The night was warm and sultry. Perhaps later it would rain, but in that moment the sky was bright with a thousand glittering stars and a glowing crescent moon.

Anne quickly crossed the tiled terrace, passing a white marble water fountain, and left the house behind. She paused in the garden, assaulted by the heady fragrance of lilac and wisteria and surrounded by beautiful, rainbow-hued blooms. What did Dom want? He was engaged to Felicity; why did he wish to rendezvous with her?

Anne laid her palm flat on her breast, as if she might ease the crushing pain there. But it did no good.

She did not know how long she stood motionless beside an ancient, full-bodied oak tree, feeling a loss so acute it reminded her of the day she learned of her father's death. The warm summer air caressed her newly dampened cheeks. Anne felt as if she were suffocating from her heartache.

Then she became aware of the sensation of being watched.

Slowly Anne turned around. Dom was a shadowy figure standing on the stone steps of the terrace, the house lit up brilliantly behind him. "D-Dom?"

He stared at her, unmoving.

Anne's heart went wild; disbelief laced her tone. This was not a joke. "D-Dom?"

Something dropped from his hand—a crushed white fragment, a handkerchief, perhaps—as he strode toward her.

Anne could not move. He paused in front of her, his expression strained, intense—unsmiling. Anne's body seemed to sway slightly toward him.

His gaze was so penetrating that Anne thought it pierced to her very soul. "Anne."

He had never addressed her by her name before. Anne failed to reply. She was trembling, wondering what he wanted with her.

"What is wrong, Anne?" he asked.

"I . . . am hiding."

His jaw flexed. "This is a party." His gaze remained

fixed on her face. "Parties are supposed to be amusing."

She bit her lip. "This one isn't."

His gaze was on her mouth now. "No, I guess it isn't—not for you."

Anne froze. Did he know? Had he sensed her thoughts? Could he know that she loved him? That she would die loving him? Anne quickly decided that she was imagining it. "I . . . I wish to offer con-congratulations," she said huskily.

He stared into her eyes again. She could see the pulse beating in his temple. "Do you?"

"Y-yes."

He suddenly jammed both of his hands into his pockets. The movement caused him to shift, and moonlight suddenly played on his sapphire studs. The row of precious gems glinted on his shirtfront. "You are too noble."

Anne inhaled. *He did know.* "No. I . . . am not . . . not at all." She wished she could stop stuttering. But she was so nervous—and the fact that he was staring at her mouth again did not help at all.

"How old are you, Anne?" he asked abruptly.

She licked her lips. "Eighteen," she croaked, lying.

"You look younger. Far younger." He turned his head away, so that she saw only his perfect profile in the shadows.

Anne felt the air leave her chest in a rush. "I'm seventeen," she confessed in a whisper.

His head whipped around, his amber regard piercing. "You are only a child."

"N-no!" Anne stammered. "I am n-not! I am al-almost eighteen, truly!"

"Tonight," he said harshly, "you are seventeen, not eighteen—a child." Suddenly, inexplicably, his expression softened. "This will pass, Anne. I promise you that."

Anne stared into his hypnotic eyes. "No. This will *never* pass."

He stiffened. His gaze slammed to her mouth, then quickly lifted. "Let me take you back inside, now. Before our disappearance together is commented upon."

"Do you love her?" Anne heard herself ask. And then she wanted to kick herself, hard, but she also wanted, desperately, to know.

"No." His hand lifted, was suspended in the air. Then ever so gently, he cupped her cheek.

Anne froze.

He had never touched her before. His touching her cheek was the most exquisite sensation Anne had ever felt. Her eyes drifted closed. She could not stop herself, and her face turned slightly, more fully, into the curve of his warm, callused hand.

"No," Dom said hoarsely, again. "I do not love her." His hand suddenly fisted. Anne's eyes flew open, collided with his. Her breath caught; his eyes glittered in a manner she had never seen before. His knuckles brushed over her jaw. "Love is not, has never been, the issue."

Then his knuckles brushed over her moist, parted lips.

Anne whispered his name.

"Have you ever been kissed, Anne?" he asked roughly. His fist, against her mouth, shook.

Anne shook her head wordlessly.

He stared, his fist pressing against the curve where her neck met her shoulder. And suddenly his hand opened, wrapping around the back of her neck. "Then I have the great honor," he whispered, bending toward her, "of being the first."

Anne waited, unable to smile, quivering with expectation.

He brushed his mouth over hers, barely touching her lips. Anne was disappointed. And then his mouth whispered over hers again, as quickly, as briefly. Anne's hands found his shoulders. He stiffened, his cheek against hers.

And then his mouth opened wide, took hers. Anne cried out.

He crushed her powerfully in his arms. His mouth held hers open, pressing, pulling, sucking on her lips. Anne stopped thinking. She pressed herself into him, against him, gripping him back as tightly as she could, taking every bit of his kiss, every way he offered it. Suddenly his tongue touched hers. As suddenly, it withdrew.

Anne gasped.

He ripped his mouth from hers, panting. "I must take you back," he cried harshly. He tried to push her away.

"No!" Anne raised herself up on tiptoe and caught his mouth wildly with hers.

He froze. But only for a second. As she kissed him, awkwardly, frantically, his arm locked around her waist in an unbreakable grip. And then his mouth was open, hot, moist, devouring hers ... and they tumbled to the grass.

A few moments later, Anne's cries filled the night.

## Chapter 1

*Waverly Hall, 1856*

*I*t was a perfect summer day: warm, sunny, cloudless. Perfect except for one fact. It was the day of the marquis of Waverly's funeral.

His death had been both sudden and unexpected. He had only been fifty years of age, and his health had appeared to be good. And his father was still hale at seventy-four. Then, very suddenly, he had become ill with the influenza. Within days he was dead.

Because Waverly was being buried in the country, only a hundred mourners now gathered at the grave. The local gentry, squires and tenant farmers, rubbed elbows with dukes and earls, and they in turn brushed up against the entire village population of Dulton: bakers, butchers and furniture makers, dairymaids and shepherds. No one had come out of affection for the late marquis. Philip St. Georges had been a reclusive scholar, one who had spent most of his time out of the country journeying to exotic places. Respect brought some. Duty brought everyone. Duty to Waverly—and duty to his father, the duke of Rutherford. Even the queen had sent her regrets.

But one and all murmured about how odd it was, that Philip had specified that he be buried in the country

11

at Waverly Hall, instead of at the mausoleum at Rutherford House with his many illustrious ancestors.

Anne did her best to comfort the duke, who had become her support during the past few years. She slipped her arm around him while he wept for his only child, his only son. And although Anne had never been close to, or even fond of, Philip, she had become fond of his father. His grief became her grief. Her vision blurred as the pallbearers appeared, the coffin on their shoulders.

She had only attended one other funeral in her short life, and that had been her father's, when she was ten years old. Anne remembered far too vividly the pain and anguish and grief. But that funeral had been nothing like this one. Her father had been a drifter and dreamer without means, and she had been completely alone, without any other family, and only a handful of neighbors she did not know had attended the brief, bare ceremony in Boston. No one had come to the grave except for the preacher. Soon after, she left America, never to return.

Anne gripped the duke's arm more tightly, stealing a glance at his ravaged face. She sympathized with him completely, wished to take away his pain, even though she knew she could not. These past four years he had been her dearest friend.

Waverly's wife, now the dowager marchioness, tossed a single white carnation into the grave. Clarisse's face was as pale as the finest ivory, her blue eyes sheened with tears, but she held herself erect. No one approached her to comfort her, no one dared—not even Anne, who wanted to, in spite of their differences.

Dirt began to spill on top of the coffin.

The crowd rippled. Restlessly, or for some other reason? Anne did not care. She had been careful to ignore everyone all day, as they had ignored her for so many years, but because she stood at the duke's side, it had proved impossible. The villagers who had laughed at her and condemned her through the worst period of her life, the gentry who gossiped about her but never came to call upon her, the nobility she had not ever met because she did not dare go to London, not even once, one and all now pressed her hand and murmured their condolences. Almost fascinated, Anne watched each mourner turn to the duke. Their expressions changed. The villagers were anxious, the tenants reverent but nervous, the gentry respectful but still, somehow, cautiously reserved. His own class was respectful yet openly concerned. More than a few of his peers embraced him warmly. Anne felt another surge of sorrow, but not for herself, for him.

The crowd seemed to shift uneasily. Or was it with curiosity? A murmur seemed to follow in its wake. Anne became aware of heads turning. Her gaze turned as well.

And for one instant, she thought her entire world had disintegrated.

On the ridge above the grave, Anne saw the black lacquer coach with the huge silver Lyons crest emblazoned upon its door. Four black horses champed at their bits in the traces. Two coachmen in black-and-silver livery held the reins, and two footmen, similarly uniformed, stood upon the back runner. The door was flung open.

Anne became utterly still. It seemed that even her heart ceased to beat.

And Dominick St. Georges stepped from the coach and paused, silhouetted sharply against the brilliantly blue sky.

Anne began to shake.

His golden head was bare and held high. His broad shoulders seemed impossibly wide, his legs longer than Anne remembered. He was too far away for Anne to discern his expression. But Anne did not have to see his face to recall his every feature. His was a face she would never be able to forget—no matter how much she wished to.

How she hated him.

Because of him, she had suffered for the past four endless years, accepted by no one, condemned as something she was not, considered an outsider, notoriety clinging to her like her very own clothes. Because of him.

And he had not shared her shame.

Anne could not move, she could not breathe. *He had come back.* She had not been sure that he would—not even for his own father's funeral.

Her breathing was jerky now, small, sharp, hurtful little breaths. And she had thought he could not affect her any more, but no, she was wrong. He could still affect her, as much as ever.

Anne told herself that she would be strong now, especially in front of the crowd who had gathered to lay Philip St. Georges to rest. In front of the crowd who had accused her years ago of being an American adventuress. If she appeared shaken or distressed, everyone would think that she still loved him—perhaps he would even think it, too. Anne had learned the hard way how to be strong—it had been a matter of survival.

Heads were turning her way, gazes darting from Dom to herself. Anne could not help but feel a flash of bitter dismay. They had caused a scandal four years ago, but he had not suffered, oh no. She was the one who had been made an object of lewd speculation, a target of stares and whispers—she alone. She was the one who had been grievously betrayed. And now he had dared to come home.

Anne would not have it.

Dominick St. Georges stared down at the somberly dressed crowd standing at the graveside below him. He stared out of wide, shocked eyes, unable to believe what he was seeing.

The horses behind him were blowing, their hides coated with sweat and mud. Dom had been in Paris when his father had fallen ill. News of that illness had reached him two days ago. Dom had left France immediately. He had been traveling hard for two days and two nights.

But the missive had not said that his father might die.

Dom felt dizzy. Disbelief overwhelmed him. The gentlemen in their black frock coats and hats, the women in black bombazine. The minister, standing over the open grave. *Good god, the marquis was dead.*

His father was dead.

Dom reeled. He was aware of someone coming up behind him—his valet, Verig. "My lord, sir," the small blond man said.

"Leave me," Dom said hoarsely.

Verig returned to the coach, his expression one of grave worry.

Dom had not been home in four years. Tears suddenly filled his eyes—and he was not an emotional man. He suddenly cursed himself for staying away, for everything—for not even knowing his own father.

He could not even claim to have loved Philip. He had been raised by nannies and tutors. He had seen his father every day for a precise ten-minute interval just before supper, but only to be interviewed about his studies, and only when his father was in residence at Waverly Hall, which was rarely. His father had been a scholar of antiquities who loved to travel. He had been abroad most of the year.

And Dom had gone away to Eton on his twelfth birthday, and from that moment, he came home as rarely as his father. Sometime just before Eton, or perhaps just afterward, he had become as indifferent to Philip St. Georges as Philip was toward him.

They were father and son. But they had not had any kind of relationship.

Dom did not feel indifferent today, though.

He rubbed his stubbled jaw with his hand. He felt ill, enough so to vomit, but fortunately he had not eaten anything since last night. How could this have happened? How could Philip have died? He had only been fifty years of age. He had been slim and fit, he had never suffered much illness during his lifetime, even though he had traveled so often to places as disease-ridden as Bombay.

With an effort, Dom moved his legs and walked to the very edge of the ridge. He stared down at the mourners.

Now he would never know his own father.

Dom did not have to search his memory to recall their last encounter—on Dom's wedding day. A day Dom avoided thinking about as a hard-and-fast rule— but today was an exception.

*He stood with his father and grandfather on the steps of the small country church in the village of Dulton, greeting the guests—who numbered but two dozen relatives. Still, they were distant relations, already envious of what they did not have, and Dom was the object of numerous stares and whispers. He had already decided to pretend that nothing was wrong. To pretend to be oblivious to the scandal he had created, right there in the heart of Rutherford's estates, right there in his very own home.*

*"Perhaps you might smile, Dominick," Philip suggested under his breath as they began greeting their guests.*

*"What do I have to smile about?"*

*"You created these circumstances yourself," Philip said calmly, ignoring the pointed accusation. "Perhaps you might think to cultivate a conscience, Dominick."*

*Dom's temples throbbed. He already despised him-*

*self. "You will not believe this, but I do have a conscience."*

*Philip's laughter was highly cultivated. "Perhaps you should have heeded it years ago—or at least during your engagement party to Felicity."*

*He inhaled, turning very grim. The pounding in his head increased. "Touché."* They had been careful never to discuss that night—not after he had first been discovered with Anne Stewart in a highly compromising position.

*"Of course, your conscience or lack thereof does not matter to me. You will conduct yourself as you choose— you always have. I do hope, though, that one day, when I am dead, you will behave in a more fitting manner, one appropriate to your station."*

*"I didn't know that you were at all concerned about my behavior," Dom said tersely.*

*"I am not," Philip said. "Except for the fact that you are* my *heir, and all that you do reflects upon me."*

*Dom was silent. What had he expected on his wedding day? A hearty embrace? Some sign of paternal affection—of real caring? "Isn't it a bit late for fatherly advice,* Father?*"*

*"Undoubtedly." Philip's tone was bland.*

The black-clad mourners in the cemetery below Dom suddenly filled his vision, sweeping him from the past. Dom tried to control his trembling. The last time he had seen and spoken with his father, his father had spoken of his own death. How ironic it was.

Dom forced his memories of those last few shared words aside. But the guilt remained, intensifying. And he already had enough guilt—and regret—to last an entire lifetime.

He inhaled deeply, fighting for equilibrium until he found it. His gaze moved over the familiar countryside. It was a warm and sunny summer day. The sky sharply blue, the grass lushly green, and flowers were in bloom everywhere one looked. The terrain was a series of gentle slopes, Waverly Hall a pink-and-white blur just visible in the distance. Several miles behind the Hall, one would find the Channel coast. To the north, the hills rose far more dramatically, laced with hedges and stone walls, dotted with sheep and cows.

Dom's gaze returned to the grave. It appeared obscene. It was a dark, wet, reddish brown hole, and it seemed to Dom very much like an oozing, gaping wound in the fertile countryside. He was not given to prayer—he had stopped believing in God during the war—but the urge to pray overtook him now.

He whispered, "Dear God, rest my father's soul, help him find peace—bless him. Amen."

His gaze blurred thickly. Dom blinked furiously, until he could see. His regard riveted on one of the mourners. Taller by a head than those around him, the duke of Rutherford stood with his white head bowed, his black-clad shoulders shaking, a handkerchief pressed to his mouth. He was weeping visibly.

Dom swallowed. His grandfather had been far more fatherly toward him than his own father had ever been.

The coffin was already in the ground. It was a rich shining mahogany, polished to a high sheen, and wreathed in white carnations. Dom's heart clenched. His mother had made sure the casket was displayed to perfection. She never erred when in the public eye. Sometimes he had sensed that she was afraid of committing some terrible and public mistake. She was always elegant and genteel, gracious and ladylike. He could not fathom how she kept up appearances so, especially now. But he understood why the endeavor was so important to her. Clarisse St. Georges had been born a vicar's daughter, but to look at her now, no one would ever guess.

Had Philip lived, Clarisse St. Georges would have made a graceful duchess one day. Dom strained to see if his mother wept, but, as she wore a full veil, that was impossible. He did not think she would grieve openly. He was not sure she would grieve at all: she and Philip had lived apart for years.

Dom stared fixedly at the casket now being lowered into the grave. Too late, he regretted his soul's empti-ness—he regretted not loving his own father the way a son should. Too late, he regretted the past—all of it.

If only she could forget that one single moment of explosive passion on that long-ago sultry summer night in the gardens behind Waverly Hall.

But she could not forget. Nor would she, ever. Not until she herself died. It had been the culmination of all of her dreams, of her wildest fantasies. That night, Anne had known that he loved her the way that she loved him.

Only to find out two weeks later how horribly wrong—and naive—she herself had been.

Anne realized that she was staring. She had been staring at Dom St. Georges for far too long—while the mourners stared at her.

Anne squeezed her eyes closed, perspiring beneath the many layers of clothing she wore. She reassured herself that he was not intending to stay for very long at Waverly Hall.

She would not allow it.

But Anne could not help herself, and when her eyes opened, her gaze turned straight ahead in the direction she had avoided facing ever since arriving at the ceme-tery. Felicity had chosen to wear a dove gray dress instead of black, and she had never been lovelier. Or was it merely that, after four long years, Anne had failed to recall just how astoundingly beautiful her cousin really was? She was picture-perfect. Her pres-ence made Anne feel shorter, darker, more childish, and far more awkward than she had felt in years.

Anne lifted her chin and held her head high. She was twenty-one. She would never be a child again. Dom had made sure of that. She need not be intimidated or anxious or even afraid now. Felicity would probably return to London soon, too. She hardly ever came to the country. Anne wished them both gone, immediately.

Felicity had also espied Dom and was staring openly at him. It was easy to read the emotions in her eyes. Anne's heart sank. The past became the present with storming force. Felicity still wanted Dom. Anne told herself that it did not matter—that she did not care.

She was trembling now. She felt faint. She wished she were not there, at the graveside. She wished to be anywhere but there. If only Dom had not come home. But Anne was only deluding herself with such thoughts, and she knew it. The truth was that she had been waiting for Dom to return for a very long time. She had been waiting for four years to have her say—and her revenge.

She would *never* forgive him.

Anne's arm was still around the duke and she knew the moment that he espied his disreputable grandson. Rutherford stiffened. In that instant, Anne realized that Dom was wearing a tweed hunting jacket, riding breeches, and muddy Hessian boots. Her eyes widened. Would he never cease to be irreverent—even at his own father's funeral?

"He needs to be brought to heel, Anne," Rutherford said pointedly. As if instructing her that *she* should be the one to take on the impossible task of taming such a man.

Anne felt her cheeks heating at the mere notion. "He needs to be horsewhipped," she snapped. Her trembling was worse—she was actually shaking. "How could he come in such attire? Or is he planning on attending a foxhunt later today?"

The duke reached out and squeezed her hand, very

briefly. "We've got plenty of whips in the stable. Feel free to choose one. If you want, I'll help you." But his tone betrayed his affection for his only grandchild.

Anne did not laugh even though the idea of whipping Dom as one might a very bad boy gave her a twinge of satisfaction. Anne realized that she was hugging herself.

He had come back. Surely he did not think to stay?

After all, four years ago he had left without even the slightest good-bye. Coldly, carelessly, callously. And in all the years since then, he had not bothered to return, not even once. He had not sent her a single message. Not even an apology, which was the least to be expected, even were it insincere.

If he intended to stay, Anne knew she would have a battle on her hands.

Grimly, Anne stole another look at Felicity—and was shocked to find her cousin watching her. Immediately Felicity looked away, but not before Anne had remarked both her excitement and her air of calculation.

Anne's agitation knew no bounds. Dom's return was distressing enough, but clearly Felicity thought to continue matters with Dom where she had last left them four years ago. She began to breathe harder now, watching as the final shovelfuls of dirt covered the grave. The crowd was dispersing, the ladies and gentlemen moving to their waiting carriages, a few men pausing to speak with the duke. Glances continued to be sent her way, though, too, and then at Dom, standing up there on the ridge. Anne knew that they were being talked about. She could not wait. The situation was untenable—impossible. Lifting her skirts, she ran to her own victoria and hurled herself inside. Picking up the reins, she cracked them, hard.

The victoria jerked off, the chestnut mare trotting briskly forward. Anne dared to look back over her shoulder. Her fear increased. The black lacquer coach with the silver Lyons crest was gone.

Anne leaned forward, slapping the reins again, urging the mare to a more rapid pace. The filly broke into a canter. The victoria jumped over the dirt road. Trees raced by. Waverly Hall appeared ahead of her, a large brick Georgian house with six plaster pillars supporting a huge temple pediment, set amongst stately oaks. There were already a few carriages and broughams in the circular drive in front of the grand residence, but the black Lyons coach was not among them.

A groom came running to take the mare's bridle.

Anne leapt from the victoria, ignoring the startled looks of her neighbors as they ascended the front steps. Anne ran past them, skirts held high, giving everyone a glimpse of her white stockings and black leather shoes. As she careened into the wide foyer, the butler met her there.

"Bennet," she shouted, "Lyons is here. Do not allow him into this house!"

Bennet turned a ghostly shade of white. "My lady, er, I beg your pardon?"

Anne was turning red now with her rage. Very carefully, so that there would be no mistake as to her meaning, she enunciated every syllable of every word. "Do not allow Lyons into this house. The new marquis is not to set a single foot inside. Dominick St. Georges is forbidden entry. Is that clear?"

The butler nodded, his eyes bulging, sweat appearing upon his brow.

And Anne strode down the corridor, fists clenched, hardly satisfied. Dom had better not dare to even try, she thought grimly. He was not welcome here. Not even now—especially not now.

Not after all that he had done.

And Anne did not give a damn that they were man and wife.

# Chapter 2

$\mathcal{W}$averly Hall loomed before him, a stately brick home set amidst majestically groomed grounds. Towering elms shaded the long straightaway approach to the house. Perfectly manicured lawns slid away endlessly from the drive. In the distance, to the east, there was parkland filled with fine riding trails; in the west, fertile farmland given to barley and oat crops, and gentle green hills dotted with a few cows and grazing sheep.

The house itself was surrounded with lush gardens in full bloom. But as Dom's coach rolled up the long graveled drive toward the front of the house, he did not see his home's beauty, and he did not feel any warmth.

His memories of growing up there were not good ones. But memories could be forgotten. New memories could be made. Waverly Hall was his now. Everything had changed.

Because of Philip's untimely death.

Dom forced his thoughts of Philip aside. He had guests to greet and he would not wear his heart upon his sleeve. As he stepped down from his coach he saw that the circular driveway in front of the house was packed with carriages and broughams and small country gigs, with liveried coachmen and grooms. He paused, mentally preparing himself.

The butler opened the front door a mere three inches in response to Dom's knock. "My lord."

Dom was surprised, for it was the footman's duty to admit guests. But he greeted the family retainer with a brief smile. He had known the Waverly butler since he was born. "Hello, Bennet."

Bennet did not smile. Nor did he open the door fully. Just behind Bennet's head, Dom could see the wide, high-ceilinged foyer with its elaborate wainscoting and the chequered corridor that left off of it, traversing the house. He could hear the hushed conversation of the many guests inside. He wondered if anyone was truly lamenting the demise of the late marquis. Had Philip had any actual friends? He did not think so. The thought saddened him.

Philip had been a lonely man, Dom realized uneasily. Dom wondered if he would die as ignominiously. Without any friends, unloved, and so easily forgotten.

Bennet had yet to open the door. Impatiently, Dom said, "Bennet?"

"Sir, I . . ." Bennet trailed off. A portly man somewhere in his fifties, he was clearly dismayed.

"Is this my greeting?"

"Sir, I am glad to see you, I truly am," Bennet said in a rush. "And let me offer my condolences for the death of your father. It's a terrible thing, my lord, terrible!" Bennet's eyes filled with tears. But he still made no effort to open the door so that Dom could step through. In fact, he seemed to be blocking the entrance with the angle of his body.

Dom stared. "Are you barring my entrance?" he asked in some amazement.

Bennet's face began to grow red. "The marchioness has instructed me to do so! I beg your pardon, my lord!"

For a single moment, Dom was confused. But a scant instant later Dom realized that his mother had not been the one to order him barred from the house. Clarisse was now the dowager marchioness. His wife was the current marchioness of Waverly.

*His wife. Anne.*

Dom tensed. He did not want to be reminded of her. He had spent years avoiding all thoughts of her. But she was his wife, and very shortly, he would undoubtedly encounter her. How could he not think of her?

The guilt he had lived with for four long years rose up swiftly in a familiar tide, crashing over him. So did the anger. The fact that he had married her, giving her his name, a title, while supporting her without reservation, did not mitigate either emotion. Nothing was ever going to change the past. He had lost his head, allowed lust to rule him, seducing a young girl still in the schoolroom.

To this day, Dom could not understand himself. He was a man who prided himself on his self-control. Yet Anne had so easily pierced his defenses. Dom could still see the shock on his parents' faces, and on the faces of the Collinses. He could still recall Felicity's hysterical sobbing and her mother's strident shrieks, and hear Anne's soft, barely audible weeping. He would never forget the sound.

"Where is she?" Dom asked stiffly. He could not form the words *my wife.*

"Her Ladyship is with the guests in the gold drawing room," Bennet replied.

Dom imagined her in a high-necked navy gown, braids wrapped around her head. His hands trembled; he shoved them into the pockets of his worn hunting coat. "Bennet, you have made an error. Madam would never think to keep me out of my own house. Please open the door."

Bennet was unhappy. "Her Ladyship was very clear, my lord. I must not, under any circumstance, allow you inside the house."

Dom could not believe his ears. Had Anne changed?

Impossible. "Of course you can. You must merely move your arm backward while gripping the door-knob." His tone grew menacing. "I am the marquis. I am pleased to see that you are loyal to madam, but I am her lord and master. I am *your* lord and master, Bennet."

Bennet was stark white. "I am sorry, sir," he croaked. Sweat beaded his brow.

Dom tried very hard to keep a rein on his temper. It was not easy. "Bennet, do you wish to be dismissed?" It was a bluff; Dom would never let the butler go.

"No," Bennet whispered.

"Then open the door," He moved forward—Bennet blocked his way.

Before Dom could assimilate this startling fact, Anne herself suddenly appeared behind Bennet. Their gazes instantly locked.

For just a moment, Dom was immobilized. He forgot the issue at hand. It had been so long.

And as Dom stared at his wife, images tumbled through his mind. Anne smiling at him, tremulously, worshipfully, so obviously in love with him; Anne thrashing in passion on a bed of grass as he loomed over her.

He was frozen, she was not. Anne shoved rudely past Bennet, blue eyes blazing, and slammed the door in his face.

An instant later he heard the bolt being rammed home.

Dom was shocked. And then he was incredulous, furious. He gripped the doorknob and rattled it. "Anne?"

"You are not welcome here," Anne said in a muffled voice from behind the thick oak door.

He paused, trying to grapple with the sight he'd just had of Anne—she had been stunning and she had not been wearing a schoolgirl's gown or braids—and the incredible fact that she dared to lock him out of his own home. Anne had changed. She had grown up. She was no child of seventeen anymore. But to lock him out? That was a very childish game. His tone distinctly dark, Dom said, "Open this door."

"No."

"Anne. This is my home. Open the door." When there was no response from the other side of the door, he said, very low, "I am the marquis."

"Go back to your London town house," she said, her voice choked and thick. "Go back to your mistress."

Dom stared at the heavy walnut door. For a moment he could not believe what she had said—surely he had misheard.

Wives did not speak in such a fashion. Nor did wives bar their lords from their homes.

Cursing savagely, he wrenched at the door, but quickly gave it up. It was bolted, and as long as Anne stood sentinel there, apparently Bennet would not open it.

He spun on his booted heel and strode down the front steps and around the side of the house. As he drew abreast of an open window, from inside the house, Anne drew abreast as well. Briefly his steps faltered. He could not take his eyes off her. Christ, she had changed so much! But Anne did not slow. She slammed the window shut. And glared at him.

Dom quickly recovered, but by the time he reached the next window, Anne was slamming that closed too. The look she sent him couldn't have been more eloquent. Her eyes told him to go to hell and stay there.

Their gazes clashed and locked. Dom took his time. He had begun to warm to the fight. He need not rush—it was inevitable that he would win. She could not keep him out of his house—or stop him from doing anything else that he wished.

His gaze moved over her, taking a thorough inventory now. She was still a slender woman. But whereas once she had been coltish, now her body had developed beautiful curves. Whereas once her eyes had been too large, now they dominated her triangular face perfectly. He had known four years ago that she was going to become a stunning woman. He had been right.

His gaze moved back to her eyes. They were blazing blue. She was furious with him. But the longer he stared at her, the more flushed her cheeks became. In that small, heated moment, it pleased Dom to know that she was not immune to him as a man after all. Of course, this time, no matter what she did, he wasn't going near her with a ten-foot pole.

Anne clenched her fists. "Go away," she mouthed through the window.

Hands on his hips, Dom faced Anne through the closed window. His smile wasn't quite pleasant. "Open the window, Anne," he said softly, knowing that even though she could not hear him through the glass, she understood his meaning exactly.

She shook her head and mouthed, "No."

He smiled, dangerously. Anne's eyes widened and she skittered back a few steps. Dom moved quickly to the French doors, which were open. Anne had the shorter distance to travel, and she was far more determined than he to reach those doors first. She slammed them closed. Dom took his time. Her satisfaction was evident by the time he faced her—but so was her growing fear. She had finally realized that he was playing this game to win. Smiling now, without mirth, Dom raised one booted foot. Anne froze with comprehension—and Dom kicked the glass in.

It broke, shattering all over his knee and thigh and then upon the tiled terrace floor. Anne cried out. Dom kicked any lingering shards of glass free of the door's frame. As quick as a snake, he reached through—and gripped Anne's wrist. A second later he had pulled her up against the wood frame and they were nose to nose, eye to eye.

Anne did not struggle. She stared up at him.

"You can't win, Anne, not against me," he murmured. And then he let her go. He didn't want to touch her, hold her, not even for a second. He did not trust himself, even now, when he was so determined to keep his distance from her.

"Look at what you have done!" she cried.

"Indeed," Dom said coolly. But he did not feel cold now. His heart was racing and he could still feel her breasts crushed against his chest. Grimly he reached inside and unlocked the door and kicked it open. He stepped into his home. She was rigid now, eyes huge and riveted upon his face.

And suddenly Dom became aware of the silence surrounding them, and the fact that they were alone in the morning room. Completely alone. Four years slid away. His heart beat painfully. He understood then, with stunning clarity, the real reason he had abandoned her. The real reason was not guilt, or anger. It had nothing to do with his family, and everything to do with her—and himself. The real reason was fear.

He was afraid of himself—of his reaction to this woman.

He jammed his hands into his pockets, unnerved. "Hello, Anne."

Her small bosom heaved. Her eyes sparked. "Hello, Dom."

Dom wanted to apologize for all that he had done to her—but he didn't dare. "You are looking well," he finally said, hesitating. "How are you?"

Her small chin lifted aggressively. "I am fine, thank you." Her tone was not as polite, or as composed, as his. "How nice of you to call, Dom."

She no longer stuttered in his presence as she once had, he realized. "Surely you were expecting me."

"No. I was not expecting you. As far as you are concerned, I am not sure of anything," she said.

He felt himself flushing. He understood her barbs. He could not blame her, but was angry nevertheless. "I would never miss my father's funeral."

She eyed his riding boots. "Really? Are you sure you were not stopping by while on your way to the racetrack?"

"I don't have to wear black to mourn my father's passing, Anne. I was in Paris when I received news of his illness. I came as swiftly as possible."

"Well, I do hope your trip was worthwhile," Anne said tartly.

Dom wondered if she knew about his new mistress, a French actress. He hoped not. "You seem angry, Anne."

"I'm not angry," Anne said quickly. "Whyever would I be angry?"

His gaze narrowed. "You have little to complain of. I've provided lavishly for you and the servants are certainly devoted to you. There is no cause for anger."

"Of course not," Anne cried. She crossed her arms. "After all, every woman dreams of being seduced by the man of her dreams and abandoned afterward!"

"I married you. One day you will be my duchess."

Anne choked on angry laughter and tears. "Lucky me!"

"I am sorry if I hurt you. That was not my intention."

"What was your intention, Dom?"

She was challenging him, and he already felt as bad as he could. "My intention was to marry Felicity, as my family wished for me to do. What was *your* intention?"

She turned red. She spun on her heel, about to leave.

Dom reached out, spinning her back around. Immediately he dropped his hand from her arm. "But you don't have to worry," he said.

Her gaze was wide, but wary.

"I'm not staying. I won't interfere in your life. Nothing will change."

"Good," Anne said, turning her back on him again. "Because I don't intend to allow you to interfere in my life." She stormed from the room.

Dom watched her go.

The mourners were congregated in the drawing room. As Dom entered, heads swiveled in his direction. His gaze immediately found Anne, who was standing on the far side of the room with her cousin, Patrick. He couldn't help noticing that they looked good together, Patrick being blond and handsome. He turned his regard elsewhere.

His mother was surrounded by guests. If she had noticed his appearance, she gave no sign. Dom hesitated, wanting to go to her first, yet reluctant to interrupt her conversation.

The vicar saved the day. He grabbed Dom's hand and pumped it. "My lord, how good to see you again, but how sorry I am that it is under these terrible circumstances!"

Dom nodded, well aware that the vicar was thoroughly drunk. The tip of his nose was bright red. The servants were freely serving up sherry, the before-supper choice of beverage. "Thank you, Mr. Almer."

"Will you be staying now? Surely you will stay to take over the management of this fine estate! Not that your wife hasn't done a good job, of course—"

"I am not staying," Dom said flatly. But he had caught Almer's drift. Surely the man was besotted, and had no idea of what he was saying. Anne could not be involved in the management of the estate. His gaze arrowed over the crowd, settling on Anne. She was staring at him, but when their glances met, she looked away immediately. Patrick remained at her side.

He was far too tense. Dom expelled his breath.

"Dom, how are you?" a woman gushed.

He stiffened, facing Felicity. As always, she was lovely, and as always, she stood so close to him that her voluptuous breasts brushed his arm. He shifted his body so they did not touch. "I did not know that you were coming to the country, Felicity," he said.

Her smile was sultry. "How could I miss your father's funeral, Dom?" She laid a gloved hand on his arm, gripping it, her thumb caressing his sleeve. "I am so sorry, Dom."

Since the death of her husband two years ago, she had acquired the habit of chasing him whenever their paths crossed, which, fortunately, was not often. He was adept at putting her off without being overtly rude. Now, however, she was being brazen in his own home—in front of his own guests, in front of his wife. People were staring. Dom's gaze found Anne's again. She was staring at them. She seemed abnormally pale.

He bit back a curse, shaking Felicity off his arm. He did not feel like being at the center of another scandal. "I appreciate your coming all this way merely to offer your condolences," he muttered.

Her lashes fluttered. "It was not a problem. Surely you know that, Dom. Surely you know that I would do anything you wish—should you wish something of me?"

Dom was exasperated. "My wishes are few and far between," he said evasively, turning away—and he came face-to-face with his mother.

Her eyes were alight with anxiety. Pale and blond, small and slim, Clarisse was still a striking woman, her features perfect and patrician.

Clarisse gazed past him, but Felicity was already melting away. Instantly relief softened her features. She offered her cheek to Dom, and he bent to kiss it without quite touching her skin.

"Mother." He hesitated. "Are you all right?"

Her mouth quavered. "How could I be all right? Philip is dead."

"I am sorry."

"Are you?" She studied him while twisting her crumpled handkerchief in her hands. "Perhaps you are. You cannot blame me for being surprised. You hardly knew your own father."

"I am rather surprised myself," Dom said grimly.

"Why is she here?" Clarisse gazed past several guests at Felicity Collins Reed.

Dom also stared. "Clearly she has come to pay her respects."

"She has come to cause trouble," Clarisse said uneasily. "I do not want any more trouble here at the Hall. Haven't we had enough scandal already?"

"Yes." Dom was terse. His seduction of Anne—and their wedding—had been an incredible scandal throughout the land. He was aware that he was flushing.

"What are your intentions, Dominick?"

He hesitated, his mind filling with Anne's image. And perhaps, also, with regret. "I am leaving tomorrow."

She appeared distressed by his declaration. Her gaze darted toward Anne. "I think you should defer any decision for a few days," she said softly. "It might be better if you stayed awhile, Dominick." She forced a smile, touched his cheek, and walked away.

Dom knew he could not stay. He stared, wanting to comfort her—now that he knew that she was distraught over Philip's sudden death. But how could he? He knew his own mother as well as he had known Philip, which was to say that they were almost perfect strangers.

Anne was flushed. And nothing Patrick did or said could calm her down.

"He has only just returned," Patrick said harshly, "and already he has upset you so!"

Anne did not correct Patrick's assumptions, but Dom had done far more than upset her. Her whole life, perfectly balanced for so long, had been tilted precariously on end. Anne felt as if she was about to slide off the edge of the world.

She closed her eyes, acutely aware of the fact that he stood on the other side of the room, where he was stiffly accepting the condolences of the guests. Even those ladies and gentlemen not surrounding him were turning again and again to look at him. People were also regarding Anne. How the countryside loved a scandal, and this, it seemed, was a scandal in the making.

"I feel as if this entire room is talking about Dom and me, instead of Philip," Anne muttered tersely.

Patrick stroked her hand once. He was her cousin and her best friend. "They probably are. He hasn't been home in years, and look at what happens when he does come home? Good Lord, he is a barbarian. To break down the door the way that he did!"

Anne gasped. "W-what did you just say?"

"One of the guests saw him break down the terrace door in order to get inside."

"I locked him out," Anne managed. She hadn't realized that anyone had seen their exchange.

"I guessed as much." Patrick grinned at her. "Probably not the best course to take."

"No," Anne said. "It was very foolish." But she had been so angry she had lost all sense of decorum. Locking Dom out had been sheer insanity. And all that she had done was to anger him and make a scene, causing even more gossip about them. Her gaze found his yet again from across the room. This time he gave her a long, hard stare.

Anne's heart skipped a beat and she glanced away.

She had no idea what his look meant. But it had been very male and very direct. She did not want to know.

"The sooner he leaves the better," Patrick growled.

"Yes," Anne agreed breathlessly. She ignored his jealousy. Patrick had been her confidant these past four years, and Anne had known for some time now that he felt tenderly toward her.

"Did you see him speaking with my sister?"

"The whole room saw her flirting with him."

"Well, she was in love with him herself, Anne."

Anne folded her arms across her breasts. "If I recall, she had already had a dozen offers of marriage before Dom proposed. She was about to accept one of the suits."

"I don't remember," Patrick said.

Anne looked down at her hands. She wore a simple gold band on her third finger. Patrick didn't remember, but Anne did. Felicity had not loved Dom. She had wanted him—as she clearly still did—but more importantly, she had wanted to be the duchess of Rutherford one day.

"Has he mentioned what he intends to do now?" Patrick asked.

"No." Anne lifted her hand, which was trembling very slightly, and tucked stray wisps of jet black hair behind her ear. "It doesn't matter what he intends. I will not allow him to stay."

Patrick looked at her with tolerant affection. "Dear, I am afraid that he is your master, not vice versa."

Anne stared at Patrick. "Not in this case."

"I beg your pardon?"

Anne's voice was husky but firm. "In this case, I am master here. You see"—and she smiled without mirth—"Waverly Hall has been given to me."

# Chapter 3

$\mathcal{W}$hen the guests were finally gone, Anne sank down onto the sofa. She made no move to leave the drawing room. Dom had left just moments ago, but not without sending her another long, penetrating glance, one she refused to comprehend. She was exhausted, emotionally drained. The sooner he left the better.

"This is going to cause another scandal."

Anne jerked at the sound of Clarisse St. Georges's strained voice. "I beg your pardon?"

"When word of this trust gets out, it will cause another scandal," Clarisse said accusingly. She was standing in front of the door, which she still gripped. Her knuckles were white. A large ruby ring winked from her fourth finger. One of her Persian cats was rubbing against her skirts, purring loudly.

Anne straightened slowly. "I cannot control the gossips."

"You don't care about the gossips. I never saw anyone as hard as you, Anne. I did not see you shed even a single tear in all the time since your marriage."

"That is unfair," Anne said tersely. But she was not going to tell Clarisse about all the times she had wept privately over Dom and the loss of all of her dreams. Yet Clarisse had to know. Those first few months after the wedding, when Dom had failed to return, Anne had been crushed and unable to hide it.

"What is unfair is the fact that you married my son," Clarisse snapped.

Anne stood up. Tension filled her body. She was fully aware of Clarisse's dislike of her—she had been aware of it from the day of her wedding. "But I have more than paid the price, have I not?"

"And what price is that?" Clarisse asked. "Oh, let me see—being a marchioness? Having an annuity a princess would covet? Being the sole and legal master of this Hall?"

"I have spent four years in this house without a single caller, other than the duke. I cannot even present myself in the village without being snickered at behind my back. My life has not been easy," Anne said.

"Well, what did you expect?"

Anne bit back a reply. She would never tell Clarisse what she had expected from her marriage—which was for Dom to love her for the rest of their lives.

"I dread the scandal we shall be confronted with again," Clarisse said bitterly. "I have spent my entire life trying to live correctly, but for what good?" Tears filled her eyes. "This is all your fault!"

"You exaggerate," Anne said, standing. "The trust is but a tiny ripple in the vast scheme of things. Dom will inherit the greatest patrimony in the land. Rutherford has eighteen estates. No one will blink an eye over the status of this house, and Dom still owns the land."

"Dom was born in this house. This house has belonged to a St. Georges for three hundred years. Philip and I were married here. This house should be Dom's."

Anne hesitated. Rutherford had announced the terms of the trust naming her sole beneficiary to Waverly Hall just last night. Anne had been shocked. She was still very surprised. The trust also held a generous annuity for her. But Dom retained the land belonging to the estate. Anne could not fathom the duke's motives. "What can I do? I did not ask for any of this."

"No? I think that you did."

Anne stiffened. "I do not know what you mean, Clarisse."

"I mean that Philip is dead, Rutherford has lost his mind, I am now a mere dowager, and you have this house, a handsome allowance—and Dom will not be a bother to you. How clever you are, Anne, how clever and cunning and shrewd!"

Anne was taken aback. "Are you implying that I had something to do with all of this, Clarisse?"

"You *planned* all of this! You have been planning all along, from the time you seduced my son, to your marriage, up until now—when you are not just the marchioness of Waverly, but the sole legal mistress of this Hall."

"No." Anne shook her head, horrified. "Those are terrible accusations. You are wrong. I planned nothing. And there is nothing wrong with the duke giving me this house."

"Do you deny that you have wheedled your way into the duke's deepest affections? Causing him to devise that atrocious trust?"

"We are friends!"

"Friends," Clarisse scoffed furiously, tears spilling down her cheeks. "You knew just what to do and you did it perfectly! Playing the son with him! Becoming his son! Riding with him in the mornings, discussing the London papers with him, inspecting the farms, buying that expensive machinery, and actually knowing what it's for. But I must say, discovering those inaccuracies on the ledgers was the *coup de grâce!* Catching the land agent embezzling funds was truly a stroke of genius, Anne. As was dismissing him on the spot! And now there is no land agent—and you manage one of the richest estates in England! How smart and clever you are!"

"Philip was never here. The land agent was a thief.

Someone had to manage this estate. Dom never returned. I did what I had to do!" Anne said.

"Yes, you did what you had to do," Clarisse retorted.

Anne stared, momentarily unable to defend herself.

Clarisse's stare was cold and accusing. "You planned all of this from the moment you seduced Dom."

"I did not seduce Dom," Anne said hoarsely.

"You seduced my son! You, a penniless American orphan, a nobody! Otherwise he would have never thought to marry you in a thousand years!"

Anne was blinded by a pain that was almost physical. Clarisse's latter statement was the truth. "And you have never forgiven me, have you? Not for the scandal, not for being half-American and penniless, not for marrying Dom. That is what this is about—my marriage."

"No, I am not about to forgive you for any of it. And yes, this is about your marriage to my son!"

"I am sorry you feel this way," Anne finally said. She wanted to end their conversation. "This has been a difficult day for everyone. You are distraught. Things will appear different tomorrow."

"I have felt this way ever since you married my son. I will hardly feel different tomorrow. And I am not alone in my assessment of you, Anne."

Anne stared, swallowing. "I am well aware of what the ton thinks."

Clarisse laughed. "The ton, the country, everyone knows the truth!"

"The truth is that I was in love with Dom when we married," Anne said in a whisper.

"The truth is that you are a ruthless American title hunter."

Anne was speechless. Yet this was what she had been accused of being for many years—although never so openly, never to her face. Everyone knew that her

American father, Frank Stewart, had left her with nothing, and that she had arrived a penniless orphan on her aunt's doorstep when she was eleven years of age. Conveniently, no one wished to remember her mother, Edna's younger sister, Janice, who had died giving birth to Anne. Janice had been a Stanhope. It was an old, blue-blooded and illustrious name.

Anne was the poor, orphaned American relation. The scheming hussy who had seduced her poor cousin's fiancé away from her on the very eve of her wedding to the most eligible bachelor in the land. Anne thought that both Felicity and Edna had done their best to spread the horrible lie. Neither her cousin nor her aunt had spoken with her since her wedding day. Or any of polite society.

"You bewitched Rutherford, just as you bewitched the staff—just as you bewitched Dom that night in the garden."

"No," Anne whispered faintly.

"You cannot fool me, Anne, you have never fooled me." Clarisse's small bosom heaved. "You appear ever so respectable, but that is all that it is—an appearance."

"Anything I say to you will be a waste of my breath, then?"

"Yes."

"Then I shall not even try." Anne fought for her composure. Clarisse's next words destroyed her hopes of regaining her calm.

"I wonder if Dom knows," Clarisse mused.

"Wh-what?!"

Clarisse stared at her. "I wonder if Dom knows just how clever and bold you are."

"Are—are you threatening me?"

Clarisse stared at her. "Yes, I think that I am."

Anne was dismayed, even though she need not be—even though it hardly mattered now what Dom thought of her. Too much had happened. They were thoroughly estranged. But what if Dom believed his mother? What if he had already heard the gossip—what if that was the real reason he had stayed away from her for all of these years?

"Why are you doing this?" Anne asked. "Are you trying to create a greater gulf between Dom and me than already exists?"

"I would like nothing more than to see Dom in control of this house, as he should be—with you out on your ear," Clarisse said angrily.

Anne's pulse raced. "Even Dom would not cast me out like some itinerant beggar."

"No? He has not been given cause to, yet."

Anne could not help being somewhat frightened. This was her home. She had no other place to go, certainly not back to the Collinses, nor anywhere else. Even though she was legally the heiress, she did not doubt that Dom could remove her from the premises one way or another if he really wished to do so. He was a very powerful man. "I did not want to be named heiress to Waverly Hall," Anne finally said, her tone faint. "I was as surprised as everyone when Rutherford announced the trust after Philip's death." Anne hesitated. "I was in love with Dom when we married. You have to believe that."

Clarisse laughed, the sound brittle. "You wanted to be a duchess, by God, and now, one day, you will achieve your greatest ambition!"

"No." Anne shook her head. She had wanted to be loved—nothing more.

Clarisse made an unladylike sound. "You planned everything, Anne. Next you will say that you did not send Dom that note which brought him into the garden for your tryst."

Anne stared at Clarisse. There was no note. "I did not entice him into the garden with a note."

Clarisse ignored her—or did not even hear her. She

hugged her cat so hard that it meowed loudly, and Clarisse let it jump to the floor and race away. "Dom plans to leave tomorrow."

Anne's heart felt as if it had stopped. Then it began to race far too quickly for comfort. "Tomorrow?"

"Yes, tomorrow. You chased him away four years ago, and you are succeeding in doing the exact same thing once again! When it is you who should be leaving." Clarisse's eyes narrowed. "You must be ecstatic with yourself."

This was what Anne wanted. This was what she intended. But Anne felt faint. "I do wish him gone. It would be an impossible situation if he thought to remain here ... with me."

"This is *his* home, in spite of that atrocious trust. Perhaps I will convince Dominick to stay."

Anne's eyes widened. Her heart beat faster. "No! I will not allow it!"

"Do you really think you can tell my son what to do?"

Anne hesitated. Her mouth was dry. She did not reply.

Anne was very shaken by her confrontation with Clarisse. She had not realized just how hostile Clarisse felt toward her. Yet Anne could not help but feel sorry for her; she understood what the other woman must be feeling in the wake of her husband's death. She should have sympathy for her.

Dom was leaving tomorrow, unless Clarisse changed his mind. Anne was more determined than ever, and not just because of the encounter she had had with Clarisse. Dom was not going to stay in *her* house. He had forfeited all of his rights long ago, as far as Anne was concerned.

However, the estate of Waverly Hall was still Dom's responsibility. She might have been named beneficiary of the trust, but that only gave her the promise of one day owning the actual house; the estate itself would always belong to Dom and his heirs—should he ever legitimize one of his bastards. But Anne had been managing the estate by herself. Philip had been an absentee landlord. Anne hoped that Dom would be just like his father. But she didn't know for certain. Was he going to hire a land agent? Anne hoped not.

But more importantly, Anne had been waiting four very big years to settle matters between them.

The master suite was on the ground floor of the house in the west wing. Those had been Philip's apartments, and now they were Dom's. Tension rising rapidly within her, Anne traversed the house swiftly—before she might change her mind, go to her own rooms, and lock her doors.

Outside of the pair of large, gleaming mahogany doors, Anne paused. Her pulse was racing. She was too warm. Confronting the lion in his den was foolish in the extreme.

But he was leaving tomorrow.

And there were questions burning inside of her.

Still, Anne hesitated. Her mouth had become dry. And before she could decide whether to knock or turn around and leave, the doors opened abruptly. Dom stood there, his amber eyes piercing.

Anne could not move.

His gaze slipped to her mouth, then jerked upward to her eyes. "I heard your approach," he said. "Do you wish to speak with me?" His manner was quite formal.

Anne nodded. "Your mother said that you are leaving tomorrow. If that is the case, then there are certainly matters for us to discuss."

One tawny brow slashed upward. "Really? I would think the only matter you wish to discuss is how early I intend to depart."

She squared her shoulders. "Yes, I do want to know when you are leaving."

He stepped aside. "Come in, Anne."

Swallowing, Anne moved past him, aware of her skirts brushing his thighs. Her heart beat harder now. She had never been in the master suite before, but she had never had cause to be inside it. Before, it had belonged to Philip, and now it belonged to Dom.

Anne had never even been in a man's room before.

She paused in the center of the salon, arms folded protectively across her breasts. She was careful not to look to her right, where the door was open, a portion of Dom's bedroom visible.

Instead, she glanced around at her surroundings. A gold carpet covered the floor. The ceilings were mauve with beautifully carved gold moldings. The walls were done in a fabric with a gold background and red and brown strips, small green leaves creeping up them. The furniture was upholstered in various shades of red, brown, and copper, and the mantel over the fireplace was the rich, warm color of terra-cotta.

One wall was nothing but triple-sized windows. The views were breathtaking. The gardens were just below, but the vista was of the emerald green lawns stretching away into the thickly wooden parkland. In the center of the park, Anne could see the lake shimmering, a small island in its midst, the ruins of a Norman keep just discernible above the wooded ground. Behind the park, the horizon was etched with sloping hills and a rapidly fading sky. Two stars had popped out brightly.

"Would you care for a drink?"

Dom's breath tickled her nape and Anne jumped, whirling. He stood so close behind her that her skirts whipped his ankles. He was in his stockinged feet as well as his shirtsleeves.

"N-no. Yes."

His smile was knowing. He turned away. Anne tried

not to notice how well his breeches gloved his muscular body. She averted her eyes. When he returned, he handed her a glass of sherry. Sipping from his own glass of whiskey, he regarded her over the rim.

Anne knew that her color was high. She quickly sat down on a red paisley settee. She took a gulp of sherry. "I have just had a conversation with your mother," she began—and stopped. Realizing that Dom might not know. He might not have learned yet what Rutherford had done. Although Anne wanted her revenge, she wasn't so foolish as to want to be the one to tell him that he was not the master of this house. He would be unhappy—to say the least.

Dom settled his hip on the arm of the sofa and took another sip of his drink. "Why are you so flustered, Anne?"

"I am not flustered!"

He smiled, amused. "You are my wife. In name, anyway. There's nothing improper with your being here in my apartments."

Anne stood. Sherry splashed over her hand. Had her discomfort been so obvious? It had been a mistake seeking Dom out in his rooms. It was too intimate, too unsettling. It was too agonizing—reminding Anne of what she had once, foolishly, dreamed of having with him.

"I have only come to discuss the management of the estate," she said stiffly.

"Really? What is there to discuss?"

"We have no land agent. Mr. Harvey was embezzling funds. He was dismissed a year ago—with your father's approval."

He stared at her. "If we have not had a land agent in an entire year, then how has the estate managed? Has it run itself?"

Anne began to blush. She knew that it was considered very unladylike and ungenteel to tally accounts and supervise the estate—in the village, her activities were always a great source of gossip and amusement. "It has not run itself," she retorted. "I have managed things in lieu of your father and an agent."

Dom did not blink. "Really?"

Her color increased. "Your grandfather knew. He was a big help to me, of course. Philip did not care. He was relieved, I think, to finally be absolved of his responsibilities."

Dom set his drink down. "This is fascinating. So the vicar was not as drunk as I thought."

Anne did not understand. Not his words, nor the look in his eyes. "Wh-what do you intend to do?"

He stared. "I intend to kiss you."

Anne's eyes widened.

A moment later she almost jumped out of her skin when he gripped her shoulders—pulling her forward. "I must have been crazy to stay away for four years," he muttered. "What could have been wrong with me?"

Anne was frozen with disbelief—and a sudden crazy, wild expectation.

He pulled her even closer. Suddenly her knees knocked his. Her breasts brushed his chest. "I promised myself something," he said, unsmiling, his eyes very heated now, "but I cannot keep it. I would truly be mad to keep it."

"No," Anne found her voice, remembering the past, the betrayal. "What are you doing?" Panic hoarsened her tone. "You cannot do this!"

"Of course I can," he said flatly. "I am your husband." His arm went around her. Before Anne could protest, she was clamped to his chest, and his mouth covered hers.

Anne's pulse rioted even as her mind shrieked in protest. She did not trust this man. She would never trust him again. But it had been so long since Anne had been held and touched and kissed.

And Dom was warm and strong and powerfully male. He parted her mouth with his instantly, his tongue probing, prodding. Anne's hands found his shoulders. Her mind began to become blank. Their thighs melded, their mouths fused.

Dom thrust now into her mouth, bending her backward over his arm. Somehow one of his hard, muscular thighs had become wedged between both of her legs. Anne was not wearing a crinoline. She was both shocked and mesmerized by the intimacy of his hard, virile body against hers. Anne could not breathe. Desire crested, became consuming. She moaned against his voracious, hungry, relentless lips. Somehow the past was forgotten.

Dom dragged his mouth away from hers, staring at her out of stunned eyes. "God." And then his gaze slammed to the door of his bedroom.

Anne was breathless, shivering—shaking. But she saw where he was looking—and understood exactly what she was thinking. Worse, she was thinking about it, too.

"Anne," Dom said huskily.

Briefly, Anne could not move. Her heart rate tripled. Something inside her fought to respond, and she wanted to cry out, leap into his arms, and make love to him wildly. But this man had abandoned her. Her memories returned with utter clarity. Anne wrenched herself free. "Don't."

He jerked.

She held up both hands. "Don't touch me again!" And she meant it.

He stared for a long, simmering moment. In that moment, his eyes began to cool, while Anne gained a far better grip on her own sanity. "You are my wife." He shrugged. "It would not be the end of the world if we slept together."

"It would be the end of my world," she cried. "And I am hardly your wife!"

His smile was mocking. "You are the marchioness of Waverly, Anne, are you not? That makes you my wife."

"Damn you," Anne said harshly.

Dom started. Then his gaze narrowed, becoming far colder than before. "Do you really hate me so much?" he asked slowly.

Anne pursed her mouth. Did she really hate him? She could not avoid his golden, searching eyes. Had she ever really hated him? Once she had loved him with all of her heart and all of her soul.

"Anne?"

"I dislike you."

"I see." Dom retrieved his drink. After a long draught, his gaze flashed to hers. "You didn't dislike me a moment ago."

Anne gritted. "You are wrong."

"Oh, no, madam. I know when a woman is willing."

Had Anne been holding her sherry, she might have actually thrown the contents in his face. "You do not take me seriously," she said furiously. "You never have."

"Now you are wrong," Dom said quietly, his expression strained. "I take you very, very seriously—more than you will ever know."

They stared at one another.

"What does that mean?"

Dom shrugged, looking away from her. His profile was stark, closed.

But Anne had to know. It was the real reason she had come to see him. "Tell me why," she demanded, pacing to him and jerking on his sleeve. Whiskey sloshed over the side of his glass. "Dom—why did you make love to me in the gardens that night?"

He laughed without mirth. "That's the most foolish

question I have ever heard." His gaze was razor-sharp. "I lost my head, Anne. Completely."

She stared into his eyes. For her, that was no answer—or an incomprehensible one. "You made me a laughingstock," she finally whispered, unable to keep the hurt from her tone, "and I was so very in love with you."

"I am sorry."

"I don't believe you."

He touched her chin. Anne did not move away. "You aren't a laughingstock anymore, Anne. You're a beautiful, sincere woman. A genteel, elegant lady."

"No. They were laughing at me today. Especially when you were flirting with Felicity."

"I did not flirt with her."

Anne turned away. There was no point in staying. But he gripped her shoulder, whipping her around. "Why don't you ask me what you really want to know?"

She hesitated. Her heart banged against her chest. The question burned inside of her as it had for four endless years. "Because I am afraid of what you will say."

When he did not respond, she lashed out with her fist, and it landed on the solid wall of his chest. He did not flinch. She pummeled him again. "Damn you! *Damn you!* Why did you abandon me? Why?"

Regret showed in his eyes, filled his tone. "Because I was a fool."

Anne choked, hardly hearing him. The words tumbled from her mouth. "How could you have done such a thing? How could you have abandoned me? The morning after our wedding night? How?"

"I am sorry," he whispered.

"I waited for you to come back," she cried, tears spilling from her eyes. She batted at them angrily. "I waited and waited—for years and years! *Damn you, Dominick!*"

"I am sorry, Anne, more sorry than you will ever know."

"It's too late," Anne cried.

He turned away, walking to the windows, staring out into the night. "Yes," Dom finally agreed. "It's too damned late."

# Chapter 4

𝒜nne stared at Dom's back. Just past him, the night was growing black. Stars were beginning to glitter, but Anne could also see the fog rolling in, puffs of mist floating across the lawns. Soon the house would be shrouded and invisible to any outside, prying eyes.

Regret filled her, body and soul. "It is best that you leave tomorrow," she finally said. "After your father's will is read." The words shouldn't hurt, but they did.

He did not turn, he did not answer.

"You are going to leave tomorrow?" she managed.

He stiffened, faced her. His expression was strained. "What would you do, Anne, if I said I've changed my mind?"

Anne's eyes widened. "What are you saying?"

"Maybe I don't want to leave."

She could not think of a single thing to say. But panic swelled inside of her breast. It would never work, the two of them sharing the same house. The two of them pretending to be man and wife. The two of them living together.

Dom was a worldly man. He was always associated with the most beautiful women. Even if Anne managed to survive residing with him, seeing him daily and knowing of his liaisons would destroy her.

Anne found her voice. "I want you gone. You cannot stay here."

51

His stare was hard, direct. "Yes, you have made yourself very clear. But perhaps my wants have changed."

"I don't care what you want!" she cried, and hearing the hysteria in her tone, she made an effort to control it. "It would be better for both of us if you left immediately."

His smile made her stiffen. "What are you so afraid of, Anne?"

"I am not afraid of you—if that is what you are suggesting!"

He folded his arms and regarded her with brooding tolerance. "I *am* staying. At least for a while."

"Is this your mother's doing?"

"No." He studied her. "Apparently there is much to be done here, including hiring a new land agent—and reasserting my authority over Bennet and the staff." He appeared amused.

"No," Anne said. She was shaking. "You are not welcome here."

"Need I remind you that this house is mine? You cannot order me to leave. And Anne"—his smile was seductive—"you are also one of my possessions, under the law—whether you choose to think of yourself as my wife or not."

"No," she said, her heart pumping mightily now. *"No."*

"No?" He was incredulous, mocking. "Isn't that a wedding band on your third finger?"

"That is not what I am denying. I know very well that I am your wife, in spite of the fact that we have not seen each other even once in the four years since our wedding."

His gaze slitted. "If you think to make me feel guilty, you are succeeding."

"That is not my intention."

"Then what are you attempting to say to me?"

She took a deep breath. "This house isn't yours, Dom."

He was not perturbed. "I beg your pardon?"

Anne swallowed. She had not wanted to be the one to tell him, especially not this way. "This house is mine."

He stared. "I beg your pardon?"

Anne was stiff. "It's true."

"Are you telling me that I have been disinherited?" He was incredulous.

Anne wrung her hands. "No! It's only the house. You see, there is a trust—and I was made the sole beneficiary."

Disbelief transformed his face. "I have never heard of any such thing. This is absurd. Waverly Hall belonged to my father. Who would devise such a trust, giving you, my wife, this house? I do not believe you!"

"Rutherford has done this." Anne was hoarse.

His eyes suddenly blazed. Suddenly he was towering over her. "Rutherford!"

Anne took a step backward. "Yes."

His expression changed. Clearly he was grappling with what she had told him—and then he stared at her as if he held her personally responsible for Rutherford's trust—as if he wished to throttle her.

Anne could feel his rage building. "I . . . I was as surprised as you now are!" Anne said in a rush. "Rutherford only told me last night! Dom! Don't look at me that way! You are frightening me!"

But his stare was hard and relentless.

He was furious.

It could not be true.

He was his father's sole surviving heir. Waverly Hall was Philip's single legacy to him. It did not matter that he had several other estates attached to his title of viscount, one of which was even larger and more lucrative than Waverly. Wealth was not the issue. This house was his birthright from his father.

Dom strode through the house. Not toward the front salon where the funeral guests had been so recently drinking, eating, and talking about everything other than the dead man they had just buried, but toward the back. The door to the library was ajar. Briefly, Dom paused.

This was the room his father had favored when in residence, Philip being a scholar. Dom had always avoided this room. As a boy, this was where he had been presented to his father for a brief daily purview. His father would question him about his studies. As Dom was a negligent student, he could rarely answer those questions, and usually failed to satisfy his father. Philip St. Georges had never tried to hide the fact that he expected failure from his son.

Angry and hurt, Dom had neglected his studies to an ever greater degree.

But Philip had never punished him.

Standing outside of his father's library door almost made Dom feel eight or nine years old again. And just for a moment, he thought he could feel his father's presence there, lingering in the hallway beside him. It was terribly strong, and it caused the hairs on Dom's nape to prickle with unease. Then Dom shook himself free of such fanciful imaginings, for Philip was six feet underground and Dom did not believe in ghosts. He shoved the door open.

Someone was inside, but it was not the marquis, of course. The duke of Rutherford sat in the large, wine-hued, leather-backed chair behind the heavy mahogany desk facing the door at the opposite end of the room. A faded Persian rug covered the distance between them. A sofa and two armchairs faced the black granite mantel over the fireplace, which was empty now, and hundreds of books lined the facing wall.

Dom stared at his grandfather. How old he had become. He looked his age, which was all of seventy-four years, when he had never looked his age before. His eyes were swollen and red. Dom recalled how he had wept at the grave. To Dom's shock, tears suddenly blurred his own gaze. A sense of acute loss overwhelmed him again. He would never really know or understand his own father.

Rutherford rose to his feet, coming out from behind the desk. He was a thin man, but almost six feet tall, and once he had been golden-haired like all the St. Georges men. His hair was still thick, but stark white. His gaze met Dom's.

"Grandfather," Dom said.

Rutherford looked as if he were on the verge of embracing him, but instead, he extended his glass toward Dom. His arm shook. "Here, drink this."

Dom took the snifter and tossed back all the contents. He welcomed the burn—and the following numbness. "Grandfather, are you all right?"

"No," the duke said, sinking back down in his chair. He hid his face in his gnarled hands, and Dom wondered if he wept again.

They were not a demonstrative family, but Dom wanted to comfort his grandfather, who suddenly appeared less a duke than a mere mortal, one aged and fragile and grief-stricken. He hesitated, then moved forward, kneeling by his grandfather's side. He did not quite have the courage to touch him. "I am so sorry," he whispered.

Rutherford waved him away without raising his head. His ruby signet ring caught the light, gleaming. "I'll be fine."

Pride also ran in the family. Dom rose and walked away, to pour them both stiff drinks, and to give his grandfather time to recover his composure. When he faced him again, the duke was sitting straight, and if he had been crying, there was no overt sign of it other than his puffy, bloodshot eyes.

Dom walked over and handed him a snifter. "I cannot believe he is really dead."

"Sometimes death strikes unexpectedly," Rutherford said hoarsely. "Why didn't you come home sooner?"

"I was in Paris. I came as soon as I could."

"God, I wish you'd come home under different circumstances, Dom!"

"I wish that, too."

"You've been gone far too long, Dom," Rutherford stated.

Dom's jaw flexed. "I've been very busy. I manage four estates. Unlike other men, I do not relinquish all responsibility to my agents and lawyers."

Rutherford snorted. "You could have come home from time to time. Like other men. There is no valid excuse for your staying away from Waverly Hall and your parents all these years." His gaze narrowed. "And Anne."

Dom stiffened. "Don't interfere in my marriage," he warned. "Although, if Anne knows what she is talking about, you already have."

Rutherford stood up slowly. "What marriage? You don't have a marriage, but I'll interfere now, because it's time and I'm getting older daily! The way you've treated Anne should be a crime!"

Dom struggled to keep his temper in check. "She became a viscountess when I married her, she is a marchioness now. One day she will be a duchess, Grandfather—she has hardly suffered by marrying me."

"Oh, she has suffered, all right," Rutherford thundered. His face had turned red. "She was in love with you when she married you and you bloody well knew it! She's been in love with you since she was a child and you were nothing but a too-handsome, wild, ill-mannered adolescent boy! Why did you stay away so bloody long?''

"You know I went to war," Dom replied tersely.

"Crap. You waited six months to enlist. You've been home almost a year. The truth is, you wouldn't have come home at all, would you, if Philip hadn't fallen so ill?"

Dom was furious, but he spoke evenly with a great effort. "That's right."

Rutherford stared at him for a long time. "You know, Dom, sometimes I think I understand you perfectly, and then I realize that I don't understand you at all."

Dom grimaced. "Sometimes I don't understand myself."

"I know you weren't eager to wed, but you agreed that it was time. You chose Felicity, and I did not object. Then, of course, you compromised Anne. You married her, as you had to do. You married a fine woman. Why did you leave?"

"There were reasons."

"Give me one!"

Dom hesitated. "Perhaps I could not stand myself for what I had done."

The duke stared. "You've had four years to atone for your sins. Why don't you remain here with Anne? And treat her with the respect—and affection—she is due?"

Dom looked down at the snifter he clenched in his hand. "Anne wants me gone. She despises me now."

Rutherford snorted. "She's in love with you."

Dom stared. He was aware of a sharp tremor sweeping through his body. "You are wrong, Grandfather." Then, "Is it true? Have you devised a trust giving Anne this house?"

Rutherford stared at him gravely. "There is a trust.

When I die, Anne gets the house and an annuity. The land remains yours.''

"I don't believe this."

"No? It's all very legal. I made sure of that. Before you and Anne married, my lawyers drew up a separate property agreement. Your father signed it, as did I.''

Dom stared. *Before his marriage to Anne?* "What the hell is a separate property agreement?"

"When your father died, Waverly Hall went into trust for Anne. Being as you had no heir. The Chancery Courts oversee the trust, but Anne has complete access to her property and funds upon application to the trustee.'' Rutherford held Dom's gaze. "I am the trustee.''

Dom's heart was thundering in his ears. "How could you do this to me?" he ground out. "This house should be mine. If you want to interfere in my marriage and make Anne independent, although God knows she is probably independent enough already, give her another property—but not this house, where I was born—not my father's home!''

Rutherford said nothing, but he was almost smiling.

"Do you find this amusing?" Dom shot. "And what, in God's name, are you really up to?''

"I hardly find your treatment of Anne amusing, Dominick,'' Rutherford said. "And what makes you think I am up to anything?''

"Because I know you, Grandfather. Or do you love Anne so much that you lost your head—and your sanity?''

"I do love Anne. She is the daughter I have never had. She is the finest woman I have known in years. She is warm, witty, intelligent, determined. You've been gone for four years. You couldn't possibly know what you have missed, but someone has to tell you.''

"I think I am capable of judging a woman without your interference.'' Exasperated, frustrated, Dom strode to the bar and poured himself another brandy. But he only took a small sip, because he wanted to think clearly. "What do you want from me, Grandfather?"

"I want you to treat Anne decently, as she deserves."

Dom turned and stared. "And you think that by making her more independent, by giving her my father's legacy to me, I will treat her as a husband should?" He laughed bitterly. "Think again."

"I think that Anne has suffered far more than any woman ever should, because of your callous treatment of her. I think that she deserves a property and income of her own—in lieu of a real husband. Is that not fair?"

Dom stared, livid. "I begin to see the light," he remarked, finally.

"Do you?" His tone softened. "There's more to life than tallying accounts, receiving complaints, paying bills, and racing horses, my boy. And those beautiful women you take to your bed are no substitute for a wife. Sometimes I think you make yourself lonely on purpose, Dom."

Dom was stiff. His tone was harsh. "I am not lonely."

"If you believe the company of that French actress can warm your soul, then you are a total fool," Rutherford said simply.

"I don't have to hear this."

"Yes, you do. You have to listen to me—if you want to regain Waverly Hall."

Dom's fists clenched. "Now we're getting somewhere. I want this house back. I will give Anne another house—in fact, I will give her a property ten times this size if that is what she wants."

Rutherford merely smiled.

"Well? What do I have to do to regain this house?" Dom demanded.

Rutherford smiled, but tightly. Dom realized that

sweat beaded his brow. "For a man like you, regaining Waverly Hall should be accomplished easily enough."

Dom said nothing. His entire body was rigid with tension, with expectation.

"I want a great-grandchild before I die," Rutherford said grimly, no longer smiling. "And time is not on my side."

Dom stared. He could not believe his ears.

"And I do not mean one of your bastards. Impregnate your wife, get an heir on her," the duke said, "and the trust will revert to you and Waverly Hall will be yours."

# Chapter 5

*A*nne had taken refuge in her bedroom.

Where she was haunted by an image of Dom's shocked—then enraged—face.

Anne paced across her room, a very feminine pink-and-white affair, to the window. She stared past a vase filled with freshly cut flowers from the Waverly gardens. She was feeling very much like a prisoner. After the past two confrontations, first with Dom's mother and then Dom, she was reluctant to go downstairs—she was reluctant to leave the sanctuary of her bed-chamber. Dom had been so angry when he stalked off to confront his grandfather. By now, surely, he had heard about the trust firsthand. Had he calmed down? Or was he more enraged?

Anne suspected that his temper still ran hot.

How abused and exhausted she felt. She had not asked for any of this. Not Dom's sudden return, not the trust, not Waverly Hall. And certainly not Dom's kiss.

Abruptly Anne shut off her thoughts. She had no right thinking about his kiss, none. What she should be thinking of was how to convince him to leave Waverly Hall as he had first planned.

Perhaps, now that he had learned he was no longer master here, he would realize it was best to go?

Anne pressed her hand against her mouth, the sensations engendered by his kiss flooding her immediately. Oh, God. Whom was she fooling? She hated him, she did, but she was going to be heartbroken when he left. Because a part of her still loved him—and always would.

Anne stared out into the foggy night. The stars were no longer visible; mist blanketed the night. Where it swirled around the trees and shrubs, it gave the land-scape the appearance of being inhabited by ghostly, swaying specters. Anne had lived with the fog for many years, but tonight it seemed eerie, and at once pregnant with potential and utterly desolate.

Anne closed her eyes. She had survived the past four years, and she had survived well. Waverly Hall was now her home, and she liked her life. But now Dom had returned, raising feelings inside of her which she did not want and did not like. That made Anne angry.

It also made her angry to be hiding in her room like this, out of her own fear of coming face-to-face with him again.

Anne strode abruptly across her room and down the corridor. She moved quietly downstairs. Once outside, her steps lengthened. Anne had no destination in mind. She just wanted to get away from the house and its occupants. She wanted to get away from the man she had so foolishly—and so eagerly—married.

A man stepped out from the shadows of a nearby tree. "Anne?"

Anne jumped, her palm on her fluttering heart. "Patrick! You scared me!"

Patrick Collins came to her, taking her hand in his. "I'm sorry." He stared at her closely.

"What are you doing here? I thought you'd left with the other guests."

"I'm worried about you. I don't like you being in the same house with him. Anne—are you all right?"

Anne could not smile at Felicity's brother, but she

clenched his hand tightly. She was very glad to see him now. "I don't think so."

He put his arm around her. "Has he done something?"

"Not exactly."

"Let's walk."

Anne agreed, and they crossed the dew-dampened lawns, the lights from the house guiding them. Patrick did not remove his arm from Anne's shoulders, and now Anne grew uncomfortable with the gesture. Of course, she was well aware of Patrick's feelings for her. Although he had never declared them, she thought that he was in love with her. She imagined that was why he'd been by her side constantly these past few years.

There was a maze on one side of the house, and they entered it silently. Once cut off from the rest of the world, Patrick turned to Anne, taking both of her arms in his hands. "Does he know about the trust?"

Anne nodded. "He is furious."

An expression she could not decipher flitted across Patrick's face. "He has never been crossed before. He has always gotten everything and anything that he wants. This must be a very rude shock."

"You almost sound pleased."

"I'm not pleased, I am stating truths. What does he intend to do? Will he leave?"

"I have no idea," Anne said. "He has insinuated that he has changed his mind, that he will stay—but that was before I told him about the trust."

"I have a feeling he will not take this lying down," Patrick muttered. "I am worried about you, Anne."

Anne looked up at Patrick's handsome face, saw the deep concern in his eyes. So often she had unburdened herself to Patrick. She was ready to blurt out all of her feelings again. But what would she say, exactly? When she was afraid to admit her own feelings to herself?

Anne brushed her eyes with her fingertips. Patrick made a choked sound and pulled her into his embrace. This was not their first embrace, but for the first time, Anne allowed herself to lean against him, her head upon his shoulder. His grip upon her tightened.

"Don't let him touch you, Anne."

Anne tensed. She tried to draw away, but Patrick was not willing to let her go. She stared at him.

"He used you once before," Patrick warned. "He will use you again. Or try to. I saw the way he was looking at you in the drawing room. He has intentions toward you that are far from honorable."

Anne slid free of his embrace. "Patrick, you go too far."

"Anne . . ."

"No! I am a grown woman, capable of managing my own affairs—capable of managing my own marriage."

"Really?" Patrick's mouth twisted. "I think you overestimate yourself. You have hardly managed your marriage thus far. After your wedding you were desolate. Who consoled you in the months that followed? Who counseled you?"

Anne grimaced. "You are a dear friend; there is no question of that. I am fully aware that you made a difficult time somewhat easier than it would have been." But it hadn't been easy at all. She never wanted to be so heartbroken again. She had promised herself long ago that she would guard her heart fiercely from any man offering the illusion that was love.

"Don't shut me out, now," Patrick said. "You are fodder for a man like Dom St. Georges. He has no morals. He will use you again if you allow it."

Anne took a deep breath of air but failed to calm herself. "I am not going to allow anything. And aren't you being a bit unfair to Dom, Patrick?" Her tone was slightly acerbic. "I thought you were his friend."

"We were close, once." Patrick grimaced. "We ran

together as young boys here at the Hall, as you undoubtedly know, and we both went to Eton and Cambridge. But once at the university, we moved in entirely
different cliques. And now, our paths rarely cross.
However, I do consider Dom a friend, in spite of that.''

"Then perhaps you should not be so quick to cast
stones," Anne said tartly.

"He keeps a mistress," Patrick growled. "But of
course, you know."

Anne flinched. She did know. Recently he had become involved with a very famous French actress, one
who was reputedly one of the greatest beauties ever to
grace the stage. Anne tried very hard not to think about
it. "Many men keep a mistress."

"Many men do not."

"If our marriage were different, it might matter, but
it docs not," Anne lied tersely.

"I'm sorry, Anne," Patrick conceded, recognizing
that he had won.

Anne sighed. "Why are we arguing about this? Why
am I defending him?"

"I do not know," Patrick said.

Anne wavered. "I am sorry, too. I treasure our
friendship, Patrick."

"Thank you," Patrick said gravely.

Anne smiled, somewhat forcedly, and touched his
arm. "Shall we go back?"

"Anne." Patrick did not move. "Before we go back,
let me remind you to be careful. Please. Remember
what he did to you four years ago. That is all I ask."

Anne swallowed. When she spoke, it was from the
heart. "I can hardly forget the past, Patrick. And more
importantly, I cannot forgive it."

Rutherford's game had become crystal clear. Dom
paced the terrace, watching the mist settling in over

the lawns and curling about the railing he sat upon. He cursed.

Somewhere in the distance he could hear a sheep bleating and cowbells ringing. Rutherford had gone too far. He claimed to be compensating Anne for these past four years' abandonment with the absurd trust. Yet what he really wanted was for Dom to be a real husband to Anne, to get an heir upon her, ultimately securing the dukedom for the future. Then there would be no need to "compensate" Anne for her lack of a spouse or abandonment.

Dom grimaced. Rutherford was also punishing him. Because he could have given Anne any other property, but he knew just how much the loss of this house would hurt Dom.

Dom did not want to do it. Yes, it would be a painful blow to lose his father's house, but Dom could survive that. He did not want to do it because his very nature rebelled at being manipulated by his grandfather in this fashion.

But Rutherford had every right to want Dom to sire a legitimate heir. Dom did not care about it himself. He had two bastards, a boy and a girl, and one day he could legitimize his son if he had to. Both children were well cared for, and he visited them frequently, having set up their mother near his own home in a very lavish manner. Their mother, Julia Gaffney, had been his mistress for almost five years at one time.

His instinct was to defy his grandfather and let Anne have Waverly Hall.

He would leave Waverly Hall tomorrow, as soon as Philip's will was read. He would return to Lyons Hill, his manor outside of London, where he spent a great deal of his time, his two children nearby.

Dom ran a hand through his hair. He could forgive Rutherford for wanting a legitimate grandchild immediately, but he just could not forgive him these heavy-handed tactics. Had he resorted to simple persuasion, Dom might have been more receptive. Especially because bedding Anne would hardly be a chore.

But Dom had the distinct feeling that he was cutting off his nose in order to spite his face.

"Dominick?"

Dom started at the sound of his mother's voice. He turned and fought to see through the gloom. Clarisse stood on the doorstep between the open French doors, appearing quite ethereal and utterly beautiful. Tendrils of mist swirled about her skirts. She stepped forward, pulling a black crocheted shawl closer about her. A fluffy white cat twisted itself about her skirts, almost the same color as the fog.

"Mother. Are you looking for me?"

"Yes." She hesitated. "We did not have a chance to really speak earlier, when the guests were about."

Dom approached her. "What can I do to help you now, Mother? To make this time easier for you?"

Clarisse looked away, staring out into the mist. It shrouded the grounds, reducing visibility to a few feet. "I am so worried, Dominick."

Dom wanted to comfort her. He was close enough to her to put his arm around her. Their gazes connected suddenly. Dom did not raise his arm. "What are you worried about?"

"I am worried about everything," Clarisse said tersely. "I am worried about myself, and I am worried about you."

Dom started. "You don't have to worry about me—and you certainly don't have to worry about yourself."

"Do you know about Rutherford's absurd trust?"

Dom looked away, growing rigid with anger. "Yes."

Clarisse moved swiftly to him, touching his shoulder. "Waverly Hall should be yours, Dominick," she cried.

"Yes, it should be mine, but currently it is Anne's."

"Your grandfather has gone too far. He must have lost his mind!"

"Yes, he has gone much too far, but he is not senile, Mother. He knows exactly what he is doing."

"As Anne does," Clarisse said with uncharacteristic vehemence.

Dom jerked. "What do you mean?"

Clarisse stared at Dom, her gaze surprisingly beseeching. "She has been working on the duke for years and years, Dom. She is now the marchioness, and in complete control of a very wealthy estate. You do not think Rutherford dreamed this up by himself, do you?"

"Yes, I do." Dom stared at his mother, assessing her words. "Mother, what are you trying to say?"

Clarisse flushed with anger. "Your wife is a scheming hussy! I am sorry to be the one to tell you the facts, but she is very clever and very capable, Dom. You cannot know, because you have not been here in four long years. She has spent those years wheedling herself into Rutherford's good graces, and into his heart. He adores her! He thinks that the ground she walks upon is hallowed! He thinks she can do no wrong! He has given her *your* birthright. He has played right into *her* hands!"

Dom stared at his mother. She, like most of the ton, thought Anne nothing more than a fortune hunter and a hussy. If he only considered the facts, he would think so, too. But he knew Anne somewhat. More importantly, although he wished he could forget that explosive night in the garden, it was engraved on his memory forever. Anne had been innocent and adoring. He had been the cad.

"I do not think Anne quite so ruthless, nor quite so clever, Mother."

"She was clever enough to tryst with you the night of your engagement to Felicity—and look at where that led her!" Clarisse exclaimed.

Dom stiffened. "I was equally to blame. More so, in fact. I should not have responded to her note. And I certainly should have behaved as a gentleman afterward."

"I do not blame you for falling for that hussy. You are a man—men have been seduced since the beginning of time by scheming temptresses."

Dom wet his lips. "Mother, Anne is my wife."

"You defend her, now? After she forced you into marriage—and has now received this house and an annuity fit for a princess?"

"Those were Rutherford's choices."

"You do not know your own wife," Clarisse cried. "She is queen here. She runs this estate. Long before Rutherford announced this trust, Anne controlled Waverly Hall in fact and deed. Now, with the trust, she has more than most women, but probably not all that she wants."

Dom stared.

"Do you know why she dismissed the land agent?" Clarisse was saying. "Solely so that she could run this estate without any interference!"

"She dismissed George Harvey?" Dom was shocked. "Surely my father dismissed him."

"No. Anne terminated his employment, your father paid little attention, quickly approving her decision."

"I am amazed. She has actually been running this estate. It is a monumental task, one most men could not manage themselves."

"Now you sound admiring!"

"Perhaps I am," Dom mused. "Mother, I find it impossible to believe that Anne is so cunning and so ruthless. She was innocent that night, and I alone am to blame for her seduction. It was my duty to marry her, but in the end all I did was hurt her. Now, of course, she despises me—rightly so."

"You are wrong! You do not know her! Dom, you cannot leave now."

"And why is that?"

"Things will worsen here. Even though the trust exists, if you stay, you can control the situation. Anne doesn't like me." Clarisse wiped tears from her eyes. "Where will I go if Anne decides that she has had enough of me? What will I do?"

"Mother, Anne is not going to ask you to leave this house. I will not allow it." Dom put his arm around her and pulled her close to his side. Her slim body was tight with tension. He released her after a moment. "Perhaps you would prefer to live elsewhere though. You are certainly welcome at any of my homes."

"This is my home. I like it here. I do not want to live elsewhere."

"Then you shall remain here."

Clarisse took a shuddering breath. "Please stay. Just a while. Until things settle down. Anne needs to be reminded of the fact that you are her master, Dom." She hesitated. "If anyone leaves, it should be her."

"No!" Dom said sharply. "This is her home now, too. Besides, you are being very unkind to her. Hasn't it ever occurred to you that you both have more in common than not? You both love this estate. You are my mother, she is my wife. Why can't the two of you be friends? I would appreciate it if you introduced Anne to the gentry and helped her make friends."

"What are you thinking?" Clarisse gasped.

"I am leaving tomorrow as planned. But I had not realized just how difficult it must be for Anne here in the country, alone. I wish to make amends."

"I . . ." Clarisse was pale.

"Mother, surely you would not deny me such a simple request?" His tone was deceptively soft, for Dom was used to instant obedience from everyone. He was well aware of his power, already inordinate, having become even greater because of Philip's death.

Clarisse nodded mutely. She turned to go.

Dom stopped her. "Mother, I appreciate your coming to speak with me now."

She met his gaze. "I know I was not a very good mother, Dominick. I am sorry."

"You were fine," he said, his tone suddenly hoarse. He managed a smile. "I feel that we are finally getting to know one another." His smile faded. "I did not know my own father, and now it is too late. I do not want to make the same mistake with you, Mother."

Clarisse wet her lips, nodded, and scooped up her cat, cradling it. Her mouth trembled. "When you were born, I did not want to give you over to the wet nurse. But your father and Rutherford commanded it. Later, I wanted to care for you, but again, it was commanded that the nanny have sole charge of you." Clarisse blinked furiously. "I even tried to do little things for you. Like bathe you and comb your hair. But your father insisted that the nanny perform such tasks. He insisted I spend but an hour of every day with you— an hour of his choosing, not mine. Which is why we had our teatime ritual. 'That is enough,' he said."

"No," Dom protested, his heart racing. "Why? Why would he do such a thing?"

Clarisse shook her head. "It was beneath me, they said." Clarisse's smile was fragile. "It was a lie, you know. It wasn't beneath me at all. Rutherford did not want me handling you because he never forgave me for eloping with Philip."

"God," Dom said, angry. Too well, he recalled, as a child, wanting his mother for one reason or another. But she had never been there. She had always been in her rooms. Even when he had fallen off his pony, breaking his ankle, he had been comforted by the housekeeper, the butler, and his nanny—not his own mother.

"Your grandfather can be a tyrant," Clarisse said with a flash of anger.

Dom thought about the trust. "Yes, he can."

"What are you thinking?" Clarisse asked, watching him closely.

"I am thinking about the trust," Dom said. "Do you know about the terms of the trust?"

"What terms?"

"Rutherford wants a great-grandson. If I impregnate Anne, if she gives me a son, the Hall will revert back to me," Dom said matter-of-factly.

Clarisse turned white. It was a moment before she spoke. "He is insane! This is absurd!"

"Yes, it is absurd."

"Will you do it?" Clarisse asked shrilly.

"If I decide to sleep with my wife, it will be because of other more personal reasons that have nothing to do with the trust," Dom said flatly.

"You have a son. He is a beautiful boy. You don't have to do anything you don't want to do." She appeared close to tears. "This isn't fair! Why is he trying to throw you together with that woman? What is he thinking?"

"He thinks I have treated Anne unfairly."

"She is at fault here—not you! If only we could find a way to get rid of Anne," she said tersely. "If only she would disappear—or run away like her mother did!"

Dom sighed. "If she ran away, I would undoubtedly have to go after her."

"You should not have married her," Clarisse said.

"It's a bit late for regrets."

"Yes, it is, because divorce would ruin us all." She kissed his cheek quickly. "I am going inside. Please say good-bye to me tomorrow before you leave."

Dom nodded. He watched her cross the terrace and

disappear inside the house. He was somewhat elated, in spite of being so very disturbed. He would have never dreamed of having this kind of reunion with his mother, not in a hundred years.

Dom sighed. What was he going to do about Anne? For four years he had pretended that he did not have a wife. Now that he had come home, even briefly, he realized he could not keep up such a pretense anymore. He did have a wife, a very real flesh-and-blood woman, who currently despised him—while he was, perhaps, far more attracted to her than before. Anne was an intriguing woman. Would it be so bad to be a real husband to her?

He turned and stared over the side of the terrace wall, into the thick and misty night, thinking about his parents' cold, loveless marriage and his lonely childhood. His pulse raced. Long ago he had vowed to himself that he would never need anyone. Treating Anne as she was due was only proper, and he had recognized that four years ago. But then, as now, he feared he might actually fall in love with her. And then what?

It would be far better to depart the Hall now, immediately.

Yet if he was truly like Philip, then he was incapable of love and had nothing to fear. Besides, he wasn't ready to leave Waverly Hall, not quite yet.

Impenetrable patches of fog swirled across the lawns, shrouding most of the house. Perhaps half an hour ago, Dom had seen Anne leaving the house, but he had not remarked her returning. Where had she gone?

If he did not know better, he would think she had gone to meet someone, perhaps for an illicit rendezvous. It was too damp and wet out for a mere stroll.

Abruptly he vaulted the railing and landed on the soft lawn below. He crossed the graveled drive.

He heard their voices before he saw them. Soft, low, intimate. They were leaving the maze. At first Dom did not recognize Patrick. He only saw that the man had his arm around Anne's shoulders, and that his hip brushed her skirts as they walked. And Anne was as comfortable with him as a woman with her longtime lover.

He was shocked. His blood began to pound. Anne, it seemed, had not been pining away for him these past four years.

It was then that Dom recognized his friend since childhood, Patrick.

# Chapter 6

**D**om stared at Patrick. He recalled Anne and Patrick sitting together in the drawing room, remaining that way for most of the afternoon. *Anne and Patrick?* Dom was shocked to find himself enraged.

Patrick dropped his arm from Anne's shoulders. Anne looked from Dom to Patrick and back again. Her expression had become strained. "Hello, Dom. Are you looking for me?"

Dom did not reply. He forced himself to be rational. He tried to remind himself that Anne was not, exactly, his wife. His mental gyrations failed. He smiled, not pleasantly, at them both. "Have you been enjoying your walk with my *wife?*" he asked Patrick.

Patrick was stiff. "Frankly, I have."

"That's good," Dom returned, very softly. "Because it's the last walk—or anything else—that you shall enjoy with her."

Anne gasped.

Patrick stared coldly. "Is that a threat?"

"No. It is a fact."

"You are mad," Patrick said. "Anne is not just my friend, she is my cousin. If we wish to walk together, you cannot stop us."

"I most certainly can."

"Stop it!" Anne said. "Dom—what is wrong with

75

you? For goodness sake, Patrick and I have known each other since I first came to the Collinses as a little girl. Of course we can walk together!''

"No, Anne. From this moment forward, you cannot," Dom said coolly.

"You *have* gone mad," Patrick said angrily.

"What are you accusing us of?" Anne cried heatedly.

Dom did not look at her. He had eyes only for Patrick. "You know damn well what I'm accusing you of, Patrick."

"Don't you think this husbandly attitude of yours is a bit late?" Patrick shot back. "Perhaps, had you been here these past four years, Anne might have not needed my friendship so badly?"

Dom stepped forward, shoving his body between Anne and Patrick. He wanted to hit Patrick, but kept his clenched fists at his side. Unfortunately, he could imagine Anne in Patrick's embrace, and it was not a pleasing thought. "Just how badly did she need your *friendship?*" he asked coldly. "And just how eagerly did you supply it?"

"Dom! You are behaving like a boor!" Hot color spotted Anne's cheeks. "This—this conversation is beyond decency! Patrick is my cousin!" Her color managed to increase. "Nothing more!"

Dom turned on her, his gaze flashing. "Be quiet. Stay out of this. This is between Patrick and myself. You I shall deal with later."

Anne's eyes widened.

Dom faced Patrick. "I thought you were my friend."

Patrick gritted. "I am your friend. But Anne is my friend, too."

"How obvious that is."

"You abandoned her, Dom. She did not deserve such treatment."

"We are not discussing the past. We are discussing

the present—and the future.'' Dom stared, his jaw flexing. Another emotion pierced through his soul. ''I saved your life, Patrick. Have you forgotten that?''

''How can I forget that you saved my life at the risk of losing your own?'' Patrick said tightly.

Anne glanced from one man to the other, clearly surprised. ''Dom saved your life? You never told me.''

Both men ignored her. ''Your gratitude is lacking,'' Dom stated. ''Therefore, so is my hospitality. I think you should leave.''

Patrick finally looked abashed.

''Dom,'' Anne said swiftly, ''do not do this. We are all friends. Do not make an ultimatum that you will later regret.''

Dom finally looked at her. ''Why not? What is one more regret in a lifetime filled with regrets?''

For a moment, Anne was very still, her gaze locked with his. For a moment, as Dom stared at her, he felt an odd connection with her, one that was as disturbing to him as the depth of his anger and jealousy.

Anne tore her gaze from his. ''Perhaps you should leave now, Patrick. Tomorrow we shall all be more sensible, I am sure. It had been a long, difficult day— for all of us.''

Patrick hesitated.

Dom was openly exasperated. ''I believe that my wife has now asked you to leave, as well. Good-bye, Patrick.''

But apparently Patrick could not resist one final parting shot. He smiled tightly at Dom. ''Of course I will leave. I cannot refuse *Anne*. Especially as Waverly Hall is hers now.''

Dom smiled back, dangerously. ''Patrick, let me remind you of a fact. Anne might possess the Hall, but I am the marquis. Do not ever forget that.''

Patrick turned away.

Anne hurried after Patrick. ''This will pass,'' she

assured him. "I will explain things to Dom." She shot a furious glance over her shoulder at her husband.

Patrick paused, took her hand, and squeezed it. "I hope to see you tomorrow," he said.

Anne nodded, clinging, it seemed to Dom, to Patrick's hand.

"Don't count on it," Dom ground out.

Ignoring him, Patrick strode away. Anne stared after him, as did Dom. They watched him disappear into the gloomy night. Even after he was gone, neither one of them moved, neither one of them spoke.

Dom broke the silence that smoldered between them. "I believe that you wished to explain to me?" he queried. Mockery laced his tone.

Anne turned. "You owe Patrick an apology."

Dom burst into laughter. It was an angry sound. "I owe him an apology? I believe that you both owe me one."

"In fact"—she ignored him—"you also owe me an apology."

Dom's next bark of laughter was filled with sarcasm. "Indeed?"

Her cheeks were so hot they burned. Anne's bosom heaved. She was livid. She could not remember when she had last been this angry. "You have been gone for four years, carrying on as you pleased. Now you return home—solely for your father's funeral. And do not think to deny it, because I am no fool. I know that was the *only* reason you returned. You suddenly appear here and think to tell me what I can and cannot do, whom I can and cannot see? You suddenly appear here and dare to refer to me as your wife?"

Dom folded his arms, his smile cold. "That's right." His eyes narrowed. *"Wife."*

Anne inhaled sharply. "Our marriage is a farce."

"Really?"

She tensed. Sudden intuition told her not to respond.

Dom towered over her. "You have been controlling a vast estate, Anne. Rutherford would have you entirely independent of me, as well. You are a marchioness, now, one day you will be the duchess of Rutherford—the most powerful, wealthiest woman in the land, after the queen. And you dare to tell me that this marriage is a farce? I don't think so, Anne. I think you have profited greatly from this marriage."

"I don't care about the titles," Anne managed, taken aback by his open anger. "I don't care about the wealth."

"But you care about Waverly Hall," Dom said scathingly.

She did not hesitate. "Yes, I do. I have watched over it for the past four years. Waverly Hall is my home now, too."

His laughter was harsh, biting. "But only because of your marriage to me, Anne—surely you have not forgotten my part in that."

Anne said, "How could I?"

"Just how much, I wonder, do you care about the Hall?" Dom mused darkly.

"What are you trying to say?"

He smiled coldly. "Perhaps you care so much about this estate that you have maneuvered my grandfather into devising the trust?"

Anne stepped back. "Have you been speaking to your mother?"

Dom stared.

"She doesn't like me," Anne said in a rush. "She never has, not from the day we were married. It is ridiculous to think that I could somehow manipulate your grandfather, who is one of the smartest, strongest men we both know!"

"But you cannot be displeased with his actions."

Anne wet her lips as she prepared her answer. She realized that she was hugging herself. "I did not ask for anything, not from him—not from you. But after these past four years''— she looked away, so he would not see how she was fighting to maintain control—''I would not refuse such a gift.''

His stare was relentless. "So be it. I have decided to accept what Rutherford has done."

His words stunned her.

"The house is yours." He smiled but it did not reach his eyes, and he made a sweeping gesture toward the Hall.

Anne knew better than to thank him. She did not trust him at all. He was after something. This battle— and it was a battle—had only just begun. She had the distinct feeling that he had just drawn the battle lines right there between them.

"Of course," Dom said softly, "I expect you to be generous and hospitable to my mother. Otherwise, I will oppose you."

"I have no intention of denying your mother anything," Anne flared.

He stared coolly at her, as if assessing far more than the truth of her words, as if assessing her very character.

Anne had to know. She had to know if he thought her a scheming hussy like the rest of his world did. "Ever since we married, people have been unkind. I hope that you have not paid attention to the nasty rumors. They are not true."

"If you are referring to the rumors that you are nothing but an American adventuress and a fortune hunter, no, I have done my best to ignore them."

Her heart actually skipped a beat. She was inordinately relieved. "But you have heard them."

His smile was almost frightening. "I have many friends, Anne. Most of them were so obvious in their attempts not to refer to the circumstances of our wedding and your antecedents that it was almost laughable.

I did not have to be a genius to know exactly what they were thinking.''

Her relief vanished. "They are unfair. All of them. That night in the garden, I did not plan it! I never dreamed ..." She trailed off, blushing hotly. "I didn't even know," she whispered.

He cocked a brow.

"Surely you, of all people, remember exactly what happened that night in the garden," Anne whispered desperately.

Their gazes collided, clung. Anne regretted referring to that unforgettable night—yet she would not have taken back her words even if she could have. Dom said, his gaze bold, his tone whisper-soft, "I remember."

Anne swallowed, finally at a loss for words.

"Now ... about Patrick."

"You have made a mistake," Anne said quickly. But she was relieved that he had changed the conversation. She must never broach such an intimate topic again.

"Really?"

"Patrick is my cousin and my friend. Not my ... lover.''

Dom's smile was rigid, menacing. "Anne, I am a fairly reasonable man. I can understand, even accept, the fact that you sought *friendship* with another man in these past four years while I was gone. The fault was, of course, my own. But I cannot accept a continuation of that friendship now.''

Anne's temper sizzled. "We do not have the kind of *friendship* you are referring to," she hissed, "but how dare you cast aspersions on my character, when you are the one with the morals of an alley cat!''

"Oh ho," Dom said, low. "Is it possible that you are jealous of my lady friends?''

"Never!" Anne cried. "I stopped caring ages ago about what you do and with whom you do it!''

He laughed at her. "I think you are lying now, Anne.

But I do admire your pride"—his gaze lowered—
"amongst other things."

She turned red. Anne whirled to leave. She was so
angry she did not know what she would next do if she
remained there with him. She was afraid that she might
actually strike him. He certainly deserved a good slap
for his arrogance and his impertinence.

But Dom gripped her arm, forcing her to face him.
"It is over, Anne. Stay away from Patrick."

"There was nothing between us," she panted. "Let
me go."

His grip tightened and he stared into her eyes. Anne
tensed. They stood so close to one another now that
his thigh brushed her skirts and her legs. In fact, if he
leaned forward, she would feel his breath upon her
cheek. "Let me go," she repeated, somewhat
breathlessly.

But Dom did not release her. She watched the anger
in his eyes changing. Something dark and hot washed
over her. She trembled. "You are hurting me."

"If anyone shall be your friend," Dom said roughly,
"it is I."

Anne's heart began to pound. She understood his
meaning exactly.

"Is that clear?" he whispered. And his hands gripped
her arms.

Her pulse rioted. She found it difficult to think, impossible to breathe. She should be shocked, but she
wasn't. There was still some inexplicable attraction between them. Anne did not want it, but she was acutely
aware of it, because it felt like a tight, hot, coiled wire,
wrapped around them both, and the longer Dom stared
at her with his smoky eyes, the tighter it became. She
could actually feel his pull upon her.

And the night had grown shockingly silent and still
between them. Making it far too easy for Anne to focus
all of her awareness on the man standing beside her.

Mist licked her skirts, his legs, their faces. His eyes heated dangerously.

Anne tensed. His face was closer to hers now. Very close. He had a beautiful mouth, and it was parted ever so slightly. *He was going to kiss her. And she did not have the will to push him away.*

As if reading her thoughts exactly, his grip tightened, his eyes darkened.

But she didn't really want to pull away. One kiss hadn't been enough.

One kiss would never be enough.

Not from Dom St. Georges.

"Anne," Dom whispered, unsmiling and intense, "I want you, Anne. Badly. I have wanted you since I first saw you again."

Anne expelled her breath. She hadn't realized that she was holding it. She could not manage any reply.

"And I know that you want me, too," he whispered. "No matter that you pretend otherwise."

It was true, Anne thought, and was horrified. Hadn't she learned at all from the past? "No," she said. "No," she lied.

He ignored her, covering her mouth with his.

His embrace was utterly male. It was futile to think of escaping him, so Anne tried instead to brace herself so that his body did not touch hers. This time, Dom's kiss was savage.

Anne gasped as his mouth forced hers open, as his tongue stroked furiously inside of her. She refused to respond, but her senses were exploding, rioting. His mouth was punishing but not quite hurtful, his hands hard, impossibly strong, kneading her back desperately, crushing her body to his. And his body, where it pressed against hers, was also hard, but excitingly alive. Warm, hard, male.

More than anything, Anne was aware of his lust. It was explosive. She felt it reverberating throughout his entire body, but she was acutely aware of the fact that he kept it firmly checked.

If not, she would be on the ground now, on her back, receiving him.

Anne could finally take it no more. She twisted her face away, crying out, tearing her mouth from his. She felt branded. A fire seared every inch of her body. Flames licked at every recess, especially high up between her thighs. Anne realized that Dom had inserted one of his legs there, making her ride him.

Dom buried his face against her neck, panting, his arms wrapped around her tightly, making no move to let her go.

Anne sought sanity desperately—before she did the unthinkable and returned his kiss. Before she allowed her own hot nature to rule her—before she pulled him down to the ground and on top of her. She must not let him use her—as Patrick had warned her that he would try to do. How right Patrick was.

Passion had ruled them once. Anne reminded herself that this man had stayed away from her for four years. If she submitted to him, she had no reason to believe that he would not disappear again.

Finally Anne pushed herself away from him with strength she did not know she had. He let her go. She leapt out of his arms. "No more."

He stared at her. Anne laid her own palm on her chest, hoping to still her wildly beating heart. She could not look away from him.

He broke the stare, glancing up at the sky, expelling his breath. Then he ran a shaking hand through his hair. His regard was direct. "Anne, you are my wife. I have reached the conclusion that I am not happy with our previous arrangement."

Anne froze. Surely he did not mean what she thought he meant! "I beg your pardon?"

His gaze was searing. "I am not leaving, Anne. Numerous factors have changed my mind, including my father's death. I am staying, here, with you—indefinitely.''

Anne stared. Horrified. ''No!''

He did not move, his stare hard, yet brilliant. When he spoke, it was as if he hadn't heard her. ''We will start anew, Anne. We must.''

Those were words she had dreamed of hearing, desperately, for four long years. Words that came now, far too late.

''No,'' she whispered, louder now, shaking her head. ''I cannot.''

''You have no choice,'' he said roughly, his gaze piercing. ''Because I am not asking you for either permission or approval. I am merely stating my intentions.''

# Chapter 7

*A*nne quickly outdistanced Dom once they had entered the house. She hurried toward the stairs, hoping to compose herself in her room. She could feel his eyes upon her. They were boring holes in her back. Anne's pace increased. She wanted to be alone; she needed to think.

*He wasn't leaving after all.*

Anne was still stunned by his declaration. Stunned and furious . . . and afraid.

But a door opened farther down the corridor, and the duke of Rutherford stepped outside of it. "Anne?"

Anne paused, one hand on the brass banister.

The duke came closer. "Are you all right?"

Anne imagined that she was quite flushed. Her cheeks seemed to burn. She was trying very hard to forget Dom's powerful kiss. "I am fine."

"I'd like a word with you," the duke said. His gaze strayed past her.

Anne glanced over her shoulder, and saw Dom regarding them from the foyer, arms crossed, one shoulder against the wall. His posture was negligent. But there was nothing casual, however, about the expression in his watchful eyes. Abruptly Anne nodded, and followed the duke into the library.

"Is there any chance of a reconciliation between the two of you?" the duke asked.

Anne hesitated. The duke's question was astonishingly blunt. "No. There is no chance." She was not even going to consider what Dom had suggested. Their marriage was over. It had been over for four years.

The duke sat in one of the plush chairs facing the fireplace. "Not even if I ask you to give him a chance?"

Anne perched on the very edge of the couch. "Please, don't," she said. "You know I hate to refuse you."

"There is nothing I want more," Rutherford said gently, "than to see the both of you together, happily, before I die."

Anne rose to her feet. "You are not going to die, not anytime soon, please, don't talk that way!"

The duke smiled at her. "Anne, I am seventy-four years old. These past few months I have become tired. I don't feel well. The day will come when I meet my Maker. If I can accept it, surely you can, too? But never mind, what has Dom said to you?"

Anne hesitated. "He intends to stay here, even though I have made it clear that he is not welcome."

"I am surprised at you, Anne," the duke chided. "This is Dom's home."

She clenched her hands. "I can't give Dom another chance. He doesn't deserve one."

"Maybe not, but you are the most generous woman I know—and the most sensible. Give him a second chance, Anne," Rutherford said softly. But it was a command. "What have you got to lose?"

"My heart," Anne replied simply.

"And what if you win?" the duke asked.

Anne inhaled loudly. His meaning was clear. What if she did not lose her heart? What if she won Dom's heart, instead?

A few moments later the interview was over, and Anne had not made any promises. Ridiculously, she felt guilty for being noncommittal. She was genuinely fond of the duke.

She hurried upstairs to her room, relieved when she saw no one. It had been a long, trying day, and she had no intention of changing for supper and joining the family for a formal meal downstairs. She was far too tired to spar with anyone, much less Dominick St. Georges. She was far too tired to bear his penetrating scrutiny, and his long, meaningful glances—looks she now understood.

She locked her bedroom door.

She had never locked it before.

It had been four years since she had been in the same house at night as her husband. And that last time had been her wedding night. Then, her door had been left unlocked.

Anne's temples throbbed. This was not her wedding night. In fact, she had tried very hard to forget all about her wedding night—the second most disastrous event of her life.

Anne could not help it. A tear spilled from her eyes. If only she could truly hate Dom St. Georges for all that he had done to her. But that was just it—Anne was afraid that she did not hate him at all.

*Anne waited.*

*She sat in their bed, her black hair hanging loose about her shoulders, dressed in a beautiful white nightgown from Paris, one trimmed with ribbons and lace. It was a modest gown, with long, full sleeves and a heart-shaped neckline, but Anne prayed that Dom would like it—that he would find her beautiful.*

*She leaned against her pillows, closing her eyes, remembering how handsome Dom had been in his white dress shirt and black tailcoat during the wedding and at the reception. Handsome and unfailingly polite and attentive, constantly at her side. She refused to think* about the fact that his smiles had been infrequent and strained and somewhat strange. He had not been as charming as he usually was.

But that, surely, was understandable. Because of the scandal, it had been a very small and private wedding.

The clock on the mantel chimed a single time.

Anne jerked. It was already one o'clock in the morning? Had she been waiting for Dom for almost two hours? She sat up, suddenly concerned, even anxious. Where was he?

Then it occurred to her that he might still be downstairs with his relatives, celebrating their wedding.

She relaxed slightly, but got up and crossed the dark room, which was only lit by candles. It was a warm summer night and her windows were open. Anne looked out, straining to see and to hear.

But she saw no lights spilling from the ground floor of the house below, and she heard no sound other than crickets chirping. The reception had clearly ended. All the guests had departed, the family had gone to bed.

Anne stiffened, touching the windowsill, uneasy. A crescent moon winked at her from the blue-black heavens above her head.

This made no sense. Where was Dom?

Foreboding made her stiffen, and chilled her to the bone. Anne hugged herself. Surely the party had just ended; surely he would appear at any moment.

Slowly Anne recrossed the room and climbed into the four-poster bed. She saw now that the two candles on her bedstand were burned a third of the way down. She sat staring into the dark.

Waiting.

And she continued to wait, even after the candles had burned themselves out, even as the horizon began to brighten, growing colder, and stiffer, and sicker, with every passing moment.

Dom did not come.

*It wasn't until much later that Anne heard the carriage and rushed to the window. The black Lyons coach with the silver crest rumbled away from Waverly Hall, drenched by the rising sun.*

*Anne was drenched in tears.*

Anne sat stiffly in her bed. There was no point in dwelling on the past, unless it was to remind herself of how badly Dom had treated her, how he had carelessly tossed her aside like a toy he'd grown tired of. Now Dom had told her that he wanted her and that he wanted to start over, but that was impossible. Only a very foolish and naive woman would agree to a reconciliation.

He had told her that he was home to stay. She did not think herself up to the task of forcing him to leave Waverly Hall, but if she remained strong, if she continued to rebuff his advances, surely he would soon tire of this latest game and leave.

And surely it was just that, a game.

For Dom could not be sincere. His interest in her was too sudden. He wanted *something* . . . but Anne could not guess what.

Anne covered her breast with her hand. Her heart was racing. She felt trapped. She must not allow him any intimacy with her, she knew that. But he was, without doubt, a master of seduction. She did not delude herself by thinking herself his equal when it came to opposing him in games of love. Especially because he was so very attractive. In games of love, she could not possibly win. Therefore, she must not play.

Anne released a long, shaky sigh. How easy it was to make an avowal, how hard it might be to keep one. But her life was at stake. She must remain strong—she must remain set against him.

A short time later, before Anne could do little more than wrestle out of her dress and hoops with the help of Belle, her maid, she became aware of footsteps coming down the corridor outside of her bedroom. Intuition told Anne to whom those footsteps belonged.

He knocked on the door to her room. "Anne?"

She regained her senses then. Anne rushed to her armoire and flung on a silk wrapper. Anne nodded and Belle opened the door. "What do you want?" she cried.

Dom smiled at her.

Anne did not smile back. "What do you want?" she demanded again. "Why aren't you downstairs taking supper with your mother and grandfather? Supper is always served at eight—and it is eight o'clock now!"

"As your husband, I thought it only fitting that we dine together. Especially as this is our first night together in years." He finally looked at Belle. "You are dismissed."

Before Anne could protest, Belle fled.

Dom smiled at her.

Her heart skipping, Anne rushed to close the door in his face—but he stepped forward, bracing it open with his hard thigh. Anne's anger died. Her fear bloomed.

"Why are you so resistant?" Dom asked softly. "Can I come inside? I wish to speak with you, Anne."

"No! We have nothing to talk about." Her eyes were very wide. Surely he did not think to exercise his marital rights now, when he had failed to do so for four very long years!

He eyed her, then stepped past her into the room.

Very conscious now of the fact that she wore nothing but a chemise, corset, and drawers beneath her wrapper, Anne clutched it closed at the throat. She could feel her pulse throbbing there against her hand. Dom, meanwhile, strolled around her room, glancing about as if curious about her few possessions. Anne watched him, filled with apprehension. She wet her lips. "This isn't right."

He glanced at her. "I cannot think of a single soul in this house who would object to my being here."

Anne said, "I can."

His brow arched upward lazily. "Really?" he asked.

How very comfortable he was in her room. But Dom, of course, had been in the private rooms of numerous women. While Anne had never had a man in her room before. "Yes." Her chin lifted. "I object."

His gaze held hers. "Your objection is overruled," he said softly.

"But this is my house."

His regard became piercing. "Do not challenge me, Anne."

She retreated instantly. "Of course, I gladly share it with you."

He eyed her for a long moment, clearly doubting her sincerity. When his gaze lowered, Anne had the uneasy feeling that he could see through her dressing gown. Finally he glanced around her room. "You do not have many things."

"I am a simple woman. My needs are few."

Dom smiled at her, and it crinkled the corners of his eyes. Anne's heart jumped erratically. "Most women have few needs, but more possessions than they know what to do with." His glance swept the room again, which would have been bare because there was no bric-a-brac about, except for the fact that Anne had flowers from her garden everywhere. Roses, lilies, hyacinth. He sniffed the air with obvious appreciation and abruptly skewered her with his regard.

"As you would know, being so well-acquainted with so many women," Anne heard herself say testily.

He laughed. "Are we back on that tiresome subject again? Anne, do you have an inordinate preoccupation with my private life?"

She was beet red. "No. I most certainly do not." She wished she had not spoken so impulsively.

Still smiling and amused, he said, "Shall I have Bennet bring our supper to your room?"

"No!" She was aghast.

"I had a suspicion you would refuse me." His smile faded. "I was very serious earlier, Anne."

She did not like his serious tone. "So was I."

"Ah, but women are allowed to change their minds." He was moving slowly toward her. Anne had lost all power over her limbs, and did not back away. He paused when only an inch separated their bodies. "I'm here to stay, and I want to start over." He reached out and covered her hand, which still gripped her wrapper at the throat, with his. His smile was infinitely seductive. "This is as good a time as any to begin anew."

"Perhaps, for you," Anne managed, unable to look away. "But not for me. Please leave. I am going to bed."

Instantly she regretted her words. Dom glanced past her at the four-poster bed and smiled, his eyes gleaming. "Now that is an even better idea than taking our supper here together."

"I am going to bed alone," Anne gritted.

His answer was to pull her hand away from her neck. Her wrapper opened there, revealing an expanse of ivory skin on her throat and upper chest. He continued to pull on her hand, raising it toward his mouth. He kissed first one knuckle, then another.

Anne uttered a small cry and fled across the room, putting its entire distance between them. A wet heat was gathering between her thighs. "It is over, Dom, over. You must leave me alone! I do not want you, and I do not want this!"

"It's hardly over, Anne, and you realize it as well as I."

She shook her head. "Why are you doing this? Why are you hounding me this way? What do you want?" she demanded. "Why have you decided to stay?!"

He stared. "Perhaps I failed to recall precisely how well suited we are. And now that I have returned, it is glaringly obvious."

"We do not suit. Not at all."

"Shall I prove you wrong?"

She backed up a step. "I have changed. I am a woman now. A worldly woman—too worldly for the kind of feelings you think to arouse in me."

His expression darkened. "Do not remind me that you are worldly, Anne."

"You have misunderstood me, again. Patrick is not my lover. I merely meant that you have destroyed my innocence. You ruined the last of my happy dreams from childhood. You forced me to grow up, Dom, no one else."

He stared at her coolly. His hands found his hips. "You know, if I recall correctly, I didn't, exactly, destroy your innocence."

It took Anne a moment to realize what he was referring to. She flushed. "I was speaking in the broadest sense of the word."

He eyed her. "I have already apologized to you twice for hurting you, Anne. I agree with you. I have been a bastard—I should not have stayed away. Where is your Christian soul? Isn't it your religious and moral duty to forgive me now?"

Anne's eyes widened.

"What would you do if I got down on my knees and begged for your forgiveness?"

She started. "You wouldn't."

"No, I have far too much pride."

Anne was swamped with relief. It would have been very hard to refuse him, but forgiving him would have been a matter of rote, because she had no forgiveness in her heart for him. Not now, not ever.

"You're an intriguing woman, Anne. I am completely intrigued." He smiled. "I also admit that I do not care for Patrick's interest in you. But now that I am back, he will undoubtedly redirect his attentions."

"Is this about Patrick?" Anne asked. She was incredulous.

Dom did not reply. Staring at her, Dom walked over to her and did not stop until his knees touched hers. By then, Anne's eyes were wide, her back rigid, her fists clenched. "I think you still have a great deal of affection for me, Anne."

She was breathless. "No."

"Yes." He smiled then, and it was infinitely engaging—infinitely seductive. "Shall we test my theory?"

Anne shook her head, but it was too late. He bent over her. Anne's spine flattened against the wall. Boxing her in, he raised both palms and laid them flat on the wall on either side of her face. "I think you want me," he whispered. "And I definitely want you."

"Don't do this."

"I won't do anything that you don't want me to do," he promised her, but he was looking at her mouth, staring at it. He said, "I can already taste you, Anne. I want another kiss."

Anne's pulse rioted. "No."

Their gazes locked for a heartbeat. He bent over her, but Anne managed to jerk her face aside. His lips landed on her cheek.

"Stop. Stop now," she whispered hoarsely, trying to push his hands away. His thighs burned her legs through her silk wrapper and drawers. She was on the precipice of a cliff and she knew it. If he did not leave her alone, soon, she would yield to him—perhaps with far more than just her body. "I can't!"

Dom lifted his head, but continued to grip her arms. He stared at her, grimly. "What do I have to do, Anne? I have apologized. I have returned. I want to make you my wife in more than name, now. I would not be a bad husband. I am a responsible man. What do I have to do?''

"There is nothing you can do. Once I wanted you more than I wanted anything, but I am older and wiser now." To her horror, tears spilled from her eyes.

"I see. No matter what I wish, no matter what I say, or promise, or do, you will not give me another chance."

Anne stared, crying silently, not quite able to get the word "no" out.

"You know, Anne," he said after a moment, "there is a physical attraction between us that is not usual. It could be a beginning if you would let nature, so to speak, take its course."

His words infuriated her and she embraced her anger with desperation. "I am not one of your *trollops* to give in to *nature*."

"Hardly," he agreed, his eyes darkening. "You act much more like a frightened, ignorant *virgin.*"

Their gazes clashed. He meant it as an insult, and Anne found it highly insulting.

She squared her shoulders, hoping to kill him with the frost of her stare. "You may leave now."

Dom straightened, dropping his hands. "Very well. I learned in the army when to retreat." He wasn't smiling. His tone wasn't friendly. His eyes were cold. "I do not pursue where I am not wanted."

"That is just wonderful," Anne snapped, furious with him, but also furious with herself, because now she was distraught.

"Only a fool would wait for an invitation that will never be offered," Dom said over his shoulder, pacing to the door.

"Or a gentleman," Anne flung. "Which you, of course, are not!"

He wheeled on the threshold of her room. "You wish to fight with me, do you not?"

"All right!" she cried. "I do want to fight—now get out!"

"I'll leave. But not until you answer one question. Was Patrick ever your lover?"

Anne wanted to throw something at him. There was nothing handy except the vase full of flowers, and she fought the temptation. "No."

His expression changed. "Anne, you're not still a virgin, are you?"

Anne inhaled. The flowers were tempting. She closed her eyes, wrestling with the urge—and lost. With all of her strength, Anne flung the blue-and-white vase at his head.

He ducked and it hit the wall instead.

# Chapter 8

*A*nne could not believe that she had so lost her head that she had thrown a vase at Dom. His eyes were wide as well. They both stared at the shattered porcelain, broken flowers strewn amongst the blue-and-white shards.

Dom's jaw ground down. His gaze pierced Anne. "I only asked you a question. If you didn't want to answer, all you had to do was say so."

Anne looked at Dom. "Yes, Dom, I am still a virgin."

He jerked.

She held her head high, praying that she would not blush. "You see, although you have been unfaithful to me, I have not been unfaithful to you."

He blanched. "*Christ.* How you make it sound."

Finally she gave in to an overwhelming urge and hugged herself. "It sounds exactly the way that it is." Her next words tumbled forth, unbidden. "Perhaps you should return to London, to Margaux Marchalle."

Dom started. Then his eyes narrowed and he crossed his arms. "Margaux Marchalle."

"The famous French actress."

"I know who she is."

"I would hope so."

"The real question is, how the bloody hell do you know who she is?"

"How could I not know when the two of you have been seen together everywhere these past two months?"

"But you are not in town." His eyes flashed. "Tell me, Anne, how is it that you are so well informed? Have you hired runners? To spy upon me? To keep track of my affairs? Has my private life become a hobby of yours?"

"No. I have no need of runners. Not when you dally with an infamous actress."

"I see. You are a woman who enjoys gossip. A woman who takes gossip to heart."

"That's not fair!"

"Perhaps you are not being fair."

Their gazes locked.

"Do you deny your relationship with her?"

Dom cursed. "Before, I found your interest in my private affairs amusing. Now I am finding it highly annoying."

"Then perhaps you should keep your affairs private?" Anne asked too sweetly.

"Your jealousy is evident, Anne."

"I am hardly jealous of a . . . a . . ."

"An actress?" Dom supplied. He was laughing now.

"A tart!" Anne almost shouted, flaming. "Will you not admit that she is your mistress?"

His laughter died. Dom's eyes flashed. "This is not only very dangerous territory for you, Anne—it is very unseemly as well."

"It is hardly as unseemly for me as it is for you. Although you will one day be a duke, so society will tolerate whatever you do—even if it is flaunting a woman like Margaux Marchalle."

He stared coldly. "You know, Anne, when you decide to be a real wife to me, in every sense of the word, then you will have the right to ask these kinds of questions—but not before then."

"Well, that is never going to happen," Anne said

fiercely. "And I do not need to ask these questions, for I already know the answers."

He said, low, "Continue in this vein, Anne, and I might think you far more than jealous. You sound like a woman scorned—a woman in love."

"Hardly." Anne protested far too shrilly.

His smile was knowing. "I see. Well, at last we are getting somewhere."

She wet her lips. "I am not jealous of your women. I am not a woman scorned. I scorn you!"

"I do not have *women*. And you are not very scornful when we kiss."

"That's because you are so very experienced at kissing." She was panting.

His jaw ground down. "Maybe I will decide to gain even more experience by making love with you."

She backed away. "Save y-your k-kisses for your mistress."

"Perhaps I will. If you continue to reject me."

She froze. Finally, stiffly, she shrugged. "You may see whomever you like. And you may dispense your kisses—and all else—where you wish."

He folded his arms and leaned against the wall, stepping on the flowers, crushing them. "How generous you are, Anne, giving me permission to manage my private life as I please."

"Other wives might not be as liberal," Anne said tersely.

"Other wives would not deny me my marital rights," he returned very softly.

"Is that why you came here tonight?" Her pulse raced so hard it made her feel faint.

"And if I did?" But his tone was mocking.

Anne was frozen. She could not think of a single retort.

He was angry. "Relax, Anne. I am not that big a cad to come knocking on your bedroom door after four long years and demand my husbandly rights. I came to share supper with you, remember. I came to reconcile with you."

Anne made a scoffing sound. "You came here to seduce me!"

His gaze darkened. "Believe what you will. But if seduction was my intention, know this: you would not be standing there on the other side of the room." His gaze moved to the bed. "If seduction were my intention, we both know where you would be right now. And you would be on fire, Anne. I would be making you burn."

Anne gasped and turned red. "Get out!"

His jaw flexed. "Gladly." But he did not move. "If I were you, I would keep in mind the fact that I am a healthy man, and your continued rejection might very well send me into the arms of another."

He turned and strode through the doorway, then paused, facing her again. His eyes flashed. "Make up your mind, Anne, about what you want. Because if you still want me, you now have the opportunity."

Anne stared in dismay.

He slammed the door closed.

The smell of something burning awoke her. Slowly, in stages.

Anne was exhausted, but she had not fallen immediately asleep. Her thoughts refused to stop, and they were focused on Dom. Her emotions roiled, at once hot and deep, and so very contradictory. When she did finally doze, her dreams were also about Dom, and they were nightmarish, because in them she knew he was sincere, and she allowed him to seduce her, eagerly accepting his embrace. Yet even asleep, a part of her brain shrieked in protest at the folly of her surrender.

Then, much later, she slept deeply, dreamlessly, in utter exhaustion.

When an acrid, charred odor began to tease her nostrils, Anne burrowed deeper under her blankets, not wanting to awaken. Her body felt like lead, impossible to move. Her mind was thick, muzzy. But the smell became stronger, heavier, unpleasant. Anne wanted to ignore it.

She was dreaming again, she decided, but this time she was dreaming about a fire.

She had become hot. She kicked off her thin, summer-weight covers.

The bitter, charred stench continued to assault her nostrils. *Wake up!* Anne's brain screamed. Suddenly Anne's eyes shot open. She began to cough.

The fire was not a dream. Something was actually burning, right there inside her bedroom.

Anne jerked upright. In the same instant, she saw that the tablecloth on her bedstand was aflame. Red fire was devouring the lace covering, licking the wooden table, and threatening to leap the small space between the stand and her bed. As Anne watched, something on her nightstand burst into flame, brilliantly, explosively. Her white roses.

Crying out, Anne jumped to the floor, her pillow in hand. She beat at the flames with her pillow. The kerosene lamp crashed to the floor, its porcelain base breaking. The beautiful Waterford vase which had held her roses also fell, but did not break. Anne continued to swing the pillow fiercely at the flames. The stand banged up against the wall. Her books thumped to the floor. Her china teacup and saucer fell, shattering.

"Anne!" Dom shouted, crashing open the door to her room.

The flames were finally out. Anne stood, gulping air, staring at the destroyed nightstand and the broken objects scattered on the floor.

Dom charged to her side, pushing past her. "What the bloody hell happened?" he demanded, then he turned and swiftly picked up a kerosene lamp from the bureau. A moment later he had lit it and was holding it aloft. "Good God," Dom said. "The damn candles must have overturned."

Anne stared at the mess that was now illuminated. She began to tremble. The tablecloth had been destroyed. Her books were badly burned. Had she not awoken, the blankets on the bed would have caught on fire. Anne did not like to think of what would have happened next.

Anne made a harsh sound, bending to pick up her edition of *Moby Dick*. The fine leather binding was charred black. She cradled it to her chest, then espied one of the roses, burned to a crisp but still in one piece. Her gaze riveted upon the blackened, obscene flower; the book slid from her hands without her even knowing it, thumping to the floor at her feet.

"Anne." Dom had set the lamp down and now he approached her, pulling her into his arms. Anne could not tear her gaze from the black, shriveled rose.

"Anne," Dom said huskily, his hand cupping the back of her head.

Anne became aware of him and the fact that she was in his arms, held tightly, reassuringly, and she looked up into his amber eyes and saw his deep concern.

"You could have been hurt." His voice was hoarse. His arms tightened around her. "Thank God you're all right."

Anne choked back the urge to cry. There was no reason to weep over her white roses, or over the small accidental fire, either. She lowered her cheek against Dom's chest. It was naked.

"Ssh," Dom hushed, his big hand stroking over her head and down the fat, thick braid of her hair. It had been bound loosely, and wisps of it were already coming undone. "It is just the shock that is distressing you. You are all right. Nothing happened. It is over now."

His gentle stroking and soothing tone had the effect of causing a surge of gratitude to well up in Anne. Gratitude, and something more. She pressed her face against his bare chest. His skin was almost as smooth as the finest velvet. She had not realized that he was mostly undressed. He was only wearing a black-and-burgundy silk robe. It was knee-length, and his legs were bare. Anne closed her eyes so that she would not see anything that she should not.

Suddenly she wondered how he had been outside of her room just when there had been a fire inside of it. She looked up at him, and he must have seen the question in her eyes. "I was downstairs, reading," Dom said. "The library is directly beneath your room. You made a commotion, Anne. Good God, I thought you had an assailant in your bedroom!"

"No," Anne said weakly. She was glad that he was there with her, even though her mind was warning her to keep up her defenses.

Dom sat down on her bed, bringing her with him, holding her close. "Sssh," he said again. "It's all right, now, sweetheart."

*Sweetheart.* The endearment twisted Anne's heart, which was beginning to pound too quickly now. Anne sensed that she was in danger, and it had nothing to do with the fire. "Dom, I think you should leave," she whispered roughly. But even as she spoke, her fisted hand, against his flat, tense belly, covered only by a thin layer of silk, uncurled.

She felt him tense even more.

Her gaze crept over. His robe gaped open, revealing his flat, muscular chest. Anne had a glimpse of his equally flat, hard abdomen.

Anne closed her eyes tightly, shocked by the sudden, insane tightening and aching of her very own loins.

"Do you really want me to leave, Anne?" Dom

whispered, tilting her face upward with one strong hand.

Anne's eyes flew open. Her heart banged wildly. Suddenly she wanted a safe haven. She wanted to remain there in his arms forever. It felt so right. Dom felt so right. The past had slipped away, as if it had never existed.

His large hand stroked over her hair, his fingers lingering on the plaits of her braid, then freeing them. "Anne?" His gaze locked with hers.

Anne understood his question; she did not want to answer. She had become very tense now, very warm. Her pulse was running wild.

How could she ask him to leave when she wanted him so desperately?

It was a night for sinning. Black, thick, silent, the air still acrid. Shadows danced about the room.

Dom had paused in the act of loosening her hair, but when she did not respond, when she did not tell him to stop, to leave, he continued, slowly.

It was a night filled with magic—a night for lovers.

"Anne," he whispered thickly when her hair hung thick and straight and blue-black to her waist. His palm stroked over it, shaking. "You have beautiful hair." Dom's eyes were golden, glittering, heated.

Anne could not look away.

Dom shifted, cupping her face with his hands. Anne did not move, did not protest. Her mind had shut down. Their gazes held, sparking.

Dom's nostrils flared. He bent his head. When his mouth touched hers, Anne sighed. Long and low.

An instant later she was on her back, Dom on top of her, pressing into her, his mouth hot and hard on hers.

Far, far back in her mind, she knew that she would regret this night. But she refused to consider the thought. Not now.

Anne welcomed him. Her nails scraped down his

silk-clad back. Dom groaned, his tongue thrusting past hers, raking hers. Anne's knees came up, apart. Dom's hands moved down, covering her breasts possessively, then pushing them up and against the fine fabric of her nightgown. Anne broke their kiss, crying out, when he began to knead them. Her body no longer belonged to herself. It was a wanton's body, starved and desperate for a man—starved and desperate for this man.

Dom's mouth moved to her breast. Through her nightgown he tugged her nipple between his teeth. Anne gasped, arching beneath him eagerly. Dom was already pulling her nightgown down her arms, baring her upper body, baring her breasts. Anne thrashed eagerly, her hands finding his head, her fingers threading through his hair. Then his mouth was on her breast again, and a moment later her nipple was being sucked between his lips. Anne held his head there forcefully. Dom groaned hoarsely.

Anne heard herself making small, breathy sounds.

Dom slid his hand down one hip, then lower, down her thigh. Anne jerked. Ignoring her, suckling her nipple with determination now, he began to stroke her thighs and the juncture between them, without lifting the skirt of her nightgown. Anne began to pant. His palm brushed the cotton covering her sex, again and again. And then his hand was under her clothes, his fingers sliding between her lips, searching her out.

A brilliant explosion wracked Anne. Her body came up off the bed, shuddering. Moans spilled from her lips.

When she lay in a boneless heap amongst the pillows once again, she became aware of Dom lying beside her. He was stroking her hip and stomach lightly, but his eyes were twin fires, his jaw was tight, his body was rigid and stiff, his robe open past his waist, revealing his navel, a fine sheen of perspiration gleaming on the flat slabs of muscles there. Anne's gaze met his.

The enormity of what she had done started to dawn upon her.

And Dom moved. He bent over her before she could say a word, his mouth seizing hers. Anne's protest died unspoken.

"Anne," he said harshly. He moved on top of her, framing her face with his hands. Briefly he stared into her eyes, his hard, stark, determined. There was no mistaking the fact that he was hugely aroused. His manhood was massive—Anne had been compelled to glance down—and it prodded her belly now. Where he touched her, her body flamed.

Anne's eyes fluttered closed. She arched for him.

He covered her mouth with his again hungrily. Anne could feel the explosive power he was just barely restraining. His big, powerful body shuddered once on top of hers. The ripe tip of his phallus rubbed against her sex.

He kissed her endlessly. His hands moved over her, knowingly. He stroked her throat, her arms, her breasts, and their enlarged, pointed tips. He caressed her hips, her belly, her swollen, aching lips. Anne was moaning now, unable to stop. He palmed her.

"Anne," Dom commanded.

She gasped, somehow opening her eyes and barely focusing on him.

"I want you."

She whimpered.

"I'm going to take you now," he said harshly.

Anne could not reply.

His knees opened her legs, spreading them. Smooth and fluid and practiced, he pushed his bulk inside her. Anne's eyes flew open, meeting his gaze.

"It will only hurt for a moment." His smile was brief and very strained. It was not reassuring. He plunged into her.

Anne cried out, gripping his shoulders, and then the

brief stabbing of pain was gone. Dom had paused, his neck corded, the muscles in his shoulders, chest, and biceps bulging. And then he began to move.

"Anne," he cried. "Anne." He began to thrust in a steady rhythm. Sweat streaked his brow, dripped onto her shoulders. He paused to find her mouth, her throat. His body was shaking. He made a sound, one filled with harsh need. His thrusting rhythm increased.

Anne gripped him tightly now. Hot desire budded inside of her, coiling up tight, and tighter still. Anne cried out. She understood the precipice he had poised her upon.

Dom gasped, pausing inside of her.

Anne's gaze flew open—their eyes met. His were mirrors of savage lust and equally savage restraint. His face was strained, perhaps with pain. Certainly with determination. The tendons and muscles in his neck and shoulders bulged. His smile was brief, meant to be reassuring, yet it was so intense that it was almost frightening.

Slowly, Dom withdrew his penis from her, inch by inch.

Anne gasped. And just as slowly, he slid inside her again. He bent, tongued her nipple repeatedly. Then he painstakingly began the entire process again.

Within moments, Anne could stand his exquisite torture no more. She shattered.

And then Dom gripped her hips and began to plunge fast and hard. Anne was shocked by his power, by his violence. He no longer attempted to hold himself in check. Her gaze flew open, and she was mesmerized by his starkly rigid face. She was part of a whirlwind, one she could not stop even if she wanted to. And then his eyes opened and he gasped her name. For a heartbeat, she saw something that defied the past, at once brutal and gentle, stoic and desperate. Need.

Dom moaned, shuddering on top of her, pulsing inside of her, collapsing.

As he lay on top of her, panting, Anne swallowed dryly, holding his sweat-streaked back tightly beneath his robe. Her mind was functioning now, and Anne was afraid to listen to her own thoughts. But there was no avoiding them.

*Oh, God, what had she done?*

Dom finally moved, sighing and stretching out on his back beside her like a big, sleek lion. Anne did not move. She was afraid even to breathe.

His eyes were closed, his lashes thick and fanlike on his cheeks. His breathing subsided as he fell asleep. But just before he did so, his hand crept out, closing the distance between them, covering hers.

Anne wanted to pull her hand away, yet she did not—needing comfort from him now as much as anything else.

When he was asleep, Anne finally pulled her hand free, fixed her nightgown, and climbed out of the bed. She stared down at him.

Moonlight spilled through the open windows and played upon his face and body, the black-and-burgundy silk rippling in disarray about him. Anne's heart clenched. He was a glorious man, his face handsome enough to take her breath away even now, after all these years, and his body was every bit as beautiful, mostly hard, sculpted muscle. He was an irresistible man.

She turned and walked to the chaise in the other corner of the room, picking up a mohair throw on the way. She curled up there. Tears burned her eyes. *What had she done?*

Perhaps their union had been inevitable. But now what?

Nothing had really changed. She still did not trust her own husband. She could not trust him with her heart—giving him her body was quite enough.

## Chapter 9

*R*utherford was sipping black tea and reading yesterday's *London Times* when Dom entered the breakfast room.

It was one of the most cheerful rooms in the Hall. Two walls were paneled in honey-colored oak, a third wall was papered in a bright yellow floral print, and the fourth wall was entirely made up of windows. Sunlight poured into the room, gilding the blue-and-gold Persian rugs and the pale blue silk draperies. The sound of birds singing their morning songs could be heard quite clearly, and outside, the gardens were a mass of vivid rainbow hues.

Dom went to the sideboard and filled a plate with buttered toast, eggs, bacon, and kidney pie. Facing his grandfather darkened his already turbulent mood—a mood he did not quite understand. His intention had not been to seduce Anne and, while last night had been far more than pleasurable, he felt like a heartless bastard.

When he sat down, the duke laid his newspaper aside. "Good morning, Dom. Did you sleep well?"

"Surprisingly well," Dom growled.

The duke studied him. Dom attacked the kidney pie. Although he did not like Rutherford's tactics, he loved his grandfather, he always had. The duke had always

110

been the one to applaud his behavior when it was merited. Those times had been rare when he was a rebellious boy, but Dom could remember each and every one. Too, his grandfather had also been the one to chastise and scold him. Those times had been numerous. Dom treasured them, as well.

Even as a small boy, he had known that his grandfather cared. It had almost made up for his father's indifference.

"Did Anne sleep well?" Rutherford asked.

Dom laid his fork and knife down. "Are there no secrets in this house?"

"I imagine that there are a few." The duke smiled.

"Anne is still asleep," Dom said flatly, recalling the fire. Fortunately it had been put out before it could cause any serious damage. Not only was she asleep, she was asleep on the chaise. He had woken up alone. Her gesture did not need much interpretation. She still intended to resist him. She was not happy with what had happened. Finding her asleep on the chaise had been very annoying—and not just because he had woken up thinking of making love to her again.

"I'm glad to see that the two of you are starting to smooth things over," Rutherford said.

Dom sighed. "Don't become too excited. We have barely started to smooth things over, as you put it."

He attacked his food. Why was he so upset? Anne was as much to blame for their consummation last night as he was. Perhaps he was angry because it had been so damnably good. And because he knew that Anne still intended to fight him. "Hell," Dom said, tossing his napkin aside.

But Rutherford was engrossed in the newspaper.

Dom stood and walked to the window and stared outside. He stared for a long time, trying not to think and failing. His head was full of Anne, and what he was doing to her. His decision to stay and reconcile had been an impulsive one. He could not help thinking that she deserved far more from a man than she would ever get from him.

And now she might become pregnant. He would not be displeased. But if she did give him an heir, he was going to turn Waverly Hall over to her legally forever.

"Why didn't you just ask me to sire an heir?" Dom finally asked. "Instead of using blackmail?"

Rutherford laughed. "Oh, and would you have agreed?"

"Maybe."

The duke snorted. "You would have told me to go to bloody hell and stay there. We both know you only came home because your father was ill, with no intention of remaining here any longer than necessary."

"Had you had a little patience, none of this would have been necessary. It was inevitable that I try for an heir one day."

"Old people have no patience."

Dom made a cynical sound.

But the duke appeared very satisfied. "So does all of this mean that you are staying here, with your wife, for a while?"

"Yes," Dom said.

"Your father's solicitor has requested a meeting with the family this morning. He should be here at any moment."

"What could Philip's will possibly contain?"

"It is just a formality," Rutherford said.

"What has been going on in my absence?" Dom asked. "Why don't Anne and my mother get along?"

"Anne gets along with everybody. Your mother, on the other hand, is difficult and demanding."

"My mother has earned her position and is entitled to whatever it is she wants," Dom said. "Especially now. You know, she told me yesterday that you have never quite accepted her."

The duke stared. It was a moment before he spoke. "Philip married without my prior consent. They eloped. I did not approve."

Dom imagined that he must have been furious at being so defied. "And you still disapprove, after all these years?"

"Yes, but not for the reasons you imagine." The duke rustled his newspaper. "Clarisse is hardly important, Dom. What is important is your relationship with Anne."

"You mean," Dom said dryly, "what's important is that I am bedding my wife."

"I am entitled to my peccadilloes." Rutherford smiled.

"What are you talking about?" Anne said from the doorway. Her face was flushed.

Dom jumped to his feet. "Good morning, Anne."

She stared at him, but not at all the way a lover should the morning after, and then at the duke, as coldly. "I could not have heard correctly."

Rutherford also stood. "And what is it that you have overheard? There is no reason for you to be upset, Anne." His tone was mild.

Her eyes flashed as she strode into the room. "I am too embarrassed—and too furious—to even repeat what I have heard!" She cried. "B-but," she sputtered, "what Dom and I d-do privately is not your concern!"

Dom was worried. Anne did not know about the outrageous terms to Rutherford's trust, and he did not want her finding out about them now, after last night—or at any other time.

But Rutherford said smoothly, "You are wrong, Anne."

"Wrong!" She gave Dom a look that would have killed a lesser man.

"Dom is my heir. And I am an old man. Of course it is my concern whether or not the two of you are sharing a bedroom," Rutherford said. "You do have a *duty,* Anne. Your duty to this family is to provide Dom with an heir."

Anne's face turned a brighter shade of red. "Well, you may wish for whatever you choose, but you are going to have to wait a very long time to see your wishes come true—if not forever!" She turned her back angrily on them both, moving to the buffet.

Dom and Rutherford exchanged glances. Dom went up behind Anne, laying a hand upon her shoulder. She whirled. Rutherford chose that moment to exit the room.

"Anne," Dom soothed, "there is no reason for you to be so distraught."

"No?" She batted his hand away. "The two of you are scheming over our private life! I am livid."

"But he is the duke. He has every right to be concerned about the future of the dukedom," Dom said in a liquid tone.

"And you will play the fiddle because he demands it?"

Dom's gaze hardened. "I never do anything I don't wish to do for myself."

"Oh, really? So it is a happy coincidence, then, that you wanted to bed me when your grandfather wishes it as well?"

Dom's own smile had faded. "Anne."

"No!" She cried. "You seduced me last night to please him. You didn't want me—you wanted an heir."

"That's not true." Dom reached out quickly and gripped her arm, halting her.

"It is true," she spit. "All right. Let's talk. Let's talk about how unscrupulous you are."

"There was the fire, you were upset. It just happened, Anne."

"It hardly just happened," she countered.

"Sometimes it just happens between two people who are enamored of one another," Dom said firmly.

Hot color mottled her cheeks. "We are hardly enamored of one another. You seduced me, Dom. You may have gone to my room because of the fire, but you took advantage of the late hour and my fright."

Dom could deny that he had seduced her, but he had taken advantage of her. "What difference does it make?" he asked quietly. "My grandfather is right. We both have an obligation that transcends our personal desires. It is time for us to fulfill our duty, Anne."

"I am American, remember? And I don't give a damn about heirs and dukedoms," Anne said furiously. "And I am not about to start over with you until you have proved yourself to me!" she shouted.

"I see. So we are back to square one?"

"Yes."

"In spite of the fact that you were as eager to consummate last night as I was?"

She flushed. "I was . . . overcome."

He had to smile, eyeing her. "To say the least."

Before she could protest, he touched her mouth with his fingertip, silencing her abruptly. "We were both overcome, Anne. Why deny ourselves what we find mutually desirable and mutually satisfactory?"

She gazed at him murderously. "There is nothing—*nothing*—mutual between us. You are heartless, ruled only by passion and self-interest. I happen to have a heart, Dom, and I intend to keep it intact."

"You are afraid of falling in love with me again."

"No."

"Then what are you afraid of? I am promising to be a responsible husband."

"A responsible husband." Her tone was bitter. "For the last time, I don't trust you. I don't forgive you. I don't want you." Her eyes were blue flames. "Go back to town, Dom. Go back to *her.*"

His eyes widened. Incredulously, he said, "Again we digress to the subject of other women?"

She did not respond.

"Anne—what if I told you that Margaux, and the others, are all in the past? That I will be faithful to you?"

She froze. Her skin suddenly appeared translucent.

Dom wet his lips. "Well?"

She inhaled. "It would make no difference."

He was terribly disappointed, but quickly shoved his feelings aside. "I see."

"Do you? Do you really?" Anne turned abruptly and left the room.

Dom stared after her.


The family had gathered in the library, Clarisse joining them. The family solicitor was a tall, thin, middle-aged man. Canfield shook hands with the men, greeted the ladies. Everyone sat down, Clarisse and Anne on the sofa, Dom taking a chair beside them, the duke choosing to sit behind the desk. Canfield remained standing. He cleared his throat.

"This will take but a moment. May I begin?"

Rutherford nodded. Dom found himself looking at Anne, but she was ignoring him as if he did not exist. Clarisse appeared tense.

Canfield quickly read the will. As it was very short, it took him a matter of minutes, "I, Philip St. Georges, marquis of Waverly, earl of Campton and Highglow, baron of Feldstone, and heir to the dukedom of Rutherford, being both of sound mind and body, do hereby bequeath my entire unentailed fortune, consisting of some eighty thousand pounds, to my dearest friend, Matthew Fairhaven. To him I also bequeath Waverly House in London, and all that it contains.

"To my beloved and loyal wife, I leave nothing.

"To my only son, I leave my private journal.

"Signed and witnessed on this day the fifteenth of September, eighteen hundred and fifty-two, by Lord Charles Gurley and myself." Canfield laid the will aside, the paper rustling loudly.

A vast silence filled the room.

Clarisse was on her feet, her face utterly white. But she said not a word.

Dom had not expected anything of consequence to come from this reading of the will, but he was also standing, stunned. He finally found his voice. "Who the bloody hell is Matthew Fairhaven?"

Canfield looked at Dom. "He is, as the will states, your father's best friend."

Dom stared. He could not believe his ears.

Clarisse still said nothing.

Anne sat very still, looking first at Dom and then at his mother.

And then, through his surprise, Dom felt the hurt and the anger. Dear God! His father had left everything to his friend—and not a single cent to his wife or to his own son. He staggered with the realization, and abruptly sat back down.

Clarisse, meanwhile, walked away from everyone, her head held high, her back to the room. She stared out at the magnificent Waverly gardens.

Dom stared after her. Anne was the one, however, to jump up and rush to her. "Clarisse, let me get you some hot, sweet tea."

"No," Clarisse said without inflection.

Rage filled Dom. His mother had been left penniless. He had already learned that she and Philip had not made an agreement before their marriage leaving her a jointure because of their elopement, and he had left all of his savings, and Waverly House, to Fairhaven. It was the grossest insult. But no one, Dom vowed, outside of this family would ever know. He got to his feet. "Canfield, you will keep this will and its contents utterly confidential."

"Of course." Canfield was bland.

But that was not enough for Dom. "Otherwise, you shall answer to me," he said bluntly.

The duke moved to stand beside him. "Dom, I am sure that Mr. Canfield will keep all that has happened this morning privy to himself." His tone was equally dire.

Dom hardly heard. And it was not Canfield he really wished to shout at and berate. It was Philip.

He glanced at his mother's rigid back again. She had not moved from where she stood staring out of the window. How could Philip have done this to her? They had been married twenty-nine years. Had Philip sought somehow to punish her from the grave? But for what?

Once they had loved one another enough to elope. Had they hated each other by the time Philip died? Dom had been aware of their apathy toward one another. But he had not thought them to be hate-filled.

Clarisse finally turned. Her face was devoid of expression, resembling a beautiful, waxen mask. "It doesn't matter."

Dom shook. "It matters," he said roughly. He crossed the room and put his arm around her, briefly squeezing her shoulders. "Mother, I do not want you to worry. I will make arrangements for you. Nothing in your life will change."

Clarisse looked into his eyes. "Thank you, Dominick."

Rutherford sighed. "Well, Canfield, you have certainly surprised each and every one of us."

Canfield flushed with embarrassment. "I tried to counsel Philip to do otherwise, but he was adamant."

"He was a fool," Rutherford said. "He is still a fool."

"Lord Waverly," the solicitor said.

Dom realized that Canfield was holding a parcel out to him. "What is that?" he asked—although he knew.

"As the will said, your father left a journal. It is yours." Canfield smiled at him.

Dom stared at the paper-wrapped bundle, one the size of a thick book. He could not move. *A journal?* He had not known that Philip kept a journal. But there it was, his father's own diary. The chance to finally know him.

Canfield laid the parcel on the side table, glanced at his pocket watch. "I really must be going. I am so sorry to present you with such a disturbing will."

Dom did not see him shake hands with his grandfather, or hear him murmur a farewell to his mother and Anne. He was staring at the parcel that contained his father's journal. He was riddled with tension and curiosity.

But Dom was also filled with a deep foreboding.

Something was not quite right.

Canfield was leaving, and looking at him expectantly. Dom's hand was steady in spite of his trepidation as he bid the solicitor farewell. He did not walk him to the door. He remained in the study, alone, as his grandfather, his mother, and Mr. Canfield left the room.

Anne remained. But Dom wished that she would also leave.

"Dom, are you all right?"

"Yes, I am fine."

"It is only a diary," Anne said.

He had not realized just how astute Anne was. He forced a smile. "I look forward to reading it." But he was recalling the terms of the will and its unmistakably biting tone.

Anne stared. "I had better go. Your mother is in shock."

"As she should be," Dom said grimly, furious with Philip again.

At the door, Anne paused. "Dom, are you sure that you are all right?"

He looked at her. "Do you want a confession, Anne? No, I am not quite all right. My late father has just delivered a very rude blow to my mother—and to me as well. I did not know my own father at all. He was a stranger to me. He did not love me, I am certain of that, but I also think that he did not particularly like me. And now he has left me his journal. Why?"

A moment passed, in which they stared relentlessly at one another, Dom flushed, Anne pale. "I am sure that he loved you, Dom . . ." she began.

He waved his hand, dismissing her. "You are wrong." He picked up the diary. "In any case, I shall soon find out, won't I?"

Anne stared, appearing as if she wanted to say something, but thought the better of it. She nodded and left.

Dom stared only at the journal in his hand. What did Philip wish to tell him? Whatever it was, he had no real choice in the matter. He would ignore his strong premonition warning him against reading the diary. His father was dead, but wished to speak to him from the grave. Dom could not refuse the strange, untimely summons.

Clarisse stood frozen outside the library, pressed against the red-and-gold-striped wall. She could not believe what had just happened. And she did not give a damn about the eighty thousand pounds. Not now, not anymore.

Perspiration beaded at her temples and along the edges of her black lace hairnet.

*Her husband had kept a journal!*

Dear God, what could Philip have been thinking of? And what had he written in those pages? *The fool!*

She inhaled loudly, the sound sharp. Abruptly Clarisse realized how it would appear to a servant should she be discovered standing like this in the hallway, spying upon her own son. Instantly she moved away from the wall to stand in the center of the hall, pale with fright now.

And what was Rutherford thinking of, to allow Canfield to give Dom that journal? Had the old man finally lost his mind? Had he gone senile, at last? *What if there was something incriminating inside of it?*

Dom must not read it. No one must read it!

Clarisse lifted her heavy black brocade skirts and raced a short distance down the corridor, stepping into the empty drawing room. She waited and waited and was finally rewarded when she saw her son passing down the hallway—carrying Philip's journal. Dismay made her feel faint.

Clarisse watched Dom walk upstairs. Undoubtedly he was taking the journal to his rooms. She must think of a way to retrieve the journal—*before* Dom read its contents.

Clarisse was frozen beside the door in the drawing room. Her heart thumped so heavily that it hurt her. The minutes seemed to go by with agonizing slowness. What was Dom doing? Surely he was not glancing through the diary now? Damn Philip! Damn Rutherford!

Clarisse was flooded with relief when she saw Dom coming back downstairs. She shrank back against the wall so he would not see her as he passed the open doorway. But he did not return her way; he went into the foyer instead. She heard a murmur of voices, his and Bennet's, and then the front door opening and closing. He had gone out.

Clarisse waited another heartbeat, then dashed into the corridor and up the stairs. She realized how she must appear, tripping on her skirts like a madwoman, and she forced herself to slow to a sedate pace. Her heart beat harder now than before.

She entered Dom's room as casually as possible, then, when she saw that his valet was not present, that she was alone, she shut the door and locked it.

Her gaze scanned the room. She spotted the thick, paper-wrapped parcel instantly. It was lying on the bedside table. *Thank God.*

The parcel containing her husband's diary seemed to sear her hand. Clarisse clutched it to her chest, rushing back to the door. Carefully she unlocked it, cracked it, and peered outside. But no one was there to remark on her odd behavior.

She slipped from her son's room. And as she hurried down the hallway and the stairs, curiosity began to assert itself through the haze of panic and fear.

What *had* Philip written about?

His life had certainly been eventful and far from ordinary, what with all of his travels. Perhaps the journal was nothing more than the descriptive passages of Philip's numerous journeys.

But Clarisse did not think so. Had he written about her? If so, what had he said? Had he written the truth? *Had he even known the truth?*

Clarisse inhaled. To this day, she wasn't sure if Philip had really known. She suspected that he had. But he had never revealed his feelings to her, and surely if he had known, he would have been enraged?

She would not burn the journal, not quite yet. She could not. She would read it first, and then she would burn it—if she had to.

For if the truth were revealed, it would destroy the entire family. No one would be able to survive the ensuing scandal. No one.

## Chapter 10

$D$om had disappeared after the reading of his father's will. Anne had seen him cantering away from the Hall on one of the stable's hunters, heading not toward the park with its many fine riding trails, but toward the distant hills. Anne knew that Dom was disturbed.

She could not help but feel sorry for Clarisse, both for the predicament she had been placed in and for the humiliation Philip had forced upon her from the grave. But Anne was not surprised by Philip's actions. She had realized years ago that there was far more to their relationship than met the eye.

But she did not want to feel sorry, or anything else, for Dom. Anne was compassionate by nature, however, and he had recently lost his father. It was going to be very difficult to remain aloof given the startling new circumstances of Philip's will. But Anne was determined.

Anne was closeted in the land agent's spacious office, which she had taken over as her own office a year and a half ago. It was terribly hard to concentrate on the books.

Anne removed her reading glasses with shaking hands. Dom wished to bed her in order to sire an heir. How despicable he was! And Anne did not care that, by law, he had every right to an heir, and that it was her moral duty as his wife to give him a son.

How could she have let her guard down even for an instant? Allowing Dom into her bed was the stupidest thing she had done in four long years. She had not trusted him—and she had already been proved right.

Anne covered her face with her hands.

After a moment she regained her composure. Perhaps she would not have succumbed to Dom's charm had she not been so distressed by the accidental fire. Anne still could not comprehend how the two candles had overturned. Had she thrashed about in her sleep, knocking both of them over? It was the only possibility, for last night Anne had checked and found all of her bedroom windows closed. No strong gust of wind had been responsible.

She shoved the incident from her mind. She had more important matters to attend to. Philip's sudden death had interfered with her daily routine, and she was behind in the balancing of the estate's accounts.

Anne forced herself to stare down at the numbers on the ledger before her, instead of out the window. It hardly mattered. The numbers refused to add up, multiply, or divide correctly. Anne finally shoved the account book aside with a soft, unladylike oath.

She was relieved by a knock upon her door. Her first suspicion was that it was Dom. "Come in," she called tersely.

Felicity entered the room.

Anne tensed. Felicity's appearance was unexpected. Felicity had not said hello to her at the funeral service, at the grave, or, afterward, at the house. Anne had not spoken with her in four years—not since that terrible night when she and Dom had been discovered in the gardens and been torn apart by their families.

But that had been a long time ago. Since then, Anne had married Dom, been abandoned, and grown up. Felicity had also wed, and was now, recently, widowed. Anne's heart filled with sudden hope. How she wished that Felicity was calling to let bygones be bygones, and to resurrect their old childhood friendship. Anne could use a good friend right now to confide in.

"Hello, Anne," Felicity said.

Anne heard Felicity's tone and saw her face and knew that her hopes were farfetched. "Hello, Felicity. This is a surprise."

"I am sure that it is." Felicity did not remove her gloves. She was wearing a dark red gown that was probably lovely in the evening, but was far too harsh in daylight. Still, she was boldly blond and flamboyantly beautiful, as always. Anne could not help feeling small and dark and plain in comparison.

"Actually, I have come to see Dom. Do you know where he is?" Felicity asked, her tone quite condescending.

Anne slowly rose to her feet, but did not move from behind her desk. "What do you want with my husband?" she heard herself ask. She flushed at her own choice of words.

Felicity shrugged. "We are old friends. Perhaps I wish to reminisce."

Warning bells screamed inside of Anne's head. Felicity and Dom were hardly old friends. Felicity was a jilted bride—and a very beautiful widow. It was not correct for her to call upon any gentleman. It was not correct for her to call upon Dom. Anne was now aware of the gleam in Felicity's turquoise eyes. She did not care for it.

"Dom is out," she said too tartly.

"Indeed? Have you chased him away again, so soon?"

"That is unkind, cousin."

Felicity smiled, but it was more a baring of her teeth. The two front ones overlapped slightly. "Really? Oh, let me recall, it was so kind of you to entice Dom into the gardens on the eve of my wedding to him!"

Anne was perspiring. "Felicity, I said I was sorry before. I shall gladly say it again."

Felicity no longer attempted a smile. "But you are not sorry, Anne. You are the marchioness of Waverly, the countess of Campton and Highglow, the baroness of Feldstone. You are the viscountess of Lyons. One day you will be the duchess of Rutherford. And"—her tone rose dramatically—"you have somehow maneuvered Dom out of this very house. Waverly Hall is yours now. Do not tell me you are sorry!"

Anne stared. Patrick must have told his sister about the trust. Anne wished he had not, but she herself had failed to ask him to keep the matter confidential. Her chin lifted slightly. "You are right, Felicity, I am not sorry. Now, I have many affairs demanding my attention. Perhaps you should leave?"

But Felicity made no move to go. "You never cease to amaze me, Anne. First playing the hussy with Dom, then playing the man. No wonder he so quickly lost interest in you."

Anne stiffened. Felicity's words really hurt. Anne knew that she was as far from the current feminine ideal as was possible. Plump, blue-eyed blondes like her cousin were all the rage, especially ones who knew how to flirt and paint watercolors. Anne had always known that her interest in books and horses was unladylike. As was her interest in the estate—and her ability to manage it well. Yet it was a challenge which she thoroughly enjoyed. One she would not, could not, give up. But surely Felicity was right. Not only was she small, dark, and plain, she was very unfeminine, and perhaps that was the real reason Dom had left so long ago.

Only to return now to get an heir.

Anne ducked her head, so Felicity would not see just how crushed she was. But she would not wallow in self-pity. She had a very good life, even without the man she had once loved.

But Felicity laughed. "You haven't changed at all, Anne. You are still an odd, awkward girl."

Anne's temper flared. Yet her tone was polite and controlled when she spoke. "You have changed, though, Felicity."

"Yes, I have. I am a wealthy widow now, and considered one of the ton's Reigning Beauties."

Anne was certain Felicity spoke the truth. "I know that you have not forgiven me for what happened in the garden that night, and for marrying Dom. I also realize that you are petty enough to never forgive me, even though your own life has been, as you have pointed out, so very successful. But I do wish for peace between us."

Felicity's pale brows rose. "Forgive you! Oh, come, how could I not forgive you, dear Anne? I married a wealthy man, and while you may have married the heir to a dukedom, he abandoned you, making it clear to the entire world that he only married you because he had no choice in the matter. Everyone knows that you lured him into the garden and seduced him in order to force his hand, Anne. And while everyone thinks that you are a scheming American capable of ruthless seduction, I know the truth. I know that you have been in love with him, pitifully so, since you were a child. I know just how crushed you were when he chose me instead of you—and I know how crushed you must have been when he left you the day after your wedding. I wonder if he would have even bothered to come back if Philip hadn't died?" Felicity tossed her head and laughed. "I have felt nothing but pity for you, Anne. So you see, there is actually nothing to forgive."

How cruel Felicity was. She had not mellowed with time. Anne almost responded in kind, but refrained from engaging in a demeaning debate. Besides, if she had survived the cruelty of Dom's abandonment, she could survive Felicity's mean, pointed barbs now.

Anne took a fortifying breath. "Felicity, it is time for you to leave."

Felicity shrugged. "I will wait for Dom in the house."

"He has gone riding. I have no idea when he will return."

Felicity laughed. "I do not mind waiting, Anne. I have offered Dom my condolences, but I haven't yet *consoled* him. I have been waiting a very long time."

Anne stared at the woman in the garish red dress. Finally, Felicity left. Anne sank down in her chair, gripping the edge of her desk. Felicity had made herself very clear. She was a widow now, and she was after Dom.

She had every intention of jumping into his bed. Anne could not help but think that she would succeed. Too well, she recalled Dom's very blunt threat. He had openly told her that if she continued to rebuff him, he might very well seek out another woman.

Anne was dismayed. Her carefully ordered life was crumbling around her.

Worse, she recalled now, with utter clarity, Felicity's threats—made four years ago.

*One moment, Anne was in utter ecstasy. The next, in complete confusion.*

*Dom leapt away from her. Anne lay in the grass, not understanding—until she heard shocked voices approaching. And one of them was her aunt's strident, angry tone.*

*"Anne, quickly, get up, someone saw us!" Dom said urgently, lifting her to her feet and yanking down her skirts. He began quickly tucking in his own shirttails and fastening his pants.*

*Anne blinked at him out of dazed eyes, unmoving. Her body felt heavy and drugged.*

*He cursed and jerked up her bodice, but it was torn, and it failed to stay up. "Hold up your dress," he hissed.*

*Anne obeyed as Edna Collins burst into the garden—followed by Philip St. Georges and the duke of Rutherford. Edna immediately halted, so abruptly that the two men careened into her. But she was big and sturdy and she did not move, staring at Anne, wide-eyed.*

*Anne yanked up her gown, horror rising up in her, and she stumbled backward a step. Dom moved in front of her, his stance rigid and wide. He did not say a word.*

*Anne began to shake. Bile rose up in her throat, choking her.*

*"Oh my God," Edna whispered in utter, abject horror.*

*Philip said nothing. He stared at Anne and Dom in absolute disbelief.*

*"Dom!" Rutherford barked. He strode forward, gripping Dom's arm, shaking it. "What the hell has happened here?"*

*It was a moment before Dom answered. And when he did, his tone was very cool. "Apparently, I have just done the unthinkable."*

*Edna cried out. She moved past Dom, her hands closing hurtfully on Anne's wrist. Anne whimpered as she jerked her forward. "Slut! Hussy! This is how you repay me for all I have given you!" Edna shouted.*

*Anne understood exactly what was happening now—exactly what her crime was. Felicity was engaged to Dom. And even though Anne loved Dom desperately, she had allowed him terrible liberties—during his engagement party to her cousin. Anne was horrified. She was sick. Hot tears of shame filled her eyes. She did not know what to say, or what to do. She glanced be-*

seechingly at Dom. He was watching her, his expression rigid, his amber eyes unreadable.

And then she heard Felicity panting as she ran toward them, followed by Patrick, Clarisse, and her father, Jonathan. "Mama, Mama, what is happening? Oh, God," she cried and stopped. She stared at Anne and Dom.

Jonathan automatically put his arm around her. Felicity turned toward him, her head on his chest, weeping loudly now.

"I . . . I'm sorry," Anne whispered brokenly, tears streaking down her cheeks.

"Slut! Slut!" Edna shouted, her fists clenched—raised.

"Don't," Dom warned Edna, his jaw flexing.

Edna did not even look at him; she had eyes only for Anne.

Anne began to weep, silently, in unbearable anguish.

"You have done enough this night. Come with me immediately," Rutherford said in a tone no man would ever dare disobey. He leveled Edna with a cold, authoritative stare. "Anne is hardly to blame. My grandson will take full responsibility for all he has done. You shall undoubtedly hear from him on the morrow. I suggest now that you leave. Without reentering the house." He inclined his head, then turned toward the brightly lit-up house, his hand still clasped on Dom's arm. Philip and Clarisse followed them.

Anne took half a step after Dom as Dom was half-dragged away by his grandfather—looking over his shoulder at her one last time. Their gazes met, held. Perhaps Anne would have followed them. She did not want Dom to leave her now. But Edna pulled her up short. "Little scheming bitch!" she shouted, striking her hard across the face.

Anne cried out, and then Edna's palm lashed her face again like a whip. This time Anne fell to the

*ground from the blow. But as Edna bent over her, strik-*
*ing her a third time, Anne did not try to defend herself.*
*She deserved the punishment, she knew. And no one*
*tried to help her.*

*Finally Edna stopped hitting her, panting now from*
*the energy she had expended. "Get the carriage, Pat-*
*rick. We are going home." Her ice-cold gaze turned to*
*Anne. "I knew it. I knew you were exactly like your*
*mother," she spit. Then she left her alone with her*
*cousin.*

*Anne turned a pleading gaze upon Felicity. "Felic-*
*ity," she whispered through her split lip. "I am sorry.*
*But I love Dom. You know that."*

*"I hate you," Felicity snarled. "And if it is the last*
*thing I do, I promise you, I will get even."*

*Anne inhaled.*

*"You are going to be sorry, Anne," Felicity cried.*
*"Very, very sorry!"*

Dom had raced the chestnut hunter for miles, jumping hedges and stone walls, coops and streams. But he
was a superb rider, and he had chosen the finest horse
in the stable. There was nothing reckless about the fast,
hard ride. Rather, it was a perfectly executed ballet of
motion, with man and horse in complete synchroniza-
tion.

Finally Dom slowed the chestnut to a walk, slipping
off his back. He stroked his sweaty neck, crooning to
him, words of praise the gelding deserved. Clearly understanding that his performance had been excellent,
the horse snorted and nuzzled Dom's hand.

Slowly Dom led the hunter across the meadow. Far
in the distance, below a patchwork of fields crisscrossed
by hedges and stone walls, dotted with sheep and grazing cows, he could just make out the numerous white
outbuildings of the Hall, its stables, and the red brick

house with its huge white pillars. His heart seemed to tighten.

Dom remounted abruptly and walked the hunter back to the house, his mind filled now with all that had happened since he had arrived home just a day ago. He was dismounting when he saw Felicity hurrying toward him in a bright red dress. Dom was annoyed; he doubted he would be able to hide his annoyance.

Felicity smiled. "Good morning, Dom. I was hoping to see you before I left."

"Good morning."

He handed the hunter to a groom, instructing the horse to be walked another ten minutes and then to be rubbed down. Felicity laid her small gloved hand upon his arm as they turned toward the house. "I was calling upon Anne," she said.

Dom glanced at her. "I wasn't aware of the fact that you and she were still friends."

Felicity smiled, holding his arm. Her skirts brushed his leg. "Of course we are friends; we are cousins, remember? Surely you do not think I would hold a grudge against her after all these years?"

His gaze was direct. "Actually, I did."

Felicity's eyes widened. "You are not a gentleman," she said, but the protest was coy.

"And I have no ambition to be one," Dom remarked calmly.

Her lashes lowered, then lifted. "Yes, I know, everyone knows. Your open disdain for rules is terribly exciting, Dom," she said in a low tone.

He laughed. "Come, Felicity, there is nothing exciting about a man so absorbed with his estates and racing stable that he has no time for balls."

"I would love to see your racehorses," Felicity said breathlessly. She was clinging to his arm now.

He was amused. "Really?"

"Really. I have heard all about your fine stable."

She held his gaze. "Perhaps you would give me a special tour?"

His mouth was curved into a wry smile. He knew exactly what she wished to do in his stable, and it wasn't seeing his horses. Even were he not involved now with his wife, and even had he not been keeping a mistress in town, he would have turned her down. Felicity did not appeal to him. She never had—not even when he had originally decided to make her his wife. Then he had been more interested in joining his stable with the Collinses' stud farm.

"I am moving my stable here," he said truthfully. He had decided that this morning.

"When will your horses arrive?"

He eyed her. "In a few days."

She smiled, hugging his arm to her full breast. "Then I can have my tour here."

He inclined his head. "You shall undoubtedly be disappointed."

She smiled at him. "You could not possibly disappoint me, Dom."

Dom was about to respond when he saw his wife step out of the land agent's office and stand on the small front porch, watching them approach. Her arms were folded over her chest. She was not smiling.

"Hello, Anne," Felicity called cheerfully. "Dom and I were just having a chat."

"Indeed," Anne said stiffly.

"Felicity has taken a sudden interest in my racing stable," Dom said, his gaze glued to hers.

"I see."

"Dom will give me a tour of it when it arrives. He is bringing his stable here," Felicity said with enthusiasm.

"Oh, really?" Anne said.

"I am going to leave today," Dom told her, uneasily. "But I will be back as soon as possible."

Anne shrugged as if she did not give a damn.

"Anne is busy with her books." Felicity laughed. "Aren't you, Anne?"

Anne said not a word. Her mouth a tight, thin line, she turned her back on them both and stalked back into her office. Dom expected her to slam the door. She did not.

Dom cursed silently, though, and extricated his arm from Felicity's clinging grasp.

"Really, Dom, how do you put up with a wife like that? She is so mannish! No lady that I know would dare to run an estate."

He stiffened. "Anne is hardly mannish. But I understand that she is adept at managing the estate."

"And you approve?"

"I do not disapprove." That was the truth. He was rather proud of her interest and abilities, even though it was very eccentric. However, he would never be the one to call the kettle black.

"But surely you cannot be happy with what your grandfather has done," Felicity said in a breathy tone. "Good lord, Waverly Hall is your legacy from your father! If I were you, I would be furious with Anne."

Dom halted. "How do you know about the trust?" Now he was furious. When word of this got out, he was going to be the butt of everyone's jokes.

Felicity watched him closely. "I am sorry, Dom. My brother told me."

"Patrick!" Dom's anger surged forth hotly. He knew damn well who had told Patrick about the trust. Did Anne think to make him look like a fool?

If their friendship had not already ended, it would end now. Dom could put up with a lot, but not a disloyal wife.

"My brother dotes upon your wife," Felicity remarked.

Dom whirled. "Yes, that has been abundantly clear."

Felicity did not seem taken aback by the vehemence

in his tone. Her eyes were wide, innocent. Her voice, when she spoke, was more childish than before. "Dom, I think Anne is quite smitten with him."

His jaw tightened. "Felicity, my wife is not your concern."

"He has remained in the country these past four years," Felicity said lightly. "What is there for a bachelor to do in the country all year long? I do not know of any bachelors who remain in the country; at the very least, they come to town for the Season. But not Patrick."

"They are friends, nothing more," Dom said dangerously.

Felicity's eyes widened. "Dom, you—of all people—believe such a thing?"

It did sound ludicrous, and it was almost unbelievable—except that Dom had bedded Anne last night and she had been a virgin. He could not, of course, tell Felicity that. But he wondered now if Anne wanted Patrick—the way he wanted her. "My wife is a lady," Dom said tightly. "And it is remiss of you to suggest otherwise."

"I just thought that you might not be aware of what has been happening," she said, wide-eyed.

"Nothing has happened." Dom was grim. If Felicity believed the worst, then others did as well. "Perhaps you should worry about your own behavior, Felicity, instead of Anne's?"

She gasped.

Dom's smile was mocking. "Surely you do not think to slander my wife and have me meekly accept your condemnation?"

She no longer held his arm. "I wasn't aware that you were so attached to your wife," she cried. "After all, you have left her here alone in the country for four years."

"Then you are mistaken," Dom said.

Felicity flushed. "Dom, I am sorry. I am only trying to be your friend."

His gaze met Felicity's. "I don't think so, madam. Now, if you would excuse me, I believe that there are some matters I must discuss privately with Anne."

Felicity stared, dismayed.

Dom turned away, and met his wife's gaze through her office window. Anne was pale, her posture rigid, but her blue eyes were blazing.

Neither noticed that Felicity's eyes were blazing as well.

Anne walked back to her desk, sat down, and began studying an account. She was acutely aware of Dom entering the office and pausing on the threshold. She spent several minutes ignoring him. Finally she glanced up. "You are looking for me?" Her tone was businesslike. But images of Felicity hanging on to his arm, pressing her big bosom against him, smiling up at him, assailed her.

"Yes, as a matter of fact, I am."

Anne glanced up again and stared coldly at him over the bridge she made with her hands. She reminded herself repeatedly to remain composed.

Dom remained standing with his back against the doorjamb. His posture was negligent; his eyes were not. "I have decided to go to London to bring my horses here."

"Oh? So you are really staying?" Her tone was mocking.

His gaze darkened. Very softly he said, "I believe I have already made myself quite clear on that point. Last night."

Anne stood abruptly, flushing. "You are wasting your time if you remain here."

He cocked a brow. "Really?" Now he mocked her. "Last night was hardly a waste of my time."

Anne clenched her fists. "I am not going to bed with you again, Dom."

He stared.

Anne gathered up her courage. "I wish for us to have a civilized marriage, one of convenience." When he continued to stare at her, without saying a word, she added, "A marriage in name only."

He remained silent. But his golden gaze had narrowed to tiny topaz slivers.

"M-many couples have such an arrangement, and I-I am sure that you know it better than I." She took a step away from him. He was smiling now—and it was menacing and frightening. "A-aren't you going to say something?"

"No."

She inhaled.

"Did I make myself clear?" Dom asked tightly.

"You cannot force me to sleep with you!" Anne cried.

He bared his teeth again. "I have no intention of forcing you to do anything, madam wife. But I have every intention of sleeping with you."

"But I don't want you!" Anne cried.

"Who are you trying to convince?" Dom asked softly.

"Get out."

He moved away from the wall. Anne tensed as he strode across the short space of her office, not stopping until his thighs made contact with her desk. He leaned forward, his hands on the table. They were eye to eye, and nose to nose. But he was so much larger than she that she felt small, diminutive, and powerless.

"You want me as much as I want you."

"No. And you are only dancing to Rutherford's tune."

"I don't dance to anyone's tune," Dom warned. "I want you. And I think I proved that last night."

Abruptly Anne tried to turn her back to him; Dom moved around her desk in the blink of an eye and jerked her back around. "I want you now, Anne."

Anne's eyes widened. "Don't be ridiculous."

His eyes narrowed. "I am not ridiculous." Suddenly he gripped her arms and pulled her up against his body. Anne wasn't wearing crinolines and she gasped when his hard loins came into contact with her belly. Her eyes widened; she found it difficult to breathe.

"That's right," he said very softly. "I want you, right now, and badly, too."

"Let . . . me go."

He released her.

Anne backed away from him. She stared at him, her back against the wall. She was trying very hard to keep her eyes on his face—when they wanted to roam below his waist. "What will it take for you to leave?"

"I beg your pardon?"

"What will it take for you to leave me and Waverly Hall?" Anne cried desperately.

He stared at her, not answering.

"Surely there is something!"

His mouth twisted. His eyes became as hard as topaz stones again. "One week."

"I beg your pardon?" she croaked.

"One week. Come away with me for one week. And during that time, you will not deny me anything."

It was Anne's turn to be stunned. She touched her breast, hoping to still her thundering heart. "I was thinking about something else," she whispered.

"And I am thinking about your body."

Anne shook her head. "I would never agree to such an absurd scheme."

"Why? Afraid?" He mocked.

"Yes! No! If your lust is so huge, you will have to go to one of your other women." she cried, this time glancing at his groin. His breeches gloved him; he was still visibly aroused. Anne turned red. "I am sure Felicity would be more than willing to accommodate you."

"But I don't want Felicity," he said dangerously. "I want you."

Anne forced the words out. "But I don't want you."

"Liar." He smiled unpleasantly. "You could have annulled the marriage at any time in the last four years. But you never did. Admit the truth, Anne. Admit to me why you failed to annul the marriage."

Anne gripped her hands. She dared not answer. Not even to herself.

"Tell me," he challenged.

She knew what he wanted her to say. She wet her lips. "I know what you are thinking. But you are wrong."

"Am I? I don't think so." He moved forward again, trapping her between her desk and the wall. "I think you loved me even after I left you—and that you have been waiting all these years for me to return."

"No."

"Then there is only one other possibility," Dom said darkly.

Anne stilled, dread growing within her.

"And that is that you are the scheming fortune hunter the gossips think you to be."

Anne felt faint. Her knees actually buckled. "No," she whispered.

"Then which is it?" His mouth curved without mirth; his eyes flashed. "Either you are ruled by your heart or by unscrupulous plotting."

He was right. Anne felt trapped. "Leave. Get out. Now."

"Anne . . ."

"Leave!" She cried. "Go away. Please!"

He straightened. "Very well. I am going to London, but I will be back in a few days. In the meanwhile, think about my proposal."

"I've already thought."

He ignored her. "One week, Anne. And if you are not happy with our marriage afterward, I will leave you alone, as you have asked me to do."

## Chapter 11

*T*he duke of Rutherford heard the rumble of carriages and the clip-clopping of horses' hooves on the drive outside, and he walked to the window in the drawing room. He smiled when he saw Dom astride a beautiful gray hunter. Another gentleman rode beside him on an equally superb mount. Rutherford thought he recognized the earl of Harding's second son, Ted Blake. Behind the two men was the Waverly coach, pulled by six matched blacks, two liveried coachmen driving it, two liveried footmen standing on the back running board. Dom's entourage consisted of two more wagons as well, with numerous servants and grooms. Amidst them were several Thoroughbreds, blanketed, their legs wrapped, including one magnificent seventeen-hand black colt.

Dom had been gone for three days, and Rutherford was very glad to see him return. He had had some small doubt, after all, thinking that Dom might stay away. But he had returned. And Rutherford suspected it was less because of the terms of the trust than it was his growing interest in Anne.

The duke smiled.

He was an old man. He would not live forever—he had no wish to live forever. He knew when it was time to let go. But that time, although fast approaching,

141

wasn't there quite yet. The dukedom was not secured for the future. There needed to be an heir.

The duke was as much a romantic as he was a pragmatist. He loved his grandson dearly. He had never been able to forgive his own son Philip for denying the boy the affection that he had craved. Even though he had understood why Philip had been cold and uncaring, and entirely self-absorbed. Philip had been within his rights, but still, Rutherford could not forgive him.

Perhaps, though, Philip would have been a different man had his mother, Sarah, not died of fever at the very young age of thirty-one, when Philip was ten years old. The duke had—selfishly—never remarried. He had been unable to bring himself to marry again after Sarah's untimely death. He was a man who could only love once.

Anne was Sarah's niece. Her mother, Janice, had been the youngest of the Stanhope sisters, born twelve years after Sarah, the oldest. At Sarah's insistence, the duke had sponsored her come-out. He had given her the most extravagant debut ball that the kingdom had ever seen. And Janice had been so lovely that night, just seventeen, so innocent but filled with so many dreams. She had run away to America the following year.

Anne was so much like her mother. Janice had married Fred Stewart, an American adventurer from Philadelphia, and they had traveled across the country together for a half dozen years. The duke had not been able to locate Janice to tell her of her sister's death. Many years later, she had written to him from Boston, where she and her husband had finally settled. They had no children, she had miscarried three times, and she and her husband had opened up a boardinghouse. Rutherford could tell that she was unhappy even though she stressed again and again how wonderful Boston was. He was enraged that she had become an innkeeper's wife, enraged that her husband had done this to her. It was the only letter she ever wrote to him. The next letter posted from America was written by Stewart himself. Janice was dead. She had died giving birth to the child she had always wanted, a baby girl, Anne.

Eleven years later Anne appeared at the Collinses, a skinny, silent orphan left without any means. The duke tried to ignore her presence there. He did not want to meet her, to know her, or even to like her. He held her as responsible for Janice's death as he did Fred Stewart.

But one day the curiosity that was eating at him dictated that he call upon her. He took one look at the small child, who was clearly grief-stricken, and his heart opened to her. Somewhat cautiously, he made it his business to know how she fared. As she matured, he realized that she was exactly like her mother, not just in appearance, but in her heart and soul. Her spirit was warm, generous, and sincere.

Yes, he was a romantic as much as he was a pragmatist.

He had decided years ago that Dom and Anne belonged together. Not because they suited, which they did, or because Anne was so in love with Dom. But for his own selfish, private, zealously guarded reasons.

And the duke had made a vow. He would do everything in his power to bring the two of them together—and he was one of the most powerful men in the land. It might be the last worthy thing he accomplished before he died, but he would see Dom and Anne reconciled. It was his way of making good his very personal debt to Janice Stanhope Stewart.

Dom was back. She replaced her spectacles. Her hands trembled. He had returned. She had not been sure that he would.

She could pretend to herself that she was dismayed. But it was only partially true.

Anne could not concentrate on the tenant's written complaint which she was reviewing. Her gaze kept lifting, darting to the window. Her heart beat unsteadily now. Dom was no longer in sight. Yet she knew he was outside with the other gentleman, because she kept hearing the low rumble of their voices. Anne was resolved to ignore the distraction.

Dom's laughter sounded, warm and rich and slightly sandy—and very seductive.

It brought searing images of the night they had spent together instantly to mind.

Anne stood up. She removed her glasses; she smoothed her hair, which was knotted in a chignon. Dom had returned, with several of his racehorses. He really intended to stay, no matter that she had made it clear that she did not want him here. And he would be expecting an answer.

Anne inhaled, made up her mind. She need not hide in her office. Dom and his gentleman friend were standing by one of the paddocks when Anne walked outside. A beautiful black colt, one Anne judged to be about three years old, was trotting in circles around it. His tail was raised and streaming like a banner behind him, his neck tightly arched. He whinnied and broke into a gallop. Anne knew horses. This one was clearly showing off.

"If only he would be so docile when he had a rider upon his back," Dom commented dryly.

"Fortunately you have found a jockey who can control him," Dom's friend responded.

"Yes, and now he should start winning his races."

Anne could not help but admire the colt as she overheard their brief conversation. This colt had been bred for speed and stamina. This colt had the look of a champion.

But Dom had turned. "Hello, Anne," he murmured. His gaze moved over her inch by inch.

Anne's attention riveted upon her husband, the horse forgotten. "Dom." She kept her tone perfectly polite. She could not help smoothing her skirts with her hand and coloring somewhat in response to his unwavering stare. His thoughts were all too clear. He was also remembering that night.

"May I introduce my friend, Lord Theodore Blake? He is the earl of Harding's second son," Dom said.

Anne smiled warmly at Blake. She had not smiled at Dom at all.

Blake took her hand and lifted it. His eyes were warm, admiring. "I have been looking forward to meeting you, Lady St. Georges. Dom's absolute silence on the subject of his wife—and his determination to return to Waverly Hall as quickly as possible—assured me that I would find a very lovely woman awaiting him."

"Thank you," Anne said. Clearly Blake was a rake, used to tossing about compliments the way boys tossed balls. He was a handsome man, his complexion fair, his eyes blue, his hair almost as black as hers. When he smiled, which was frequently, he had two deep dimples. His flattery might be nonsense, but his charm was hard to resist. Anne suspected she would come to like him in time. "You are too kind, Lord Blake."

"Just Blake." He winked. "All my friends are irreverent when it comes to my illustrious antecedents."

Anne had to laugh. "There is always Theodore."

"Good God, no!" Blake cried with mock distress.

Anne smiled again, warmly. "Then Blake it shall be."

"That's enough, Blake," Dom growled. "Save those dimples for another woman."

Blake grinned. "My, surely you aren't jealous of my sharing a few words with your wife, old man?"

"Hardly," Dom scoffed. His gaze moved back to Anne. It was very intense. "I am sorry that it took me a day longer than I anticipated to return."

"Did it? I hadn't noticed." Anne shrugged as if she had not been sleepless each and every night that he was gone, wondering where he was, thinking about his question—and if he would really come back.

"I have invited Blake to stay a few days," Dom said. "To help me with Lucky's training. You do not mind?"

"Of course not," Anne said, her gaze going back to the colt. "He appears superb."

"I have bred him myself," Dom said. "And he is the fastest colt I have ever seen."

"But?" Anne queried.

"Until recently, he was very difficult to ride. However, I believe this horse could be a great champion."

"I would not be surprised," Anne said.

Dom stared at her steadily. "Do you know something about horses, Anne?"

She held his gaze. "Yes, I do."

A moment passed as they stared at one another. Anne's heart raced.

Then Blake looked past Anne. He whistled. "Who is that?"

Anne turned, as did Dom. She forced her expression to remain impassive. Dom sounded as carefully neutral as she was trying to appear. "That is Anne's cousin. I cannot believe you haven't met Felicity Collins Reed."

"Harold Reed's widow? No, I haven't been that lucky." Blake grinned. "But I have heard about her, and she is as lovely as rumored. Is she as cold as they say?"

Anne found herself exchanging a long glance with Dom. He turned and grinned at Blake. "I am sure she could warm up to the right gent, Blake. Come, I will formally introduce you." Dom smacked Blake's shoulder. "In fact, I shall invite Felicity to supper so that you do not chase after my wife."

Anne watched them walking toward Felicity, who

had not appeared even once at Waverly Hall in the few
days Dom had been gone. She knew why her cousin
had appeared now. Anne did not want to be angry, or
to feel threatened, but she did.

Anne watched Felicity smile at Blake—and then turn
all of her attention to Dom. She turned away abruptly,
leaning on the paddock railing, staring at the black colt.
He had been nibbling grass a few feet away from her,
and now he lifted his head and stared at her out of
luminous and watchful brown eyes. Anne tried to smile,
and failed.

"Hello, boy," she said softly. "My, you are a
beauty. Is it true that you are also a bit of a rogue?"

The horse listened, its ears erect, unmoving. Only its
large nostrils moved, quivering.

"So tell me, beauty, what am I going to do?"

Lucky snorted, his ears going back.

Anne felt Dom's presence at the exact same time.
She stiffened.

"I hope it is my proposition which you are discussing with my horse?" Dom said softly, his breath
feathering her neck.

Anne turned, a mistake. He stood so closely behind
her that now her skirts covered his boots. But she could
not move backward, for the paddock already pressed
against her spine. "Your proposition?" She shrugged
as if she did not even remember his shocking proposal.

But she did.

Oh, she did.

One week, in which she would do anything he asked.
One week, which she would spend with him. Anne
knew what he wanted from her.

"Well?" Dom asked.

"I haven't thought about it," Anne lied. It was all
she had been able to think about since he had left.

"Then think about it now," Dom said, his gaze
piercing.

*    *    *

Clarisse had a new suite of rooms in the Hall's south wing. Although she had shared the master suite with Philip since the first day of their marriage twenty-nine years ago, Clarisse had moved into the dower apartments as she was expected to do.

Now she left her apartments, her heart pounding with anticipation. In her hand she clutched Philip's diary.

She paused outside of the library doors, which were open. The duke of Rutherford was standing with his back to her, staring through the windows outside. Her heart rate increased. She was well aware that Dom had just returned. "Your Grace," she said coolly.

He turned. He did not smile in a friendly manner. But then, they were hardly friends. "May I have a word with you?" Clarisse asked with a patently false smile.

"Come in." He nodded, his glance touching the red leather volume in her hand. "What is that, Clarisse?"

She no longer smiled. "Why, it is Philip's diary, of course." Her eyes were very bright.

"Dom gave it to you to read?" Rutherford's golden eyes were piercing.

Clarisse stared at him and replied without hesitation. "No. I borrowed it."

"I see. You took it without his permission."

"Yes! Apparently he did not even know it was missing—he left so precipitously. Don't you care?" she cried accusingly.

His face rigid, he crossed the room, and closed the doors she stood in front of. "You know that I care about Dom greatly."

"That is not what I mean!" She raised the tome and shook it at him. It wasn't often that Clarisse lost her control and allowed her hatred of Rutherford to show, but it showed now. "Don't you care what he wrote about? Don't you?"

"Of course I care."

"Philip knew."

Rutherford did not flinch.

"He never says so explicitly, but he drops hints, he knew—and he hated this entire family."

"I am aware of all of that."

Clarisse gasped. But she could not stop herself. "Did you know that he hated you most of all?"

This time an expression of anguish clearly crossed the duke's face. "Yes. I knew that, too. Return the journal to Dom."

Clarisse backed up. "My God, you are mad! You want him to know!"

"Perhaps I do."

"No," Clarisse said, shaking her head. "No. I am burning it. You are a fool!"

Rutherford hesitated. Sometimes it was better to let sleeping dogs lie. But he was an old man, with many regrets, and if he died before Dom learned the truth, Dom would never discover it, because he knew bloody well that Clarisse would go to *her* grave with her lips sealed.

"I think that this is Philip's revenge," Clarisse said vehemently. "It is his revenge on all of us. On you, on me, on Dom—on the world. He was a bitter man, a hate-filled man. I am frightened thinking about the kind of self-control he had, never revealing what he clearly knew. No wonder he traveled constantly! He hated Waverly Hall as much as he hated all of us."

Rutherford's nostrils flared. His jaw was tense. He would trust his gut now. "Return the journal to Dom, Clarisse."

Clarisse automatically hugged the diary to her breast. "It must be destroyed."

"Why? Because you have more to lose than any-one?" His eyes narrowed. "Return the journal to Dom." Abruptly he walked past Clarisse and left the room.

Clarisse stared after him. Tears filled her eyes. God, she *hated* him. But he was one of the most powerful men in the land, answerable only to the queen and God, and even she did not dare disobey him. No matter how she wanted to.

But, one day, she would have *her* revenge. She had been biding her time for twenty-nine years.

When Anne came downstairs, everyone had already gathered in the drawing room. Her gaze found Dom immediately. He stood with Blake beside the marble mantel over the hearth, chatting; each held a glass of sherry in his hand. Felicity stood with them, her voluminous gold skirts enveloping Dom's legs. She was laughing at every other word he uttered. And her gown was so low-cut that she was in jeopardy of exposing herself with every breath she took.

Anne fought to appear indifferent.

Rutherford sat on the gold brocade sofa. He was speaking with Patrick, who sat beside him. Patrick stopped in mid-sentence, caught Anne's eye, and smiled. Anne realized that he must have escorted Felicity to the Hall, although a widow had every right to attend a dinner party alone if she wished. Anne was very glad to see him now.

Anne entered the room. She did not look toward Dom and his group, although she knew his eyes followed her. She went straight to the duke, curtsied fractionally. "Good evening, Your Grace."

He got to his feet with an effort. "Good evening, Anne." He kissed her cheek.

Anne turned to Patrick. "This is a surprise."

"A good one, I hope?"

"A wonderful one," she returned, smiling. Past Patrick, she saw Dom staring at them. His easy smile was gone.

Anne smiled more brightly. "It has been a while

since you stayed for supper. Will you escort me tonight?''

Patrick laughed and took her arm. "Certainly."

Anne saw that Dom was angry. Her own pleasure heightened dramatically. A small voice inside of her head told her that she was behaving like a child, worse, like Felicity, but Anne had never flirted before—and had never seen Dom stare at her with such open jealousy. It was a heady moment. But how could he be jealous of *her*?

That would have to mean that he cared, even if it were merely a matter of masculine possessiveness.

Anne could not assimilate such a concept.

Dom had turned his back on her now. Anne quickly grew dismayed. Felicity was whispering in his ear, and it seemed to Anne that her lips were very close to his cheek.

Anne's pleasure died. Despite her bravado before Dom, she was not a worldly woman, and she was not a flirt. She was also not endowed with all those assets men seemed to treasure so much. And she was clad in ugly black from the tip of her toes to her chin out of respect for her father-in-law. She was a fool to think, even for a moment, that she was making Dom St. Georges jealous. Not when he had a woman like Felicity hanging on his arm. Not when he had that French actress waiting for him in London. And two children from his previous mistress.

Rutherford moved to stand beside her. He put his arm around her and steered her away from Patrick. "Your every emotion is showing, my dear."

"Am I so obvious?" Anne thought that her voice sounded too thick with impending tears. She coughed to clear it. "I am a ninny, worse," she said angrily.

"You are hardly that. Felicity is the ninny," Rutherford said.

"She is stunning. I am plain. It's the luck of the draw. Dom finds me hardly worth a thought."

"To the contrary, I think he is terribly jealous of your friendship with Patrick."

Anne couldn't help but grow hopeful. But she did not want to have hope—not where her husband was concerned. "I thought so, too," she admitted. "At first. Until I realized how silly the very idea was."

"It is hardly a silly idea, Anne." He patted Anne's shoulder. "My dear, you are a lovely woman, far lovelier than most women, and far lovelier than your vapid cousin. Good God, you look exactly like your mother, Janice, and she was a great beauty in her day."

"Do you really think I look like her?" It was almost inconceivable.

"Yes, I do. While Felicity resembles Edna. In personality as well as appearance. Dom is not a fool, Anne."

Anne did not know what to think. She turned so she could stare at Dom—and found his piercing gaze trained upon her. Their gazes locked. Anne found it difficult to breathe.

"Would you like some advice?" Rutherford asked pleasantly.

Anne nodded.

"I would continue doing exactly what you have been doing, and forget Felicity, for she cannot compare to you in a hundred years."

Anne smiled. "You are too kind."

"No, I am an old man, and old men tend to be honest, as they have little time for lies."

Anne grew distraught. "Please do not speak that way, Your Grace."

"Why? I am not afraid of dying, Anne. I have lived a good life."

Anne did not know what to say. There was a faraway look in his eyes, now. Anne imagined that he was think-

ing about his wife, the Duchess Sarah. It was common
knowledge that the reason the duke had never remarried
was because he had never been able to get over the
loss of his first and only wife.

"I wish I had known the duchess," Anne said softly
"What was she like?"

The duke's eyes cleared. He seemed startled.
"Sarah? She was a good wife and a good mother. In
fact, she was quiet and warm, like a gentle late spring
day. The first time I saw your mother, a few months
before the debut I gave her, I was so surprised." He
coughed. "There was such a strong resemblance between the two sisters, yet, they were as different as
night and day. I quickly realized why. Everything about
Sarah was soft and quiet. But Janice, well, she was like
a bright light, a shining star, warm, generous, sincere
to a fault—yet always laughing and gay. Everyone was
attracted to her. Men and women, young and old, and,
of course, children. She wanted children very badly,
you know."

Anne stared speechlessly. In all the years she had
known the duke, she had never heard him talk this way.

He smiled. "Although a dozen years separated them,
they were close. Janice worshiped Sarah, and Sarah
adored her. She had great hopes for your mother, dear.
Janice could have married a great nobleman. She could
have married anyone she chose. She was the reigning
debutante that year. She had dozens of offers for her
hand—she turned them all down." His smile faded.

"I did not know," Anne whispered. Her eyes were
wide, riveted upon the duke's face.

His jaw clenched. "It broke Sarah's heart when she
ran away. She was only eighteen. She left a short note
for Sarah and myself. As you know, Sarah died the
following year."

"And my mother married my father."

"Yes," the duke said grimly. "I am sorry, I know

you miss your father and that you loved him, but Janice deserved a better life than the itinerant one she led with him.''

''My father loved her,'' Anne whispered, staring at the duke.

He sighed heavily. ''Everyone loved her,'' he said.

Anne stared. Stunned. Suddenly wondering if the duke had also loved Janice—but far more than was seemly.

Supper was over. Anne was not sorry. Felicity had spent most of the evening casting long, suggestive looks at Dom, while ignoring Ted Blake, who had made repeated overtures toward her.

Clarisse excused herself early. Anne said good night to Patrick and Felicity, who were in the hallway below, preparing to return to Hunting Way, and to the duke, Dom, and Blake. She started up the stairs. But the steps creaked below Anne, causing her to pause, one hand on the brass banister.

Dom met her gaze.

Her body quickened. ''What are you doing?''

''I am coming upstairs.''

''But you have not yet had your brandy.''

He came abreast of her, standing one step below her. ''I do not want to sip brandy with my grandfather and Blake.''

Anne stared into his warm, amber eyes.

''But I will share a brandy with you, if you wish,'' he said, his gaze trained intently upon her face.

Anne came to life. ''No, thank you.'' She turned and started up the stairs, tripping on her gown in her haste.

He caught her elbow, steadying her. ''You don't have to be afraid of me, Anne,'' he said in a liquid tone.

Anne inhaled. ''I am not afraid of you,'' she snapped. ''Now let me go!''

He smiled, amused, and she did not blame him. She

had shrieked at him as if she were being accosted by
a highwayman. "After you." He inclined his head.

Very aware of him following closely behind her,
Anne hurried up the stairs. Her mind was racing. Surely
he did not think to try to seduce her tonight? Her pulse
soared. Of course he did! Dom St. Georges had no
scruples—not where she was concerned.

Anne rushed down the hall. She knew that Dom was
on her heels, his long strides easily keeping pace with
her shorter ones. Outside of her door she whirled
around, planting her back against the gleaming wood,
as if to barricade the way. Dom paused in front of her.
Slowly, he smiled.

"Good night," Anne said.

One brow rose. "I want to finish our conversation."

"What conversation?" She was perspiring. But she
had no fan, and even if she did, she would not use it.

"The one from this afternoon—and the afternoon of
my departure."

Anne decided that it was useless to feign ignorance.
"What you suggest is preposterous."

"Is it?" He laughed. "Anne, you are not a virgin
anymore, and we are married. It is hardly preposterous
for a man to ask his wife to go away with him for
a week."

She was beet red. "There were other terms."

He grinned now, clearly enjoying himself, his eyes
glinting. "Yes, there were."

"They were hardly gentlemanly."

"I am not a gentleman. I don't even wish to be one."

"But I am a lady."

"True. So why is it that you assume that I would
abuse you?"

She inhaled. She had been trying very hard not to
think about what might happen if she did go away with
him for a week. As she was far more ignorant than
informed on the delicate matters that absorbed a hus-

band and wife behind closed doors, it was hard to imagine what he might ask of her. Anne preferred it that way. "I don't trust you, Dom."

"I would never make you do something you did not wish to do yourself."

She stared, feeling her cheeks flaming again. He was so cocky! And undoubtedly his confidence was not misplaced. "I am not relieved. Because you are a sorcerer when it comes to women and you know it as well as I."

"I take that as a compliment, darling."

She turned angrily, her hand on the doorknob, wrenching at it. But Dom's covered hers a second later.

"Well? I want an answer, Anne," he whispered against her ear.

Anne inhaled, flooded with fiery sensations. He knew, of course, just what he was doing. She would refuse his indecent offer. But no words came out. Her mind was having trouble coping with the fact that she could actually feel the heat emanating from his body.

"Anne?"

She turned, a mistake. His face was mere inches from hers. "I want you to go away," she said. "I want you to leave Waverly Hall. How much clearer do I have to be?"

Anger darkened his eyes. He threw his arm around her and pulled her up against him. "And I don't want to go away," he said roughly. "How much clearer do *I* have to be?"

Anne could not answer. He had crushed her powerfully in his arms. Dom's eyes smoked. Anne understood his intentions and tried to turn her face away, but he caught her mouth with his before she could succeed. Anne cried out against his lips. He ignored her. His grip on her waist tightened; his mouth opened hers. His tongue thrust deep. His big body pressed hers hard against her door. Anne could not have moved if she had wanted to.

But she wasn't sure she would have moved even if she could have, because Dom's kiss was thrilling. In turns greedy and hungry, gentle and soft, he nipped and nibbled and sucked on her lips, finally mating with her tongue. By then Anne was melting very rapidly, and clinging to him in order to stand up. She was also kissing him back.

He ripped his mouth from hers. He was panting. "Has Patrick ever kissed you that way?"

Anne was also breathless. She was dazed. Her body was on fire, a hurtful fire, one which had reduced her to a state of savage tears. She blinked at him, gasping, "Patrick?"

"That's right," he said harshly. "Patrick. The man you spent this entire evening flirting with—in the hope of making me jealous."

Anne stared. She had followed Rutherford's advice, and she had behaved somewhat coyly with her cousin, but she had not thought that Dom had even noticed.

"Well, you have succeeded, Anne," Dom growled. "I am jealous, unhappy, and very aroused. In case you hadn't noticed."

Anne flushed. She did not dare take her eyes from his face.

"Anne?"

"What?"

"Do not ever tease me again—not unless you are willing to face the consequences."

Anne gasped.

But Dom had released her. His face was a study of competing emotions—anger, determination, hunger. He shoved open her door, standing aside for her to enter. When she failed to move, he turned and strode down the corridor. Anne watched him disappear down the stairs.

Anne's knees were weak; she released a long, shaky

sigh. Oh, God. She had been ready to give in to him, had he but persisted.

Worse, she was still ready to give in to him. Her body was an absolute traitor to her mind.

Anne turned and slipped inside her bedroom, bracing her back against the door.

She swallowed, but it was no use, her pulse still thundered in her ears. She stared at her room. A single kerosene lamp had been lit by her abigail, and the room was dark and mostly in shadow. It was utterly silent, utterly still. Only her sheer white draperies moved, fluttering in a breeze from an open window.

Anne turned and locked the door.

Oh, God. How was she going to continue like this, with Dom hounding her every night? It was inevitable that she give in to him sooner or later—she would have given in to him tonight. Anne was no match for his seductive games.

Anne moved slowly toward her bed. It was becoming crystal clear now. She could not persuade him to leave. If she really wanted him gone, she would have to agree to his outrageous proposition. All she would then have to do is to endure him for an entire week. One week ... and she would have her freedom.

Anne was terrified by the idea. And secretly, she was fascinated.

There was a secret image in the back of her mind, haunting her. Her and Dom, naked, sweaty, entwined.

Anne's nightclothes were laid out on the settee at the foot of her bed. Her bedstand, which had been damaged, had been replaced. She was not in the mood for Belle's chattering; she would call for her maid later. Anne walked to her bed, which was turned down, twisting her hands. She would lie down for a while, until she had calmed herself, and then she would ring for Belle to help her disrobe.

Anne sat down, about to remove her shoes. And then her glance landed on her pillow, and she froze.

Lying upon its pristine white center was a single, charred rose.

# Chapter 12

*F*elicity stared up the stairs, after Dom.

Blake was exasperated. He gripped her arm, and spoke in a low tone. "Would you care to take a brief walk with me outside?"

Annoyance crossed Felicity's face. "I don't think so. Patrick is taking me home."

Blake's jaw clenched. "I think your brother wishes to have a brandy with the duke."

Felicity followed his gaze. Rutherford and Patrick stood chatting a few steps away from them in the foyer. "I don't care," she snapped. "I happen to be tired."

"Really?" Blake mocked. "You didn't seem very tired a moment ago—before Dom went upstairs." He smiled. "With his wife."

Felicity was furious. Her blue eyes flashed. "You're right. I wasn't tired a moment ago—but I am very tired now!"

Blake laughed softly, then said in a louder voice, "Patrick, I am going to take a stroll outside with your sister." He ignored Felicity's gasp of indignation.

"Fine." Patrick said. "I will be in the library with His Grace."

Felicity opened her mouth to protest, but Patrick and the duke were already disappearing down the hallway. She whirled, her very bare bosom heaving. "You are insufferable."

He eyed her bow-shaped mouth. "Only when I have to be." His gaze dipped. "And you, darling, are truly beautiful."

Felicity raised her chin. "I am not interested, Lord Blake."

His eyes darkened. He took her elbow firmly in his hand. "Let's see if we can get you interested."

Felicity tried to shrug free of him, but quickly gave up, as Blake propelled her forcefully through the foyer and outside.

"Let me go," she cried.

"No." He half dragged her down the front steps and into the mist. When they stood on the lawn, shrouded in fog, invisible to anyone who might try and watch them from the house, he released her and smiled. "Hasn't anyone ever told you that it is exceedingly bad-mannered to drool after one's married host?"

Felicity inhaled. "You are the one who is exceedingly bad-mannered."

"To the contrary, I have been nothing but polite since first laying eyes upon you this afternoon."

Felicity made a scoffing sound, turned her back on him and started to march toward the house.

But she did not get very far. Blake's hand shot out. A moment later he had her completely in his embrace. Her crinolines were crushed by his legs, her bosom by his chest. "But as civility has failed to attract your interest, I shall resort to more barbaric means," he said, and he cut off her gasp of outrage with his mouth.

Felicity struggled. Blake held her in an iron grip, his mouth hard and demanding on hers. She stilled. He gentled, his tongue sliding along the seam of her lips. Felicity's hands curled around his broad shoulders. He prodded against her lips, and when she opened, he thrust his tongue deep inside, his mouth becoming voracious.

Felicity moaned from deep within her throat.

Blake slid one hand into her bodice, cupping her big breast, his thumb teasing her nipple. Then he tore his mouth from hers, bent, and sucked the tip deep into his mouth. Felicity cried out, clinging to him, her knees buckling.

Blake lifted his head and smiled. "Do I have your interest now?"

Felicity blinked at him. And slapped his face in fury.

Dom didn't even consider the idea of going to sleep. Carrying a candle, he went downstairs. His grandfather and Blake had already retired. The ground floor of the house was utterly silent, and mostly dark shadows. In the library he set the taper down, lighting a lamp. Then he poured himself a stiff drink.

Dom sat on the sofa, staring at the hearth where a very small fire burned, in deference to the cool summer nights. He tried to divert his thoughts from his wife, in the hope of cooling his ardor, which remained huge, so he could go upstairs and get some sleep. The fire cast long, flickering shadows across his face.

"Dominick?"

Dom jerked, almost spilling his whiskey. He rose to his feet. "Mother, you surprised me. I did not hear you approach."

Clarisse's smile was cursory. She stood in the doorway, clad in a long white silk robe, holding a taper aloft. Two white cats rubbed against her ankles. "Yes, you were far away, I could see that." She held out her hand. In it there was a red leather book. "I hope you do not mind. I borrowed the journal and read it."

Dom stared at the thick volume. "I was looking for the diary. I thought I had misplaced it." Actually, he had not thought any such thing. He had left the journal on his bed table, and it had disappeared. He had known damn well that someone had taken the diary, but he could not fathom who would have done such a thing. "It did not occur to me that you had taken it."

"I suppose I should have said something."

Dom accepted the diary. "It doesn't matter. You have every right to read it."

"As do you." Clarisse stared at him.

"Is it good reading?" he finally asked.

"Not particularly. Good night, Dominick." His mother turned and left.

Dom now downed most of the contents of his glass of whiskey. The familiar burning sensation hardly soothed him. He stared at the journal. *Damn.*

Now he would never be able to sleep. First Anne, and now the diary. Just wondering what was inside of the diary would keep him awake all night.

*So read it,* a small voice inside of his head said. *You can't possibly be afraid of a dead man's words.*

Dom grimaced. He flipped open the journal at random, landing somewhere in the middle. Scanning the page, he caught the words *my son,* which his eyes locked on.

He began to read the entry. There was no date.

*My son has come home, and as usual, he has not deigned to inform us first of his plans. Clarisse and I are now on our best behavior. Once again I curse Rutherford. How I would love to be rid of all pretense.*

Dom slammed the journal shut. His eyes were wide, stunned; he was filled with shock.

He did not know what he had expected, but he had never expected anything like this.

Had his father hated him? Had his father hated Rutherford? Why were Philip and Clarisse on their best behavior now that Dom had returned home? What pretense did Philip refer to?

Dom realized he needed to get a grip on himself, quickly. Abruptly he rose, walked to the bar, and poured himself another whiskey. He took a long draught, and began to feel calmer.

Dom turned and stared at the old grandfather clock in the corner of the room. It was almost midnight.

Determination seized him. He returned to the sofa, picked up the book, and opened it to the first page. This time there was a date before the entry. Dom's stomach tightened. It was the day Dom had been born.

*February 11, 1828*

*I am frightened. Clarisse has been trying to deliver our child into the world for a full day now. I do not know what to do. I feel helpless. Thank God for Father. As always, he is strong, a rock for me to lean upon. But I can tell that he is worried, too.*

Dom looked up. In the course of almost thirty years, how Philip's tone of voice had changed. He sounded like a concerned husband, and as if he cared for his father.

Dom began to read again.

*I have a son. I am thrilled. I am actually weeping with relief and joy.*

Dom stood up. He could not read any more. Something was terribly wrong.

Philip had cared for Clarisse in that first year of their marriage. And he had loved his son, too.

What had happened in the course of twenty-eight years to make him come to despise his wife so much so that he would leave her with absolutely nothing—and make sure his will openly mocked her?

What had happened in the course of his lifetime to turn him from a loving father into a near-stranger?

A voice inside of Dom told himself to leave it alone. The truth could not change the past, undo it, and make everything right when everything had been wrong.

But Dom had to know.

Dom sat down and began to read.

*December 15, 1830*

*I found the evidence I have been seeking. Yes, I was snooping, prying. The letters were kept inside of a hidden compartment in the locked drawer of the desk. It is all there. The proof of Clarisse's betrayal. Goddamn her to hell. Goddamn them.*

*How stupid I was. How stupid I am. But now I know that I suspected the truth long ago, vaguely, shortly after Dom's birth. Perhaps even before. Oh, God. I will never forgive her. I will never forgive them. I am sick, so sick, and when I look at the rifles mounted upon the wall, I am almost tempted to take one and use it to end my own wretched life.*

*I have been wronged. I tried to live by the world's rules, and they mocked me. They have wronged me. There is no justice in this world, none.*

*But I am too weak to end my miserable existence. Just as I am too weak to kill her, or him. Instead, I shall go to India. Perhaps I will never return.*

Dom rose to his feet and walked slowly into the hall. He had read most of the journal. Outside, the sky had turned gray. In the east, it was slashed with streaks of fiery orange.

His father had not committed suicide, nor had he killed Clarisse or her lover. And he had returned after a year's sojourn in India, only to depart almost immediately for the Balkans. Indeed, after that winter of 1830, he was hardly ever home at Waverly Hall.

There was a sideboard in the hall, against the wall, and hanging over it was a large, Venetian mirror. Dom faced it and stared at his reflection.

There had been times, when he was a small child, unable to get his father's attention when he so desperately wanted it, that he had wished that Philip were not his own father. As a very small boy, sometimes, he had pretended that was the case. In those fanciful days, he had imagined his father to be someone warm and wonderful, someone heroic—and loving.

Of course, as he had grown up, those fantasies had ceased, as all children's fantasies do.

Now he had reason to believe that Philip might not be his own father.

Though Philip was not direct, nor had he ever identified Clarisse's lover. He had not written whether the affair took place before or after the marriage, or even it if had continued after the marriage. But after his discovery of Clarisse's betrayal, Philip was hostile and hateful to everyone around him. Whereas in one entry he had been a concerned husband and caring father, in the next he hated his wife and son.

Could a man dislike his own son for the crimes of the mother? Blame his own son for the crimes of his own mother?

Or was that son the result of those crimes?

*Was Philip his father?*

Dom was sick. If Philip were not his father, it would explain why he had never acted like a father to him during Dom's entire lifetime. Surely Philip could not have hated his own flesh-and-blood son for his wife's sins.

Yet it was improbable. Outrageous. Rutherford knew everything—how could he not have known of this? Dom had been raised as a St. Georges. His grandfather would have never allowed him to be Philip's heir—and one day the heir to the dukedom—if he were not a St. Georges in truth. Would he?

And Dom also looked like a St. Georges. The St. Georges men were famous for their golden hair and their golden eyes and their striking good looks. As a small boy, and throughout his life, Dom had continually heard people comment on the fact that he was a St. Georges through and through.

Which shot that absurd question right to hell, because Dom's having the St. Georges traits would be an incredible coincidence if Philip were not his father.

In which case, Philip had hated him because of Clarisse, not because he wasn't his own son. Dom wanted that to be the truth. But he wasn't convinced.

*Was he a St. Georges, or was he an impostor?*

Dom stared at his reflection. Dom did not especially believe in coincidence. He did not want to believe in it now. He was too afraid to believe in it now.

Dom closed his eyes, suddenly unable to breathe. His chest felt as if it might explode. He would have to go to his mother and beg for an explanation. But what, exactly, would he say? "Mother, I beg your pardon, but were you unfaithful to Father, as he has claimed, and if so, was it before your marriage or afterward?" Clarisse would have every right to strike his face for such an unforgivable intrusion.

But it was not an intrusion.

Because the possibility had been raised by his own father's words. If he wasn't Dominick St. Georges, if Philip was not his father, then Rutherford was not his grandfather. Then Waverly Hall was not his birthright. Then he was not the marquis of Waverly, the earl of Campton and Highglow, the baron of Feldstone, the viscount of Lyons. He was not Philip's heir—he was not Rutherford's heir.

If he wasn't Dominick St. Georges, then his entire life was a sham. A monumental sham.

# Chapter 13

"*G*ood morning, Mama."

Edna Collins started. A plump, pretty blond woman in her sixties, she was sitting at the oval dining table with her son, her plate heaped with bacon, eggs, and toast. "Felicity, you are up early."

Felicity smiled, kissing her mother's cheek. She was clad in a lavender satin robe with darker purple piping and she was wearing matching satin slippers. "Yes, I am," she agreed cheerfully. She smiled at Patrick. "Good morning, dear."

He eyed her. "Let me guess. You wish to accompany me to the Hall."

Felicity laughed, leaning over the table and plucking a scone from the platter of baked goods. She picked at the raisins with her fingers. "I promise I will not be tardy. My abigail is laying out my dress right now."

Patrick shrugged. "I am leaving here at nine-thirty. If you are ready, I have no objection to bringing you with me."

"Wonderful," Felicity said, plopping down in a chair beside him.

"What is going on, Felicity?" Edna asked in a grim tone of voice. Her formidable bosom heaved. "What do you think you are doing?"

Felicity popped a raisin into her mouth, chewed it

168

with relish. "Mama, I am a grown woman now. A wealthy and independent one." She shrugged. "If Dom needs comforting, why shouldn't I be the one to provide it?"

Edna rose to her feet. "So you think to warm his bed now that he is home? Have I raised you to be a common strumpet like your cousin?"

Felicity was not perturbed. "Mama, come. I am hardly an innocent virgin. And neither you nor anyone else can tell me what to do or how to behave." She smiled at her brother, who remained impassive.

"Your next husband will have to take a strap to your pretty backside," Edna warned. "I doubt *he* will tolerate your indecent behavior!"

Felicity stood up, yawning. "There isn't going to be another husband. Why should I remarry? I am rich, young, and beautiful. I can do as I please. I would be a fool to marry again so some stupid clod can order me around." She sauntered from the room, then turned. "Don't be mad, Mama." Her smile was engaging. "I will be discreet. Besides, I owe Anne, remember?" She left the room.

Edna said nothing.

Patrick picked up his fork and continued to eat.

Anne was finishing her breakfast when Dom entered the breakfast room. It was just past eight.

"You are an early riser," Dom remarked, coming to stand besides her. "Good morning, Anne." His tone was warm.

"Yes. There is much I have to do on any given day." She rose to her feet without looking at him. "Where is Blake?"

"What does it matter? He is probably still abed." Dom reached out and gripped her arm. "Where are you rushing off to?"

"Charles Dodd promised to be here at quarter past

eight. One of the brood mares is close to foaling.''
Anne said.

"You are dressed for riding," Dom remarked.

Anne tensed. "I am meeting Patrick at ten."

Dom's smile faded. His eyes blazed instantly. "Like
bloody hell."

"We made a riding engagement last night during
supper," Anne said calmly, ignoring his tone.

"I'm sure that you did. Now you may cancel it,"
Dom said.

Anne stared at him. "Why are you being such a
fool?"

"Because I don't like my wife being the subject of
lewd gossip and nasty speculation," Dom snapped.

Anne's bosom heaved. She thought he exaggerated—
surely no one gossiped about her and her cousin! "Perhaps you should have been so concerned four years
ago, when I was the subject everyone gossiped about—
in conjunction with you."

"You are clever, Anne, and I should have thought
about it four years ago," Dom said harshly. "But four
years ago I didn't give a damn—and I wasn't jealous
either!"

Anne opened her mouth—and closed it.

"Listen carefully," Dom said. "If you don't tell Patrick when he arrives that your date is canceled, then
I shall."

Anne trembled. "There is nothing between Patrick
and me other than friendship, and no one is gossiping
about us."

"You are wrong—on both accounts—whether you
know it or not." Dom turned his back on her and
moved to the sideboard containing the breakfast buffet.

Anne did not like being dismissed. Nor did she like
Dom telling her what to do. She walked up behind him,
tapped his shoulder. He whirled.

Her tone was very sweet. "Perhaps, Dom, you might

try out that old adage which says that you can catch flies with honey but not vinegar?''

He stared at her coldly. ''I'm not interested in catching flies, Anne.''

''No, you have made your interest clear enough. And it is what I should have expected from a man with your reputation,'' Anne said, and she turned and stalked from the room.

Anne strode down the front steps of the house, her black riding skirts swishing about her. It was a beautiful summer morning, but she was too frustrated to notice. Dodd was already examining the hugely swollen mare in her large box stall. Anne managed to push Dom out of her thoughts as she entered the box, crooning to the chestnut.

A half hour later, Anne left the barn, having been assured that the mare was doing just fine. Outside the sun was pouring brightly down. It was a perfect midsummer day and she sighed. Anne began to relax. She would enjoy the ride she would now take alone, as long as she kept any thoughts of Dom and his proposal far at bay.

Unfortunately, as she left the barn, her gaze drifted toward the gardens, partially visible behind the Hall. Anne faltered, thinking about the burned rose. Her stomach tensed. She didn't want to think about it—and she had no idea what it meant.

It was very strange. She did not like the very idea that someone had gone to the trouble of placing such a strange offering in her bedroom—upon her bed. But there was no point dwelling upon what had to be a mischievous prank.

Anne dismissed her thoughts. She had given Willie, the head groom, instructions to have her mount saddled and ready for her. Anne halted abruptly. Her frisky young hunter was waiting for her as she had requested, but another hunter was also tacked up—and Dom stood holding the reins of both mounts.

Anne was angry. She strode forward, taking the reins of her horse out of his hands, being unnecessarily rough. "I do not want company," she said.

"But a mere hour ago you wanted Patrick's company," Dom said in a calm tone of voice. There was nothing calm about his glinting eyes.

"I am not riding with you," Anne said stiffly.

Dom stared at her, then cursed. "Anne, I do not want to fight. To the contrary. I want to make peace with you. Look, it is a glorious morning. And if I recall correctly, you're a good rider. Let's ride together and enjoy this perfect morning. Perhaps it will be fun if you let go of your animosity toward me?"

Anne's mouth tightened. *Fun.* What kind of excuse was that for his accompanying her? *Fun.* When had she last had fun? She could not remember. "I am not interested in having fun," she finally said.

He eyed her. "Then you are missing a great deal of life."

Anne was spared having to reply when she saw Patrick step out of the house. She had not known that he was already here. Her sudden smile died. Felicity appeared beside Patrick, clad in a bright green riding costume. She waved at Dom.

"Shall you tell him, or shall I?" Dom asked tersely.

Anne ignored him, leading her horse as she strode toward the front steps of the house. "Good morning," she called.

Patrick smiled at her, then sobered when he saw her expression. He came down the steps. "Hello, Anne."

Anne nodded somewhat coolly at Felicity, who did not bother to acknowledge her. "Patrick, I am afraid that I cannot ride with you this morning."

"Why not?" Patrick demanded, but he was already

gazing at Dom, who had come to stand behind Anne, leading his own hunter.

Before Anne could answer, Dom said, "Because my wife is riding with me."

Patrick stared.

Dom stared back.

"Oh, Dom," Felicity cried, breaking the silence. "And I was so hoping for a tour of your stable! Which," she added plaintively, "you promised me."

Dom finally looked at her. "I am sorry you have come all this way, but as you can see, I am about to go riding with Anne."

"Shall I wait?" Felicity asked.

Abruptly Anne turned away. Not caring that it was unladylike, she gathered up her reins and mounted without help, as any boy might do. Anne settled into the sidesaddle, wishing she were riding astride as she did when she was alone.

"Wait, Anne," Dom said, vaulting into his own saddle.

Anne did not answer him. Her colt was prancing about very restlessly. Immediately Anne sensed that something was wrong. But she ignored her intuition, wanting to get away from Dom. She touched her crop very lightly to the horse's flank. Blaze shot forward, as Anne intended him to.

But as the bay bounded away, he bucked once in midstride. Anne was taken by surprise—this was her personal mount, whom she had ridden for years, and he had a gentle nature. Blaze bucked again. Anne did not fall off, for she was a very good rider. But Blaze took the bit between his teeth and began to gallop.

Anne was stunned. Blaze was running away with her.

She heard Dom shouting at her from behind.

"Blaze, steady boy, easy," she murmured as he galloped down the drive. But the horse's only answer was to increase his stride.

Suddenly Anne was afraid. Blaze was galloping and out of control. Her balance was precarious at best; she could not really control Blaze while riding in a sidesaddle. Had she been astride there would have been no problem—Anne would have let the animal run until he tired. "Blaze, ssshh, easy boy, easy," she cried, trying to soothe him with her voice when she herself was becoming frightened. Her heart was roaring in her ears.

She heard Dom shouting her name again.

Suddenly Anne tensed. Blaze was racing flat out now, and he had veered off the drive. Anne gave up trying to control him. She hung on now to the pommel, determined to stay in the saddle. She could not help recalling the fate of Lady Hornby, who had fallen off a runaway horse and had been paralyzed from the waist down.

Then she saw the stone wall. It loomed in front of her, four feet high and two feet wide. Although she was a superb horsewoman, and she had taken this fence before, at this pace she could break her neck if she fell while attempting it. And Blaze might break his leg, as well.

Anne heard Dom shouting her name, but she did not dare glance over her shoulder, not even for an instant. She heard Dom's hunter coming up behind her. Anne began to pray that he might succeed in catching up to her and grabbing the colt's bridle. But he had only seconds in which to do so.

"Anne!" Dom shouted.

Blaze's great body tensed. He launched himself into the air. As he landed, he stumbled. Anne was already off-balance and riding his neck. Immediately she flew over his head.

The horse was still in motion when Anne fell over his head, in front of him. She saw his huge hooves coming down toward her—about to trample her.

She thought she was about to die.

Time stood still.

Blaze's hooves were each as large as half of her face. She saw the single huge gray hoof bearing down on her, knew he would tread over her and kill her. She opened her mouth to scream.

And felt a slicing pain beneath her breast and then the beast was gone.

Anne lay still, unmoving.

But she was alive.

Dom carried Anne from the pasture all the way across the lawns and to the house. His black hunter followed them, but Blaze had never stopped after Anne's fall, and he had disappeared in the distance.

Patrick raced up to him. "Is she all right?" he cried. "My God, is she all right?"

"She has had a knock to her head, and maybe a broken rib," Dom said grimly.

"I'm fine," Anne whispered, opening her eyes. Her face was pressed against Dom's chest. Her hands gripped his wool jacket. She tried to smile at Patrick, and failed. "I don't think anything is broken."

"Anne," Patrick whispered, reaching for her hand.

Dom increased his pace, leaving Patrick behind. By now, numerous stable boys and grooms were milling about in front of the stables, word of Anne's accident having spread like wildfire, her runaway ride and fall visible from the house.

"My lord," Willie cried, rushing to them, pale with shock. "Lady Anne?"

"Send for a physician," Dom ordered.

"I'll go myself and fetch him right away," the old groom promised.

Rutherford was rushing down the front steps of the house as Dom came striding toward them, Blake beside him. "What happened?" he demanded. "Is Anne hurt?"

"She has suffered a very bad fall. Willie has gone for a doctor," Dom said grimly.

"I'm not hurt," Anne assured the duke. But she wasn't as certain as she tried to sound. Her rib did hurt, her head throbbed, and she was in shock. How could this have happened? "Something is wrong with Blaze," Anne said. "I am worried about him."

Dom's gaze was piercing. "I will have your horse tracked down and shot—have no fear."

"Dom!" Anne cried. "He is a good horse. I have never had a problem with him before!"

His expression tightened. "Dammit, Anne, you could have been killed!"

"Blaze is out of sorts," Anne said, breathlessly. "Don't you dare shoot him."

Dom's expression softened. "I won't. I couldn't. But you are to stay away from that horse. Have I made myself clear, Anne?"

Anne knew better than to argue, and her gaze met the duke's. He gave her a silent if not grim look of encouragement.

"Yes," Anne said meekly, collapsing limply in Dom's arms. She was exhausted.

"You are not fine," Dom cried, increasing his stride. He bounded up the front steps.

Clarisse stood beside the front door, her eyes wide, alarmed. Then Anne tensed. Felicity was standing behind Clarisse. Her face was flushed. Her eyes glittered. "Anne," she said in a high, unnatural voice as Blake moved to her side, staring at her strangely.

Anne looked away from them, her heart pounding. Surely Felicity wasn't pleased that she had almost been killed? Surely she wasn't gloating?

"Sir, I am sending soap and water and rubbing alcohol up to Her Ladyship's room," Bennet said, appearing at Dom's elbow. He was ashen.

The housekeeper appeared on Dom's other side with

Belle. "My lord," Mrs. Riley said, "might I bring up cold compresses and some tea?"

"Yes. And bring some brandy while you're at it," Dom commanded as Mrs. Riley and Belle rushed off. "Blake, please see that the Collinses are escorted home."

"Right," Blake said, gripping Felicity's elbow. "Patrick?"

Anne saw no more, for Dom was pounding up the stairs. She told herself that she had imagined her cousin's excitement and odd behavior. "Dom, put me down. I can walk."

"Forget it."

Anne decided not to argue, recognizing that it would be useless.

Once inside her bedroom, Dom laid her gently down on the bed. He reached over her and began to remove her jacket very carefully. Anne fought not to wince as she maneuvered her right arm out of the sleeve. He repeated his actions with her shirtwaist. Anne began to think about the fact that he was undressing her. "Dom, where is Belle?" she managed.

"I imagine she will be up shortly," he said. He did not stop what he was doing.

Color returned to her cheeks; Anne watched him toss her blouse aside. Her corset was already loosened and he pulled it off easily. Then he raised her chemise.

Anne glanced at Dom's face, but he was oblivious to her nudity. His palm was pressing gently against her ribs. Below the bruise, exploring. Anne winced.

Their gazes met. "Does that hurt?"

"Yes," she whispered, dryly.

"You have an ugly bruise. It could have been worse—much worse." Suddenly he was still. She saw the moment his gaze wandered.

His eyes quickly lifted to meet hers. They mirrored numerous, conflicting emotions. The sudden surge of lust, and his attempt to battle it. Surprising gentleness, and dark anger. Dom stood up abruptly and paced away. Anne pulled down her chemise. The movement hurt her and caused her to gasp.

But it was Dom's open concern—and his tenderness—which were the cause of the tears in her eyes.

Dom turned and stared at her. She met his gaze. Neither one of them spoke for a very long and tense moment.

"You could have died," he said unsteadily.

"Yes."

"I want some answers."

Anne blinked at him in confusion—but he was already gone.

Dom strode purposefully to the stables. He saw that Blaze had been found. The bay was tied up with double lead lines in the corridor inside, where it was cool and dark, but clearly such a precaution was no longer necessary. The horse was exhausted. His head hung to his knees, and his sides, mottled with sweat and dirt, heaved.

Dom immediately went to the horse. "Sshh, boy, what happened to you?" he crooned, stroking the horse's strong neck and rubbing him below the ears. Blaze opened one eye, then proceeded to doze.

Dom stared at the horse while he rubbed his muzzle. He turned when Willie appeared from behind, with sponges, soap, and water. "What happened to this horse?" he demanded. But he could guess.

"My lord, this is a fine animal. He has never acted up like this before," Willie said.

Dom felt anger rippling over him. "So Anne said."

"He has hurt himself, my lord. He has strained a tendon."

Dom squatted and gently began examining Blaze's right foreleg. The tendon had been strained, it was puffy and swollen. He stood. Then, very slowly, he ran his hands over its neck, exploring. As he felt the horse's hard flesh, his gaze met Willie's, and a silent understanding passed between them. Willie had grown pale.

Dom found nothing. He moved to Blaze's other side and ran his hands up and down the horse's neck again. His hand stilled.

"What have you found?" Willie asked tersely.

"What I was looking for—and hoped not to find," Dom said sharply. He patted the animal, but stared at Willie. "Who had access to this horse today?"

"Anyone could have come inside the stables," Willie said.

Dom's jaw flexed. "But not everyone would know how to inject a horse with poison."

At the door to Anne's room, the doctor faced Dom. "She is fine. She is a very lucky lady. Not even a knock on the head—just that single bruised rib. She should rest today and tomorrow. But there is nothing to worry about."

Dom looked past the doctor, at Anne, who sat up in bed now, propped up by numerous pillows, clad in a simple pink dressing gown. It was a wonderful color on her, matching the blush on her cheeks and the soft color of her lips. It set off her ink black hair and pale, ivory skin.

"Thank you," Dom said, relief evident in his tone, never taking his eyes from Anne.

When the doctor left, Dom walked to her side and smiled down at her. "Thank God, Anne."

She held his gaze searchingly. Then, "Did Willie find Blaze?"

"Yes." Dom's expression tightened.

"Is my horse all right?"

Dom stared at her, not replying.

"Dom—you are frightening me! What has happened?"

Dom sat down beside her hip. "The animal is fine. He has a strained tendon, which will heal in time."

Anne was relieved. "I cannot understand what happened today," she said. "Blaze has never acted so wild before."

Dom was silent. Finally he shrugged. "Perhaps there was a burr under his saddle pad. Who knows? It doesn't matter." He smiled, but it seemed forced. "The horse is fine—you are fine."

Anne stared at Dom helplessly. Was it possible that he really cared for her? After all of these years, finally?

Dom must have read her thoughts. He leaned over her, one hand on each side of her hips. Anne thought he was going to kiss her, and her heart went wild, but instead, he said, "Come away with me, Anne. Tomorrow. We will go to Scotland. For one week."

Anne was mesmerized. Her heart had turned over, beating hard and fast. Somehow his current suggestion did not sound at all like his previous proposal.

"Yes," she finally said.

# Chapter 14

*T*hey were gone.

Anne and Dom had left that morning for his hunting box in Scotland.

She was so angry that she did not know what to do first. Felicity leaned against her bedroom door, her pulse racing, dangerously explosive. Outside of her door, she heard Patrick calling her name. She ignored him. He was the one who had brought her the news.

Panting, Felicity stared wildly around her blue-and-white bedroom. But all she could see was Dom and Anne, naked and passionately entwined in a bed.

She cried out, rushing to her own canopied bed. In a frenzy she ripped the pale blue velvet coverlet off, then wrenched the dozen blue-and-white pillows from its head, throwing them violently aside. But that wasn't enough. Panting, she gripped the dark blue draperies attached to the canopy, pulling on them until they ripped apart with a savage tearing sound. Felicity threw the scrap of brocade fabric on the floor.

She stomped on it.

Repeatedly.

Wishing it were Anne she stomped upon.

# Chapter 15

$T$ hey boarded the train in Dulton.

Philip had preferred travel by coach, as did his father, and there was no private Waverly carriage. But Dom had taken an entire first-class carriage for them alone. Anne entered it, crossed its carpeted length, and sat down on a velvet-covered seat. Not once did she look at him.

But she was acutely aware of him. He had entered behind her, and now he stood with his valet next to the windows, which were framed by red damask curtains, speaking quietly. Verig nodded and left. Dom closed the door behind him, and looked across the car at Anne.

Anne tensed. She had not said anything other than what was necessary since leaving Waverly Hall that morning. Last night she had accepted his offer to go away with him, but she had been in the throes of shock—or pure madness. Nothing had changed. A single act of concern and kindness on Dom's part did not, could not, wipe out her mistrust, which was based on four years' abandonment. If she chose to believe that Dom's concern yesterday was proof of any genuine interest in her on his part, she was undoubtedly poising herself for more wrenching heartbreak. Heartbreak she could not bear.

"Verig and Belle will be traveling in the car behind us," Dom said quietly, coming over to Anne and staring down at her. "If we need anything, all we must do is call."

Anne finally looked up at him. If only he were less impressive physically as a man. She nodded wordlessly.

He folded his arms. Annoyance shone in his golden eyes. "All right, Anne. You have made it clear that you are displeased as all hell. Do you want to tell me why?"

She lifted her chin. "I do not like being forced into this position."

"What position?" he ground out. "Last night you agreed to come away with me. Last night you seemed amenable to the suggestion. Last night felt like a new beginning for us."

Anne inhaled. She wanted to plug up her ears like a small child. His words somehow dismayed her. "Last night I was suffering from shock—and perhaps insanity."

"I see. But today you have returned to normalcy?" He was mocking.

"Yes, I have."

He laughed, mirthlessly. "So we resume hostilities now that we are about to depart?"

"I have no intention of being hostile to you."

"Oh, come. You can't wait to do battle."

"To the contrary." She stood and faced him, no easy task, as she was so much smaller than he. "I will do all that you ask in the next week." She began to blush. "Anything. Everything." Unfocused images flooded her mind, of her and Dom in utter abandon, his mouth on her, his hands on her.

He grimaced. "I see."

"We have agreed upon one week. One week only." She could feel that she was bright red now. "One week in which I shall ... accommodate you ... as you please.'' She could not look away from his gaze, which seemed furious. "But afterward, you will leave Waverly Hall, as you have promised.''

He stared at her, his eyes blazing. "Dammit! I wasn't referring to that damnable proposal when I asked you to go away with me last night—and you know it!''

Anne backed away. "No. I am accepting your initial proposal, nothing more.''

"Why are you doing this?'' he shouted.

She trembled. "Because I don't trust you, I can't trust you—I won't trust you.''

Dom stared at her, his eyes dark. "Well, at least you are honest. Somewhat.''

"That is more than can be said for you,'' Anne said, then instantly wished to take her words back.

His countenance became thunderous. "Oh, really? So I am a damnable liar who only thinks of self-gratification and wishes to make you naught but my sexual slave?''

Anne backed away from him, stumbling. "You—you formulated this absurd proposal!''

"That's right,'' he said flatly. His stare was hard, relentless—frightening.

Anne regretted her decision to go to Scotland with him. She gripped her own hands. "Dom ... you are frightening me.''

"Then perhaps, in the future,'' he snapped, "you should be more tactful. Why don't you shower some of the kindness and goodness you are famous for on me?''

Anne stiffened.

"But I guess I don't deserve it. I guess I'm going to be punished forever for one miserable error.'' He turned and stormed across the car.

Anne watched him, suddenly aching inside, suddenly wishing it could be different between them. But she dared not change her mind. "Dom!''

He paused at the door.

"Do we have an agreement?"

His mouth curved, but not in a smile. "You mean, will I leave Waverly Hall—and you—when we are through?"

She nodded.

"Only if you wish me to." His gaze was piercing.

Anne was relieved. "Thank you."

He laughed once, harshly. "Don't thank me yet, Anne. Because when I'm through with you, you won't want me to leave."

Anne inhaled.

Dom slammed from the car. He did not return until just before they arrived in Scotland.

Anne slept alone fitfully in the first-class carriage that night, regretting the way she had managed her single conversation with Dom, and beginning to feel dread at the prospect of actually arriving in Scotland. She did not know where Dom slept. Belle served her all of her meals. In the late afternoon of the following day the train stopped at another small village. One or two crofts could be seen just before the village, and Anne had spotted a young shepherd with his flock on a rocky hill. A row of thatched-roof, stone cottages faced the small, deserted rickety wood depot. Smoke curled out of every single chimney. A man in tweeds and a worn cap pushed a two-wheeled cart containing fagots of wood. One of the cottages boasted a faded sign, hanging at an awkward angle. Painted in nearly indecipherable letters were the words RED DEER INN.

The door to Anne's carriage opened. Anne tensed at the sight of Dom.

His stare was impossible to read. "We depart here."

Anne stood, somewhat hastily. "Where are we?"

"A small hamlet called Falkirk. My hunting box is

twenty-five kilometers from here, but we can be there before dark.''

Anne's heart sank. She had hoped that the hunting box was much closer; she was tired and looked forward to retiring for the night. But it was probably too much to hope that Dom would leave her alone. Her pulse raced. She shut off her thoughts, trembling.

Anne had no choice but to cross the car. Dom moved aside and allowed her to precede him. Verig and Belle had already disembarked. A hired wagon was being loaded with the baggage, and they were supervising the task.

Anne glanced up at the sky. It was dark, cloudy and threatening. A gust of wind tugged at her skirts and her hat. She held her skirts down with one hand, hoping her veiled black hat was secure. She found Dom watching her. ''Are we in for a storm?''

''Probably,'' Dom said. ''But the weather on the coast is unpredictable, and that is where my estate is located.''

A hansom had appeared. It was terribly old-fashioned, a leftover from an earlier era, and it looked quite neglected, its wheels rusted and its leather seats cracked, but Dom handed Anne up into the back, then settled there beside her. He called for the driver to depart. Fortunately there was a canopy over their heads, but Anne espied several tears in the leather, and hoped it would not rain yet.

They traveled away from the village upon a road which quickly narrowed and became rutted and almost impassable. They seemed to be climbing upward as they passed through rocky hills covered with heather and gorse. Neither cottage nor croft was to be seen. Anne made no comment, but as they jarred over the gaping turf, she clung to her seat. It did not matter, she was thrown against Dom constantly. He appeared not to notice, but she was aware of each and every instance of contact with his hard, muscular body.

She would not think about the coming night, though.

Anne began to hear the sea. She sat up. It was close to dusk now. She saw a lonely gull soaring above them. Her gaze found Dom's. He was watching her again.

"We will be there in another moment," he commented.

Anne nodded, glanced out of the window, and her eyes widened. They had crossed the last line of hills, which they had been steadily climbing. The landscape seemed to drop away abruptly where it met the dark horizon. Anne had expected a rustic lodge. She stared as a red stone tower rose up like a sentinel ahead of them.

"Welcome to Tavalon Castle," Dom said.

The castle had originally belonged to a Campbell. It was five or six hundred years old, Dom wasn't quite sure. As he pulled the bell rope on the barbican, waiting for someone to winch open the old, rusted portcullis, Anne stared through the iron bars, feeling as if she had stepped back in time. The castle was built of bloodred stone. The central tower was high and square, surrounded by ancient walls boasting real parapets and four short, squat round towers. She could hear the sea now, roaring loudly, just behind the castle. She could smell salt on the air. A single raindrop wet the back of her neck.

"My lord, sir!" A thin, hunched-over man in an oilskin stepped out of the heavy, scarred front door of the square tower and rushed across the thick, overgrown grass of the ward. "We were na expecting ye." It was an accusation.

"I am aware of that, Thomas. Kindly open the door," Dom said.

The ancient Scot disappeared. Dom took Anne and

led her along the thick, but in places crumbling, wall of the barbican. A heavy wood door suddenly thrust open. "A convenient modernization," Dom said, humor in his tone. "Besides, Thomas can't raise the portcullis alone."

Anne stepped through the narrow doorway and found herself inside the ward. She squinted, looking around, as Dom went with Thomas to raise the portcullis so the wagon containing their goods could be admitted inside the castle.

Anne saw that the outbuildings, although typically stone and thatch, were far more recent than the castle itself. She relaxed slightly, noticing both a light in one of the tower's ground floor windows and smoke curling from one of its chimneys. The sounds of a cow's quiet mooing drifted to her along with the tinkle of its cowbell. A crow flew over her head, and the sea thundered somewhere below her. A hand touched her shoulder and Anne jerked.

"It's going to rain," Dom said. His gaze held hers searchingly. "Come."

He took her elbow and Anne allowed him to lead her toward the castle while the wagon rumbled past them. But suddenly he veered around its southern wall. Anne gasped.

The black sea yawned below their feet, pounding the base of the cliff violently, casting thick white sheets of foam up on the rocks and into the air.

Anne inhaled, not realizing that she was clinging to Dom's arm. The wild splendor of the scene kept her riveted. Tavalon Castle was perched on the very edge of a cliff. It was almost a miracle, Anne thought, that it did not fall into the unruly sea. The ground fell away from the castle walls precipitously, sheets of sheer, jagged red rock running vertically to the black, thundering, foaming sea.

A raindrop fell on Anne's hand.

But she could not move, mesmerized. She was acutely aware of the red castle beside her, the black sea below her, and the darkening sky above her—and she was acutely aware of the virile golden man she stood beside. Anne felt his gaze upon her face. She lifted her eyes to his.

There was a question in his gaze.

Anne's body tightened. But she knew he wasn't thinking about the night to come—even though she was, although she'd resolved not to. She wet her lips, realized he held her hand. Anne took a deep breath. "What a wild and majestic place."

"Yes," Dom agreed.

"Do you come here often?" she asked, thinking that there were many facets to Dom which he chose not to reveal. This was a lonely place, majestic but lonely—just like its master.

"Hardly," he said. "It is inconveniently located, and, as you can see, quite run-down. Nor am I a hunting enthusiast. However, I am inexplicably fond of this estate." Their gazes met. "A man cannot fail to hear himself think, here. There is no escape."

"Yes." Anne looked up at the sky, which would soon be as black and opaque as the sea. A man—or a woman—would not be able to escape himself or herself in such a place. Her pulse raced. "It is going to rain."

"At least," Dom said, and as if to confirm the fact, thunder suddenly boomed right over their heads. Anne jumped.

Dom threw his arm around her shoulders just as the heavens opened and it began to pour. Lightning lit up the sky. Thunder cracked.

"Come on," he cried, and they retraced their steps, running back around the castle to the front door. It was wide open. They raced inside.

Dom slammed the door shut and bolted it.

Anne was panting and light-headed. She found herself in a large, primitive hall. The stone ceiling arched high over their heads. Faded pennants hung from the rafters. Although a Persian carpet graced the floor, it was ragged and torn and almost colorless. Two old suits of armor guarded the entrance to the hall, and a mélange of medieval weapons—swords, maces, and crossbows—hung on the walls, high above their heads. A fire blazed in a brick hearth large enough to fit a horse. Anne was soaked now; she quickly walked over to it to warm herself.

"Our chamber is the first one upstairs," Dom said from behind her.

Anne didn't know whether she was angry or just dismayed. She had expected the courtesy of separate bedrooms even if she had to share her bed.

"My lady, are you all right?" Belle asked, worry in her tone.

Anne could not smile. She stood in the center of the master bedroom, unmoving. It was a large square room, sparsely appointed, dimly lit, the floors and walls stone. What furniture there was was nondescript: a square wooden table, two rickety chairs, a pale pine armoire, and a round ottoman covered in a faded red velvet. There were several rugs underfoot, all locally woven of rough, hand-dyed wool in shades of dark green. A four-poster bed dominated the room, the blankets and pillows dark blue, a heavy red wool plaid at its foot. A fire blazed in the hearth.

Outside it was raining heavily. Anne could hear a shutter banging in the wind.

"I have almost finished unpacking," Belle said when Anne did not reply.

Anne glanced at her trunk, which was on the floor and open. "Thank you." She moved to one of the chairs and sat down. Its legs were uneven and it rocked before it settled beneath her weight. Anne's heart was pounding heavily.

She had no choice but to share her bed with Dom, but she would insist upon separate rooms. It was far too intimate otherwise. Anne realized that her body was riddled with tension. She must try to relax; it would be hours yet before he would expect her to fulfill her part of this mad bargain.

"My lady, you are wet," Belle scolded.

Anne had forgotten. Now she became aware of being cold as well. She stood, shivering. "You are right. I had better change before I become ill."

Thunder suddenly boomed right over their heads. A moment later the room turned dazzling white, lightning striking just outside the castle and the room they were in.

Anne and Belle froze, until the room grew dim with dancing shadows again.

"It's only a storm," Anne said, shaking off a touch of unease.

Belle's hand covered her heart. "Is it always like this in this godforsaken land?"

Anne understood that her maid was distressed, although her words were light. "I don't know. In truth, I have never been this far north before."

"I am not fond of this place," Belle said grimly. "What if there are ghosts lurking about?"

Anne had to smile. "Oh, Belle, there is no such thing."

"An old castle like this is bound to be haunted," Belle insisted.

Anne still smiled. "I promise you, it is not."

Belle did not appear convinced. Lightning brightened the sky outside again. Briefly Anne and Belle stiffened, while thunder drummed close by.

"Let me get you some dry clothes," Belle finally said, kneeling by the trunk. She rummaged in it, lifted a dark blue gown. Her eyes changed, gleaming. "How about this, my lady?"

Anne frowned immediately. The navy color was appropriate for mourning, but it was satin and low-cut, intended as evening wear. It was a gorgeous dress in spite of its dark color—Anne had never worn it, had never had cause to wear it. "Why did you pack this?" she asked. She had no intention of dressing now so elegantly for the supper she would share with Dom downstairs.

Belle's gaze turned sly. "His Lordship would like to see you in something less severe, I have no doubt, my lady—if you do not mind my saying so."

"I mind," Anne said sharply. She was flushed. "Do I not have something serviceable in that trunk?" Anne strode over, peering inside. "Something with sleeves? Something that will not leave half my bosom bare?" She could imagine Dom's reaction to such a dress. How flustered she now was.

Belle began to search through the trunk again. Her sigh was all too audible. Anne thought she muttered to herself, something about Anne being so lovely but determined to hide it. Anne was about to chastise her when Belle paused, still bent over the trunk, her hand inside of it. Anne suddenly frowned. "Belle?"

Belle lifted a strap of leather from the trunk. "My lady, what is this?"

Anne stared at the broken leather strap.

"I never packed this," Belle cried. "How did this get inside your trunk?"

Outside, the rain suddenly increased, beating heavily against the stone walls of the castle. Anne could not answer Belle. She stared, her heart lurching.

Attached to one end of the broken leather strap was an iron stirrup.

\*      \*      \*

Dom paced the great hall. He had been pacing for a long time now, warring with himself. He was so damn irritated—and so damn disappointed. Anne was still determined to do battle with him.

After Anne's riding accident, Dom had thought that something new and different was happening between them. It had felt as if a real bond were being forged. When Anne had accepted his offer to go away with him, he had not been referring to his lewd earlier proposal—and she had not been thinking of it either. Or so he had thought. But clearly he had been wrong.

Dom's gaze found the narrow, steep staircase that led to the second floor of the keep. He stared, but Anne did not appear. She had gone upstairs an hour ago. It was, he knew, her way of flinging her determined reluctance into his face.

Dom raked his fingers through his thick, sun-streaked hair. He had not slept at all last night. He had not been able to keep Anne out of mind. His body's response had been hardly characteristic, but all too familiar.

He had wanted her, and badly. He still wanted her. He could not understand himself. He had had many women, and he had never been obsessed with one before. Of course, none of the women in his life had been impudent little Americans with blue-black hair and huge blue eyes that too frequently mirrored both hurt and betrayal. Too well, he recalled another time when her eyes had been filled with light and laughter and love.

Dom glanced up the stairs again.

However, as much as he wanted Anne, that was not the primary reason he had asked her to come to Scotland with him. Had she refused him, he would have whisked her away anyway.

Her riding accident had been no accident. Someone who was very familiar with horses, someone with a grudge against Anne, had poisoned Blaze with a dangerous substance, one known to overexcite horses, often making them uncontrollable. Dom was familiar with the practice, although he did not condone it. But it was often done to increase a horse's speed on the racetrack by owners and trainers less scrupulous than himself.

Someone wanted to hurt or scare Anne, someone who knew horses, and Dom could not help suspecting Felicity. She had been raised around horses and knew them, although she was an indifferent horsewoman. Who else could it be? He had discussed the matter with Blake. Blake had been shocked and then angry to learn that the accident was a deliberately inflicted mishap. He had resolved to keep a close eye on Felicity, but he did not think she was the culprit.

And what about the fire in Anne's bedroom? Had that been an accident—a coincidence? Or had someone caused that, too?

In any case, until Dom had answers, he wanted Anne far from the scene of both the riding accident and the small fire. And taking her away to Scotland was hardly a hardship. It could prove very rewarding, indeed.

If Anne would allow bygones to be bygones, and give in to her sensuous nature.

Grimacing, Dom looked up the stairs again, more than annoyed. Where in bloody hell was she? It was time they ended this state of constant warfare.

He strode forward, taking the smooth, timeworn stone steps two at a time. He knocked once on Anne's door, sharply. Then he thrust it open.

Anne faced him, as white as a sheet, clad in her chemise and drawers and nothing else. Her corset, petticoats and an ugly black bombazine dress were laid out on the bed behind her. Belle peeked out past her shoulder.

"What," Anne gasped, her color returning in a rush of hot pink, "are you doing?"

He couldn't help but stare. Her chemise was lace-edged and transparent. "What do you think I'm doing?" he finally returned dryly. His gaze lifted, skewered hers. "I've come to collect."

Anne paled again. Her bosom heaved. Her nipples, he saw, were tight and hard.

Dom's smile was cool. His searing regard locked with Anne's. "Belle, you may leave. Madam will not need you again tonight."

# Chapter 16

$\mathcal{A}$nne recovered her wits just as Belle was opening the door. "Belle has to help me finish dressing!"

Dom smiled. "Why? When I'm only going to undress you?"

Anne stared, her pulse soaring.

"Good night, Belle," Dom said, a command.

Her cheeks flushed, trying to hide a sly smile, Belle backed quickly out of the room. Dom walked casually over to the door and slid the bolt down. There was a key in the lock. He turned it, took it out. All the while Anne did not move, or even breathe, watching him.

Dom turned toward her, smiling, holding the key loosely in his hand.

"Wh-what are you doing?" Anne said.

His smile widened. His single dimple dug deep. He walked over to the window. Outside, it had stopped raining, but it was a bleak, cloudy night, and the wind howled like a pack of lonely wolves. He moved the draperies aside and opened the window. A blast of cold air rushed into the room. Anne shivered. "Dom?"

He glanced at her, his eyes gleaming, then threw the key through the window.

"Dom!" Anne said.

Dom shut the window abruptly and pulled the draperies closed.

Anne stared, her heart beating explosively inside of her chest. "You threw the key away!"

He was cheerful, yet threatening. "That's right."

"You have locked us inside—together!"

He nodded, leaning one shoulder against the stone wall.

"How are we going to get out?"

"We're not going to leave." His stare was hard, penetrating. "Remember? You promised me an entire week, Anne."

"An . . . entire week." She stared, beginning to tremble. "You expect . . . you expect us to stay in this room for the entire week?"

He did not answer her. Very slowly now, his gaze roamed over her. Anne shook more fiercely, but not with fear. With anger—and with desire. Dear God, his burning eyes were undressing her, no difficult feat when she was already more naked than not. And every time she drew a breath, her silk chemise seemed to chafe her already hardened nipples, tightening them. Anne pressed her thighs together. The muscles there were constricted, tight, throbbing. "Stop," Anne said hoarsely.

Dom smiled briefly, knowingly. He levered himself off the wall. A moment later he shrugged his worn tweed hunting jacket off, tossing it onto one of the chairs. His fingers moved to the buttons on his linen shirt.

Anne came to life. "What are you doing?" she cried.

He smiled. "Undressing."

"Stop!" Hysteria made her tone shrill.

He squinted, yanking his shirt off one shoulder, revealing hard muscle and heavy bone and a slab of flat, thick chest. "Relax."

That was impossible, and he surely had to have known it. Anne's eyes were wide as he revealed his other shoulder, his entire chest, and his lean torso. Anne had not realized that his dark chest hair narrowed into an interesting vee, arrowing down into the waistband of his doeskin breeches. She froze. There was no mistaking what those breeches now contained.

"I cannot relax," she snapped furiously, turning her back on him. Fear added to her tension. Not fear of him—but fear of herself and her own body. She hugged herself, panting, licked her dry lips. Wondering if he was taking his pants off now.

She strained to hear the rustle of clothing, but heard nothing at all.

"You've seen me without my clothes before," Dom said, amused.

Anne jumped as he touched her shoulders from behind, nearly leaping out of her skin. She had not heard him approaching.

"Easy," he crooned as he might to one of his horses. "Easy, Anne, I don't bite."

She was as stiff as a board. He cupped her shoulders. And suddenly his teeth were tugging gently on one of her earlobes. "Not unless you want me to," he said in a low, seductive drawl.

He nipped her very gently.

Desire rushed over Anne, pooling in her loins.

She jerked free of his embrace, whirling to face him. It was a vast mistake. Even though he had kept on his breeches, his loins bulged unmistakably now. She flamed, looking away, but found her gaze drawn again to his.

"You are toying with me!" she accused.

"That's right." His gaze warmed as it moved down to her heaving breasts. "Are not toys an integral part of games?"

Anne stared. "I . . . do not understand." His words had a sexual meaning she was afraid to guess at.

"You will." His smile was lazy, seductive. "Come here."

Anne froze.

"Come here," he repeated, his tone more commanding.

Anne hesitated, her heart beating wildly. She was torn between her having agreed to his absurd proposal, and her unwillingness to play this kind of game with him at all. Torn between rampant desire—and abundant fear.

"Come here, Anne," he said dangerously.

Her arms folded protectively across her chest, Anne finally walked over to him.

He slid his thumb across her cheek.

"Don't," Anne managed, a plea she did not quite mean.

"Sssh." He trailed his forefinger down her neck. Anne trembled, breathing hard now, squeezing her thighs tightly together. She was hurting now. How could he make her want him so easily, so soon, by doing so little.

He understood. "Give up, Anne," he murmured.

"N-no." Her tongue had to wet her lips.

He watched, smiling. His fingertip traced her collarbone. Anne found herself staring at his mouth. Thinking about his kiss. Then his finger slid down lower. She tensed, staring at it. She knew where he was going, and she desperately wanted him to touch her breasts, and wanted him not to, just as desperately.

His forefinger glided over the bare skin of her chest above her lacy chemise. And then across the lace border, lower, around the curve of her breast. Anne bit down hard in order not to cry out. She wanted to push her breast into his hand. And suddenly his thumb grazed the aching tip of her nipple. Anne choked on a moan. Their gazes locked.

It was heaven. It was hell.

"Anne." His jaw was tight, flexed. His golden eyes

burned. "Relax. We both know you want this." He brushed his thumb over her nipple again.

Anne shook her head, unable to speak.

His thumb continued to tease and torture her. "Liar," he whispered.

Anne wet her lips. "Stop."

"Why?" His palm covered her breast possessively. "We have a bargain, remember?" He bent and touched the tip of his tongue to her nipple, through the chemise. Anne made a sharp sound.

Dom made a harsh affirmative sound and continued to lave the hard point, thoroughly now. Anne gripped her own hands, hard, closing her eyes. Pleasure washed over her. Again and again. Swelling inside her, a floodtide she could not fight. Suddenly Dom jerked her chemise down to her waist, tearing it. Abruptly he sucked the tight bud into his mouth.

"Dom!" Anne cried. Of their own volition, Anne's hands came up, clenching his head.

He laughed harshly.

And when he was finally through, Anne could not stand up. She would have fallen to the floor, but Dom caught her, holding her upright.

Her eyes opened, her gaze colliding with his. Anne was breathing heavily, but so was he. There was no mistaking the feeling of his hot, hard erection against her belly through her thin silk drawers. Anne could not move, could not speak.

"Yes," he said roughly. "I feel that way, too." He ducked his head and took her mouth in a long, wet kiss. He lifted her abruptly in his arms and carried her to the bed. Before her back even touched the mattress, his mouth was on her nipple again, sucking, tugging, then licking, laving. Anne squirmed, gasped, cried out.

He laughed, the sound triumphant. "Touch me, Anne," he demanded, looming over her.

Anne could not speak. She stared into his smoldering

eyes. She had one coherent thought—she had agreed to do anything he asked her to do, and now she had the perfect excuse to touch him as she longed to. Anne laid her palm on his chest, then rubbed the hard muscle there.

Dom groaned.

Anne slid her hand lower, over his rib cage, then across his tense, flat stomach.

His eyes shot open. "Yes," he breathed. His gaze caught hers. "Lower."

Anne finally understood—and her eyes widened, her hand paused.

"Sweet, touch me," he commanded. His tone changed. "Please, Anne."

Anne was mindless now. The devil was instructing her. She slid her hand lower. And lower still, over the very hard bulge in his butter-soft breeches.

Dom threw his head back, his hand flying to hers. He held her palm tightly against his erection. "God," he gasped. Sweat beaded on his temples.

Anne was mesmerized by the feel of his erection under her hand, and by the sight of him arched above her. It struck her suddenly that she had done this to him.

Anne was panting sharply now. She reached up with her other hand and stroked the hard slab that formed one side of his chest. Dom's gaze flew open. They stared at one another.

A moment later he was ripping open his breeches. Anne could not look away. His penis was a massive ridge of straining, swollen muscle, the tip terribly engorged. He kicked his breeches to the floor and kneed her thighs apart.

Anne wanted him. Terribly.

Dom knelt between her legs. "This is what you do to me," he said, and he gripped her drawers and ripped them off her.

Anne felt something utterly primitive flood over her

in response. She reached for him. Dom was pushing her thighs apart. And instead of thrusting his body into hers, he bent his head, and claimed her sex with his mouth.

Anne moaned.

His tongue ran over her heavy, swollen lips, then plunged between them. He began to delicately suck on her clitoris. Anne began to gasp, thrashing. He withdrew, seemed to smile against her, then teased her with the tip of his tongue. Anne arched up off the bed, a huge, guttural cry ripping its way out of her chest. But before she could float back to earth, his mouth was on her again.

"Dom," Anne gasped, wanting to push him away and pull him close at the very same time.

"We're not through, Anne." He thrust his fingers deep inside her, his tongue shrewd and cunning, laving her expertly. Anne's fingers dug into his head. She rocked back against the bed. She began to spiral upward in a frenzy of white-hot fire.

"Not yet," Dom said, moving over her.

Anne whimpered, her nails digging into his shoulders, raking down his back. "Please," she begged.

His smiled flashed, strained, triumphant. His mouth seized hers, forcing her lips open. Anne kissed him back as hungrily.

He tore his mouth from hers with a sound that was half gasp and half laugh. "Anne." He braced himself over her on his forearms, the muscles popping out under his skin. And he moved, smiling now, knowingly, rubbing the ripe tip of his penis against her slick, swollen sex.

Anne cried out.

"Yes, sweet, I know," he ground out, moving himself very slowly over her.

Anne's mind began to blank. She thrashed on the bed. Stars began to blaze in her head. "D-Dom."

"I know. I know," he soothed. "Come on, Anne. Come on."

Anne whimpered. His penis had become an instrument of exquisite torture. A huge moan worked its way out of her throat. Then Dom bent and thrust his tongue against her nipple.

Anne shattered. Screaming.

As she climaxed, Dom knifed inside of her. Fast, hard. Anne wept, another wave of pleasure, more intense than the one before, crashing over her. Dom's thrusting rhythm increased. "Bloody, bloody hell," he gasped against her ear. "I can't hold it." His mouth found hers.

Anne kissed him back, and this time, as he plunged his manhood deep inside of her, she forced his mouth open, thrusting her tongue against his, entwining, wanting to take all of him, and then even more of him, as much as she could. He shuddered on top of her. She sucked harder. He made a soblike sound. And cried her name.


Anne almost fell asleep. But Dom removed his arm from where it lay across her waist, sitting up. Instantly Anne was fully awake.

She began to think—and comprehend what had just happened and the extent of her own role in their lovemaking. Her gaze flew open.

Dom sat beside her, staring very gravely out into the night-darkened room.

Cautiously, she also sat up, reaching for the plaid throw and pulling it up to her neck. She began to blush. It was a little bit late for modesty and she damn well knew it.

Dom turned and looked at her.

Anne felt her cheeks flaming. She said nothing.

His regard was intense yet somber; it was also enigmatic. Anne could not decipher what he was thinking.

Her pulse was already skittering. She stole a glance at the locked door. Surely he was not thinking of remaining in this room with her for an entire week. In spite of her determined moral outrage, Anne tingled from head to toe imagining the event.

Dom bent suddenly and kissed her, long and hard. When he pulled back, his gaze was fierce. "I don't know what the hell is happening here, but something is happening, Anne."

Anne dared not refute him. She dared not agree.

"And right now, I also don't care," he said, catching her face with his hands. "I'm going to make love to you all night," he said roughly.

It flitted across Anne's mind as he kissed her again that she should resist, or at least pretend to. But she owed him an entire week, so what was the point? Especially when he was already stoking the heat spreading rapidly throughout her body.

He pressed her back into the pillows. His hands and mouth began an unerring quest.

Anne walked outside, alone.

The sun was shining brightly, scattering the patchwork of clouds overhead, as if last night's storm had never existed. She was not wearing a hat, and the steady breeze tugged at her hair, causing tendrils to escape her chignon and curl about her face. Anne wore a light coat and kept her hands in the pockets. It was almost noon. Anne had overslept—with good cause.

She blushed just thinking about it.

Her heart raced just thinking about it.

It tried to sing a little, too.

Anne forced her elation down. She had spent the night with Dom in order to fulfill their strange bargain—so that he would leave Waverly Hall and her. Not for any other reason. But no matter how hard she tried to convince herself of that, she was strangely elated. She could not help but wonder where he was. Thomas had said that he had gone riding earlier that morning. Anne had not awoken when he had left her bed.

Anne thought about how she had been tricked. Her bedroom door had never been locked; that morning she had learned that the lock had long been useless and broken.

Feverish tension tautened her body. She would remember last night until the day she died. And contrary to what she had expected, Dom had not asked very much of her. In fact, he had spent most of the night kissing her, touching her, tasting her—in general, pleasing *her,* as if he could not get enough of her.

It was almost as if he were consumed with love for her.

Anne forced the thought aside. She must not forget the past four years. She must not forget the fact that Dom was an experienced roué. She must not forget, most of all, that she had something which he wanted. Waverly Hall was a far more powerful aphrodisiac than her body, in all likelihood.

But a little voice inside of her head taunted her with *What if?* What if he was really consumed with desire for her? What if he loved her?

Anne inhaled, pausing beside a small corral where two hacks grazed. She must not allow her mind to wander on such a tangent again. She must keep a firm grip on reality—she must never be such a fool. She must remember what it was she wanted—why she was in Scotland at Tavalon Castle in the first place. And what she wanted was for him to leave Waverly Hall—and her—alone.

One of the horses lifted its head and snorted.

"Hello, boy," Anne said softly.

The horse stood very still, watching her out of wide, luminous eyes. Anne moved closer, wishing she had brought an apple or some other tidbit for him. She leaned on the rail—and suddenly recalled the broken stirrup that she and Belle had found in her trunk.

Anne tensed. She could not fathom why someone would have put such a reminder of her riding accident inside of her trunk. How malicious the gesture was. Yet it had only been a prank, she was certain of it. Nevertheless, Anne was uneasy.

Why would someone wish to upset her by reminding her of an accident that could have been fatal? Did someone want to frighten her? But that made no sense. Clearly it was a petty and stupid prank.

Nevertheless, Anne shivered.

She forced her thoughts to happier ground, not fully convinced. Anne glanced around. Barren hills with frequent rock outcroppings surrounded Tavalon Castle. Still damp from last night's storm, they were alternately cloaked in shadow or glistening in the sunlight. On the eastern side of the castle was the endless indigo North Sea. She saw no sign of Dom. She envied him—it was a beautiful morning for riding.

Excitement rippled through her. Why not go after Dom? Surely after last night he would not find her company an intrusion. She did owe him a full week, after all. And they were in the wilds of Scotland—she would be able to ride astride.

Anne hurried back to the castle to change. A few minutes later, clad in a dark gray riding ensemble, Anne was mounted on a big gray gelding and cantering away from the lonely red castle and the windswept sea.

She reassured herself that she was not lost. Yet she had intended to keep the castle within sight. Somehow one rocky path had led to another and then another, and although her intention had been to ride directly to the top of the nearest hill, that had proved impossible. The hills were too rocky to ride directly across on a fine mount, and Anne had been forced to choose amongst the numerous paths bisecting the countryside.

Anne halted the gray and gazed all around her. Hills and ridges rippled every which way, the indigo sea lay directly ahead of her, glistening in the dazzling sunlight, but the red sentinel tower of Tavalon Castle was nowhere in sight. A chill crept up her spine.

Nor was Dom anywhere to be seen. It had been foolish to think that, in this vast countryside, she would be able to spot him.

In fact, other than a few sheep and a soaring crow, she had not seen any other living thing.

Anne hesitated. She would have to retrace her steps. Although she had a terrible sense of direction, she had been careful to always bear right when making a choice about which path to take. It should not be too difficult to return to the castle.

But Anne kept her mount standing still as she shifted uneasily in the saddle. She could not quite identify whether she was disturbed because she might be lost or for some other reason. The hairs on the nape of her neck were prickling. It almost felt as though she were no longer alone.

Anne's gray gelding snorted.

Anne suddenly had the distinct sensation of being watched. She was suddenly certain that she was no longer alone as she had been for the past hour.

But that was ridiculous. For if anyone were about, it had to be Dom, and he would hail her immediately. Anne maneuvered the horse in a small, tight circle. There was no one in sight. Just the sun and the sky and the sea, and the endless litany of rocky hilltops and bare, faded ridges.

Anne turned the gray around, disappointed that she had not found Dom. By now Dom was probably at home. She urged the gray into a trot. And had the strongest sensation again that she was being watched.

Eyes seemed to bore into the very center of her back. And her horse snorted, its ears pricked.

Anne's heart pumped. She thought she glimpsed another rider on a ridge parallel to them, not far away. But it was just an effect of the sun and shadows; her eyes were playing tricks on her. It wasn't another rider; she was very much alone. Anne was relieved. She had been foolishly frightened.

"Let's go home, fellow," she said to her horse. "Enough of this nonsense."

She was about to proceed when a shadowy figure emerged from a cluster of boulders on the parallel ridge. Anne froze.

This time, she had no doubt that it was a rider, and he was about half a mile behind her.

"Dom," Anne murmured uncertainly. She hesitated—and waved. But the rider suddenly disappeared behind a stone wall that jagged across the hill, as suddenly as he had appeared.

But surely Dom had seen her. Surely he had been following her, hoping to catch up to her. Surely the rider *was* Dom. Anne waited, but the rider did not reappear. Anne grew very uneasy. Her pulse was pounding. If the rider had been Dom, he would have joined her by now. If it wasn't Dom, then who was out there? Trailing her? Watching her?

Suddenly Anne urged her horse into a trot, and then a canter. She was probably being foolish, but if she were accosted, she had no one to come to her aid. And this time, when she looked back, she saw that the rider on the red horse was now on the *same* trail behind her—and he appeared to be maintaining a careful distance from her.

Anne was frightened. She urged the gray into a faster canter. This time she saw that the other rider was also cantering now—pacing her.

Anne flicked her crop to the gray's flank. He broke

into a gallop and they raced down the steep and narrow, twisting path. Anne flung a glance over her shoulder. But the rider had disappeared yet again.

Anne was sweating. She slowed her horse. She realized that she had a death grip on the reins, but her fingers would not relax. An image of the broken stirrup leather flashed through her mind. Someone had gone to a lot of trouble to place it in her personal trunk with her clothes, but why? A graphic reminder of her riding accident and her near brush with death, placed where she was sure to find it.

Just as the burned rose on her pillow was a graphic reminder of the accidental fire in her bedroom.

The gray stumbled. Anne caught herself before she was catapulted over his head. It flashed through her mind that if she did not slow down, she could have another riding accident—and be thrown and break her neck. Anne pulled the gray up.

Her breathing had grown shallow. Surely her imagination was running wild! Anne glanced around—the other rider had vanished. No one was in sight.

She chided herself for her foolishness. It was ridiculous to think that someone wanted to frighten her or even to harm her. It was absurd even to dream that the fire in her bedroom and her runaway horse were anything but accidents and that the prankster, whoever he was, was anything but petty and mean-spirited.

The accidents were a set of bizarre coincidences.

No one wished to frighten her. Certainly no one wished to harm her.

She had no enemies.

Besides—she was not being followed, not anymore.

That had also been a coincidence, one which she had blown out of all proportion.

Then, to her immense relief, Anne spied the red stone tower of Tavalon Castle. Just below her, the towering and brilliantly red stone keep was framed by the bright blue sky and the shining indigo sea.

Anne urged the gray forward at a brisk trot, trying to regain her breath, wetting her parched lips. But she glanced back one more time. And Anne saw a rider silhouetted against the sky, high on a ridge above her.

## Chapter 17

*H*e entered the Red Deer Inn with swift, angry strides. The gnarled innkeeper started to smile at him, but stopped upon seeing his expression. Gingerly he held out the room key. Patrick swiped it without breaking stride, and pounded up the narrow stairs and into his small rented room.

He slammed the bedroom door closed hard behind him.

*Four years,* he raged silently as he paced. Four years he had been there for her, doing anything that she wished, comforting her, caring for her, loving her. And now this. All for nothing.

Damned Dominick had ridden back into her life, and it was as if the past had never existed.

Patrick whirled and threw his key at the wall. When would she realize that Dom was a worthless specimen of a man where women were concerned? Unreliable, selfish, self-serving? Arrogant and vain? God! He wanted to tear his hair out, he wanted to howl at the moon. He had loved Anne for years. But Anne had been in love with Dom from the moment she had arrived at Hunting Way as a tearful orphan ten years ago. Dom, of course, had not even noticed her. Like Patrick, he had been away at school, and later he had chosen to live at his extravagant town house in London. At the time, Patrick had been living in London as well. But in a dingy bachelor flat far from Mayfair's exclusive environs.

And then Dom had been summoned home by the duke and bluntly been ordered to marry. Over a bottle of brandy, Dom had confided in Patrick all of the particulars. He was resigned and would do as his grandfather wished him to do, as he had to marry sooner or later. Patrick had pointed out that his sister was still available and one of the ton's Reigning Beauties. He could not help himself. Everyone in his family would benefit from the union.

And Dom had chosen Felicity immediately afterward. It wasn't really surprising. He had grown up with Patrick and he had known Felicity all of his life. He had no need of money, so he could marry whomever he chose.

The Collins family had celebrated privately that night.

But instead of marrying Felicity, Dom had seduced Anne. And then he broke it off with Felicity, married Anne—and promptly abandoned her.

Patrick wasn't sure when he had first fallen in love with Anne. Perhaps in that first year after her marriage, when she had been inconsolable over Dom's abandoning her. Patrick had been waiting for Anne to choose him over Dominick St. Georges for a very long time.

He had been waiting for four long years.

And surely she would choose him. Surely this time, for once in his life, he would beat Dom at something—he would beat him at love.

For he had never bested Dom at anything in his entire life. And Patrick was acutely aware of growing up in Dom's shadow. Patrick had been the less noble one, the less wealthy one, the less handsome one. He and Dom had grown up together, they were exactly the same age. But Dom had had everything. He was, ultimately, heir to the Rutherford dukedom. The Collinses were titled, Jonathon was the baron of Hunting, but it was an insignificant title, and they struggled to keep up appearances. Patrick had three older brothers. He would inherit neither title nor land. He was, in fact, the youngest son of a minor, impoverished lord; he was a nobody.

It was at Eton that the differences between them had become glaring. Before, it was a matter of clothing and toys, and later, horses and village girls. But at the exclusive private school, Dom had immediately been deferred to as the leader of his class, and Patrick had only been welcome in the clique because Dom demanded that the others accept him. How painful it had been. Then they had gone to different universities, but Patrick had been miserable, and had transferred to Cambridge in his second year—where Dom was enrolled. There, as always, Patrick had watched Dom, the golden, handsome heir to the dukedom, effortlessly gliding through his studies, his professors applauding him, lauding him, his acceptance by the ton a given, every door open to him, coveted invitations always jamming his mailbox, and women, so many women, innocent and worldly, genteel or not, chasing after him. All the while Dom did exactly as he pleased. But for Patrick, there were few invitations, although Dom took him to all the fetes, and there were as few women, although Dom always introduced him to the ladies about whom he never seemed truly enthusiastic. Patrick had had to work hard at every single thing he did, and even then, he had never been first at anything.

This time, though, would be different.

This time, Patrick knew that Anne would be his.

She would choose him over Dom St. Georges.

He would see to it.

Now Patrick punched a pitcher and watched it topple to the floor, spilling all of its water. *Anne was still in love with Dom.* Why else would she have gone away

with him? Worse, by now Dom had undoubtedly seduced her. Patrick was sick; he was also furious.

But he was not ready to give up. He would take
Anne from Dom. He had tried to make her see reason,
but that hadn't worked. So instead, he would resort to
other means in order to make her see Dom as a ruthless,
terrifying bastard.

Patrick clenched his fists. He wanted to kill Dom. Of
course, he would not. Because as much as he hated him,
he also loved him as he would one of his own brothers.

But today he was so angry he even wanted to kill
Anne.

•

## Chapter 18

*A*nne whipped the gray with her crop. She leaned low over the gray's neck as they galloped down the rocky path. Stones shot out from beneath the gray's hooves, tumbling over the side of the road and into a narrow gorge beside it. The horse stumbled. Anne gripped its mane. From the corner of her eye she glimpsed the bottom of the gorge, many feet below her, a jumble of sharp rocks. She dug her heels into her horse's sides. The gray lengthened its strides.

Anne did not dare look back to see if the rider was pursuing her again.

She did not have to. She could hear a horse galloping behind her—the sound of its racing hoofbeats coming closer—and closer.

Her heart lodged itself in her throat. Anne looked over her shoulder, and saw a flash of red hide. The rider was only a few lengths behind her! She turned forward, whipping the gray's neck with her crop, terrified.

"Anne!" Dom shouted.

Anne thought she had misheard. But Dom shouted her name again as he drew abreast of her. His hand shot out, seizing the gray's bridle abruptly. Both horses came to plunging, heaving halts on the narrow path simultaneously.

Dom released her mount and spurred his bay hunter close to hers. His knee knocked her thigh. "What the hell are you doing?" he shouted.

Anne stared at him out of wide, stunned eyes, then collapsed on her horse's neck in profound relief. She buried her face in its coarse salt-and-pepper mane. Her heart was roaring in her ears.

"What is wrong with you?" Dom was still shouting. "To ride so recklessly! You could have killed both yourself and your horse!"

Anne gulped air. Her pulse finally began to slow a bit. She realized that she was shaking. Oh, God. It was Dom who had been following her after all, not some stranger intent on harm. She straightened, managing a weak smile. "I did not know that it was you."

He stared at her. His face was dark with fury. His eyes were almost black. "What?"

"I was spooked," Anne explained. She brushed a strand of hair off her mouth. "I thought a stranger was following me." She laughed shakily, realizing how ludicrous her words sounded, and how hysterical she must seem. She brushed more hair away from her face. Her chignon had become undone in her madcap ride and her thick, waist-length hair was rioting over her shoulders and down her back.

Dom's expression changed.

"But it was only you." She smiled again, more brightly. She covered her beating heart with one gloved palm. "I wouldn't have ridden that way if I had known. How silly I am."

Dom's gaze lifted and moved over the hillside behind her. Anne stiffened slightly when she realized that he was actually looking for something—or someone. But then his gaze settled on her abruptly and Anne forgot her fears. She knew she must look terribly ill-kempt. Not only had her hair come loose, but her jacket had popped some of its buttons

But his gaze moved slowly over her wind-reddened face, her flowing hair, then down her heaving breasts and the outline her legs made through her black riding skirts. A sudden warmth unfurled from the very pit of her belly. All of her muscles tensed. It was shameful. Shameless.

"Are you all right?" he asked huskily.

Anne nodded, at a loss for words.

He drove his bay even closer, his knee spooning the back of hers, his hard thigh driving hers up high on her saddle. His gaze pierced hers. "God, Anne, I thought you were going to break your neck."

Something shafted Anne, not just inside her body, but through her very soul. Anne stared back at him. There was no mistaking his concern. It was there in his tone, and it was written all over his face. It was clear in his incredibly mesmerizing eyes. All she could think was, *he cares.*

*Good God, he really cares.*

Dom's gaze darkened. He leaned toward her, his arm going around her, hard. He dragged her half off of her horse so that he could kiss her. Anne's eyes closed. His mouth was hard, demanding, hungry. He plumbed her mouth with his tongue. Anne heard herself moan. Her fists were balled against the soft wool of his riding jacket.

He tore his mouth from hers.

Anne settled back in her saddle, dazed.

His jaw flexed. He glanced around, at the rocky hill rising up behind them, and at the deep gorge careening down on the other side of his horse and the path. Anne guessed exactly what he was thinking. She was thinking it too.

He smiled crookedly. "Let's go back."

Anne nodded, gathering up her reins. But she could not help taking one glance around herself, regretting that there was not even the smallest patch of grass to serve as a bed.

What was happening to her?

She was afraid to think about it too closely. And as they rode slowly single file down the narrow path toward Tavalon Castle, her eyes remained glued on Dom's broad back.

Anne was removing her riding habit with Belle's help, mindlessly, for she was thinking of Dom. Even the sight of the antiquated brass tub, filled with steaming bathwater, smelling of roses, could not divert her from her wicked thoughts.

When a knock sounded upon her door, she stood very still, knowing who it was. Wondering what had taken him so very long.

Belle hid a smile, handing Anne a wine-colored silk wrapper, which she donned slowly and belted over her bare body. She nodded and Belle opened the door.

Dom's gaze slammed over her as if he knew she were nude beneath the wrapper. If he was aware of Belle's presence, he gave no sign of it. His golden eyes were gleaming, his tone as intimate. "May I come in?"

Her body was already fevered and ready for him. All because of a single kiss and his open concern for her—and her own ceaselessly sinful thoughts. Anne nodded. She barely saw as Belle left the room, shutting the door behind her.

Dom's gaze moved back to the bath. "I don't want to interrupt."

"I don't mind," Anne said, her tone so husky that she hardly recognized it herself. She was trembling in excitement.

Dom paused in front of her. His eyes on hers, he unknotted the tie on her wrapper. It fell open immediately. Anne was acutely aware of her breasts, her belly, and the dark patch of her femininity being exposed. Anne did not move.

Dom's gaze did. It dipped. His jaw flexed. His hand came up, his fingers grazing her cheek. "You worried me this afternoon."

Anne swallowed. She could not reply.

"You are so beautiful, Anne," he whispered hoarsely.

Anne smiled, sighing as he cupped her cheek. She knew she was not beautiful, but since last night she felt like the loveliest woman in all Creation. "Dom."

He no longer looked into her eyes. Unsmiling, his hand slid down her neck, under her silk wrapper, to cup one of her breasts. Anne fought back a moan.

An instant later his hands were curved hard around her buttocks, holding her tightly against him. He kissed her with the same rough hunger he had displayed just minutes before out on the heath. Anne kissed him back as wildly. Their teeth touched, scraped. Anne pulled his lower lip between hers gently, then more firmly. Dom's response was to grip her bottom more tightly, pulling her up his body so that her soft, swollen loins rode every single inch of his arousal.

A moment passed and Anne found herself in the bed, beneath Dom. As he braced himself above her, she was acutely aware of how utterly naked she was, and that he was fully clothed. The leather of his boots felt hard and abrasive against her calves, his breeches butter-soft on her thighs, his jacket slightly scratchy on her arms and breasts. Anne's excitement increased. As their mouths fused, she thrashed, his jacket brushing her nipple, stiffening it.

Their tongues warred, then mated. Dom shoved his breeched thigh between her legs, hard. Anne pumped against the smooth, worn buckskin, crying out, seeking ecstasy.

Dom tore his mouth free, panting. "Anne, you are unmanning me," he gasped.

Anne did not understand. Nor did she care to, for he was raining kisses on her breasts, her nipples, and on her soft, heaving belly. As he moved down her body, his jacket tickled her, his breeches teased her. Anne gasped when he nudged her mons with his mouth. She arched off of the bed as his tongue found the protrusion it was seeking.

"Forgive me, Anne," Dom rasped, rising up over her abruptly and tearing at his breeches.

"There is nothing to forgive," Anne gasped, her palm fluttering over the leather gloving his manhood. Dom panted. Their hands brushed. His erection sprang free.

"Hold on," Dom warned.

Anne dug her hips into the bed, her hands seeking the headboard behind her. As she gripped it he thrust hard and deep inside her. Anne cried out as he drove her completely up the bed.

It was much, much later before either one of them remembered the bath. By then, the scented water was ice-cold, the sky night-dark.

Dom stared into the fire blazing in the hearth.

Beyond the glow from the fire, the great hall was dark, lost in flickering shadow and absolutely silent. Dom had not been able to sleep.

Which was in itself amazing, after last night's and today's sexual excess. But Dom was too disturbed to sleep.

Had someone been following Anne today? She had probably imagined it. He had not been following her. She could not have seen him, either, as he had come across her from the opposite direction, and only at the last moment before their moment of meeting. He had not seen any other horseman upon the heath.

But Anne had been frightened, and Anne was a very sensible woman.

Dom grimaced, thinking again about the two "accidents" that had befallen Anne. And now, perhaps, she had been followed on the heath. One fact was becoming crystal clear. Someone wanted to frighten or hurt her. Perhaps someone even wanted to kill Anne.

Dom was furious. Whoever was behind the "accidents" and the stalking today would pay dearly for what he or she was trying to do. Dom would see to it himself.

Tomorrow he would go to the village alone and ask a few questions. And at Waverly Hall he already had Willie, the head groom, carrying on a discreet investigation. He didn't want his grandfather alarmed. Dom still thought that Felicity was the most likely suspect. If she had followed them here, he should be able to ferret her out easily enough. Felicity was too young and too attractive to loiter in the village unremarked. However, if Felicity had followed them to Scotland, wouldn't Blake have alerted him to the fact?

Dom had a strong sense that he was missing something, some clue perhaps—which was right under his nose.

In any case, he would not share his suspicions with Anne. He did not want her frightened when she was just beginning to relax around him.

Dom shifted in the hard chair. His Scotch whiskey remained untouched. There was another reason that he was alone in the hall brooding. He was agonizingly aware of the fact that, in another five days, his idyll with Anne in Scotland would end. And they would return to Waverly Hall.

And he was still unsure of her answer.

He stood, paced closer to the dancing fire, until its heat threatened to burn him. He stared blindly, oblivious to the danger.

He had not expected this. Not any of it. Not his own passion, not hers.

And his preoccupation with his wife was, incredibly, growing with every moment that they spent together.

What was happening to him?

He had spent his entire life avoiding relationships of any serious depth. He had been determined from a very young age to be emotionally independent; to need no one but himself. Early on he had been clever enough to know that if he did not need anyone, he could not be hurt by anyone. Growing up had been painful enough.

Yet now the worst had happened.

He was dangerously close to being obsessed with Anne.

Yet Anne was there at Tavalon Castle with him for one reason only. To fulfill her part of the bargain so that, in another week's time, he would leave her and Waverly Hall.

Surely she was not going to ask him to leave when they returned to Waverly Hall.

Dom tried to assure himself that it was an unlikely possibility. She was now consumed with him sexually—and she was a very sensual woman. But Anne was strong-willed and determined. He had abandoned her for four years—when she was young and in love with him. He would be a fool to take his success for granted. Her final rejection of him was a possibility, no matter how much Dom wished that it were not.

If she asked him to leave, Dom would be unable to avoid what he had been thus far successfully avoiding his entire adult life.

Crushing heartbreak.

Anne woke up under the wide baleful stare of a full moon.

She blinked, realizing that she slept alone. The fire in the hearth had died to a few mere embers, and the room was lost in nearly total darkness. The draperies were open, and outside the night was blue-black and bright, filled with stars glittering in the light of the incandescent moon. Where was Dom?

Anne stretched, realizing that she was stark naked beneath the heavy blankets, and smiled to herself. She should be ashamed of feeling so wonderfully wicked and so gloriously satiated. But apparently there existed a hot-blooded wanton beneath her cool, ladylike exterior.

The draperies fluttered softly.

Anne caught their movement out of the corner of her eye. It startled her, but before she could relax, she became aware of someone standing behind her in the far corner of the room.

"Dom?" Anne called.

There was no answer.

And now it appeared that no one was there. But Anne sat up, clutching the covers to her neck, uneasy Perhaps she had been dreaming. But ... "Dom?" She tried again.

No one answered.

Anne's pulse was racing. She told herself that she was alone, and because she wished that Dom was present, she had imagined him to be there. She shivered, recalling Belle's fear of ghosts. And became aware of a draft of cold air teasing her bare arms.

Anne jerked and stared at the whispering drapes. The window was slightly ajar. She had thought that it had been closed when they went to bed. The nights in Scotland were so very cool.

Anne slipped from the bed, suddenly awkward with her nudity, goose bumps prickling her entire body. She found her thin wrapper and slipped it on. It hardly warded off the cold. She quickly crossed the stone floors and closed the window. Then, groping on the table beside the bed, she found a candle and lit it. She ignored the compulsion to glance into the dark corners behind her and she hurried from the room.

How quiet the castle was at night.

She wondered if Belle were right. If it were, indeed, haunted.

Anne did not believe in ghosts, but she felt a prickling of unease. She hurried toward the staircase. How nonsensical she was being. She was alone on the second floor—the servants were upstairs.

Nevertheless, she glanced quickly over her shoulder from the top step. Behind her, the hall was silent, black, shapeless.

Anne's bare feet were soundless as she rushed down the timeworn stairs. On the landing below she halted.

Dom stood staring into the fire, his profile turned toward her. He was wearing his breeches and a smoking jacket, slippers on his feet. His astounding male beauty tightened her chest and made her breathless.

But something was wrong. Anne stared at him, not venturing any closer, for his brooding demeanor was all too apparent.

He appeared unhappy. Yet how could that be? They had shared a wonderful afternoon. He had behaved like a man in love. Hadn't she pleased him? Or was he tired of her already?

Anne's heart sank like a rock.

Dom's head moved. He turned toward her. "Anne?"

She hadn't realized that he was aware of her presence. She came forward reluctantly, almost fearfully. She forced a lightness into her tone which she did not feel. "Can't you sleep?"

His somber gaze met hers. "No, I can't."

Anne's small smile faded. Something was disturbing him—but she was afraid to know what it was. "Is there anything I can do?"

His eyes remained fixed on hers. "No."

She swallowed. "Would you rather be alone, Dom?"

His gaze softened. His mouth curved very slightly. "I'll be upstairs in a few minutes."

Worried and uneasy, Anne nodded. Suddenly Dom bent and kissed her mouth gently. She smiled, relieved at receiving that small sign of affection, and turned and hurried up the stairs and back to their bedchamber.

She climbed into their bed and blew out the taper. Now it was Anne who could not sleep. She turned onto her side, cuddling her pillow, listening for Dom.

Waiting for him—yearning for him.

Anne realized the extent of her passion for him. She stiffened, clutching her pillow to her breasts. She had only spent two days with Dom, and already she was behaving—and feeling—like a lovestruck schoolgirl.

Already she was dangerously close to falling head over heels in love with him. Even more than she had as a young girl.

The last vestiges of her happiness faded. How could she not fall in love with him? He was everything a woman dreamed of one day finding: he was handsome, charming and charismatic; he was incredibly virile, powerful yet kind; and he was also titled and wealthy.

Tears filled Anne's eyes. She reminded herself that he hadn't been kind or caring when he had married her four years ago and abandoned her immediately after.

They had only spent two days together, and she wanted him desperately—at least physically. What would happen five days from now when they returned to Waverly Hall?

Anne trembled, wondering if Dom was right. Perhaps, when the week was over, she wouldn't want him to leave. Perhaps, when the week was over, even knowing better, she would not have the strength to ask him to go. Perhaps, instead, she was going to beg him to stay.

Dom entered the room, startling Anne. She gasped, sitting up, holding the covers to her neck.

"I'm sorry," he said, holding a candle whose flame was dancing wildly. "I didn't mean to frighten you."

"It's all right." Anne stared at the taper, a dread she did not yet understand creeping over her. As she stared, the candle's flame suddenly went out.

And Dom did not come to the bed to hold her as she wanted him to. Instead, he crossed the pitch-black room, his strides brisk. "Anne, why did you open the window? It's freezing in here," he said.

Anne turned around, surprised.

The window was wide open now.

Until Dom slammed it closed.

# Chapter 19

They rode into the small village of Falkirk astride the two hacks. Dom had offered to buy Anne dinner at the Red Deer Inn. Anne had agreed enthusiastically, and she had suggested they ride instead of taking the castle's ancient coach.

They walked their horses up the short cobbled length of the main street. A burly baker in a big wool coat came to stand on the stoop to watch them ride past, calling out to them in greeting. A woman walking down the street, her apron full of eggs, also halted, in order to curtsy and smile at them. "G'day, m'lord, m'lady."

"Good day," Dom returned, smiling.

Anne smiled as well. How could she not? It had happened. She was madly in love with her husband, in spite of the past, regardless of the future. In fact, days ago she had resolved not to think about anything other than the present. She would face reality only when she was forced to by their return to Waverly Hall.

For the moment, she was a woman in love—a woman beloved.

"You are a fine rider, Anne. I did not realize," Dom said.

"I love horses," Anne responded, absurdly pleased with the insignificant compliment. And his voice had the exact effect he undoubtedly intended; her blood warmed considerably.

Dom's amber gaze was unwavering. "Perhaps we have more in common than we had thought."

Anne began to blush. Yes, they most certainly did have a number of things in common, including love of horses, but more importantly was their mutual attachment to Waverly Hall—and the shocking passion they had discovered in one another's arms.

Dom slid from his mount. He looped its reins over a hitching post, and went around to Anne. His hands settled on her waist. "Whatever could you be thinking?" he murmured.

Anne's color increased, but she did not look away. She had become so very bold these past few days. "I am thinking about all that we have in common."

He grinned, his single dimple flashing. "You are a woman after my own heart, Anne," he said, pulling her off her horse. "For I am thinking about the very same thing."

In that single instant, Anne found herself in the circle of his arms. Her pulse skittered and raced. She could feel the hard length of his legs pressing through her skirts, against her thighs, as she had chosen not to wear her crinolines while in Scotland. His mouth was very close. His beautiful, dangerous mouth. Anne wanted a kiss—but they were on a public street. Then Anne told herself that no one could really see them, as they stood between their two big horses. Yes, she had become bold and shameless.

And as if reading her mind exactly, Dom's grip tightened on her arms. "Anne," he whispered, bending his head.

Anne closed her eyes and accepted his kiss, clinging to the lapels of his faded tweed jacket. It was a brief, gentle union, but Anne's body warmed from the very top of her head to the tip of her toes.

She smiled at her husband. "Our behavior is so shameful."

"No," he said, his smile easy. "I do not abide by the current morality, that one must make love fully clothed with one's eyes closed. And had you an inclination to propriety, I would have done my best to break you of it."

And he would have succeeded, Anne thought. "Well, you must admit, then, that our behavior is scandalous."

"I do not care, and no one is watching us, anyway," Dom smiled.

Anne was about to agree when her own smile faded. She recalled the open window of two nights before. Either Tavalon Castle was haunted, as Belle had suggested, or someone had been inside her bedchamber while she was downstairs with Dom—and perhaps even before, while she slept. Either possibility was outrageous, absurd. And very frightening.

"Anne?" Dom prodded.

"I was thinking about the window in our bedchamber being open the other night," she confessed.

He reached out and smoothed his hand over the top of her head. She wore a coronet of braids today. "I thought we went over that. You were dreaming about shutting the window, Anne, that is the only explanation." He smiled at her. "No one could get inside Tavalon Castle after dark, unless you wish to make a case for ghosts."

Anne nodded, uneasily. Perhaps it *had* been a ghost. But she was not reassured.

They dined on roasted venison and baked salmon fillet. Accompanying the main course was spinach gratinée, yams roasted in honey and butter, and a delicate salad of mixed greens with a delicious dressing Anne could not decipher. She sipped sherry, Dom drank half a bottle of red wine. They both declined dessert.

Dom leaned back in his chair. His eyes were warm, golden, lingering upon her—as they had all that day.

Anne had never felt so connected to another human being as she did then. Loving someone—and being loved back—was a wondrous thing.

Anne dreaded returning to Waverly Hall.

He leaned forward. "Anne, we go home in two days."

So he was thinking about it, too. Anne tensed. "Yes."

His smile was gone. He reached for her hands, enfolded them. "It has been a very fine week."

Anne did not want to continue this conversation. She did not want to broach the future. Not yet. They had two days left. "Yes, it has been a lovely week," she said unsteadily, averting her gaze.

He was silent.

Anne dared to look up. Dom had removed his hands from hers, and now he was studying them. As if he were dismayed, even hurt, by her and what she had promised to do.

Anne suddenly hated Waverly Hall. She hated the past. She did not want to be reminded of it. She wanted her life—all of it—to be the present as they were living it now. She did not want to go home and become sensible, strong-willed Anne, a woman capable of sending Dom St. Georges away. She wanted to the newly discovered Anne. Fiery and passionate, feminine and loving.

Oh, God.

Dom's gaze lifted. "Anne, we have to talk about it."

Desperation flooded Anne. "All right."

He hesitated. "What are you going to do?"

His golden gaze was steady, unwavering. Anne thought about how he had held her that morning after making love to her. Anne thought about the way he looked at her these days, with warmth in his eyes. Warmth, and perhaps real affection, perhaps even love.

Her pulse sped dangerously. Surely she could not send

him away? Not when she loved him so very much—not when they were on the brink of something wonderful and exciting? Not when a real future beckoned them?

"Anne?" Dom said very seriously.

But four years was a very long time. Anne blinked at him to clear the moisture from her eyes. "If I had any sense, I would send you away."

"But?"

She trembled. "I don't want to send you away, Dom. Not now, not ever."

Triumph lit his eyes, his face. He reached across the table and gripped her hand, clearly exultant. "Anne."

She shook her head, feeling faint from the anxiety of making such a monumental decision. "Dom, stop. I cannot decide now. I am only telling you how I feel."

He stared. The fierce light faded from his eyes. "I see."

His disappointment was all too apparent. Now Anne reached for his hand and clung to it tightly. It was on the tip of her tongue to blurt out her love to him. But the caution born of four years' waiting made her hesitate, as did the fact that he had never spoken of love to her, either.

He smiled, shrugged. "I guess I'm just going to have to try a little bit harder to persuade you to let bygones be bygones," he said lightly.

Anne relaxed. "There is nothing in the rules which says you cannot," she smiled. And she stroked his hand lightly with her fingertips. Wanting him to know how she felt, even if she could not tell him with words.

"Then let's go home," he said, signaling the inn's proprietor. But the afternoon was not the same.

The future was catching up with them and they both knew it.

The Waverly coach had picked them up in Dulton at the train depot an hour ago. Pulled by six glorious matched blacks, they were traveling alongside the weathered brick wall which formed the boundary of the immediate estate. Waverly Hall was growing more visible now, a large, brick Georgian home with massive white pillars and numerous outbuildings. In the past, Anne had always been warmed by the sight of the magnificent house. Not this time.

She looked at the outlines of the place dispassionately. Since she had awoken that morning everything seemed duller, colorless. She was remembering, far too vividly, the morning after her wedding as she watched Dom leaving at sunrise. Never had she been so crushed. The pain had been physical.

The new Anne, the woman who had been so thoroughly loved this last week, trusted him completely. But the other Anne had returned with a vengeance, the Anne who had seen four winters pass without a husband, and she was frightened and wary and filled with doubt.

How could she do it? When she loved him so?

But how could she not? When a part of her refused to trust him?

She glanced at him. Since they had awoken on the train, he had behaved like a distant stranger. Formally, civilly, but with no warmth at all. Now his jaw was tight, flexed. He had not shaved that morning, and the shadow of his beard darkened his tense jaw. He sat carefully on his side of the velvet-backed seat, so that his legs did not even brush her skirts. He had not touched her since he had made love to her last night somewhere in the north of England as the train sped through the moors beneath a cloudy, night-darkened sky.

Anne was finding it hard to breathe. She fought for calm. She fought not to cry. She thought about the week she had just spent with Dom. He had to love her—as much as she loved him.

If only he would hold her now, and tell her just how much he loved her.

But once, four years ago, she had thought he loved her, too. And he hadn't loved her at all. In spite of his passionate lovemaking in the garden on the eve of his wedding to Felicity. In spite of his marrying her two weeks later.

"Anne," Dom whispered.

Anne jerked. Their gazes collided, Dom's suddenly stark. "Come here," he whispered.

Anne did not hesitate. As he reached for her, she flung herself against his chest.

But it was not an embrace which he wanted—or which she wanted, either. His hands were hard and hurtful, moving down her spine, crushing her against him.

Anne's fingertips dug into his neck. Their mouths fused. Dom's body drove Anne down, onto her back. His muscular thighs wedged hers apart.

She accepted his tongue, his teeth, whatever he wished to give her. His mouth moved to her neck. Anne arched backward, gasping, as he pushed her high collar down and kissed her throat. His hands molded her breasts beneath her jacket and dress. His mouth followed his hands.

And as he kissed her through her clothing, he was groping beneath her skirts. His palm brushed the open crotch of her drawers. Anne cried out when his finger slipped deep inside of her.

And then she was helping him move the masses of fabric away, panting, lifting her hips so he could untie her crinolines. He practically ripped the flexible cage from her.

Anne gripped Dom's shoulders, her skirts and petticoat bunched around her waist, unaware that she was crying. Dom tore open his breeches and thrust deep inside of her. Her tears wet his cheeks.

They bucked wildly together on the velvet seat. Anne cried harder, realizing that her emotions were so frazzled now she would never find the ecstasy she wished to escape to. Suddenly Dom froze over her, his arms around her, holding her tightly, his weight crushing her into the seat. "Anne?"

If she spoke, he would know that she was crying, so she buried her face in the nook made by his shoulder and neck.

"Don't cry," he said harshly. "Please don't cry."

Anne wept.

The coach bounced heavily over a deep rut, dislodging their bodies. It did not matter. Dom was no longer aroused. But Anne did not want to move. Keeping her eyes tightly closed, she gripped Dom even harder. His embrace also tightened. She felt his mouth on her cheek. She could taste the saltiness of her own tears on the corners of her mouth.

"Don't cry," Dom said again, anguished. He lifted his face so they could stare into one another's eyes. Then he bent and kissed the tears on her cheeks.

Oh, God! Anne had never loved him more. And she held him tightly, desperately. Loving him with every fiber of her being. Loving him so much that it was painful. Even if he did not love her the same way.

She would take a chance.

She would trust him now.

She would not ask him to leave.


They did not arrive at Waverly Hall immediately. Wisely, Dom ordered the driver to stop before they reached the house, and helped Anne don her crinolines and adjust her clothes and hair. He was grim. Anne wanted to tell him what she had decided, but he forestalled her. "We will speak at the house." He avoided her eyes now.

"Dom," she tried again

But he refused to look at her, ordering the coach forward.

Anne settled back on the seat. He was right. This kind of discussion should wait. Things of such import should not be rushed.

The coach came to a halt on the circular drive in front of the house. Two liveried footmen helped Anne alight. Dom followed her. Bennet stood on the porch, as impassive as ever, but Anne knew him well and could tell that he was pleased that they were home. Before Anne could smile at the butler, Dom slipped his arm proprietarily around her waist, and guided her forward. Anne was so thrilled by his surprising and public show of affection that she was at a loss for words. But still, he refused to make eye contact with her.

"My lord, my lady," Bennet bowed.

"Good day, Bennet," Dom said. "Is my grandfather still in residence?"

"No, my lord, he left shortly after you and the marchioness departed for Scotland."

"Did Belle and Verig arrive?" Dom asked. They had been sent ahead a day earlier.

"Yes, sir. The master suite is ready. Hot baths have been drawn."

"Very good." Dom glanced at Anne, then turned to Bennet. "Per my instructions, have my wife's belongings been removed to the master suite?"

"Yes, my lord."

Anne managed not to gasp. Bennet was stepping aside so they could pass. This time he was unsuccessful at hiding a happy smile.

Anne stared at Dom, who pretended not to notice. Apparently he had not waited to see what she would do upon their return to the Hall. Quite clearly, he had issued orders from Tavalon Castle, taking charge of the matter himself. She should be offended; she was absurdly thrilled. It struck her then that had she asked him to leave, he might have ignored her and his part of the bargain. "Dom," she began, but not in protest.

His gaze was as hard and bright as diamonds. "We have much to discuss. Why don't we do so over tea in the library, after you have had a chance to bathe and rest?"

Anne nodded. His formality did not disturb her. He still did not know that he had won—yet his victory was ultimately hers. "Four o'clock?"

"Fine," he said. Then his eyes darkened, and suddenly he kissed her on the mouth, in front of the coachman, the two footmen, Bennet, and anyone else who might be there to see.

Anne went directly to the master suite. In the large, marble-floored bathing chamber, a hot bath in a porcelain tub awaited her. Refreshments had been placed on a small table set for two in the suite's drawing room. Belle moved about an adjoining chamber, one traditionally used exclusively by the marchioness, unpacking Anne's belongings. Anne felt like skipping about the lavishly appointed suite like a small, ecstatic child. Now that she had made her decision she felt incredibly free, light and weightless. It was as if a great burden had been magically lifted from her shoulders. And as Anne glanced out of the triple-sized windows at the rolling lawns and the lush parkland, suddenly it was so good to be home.

Someone knocked on the two heavy mahogany doors. When no one appeared to answer, Anne crossed the room and opened the doors herself. She was surprised to find the head groom standing there. Her gaze widened. "Willie, come in. Do you wish to speak with the marquis?"

Willie came in somewhat reluctantly, holding his cap

in his hands, twisting it nervously. "No, my lady. I wish to speak to you but a moment if I may."

Anne was perplexed. "Of course." Her smile was gracious.

Willie glanced around, but not at the opulent surroundings. Belle was visible in the other room. "Might we speak privately?" Willie asked anxiously.

Now Anne was very curious, and she nodded, closing the door to the adjoining chamber. "Is something wrong, Willie? And how can I help?"

He wet his lips. "Yes, ma'am. Something is wrong— very wrong."

When he did not continue, Anne smiled at him gently, unperturbed by his ominous tone. "You need not be afraid to speak openly to me."

"But I am afraid," Willie cried. "Lady Anne, since you have been gone, I have been so worried, I swear I have not had a single night of rest! But I promised the marquis not to say a word to you. Yet I do not think that is right. I think that I must tell you the truth."

Anne did not understand. Whatever could Willie be talking about? Her intuition was warning her that this would not be pleasant. And her loyalty to Dom remained strong; but it warred with her sudden need to know what Willie wanted to tell her. "Willie, you should not disobey the marquis. I am sure that he had his reasons for asking you to keep certain matters confidential." But she was more disturbed now than before.

He stared at her beseechingly. "But you are my mistress—and I am afraid for you."

"I do not understand," Anne said slowly.

Willie looked as if he wanted to cry. "It wasn't an accident, Lady Anne," he said in a rush. "Blaze's running away with you wasn't any accident!"

Anne blinked. "What are you saying?" How uneasy she had become. Scattered images flitted through her mind—two overturned candles, a charred rose, Blaze's hoof coming down toward her just before it grazed her rib, the broken stirrup leather, the open window. "Willie?"

"Someone poisoned Blaze with morrow root, my lady. It makes horses go wild. It made Blaze go wild."

Anne found it strangely difficult to comprehend Willie's words. She felt frozen inside of her mind. But she knew a little about morrow root, enough to know that it could have caused Blaze to become uncontrollable— to run away with her. "This is impossible," she said hoarsely.

"No! The marquis knows. But you musn't tell him that I told you!"

Anne sat down abruptly on a chair. "Dom knows?"

"He found the spot where Blaze was injected on his neck. I saw it, too. And later, after the two of you left, I found the syringe in a pile of garbage behind the kitchens where the servants eat."

It was beginning to dawn on her. Someone had injected Blaze with poison. "But why?" Anne whispered. "Why?" Yet even as she asked the question, she knew.

"Someone wanted to hurt you, my lady," Willie cried. "Perhaps even kill you!"

Anne was reaching the same conclusion and she stared at Willie in horror.

Anne was pacing. Someone wanted to frighten her. Or do far, far more. Did someone actually want to hurt her? Had the fire in her bedroom been an accident—or a deliberate act of arson?

Blaze had been injected with a deadly substance. That was hardly a prank. She could have been killed. Anne thought again about the broken leather stirrup which someone had placed in her trunk. Oh, God.

Someone had access to her horse—and to her private belongings.

Had someone gone into her bedroom while she slept

and set the fire? Clearly, someone *had* gone into her bedroom in order to leave a charred rose afterward!

Anne sank into a chair, a mass of quivering nerves, sick and frightened. Now she thought about the feeling of being watched that night in the castle. Had someone been lurking in her bedchamber while she slept? Given the fact that someone had stolen into her bedroom at Waverly Hall to leave a charred rose there—and perhaps even start a fire—it was very possible. She found it difficult to breathe.

What was happening?

Why was it happening?

And someone had been watching her the day she had been riding alone on the heath—Anne was certain of it.

Perhaps it was all coincidence.

But Anne did not believe that. Something *was* happening. Someone was out there, trying to frighten her, perhaps even trying to hurt her. But surely no one was trying to kill her, as Willie had suggested. That was absurd!

She had no enemies. Or did she?

Felicity hated her for stealing Dom away from her four years ago. She had not even tried to hide her hostility. And Felicity knew horses. Felicity had threatened revenge.

Oh, God. Had Felicity tried to hurt her? Could Felicity have followed Dom and Anne to Scotland?

It was ridiculous.

Or was it?

Anne was breathing harshly. She was alone in the suite. Willie had left after Anne had promised not to tell Dom that he had revealed the truth behind her riding accident to her, and she had ordered Belle out, too. But suddenly she did not want to be alone. Suddenly she wanted Dom. She would confide in him. He would protect her—and solve this mystery.

Anne heard a knock on her door. She rushed to open

it, expecting Dom, already flooded with relief. She swung the heavy doors open, and her face fell.

Clarisse stood there in her black bombazine dress, two Persian cats at her feet. Her gaze widened when she glimpsed Anne. "Are you all right? My, Anne, you are as white as a sheet."

Anne backed up, into her room. It immediately occurred to her that Clarisse was not very fond of her either, and she was an excellent horsewoman—but now Anne knew her panic was running away with her, because Clarisse was not a sick, malicious person, and she could not have followed her and Dom to Scotland, that was preposterous. As preposterous as the idea that Felicity had followed them to Scotland.

*How clever you are, Anne. . . . The truth is that you are a ruthless American title hunter.*

Anne licked her lips. She would ask Bennet if Clarisse had been at the Hall these past ten days. "You wish to speak with me?"

"Yes, I do." Clarisse moved into the room. "I am very disturbed, Anne."

Anne could hardly focus on what Clarisse was saying. She had to fight for even a shred of composure. She needed Dom.

"I have learned something utterly terrible while you and Dom were gone." Clarisse stared at Anne. "It is unconscionable, and as much as I love my son, I feel morally obligated to tell you the truth."

Anne began to tense. She did not need to hear anything disturbing about Dom now. "Clarisse, I am really very tired from the journey home. Could we not speak later? After supper, perhaps?"

"No, Anne, we must speak now. You must know, as you are the very crux of the matter."

Anne stiffened. "I do not understand."

"It is very simple. Rutherford devised absurd terms to the trust giving you control of Waverly Hall.

Amongst the many stipulations, there is one way in which the trust can be broken, the rights to Waverly Hall reverting to Dom."

Anne did not like this.

"He didn't tell you, did he? About the terms of the trust? About what he must do in order to regain his birthright?"

Anne began to feel very sick. She warned herself now that whatever it was Clarisse was about to say, it would hurt her terribly. But the warning did no good. "What does he have to do to regain the Hall?"

Clarisse smiled. "All he has to do is get you pregnant, Anne." Her brows raised. "Which I imagine he has already done."

# Chapter 20

*Rutherford House*

$\mathscr{A}$nne arrived at the Duke's townhouse a few hours later.

She had fled Waverly Hall immediately, without any belongings, dragging Belle out the front door and to a carriage she had hastily summoned. She hadn't quite puzzled through everything yet, but two things were quite clear: Anne was a woman seduced and grievously betrayed, and she was a woman in danger. Her instinct was to run and she heeded it without question.

Miraculously, she did not encounter Dom until after she was in the Waverly carriage, the doors locked, the vehicle speeding away from the house.

She heard him shouting.

Anne turned stiffly and stared out of the window. Their gazes met. Dom had been running after her, and now he halted, scattering the small stones of the drive. "Anne!"

Anne's heart felt like it was bleeding profusely, but her body—and her mind—felt heavy and lifeless, like lead. She stared back at him, saying nothing. At that moment, there was nothing she could possibly say.

He had broken her heart twice. After that first time,

she had never dreamed he could hurt her as badly again. But she had been wrong.

"Anne!" Dom cried, his eyes wide and shocked.

But her carriage did not stop, and it left him standing in the dust.

Anne had had six hours during the journey to London in which to regain her composure, but she had not recovered. It no longer seemed consequential to her that someone wished to hurt her, perhaps even kill her. She was physically safe now, anyway, the would-be attacker far away in the country. What mattered was that Dom had betrayed her again.

The man she had loved since she was a young girl— the man she had never stopped loving, if she dared be honest with herself—had treacherously and ruthlessly feigned affection and passion for her which he did not feel, solely to regain his birthright.

And what about the duke? Anne had thought him to be her friend. His role in this farce was despicable.

Now Anne waited for the footmen to open the doors and allow her and Belle to descend to the pavement. She was trembling. While she intended to take up residence in a hotel—what other choice did she have?— first she had a few choice words to deliver to the duke.

Rutherford House was a palace. The St. Georges mansion, located on Belgrave Square, sprawled across an entire block and was four stories high if one included the attics. Built of pale beige stone in Elizabethan times by Robert Smythson, it was an architectural rarity because it had never been added onto since then. A huge central dome dominated the imposing structure, rising another fifty feet into the sky, and was flanked by two smaller domes on the house's either side.

"My lady, please, won't you tell me what has happened?" Belle asked, tears streaking her cheeks.

Anne turned. The anguish threatened to rip her apart.

It was very difficult to speak. "I cannot talk about it," she choked.

Belle wept into her hands.

"Madam Marchioness."

Anne could not smile—she doubted that she would ever smile again—but she nodded for the footman to open the door. The two footmen helped Anne and her abigail from the Waverly carriage and escorted her up the imposing stone stairs—which boasted seventy-three steps—to the mansion's black, oversized front doors. The gold Rutherford crest was emblazoned on each one, as large as Anne herself. Two liveried footmen pretended she did not exist, standing on either side of the closed doors, staring vacantly straight ahead. Rutherford's butler appeared instantly.

"My lady," he bowed. He stood aside so Anne could step into the foyer, which boasted white marble floors streaked with veins of real gold, white-and-gold walls, and a gilded, domed ceiling numerous stories above her head. "His Grace is out presently. Might I bring you refreshments in the drawing room?"

Anne forced herself to respond without bursting into tears. "Caldwell, I will wait."

He did not blink. "Of course, my lady."

"Ready a room for Her Ladyship," Belle ordered. "Madam is not well. I think she must lie down."

Caldwell was instantly concerned. "Shall I send for the physician?"

"Yes," Belle cried, wringing her hands.

"No," Anne said sharply, her tone husky. "No. I cannot . . . I am not staying here."

"My lady," Belle protested, "where will we go?"

Anne could not answer. She had fled in such haste that she had not taken her pin money, but she thought that a personal IOU would suffice in order to gain a suite of rooms. But Anne was not familiar with London—she did not even know of a hotel for her to go to. She gulped air. "C-Caldwell, do you know of a hotel appropriate for myself and Belle?"

Caldwell lost his impassivity. "I beg your pardon?"

"A hotel," Anne managed.

He recovered. "The Cavendish Hotel is quite elegant, or so I am told."

Anne nodded, turning away, blinking furiously. Tears would do her no good now. She followed the butler into a salon, oblivious to her lavish, gilded furnishings. Anne walked to the window and stared out of it. But she saw nothing.

Caldwell brought in a cart containing tea and cakes. Anne did not move. She ignored Belle's attempts to get her to sit down or go upstairs and rest. And finally she was rewarded with the sight of the Rutherford coach. Pulled by six white horses, the gilded white lacquer coach glided to a stop on the street below, and the duke of Rutherford alighted.

Anne was facing the door when the duke entered the drawing room, his expression concerned, his eyes riveting upon her. "Anne? What is wrong? Caldwell says you are ill."

Anne stared. A fresh onslaught of pain prevented her from speaking.

"Anne?"

"I thought you were my friend," she finally said. Her tone was hoarse.

"I am your friend. I love you as if you were my own daughter."

"Don't!"

He stared. "Dear God, Anne, what is wrong? What has happened?" But Rutherford did not cross the room and approach her.

Anne did not move, either. But tears spilled down her cheeks.

"Anne, what is it? Where is Dom?"

Anne cried out, fists clenched, and she began to weep

uncontrollably. Rutherford moved. He strode to her and took her in his arms, cradling her. Anne sobbed and sobbed . . . until she felt the first budding of anger.

"Damn Dom," she gasped, and she struck the duke with both fists on his chest.

His eyes widened.

"Damn Dom!" She shouted, loudly now, and she lashed out again and again.

Rutherford caught her wrists. "What has happened?" he demanded.

But Anne was enraged. She stared at him—but saw Dom, who had loved her, teased her, charmed her, so damn thoroughly—all in order to regain Waverly Hall. And then her vision cleared and she saw the duke— who had devised the absurd trust to begin with.

"You!" She shouted. "You are as much to blame as he is!"

Rutherford released her warily. "What have you learned?"

Anne brushed her hand across her eyes. She was panting, fists clenched. "I learned all about the trust."

"I see."

"I will never forgive you—and I will never forgive *him.*"

They stared at one another.

"I did it for you, Anne—just as I did it for him."

"No." Anne's laughter was bitter. "You did it for the dukedom. You did it for yourself. You did it because you want to know, before you die, that Dom has an heir. Damn you!"

The duke stiffened. "I do love you, Anne. Just as I love Dom. I want the two of you to be happy together."

"Happy? Dom and me?" Anne laughed hysterically. "That is impossible—especially now!" She faced him. "You do not even know the meaning of the word love."

Pain appeared in the duke's eyes. "How wrong you are."

Anne hesitated. "If you loved me, you would not have used me—and if you loved Dom ..." She broke off.

"I do love Dom, and I want to see him happily married with little children running at his feet. Legitimate children. Your children. And I love you Anne. You are ... Sarah's niece. I have always loved you."

An image flashed through Anne's mind, of one crisp autumn day a few months after she had first arrived at Hunting Way. She was eleven years old and so terribly lonely, and still overcome with everything that had happened. Now Anne remembered the tall, aristocratic man who had called on her that very day, asking her if he could do anything for her, his eyes kind and concerned.

The duke was speaking. "I also believe that Dom loves you."

Anne flung off her momentary confusion. "He loves something, and I believe it's Waverly Hall."

"You are not being fair, Anne."

"Stop!" Anne held up her hands. "Don't you dare continue! You are the one who is unfair!"

"I do not agree." Rutherford was firm. "Anne, you are very upset, which is understandable. But in time you will calm down. Surely by then you will begin to see that what I have done is not so terrible. I am within my rights to want a grandson. Furthermore, I don't think Dom's interest in you has anything to do with Waverly Hall. Did not the two of you enjoy yourselves in Scotland? Did you not achieve a reconciliation there? Surely you both learned how well suited you are to one another?"

Tears abruptly filled her eyes again, but Anne also shook with rage. "Yes, we did. Perhaps I am even increasing. There. Are you happy? Now Dom will have an heir, the dukedom is secured, and he can also have

Waverly Hall back—because I don't want it!'' She turned away.

"Anne, you are a sensible woman, and you love Dom. I think you will come to the correct conclusion in time. In the meanwhile, use this house as you would your own."

"I am not staying here."

The duke started. "What can you possibly be thinking of, Anne?"

She tensed her shoulders. "I am going to the Cavendish Hotel."

The duke's eyes widened. "I will not allow it."

Anne's head shot up.

"Anne—I know you are a generous person. I know you do not seek vengeance. But if you stay at a hotel, you will air all of our problems—and it will be quite the scandal."

Anne inhaled. He was right. Anne had not been thinking clearly. Other options filtered through her mind. She could not return to Waverly Hall—it was a matter of principle. She would not go to one of Dom's other estates. She knew Edna would never allow her to return to Hunting Way, and Matthew Fairhaven possessed Waverly House in London. She had no choice.

"Very well."

Rutherford sighed, as if relieved. "I would like to talk to you again later today. After you have had some time to adjust to what you have learned."

"There is nothing to talk about."

The duke's face fell. "Anne—I do love you— dearly."

Anne refused to answer. She hugged herself, swept up in another wave of painful emotion. When he had left, she sat down. Her knees were shaking.

It was only when she turned, thinking herself alone, that she saw Belle, standing in the far corner of the room.

"Oh, my lady," Belle whispered.

"I will be fine," Anne lied.

Belle rushed to her and did the unthinkable—embracing her. Anne hugged her back. "Thank you, Belle," she whispered shakily.

"What can I do to help you, my lady?"

"I don't know. I must think." Then she spoke, almost to herself. "I need my own solicitor. I refuse to be the beneficiary of this trust any longer. I do not want the Hall." She grimaced. "I can never return there."

"Oh, Lady Anne," Belle cried, "everyone loves you so, if you don't mind my being bold, and you love that house and all the staff!"

Anne's heart clenched. "It doesn't matter. Waverly Hall belongs to Dom, and even if there is no legal way to return it to him, he will control it by my default."

"What are you going to do?" Belle asked fearfully.

"I shall find a flat here in London. My marriage is over, of course."

Belle's eyes widened. "Surely you are not thinking of . . . divorce?"

"I would never destroy the family with a divorce. Besides"—her eyes grew moist—"what if I am with child? It is certainly a possibility."

Anne touched her flat, hard belly. If she were pregnant, she would be happy, because she had always wanted children. If not, she would survive being both childless and alone. For she and Dom would live apart, leading completely separate lives, Anne was resolved. Dom was never going to touch her again.

Anne brushed at her eyes. Impossibly, she still loved Dom—a ruthless, cold-hearted stranger.

"My lady, what can I do?" Belle whispered brokenly.

Anne inhaled. She had to deal with the probability that a person was seeking to harm her, too. "Belle, do you remember my riding accident—and the broken stir-rup we found in my trunk afterward?''

Belle nodded.

''It was not an accident, Belle. Someone was trying to frighten me or harm me,'' Anne said. And she proceeded to tell Belle everything.

Belle's lower lip began to tremble. ''What are you going to do? You must go to your husband, my lady, you must! No matter what he has done!''

''No. Never.'' Anne stood, holding the back of the chair firmly. ''Go back to the Hall. I will send two notes with you. One is for Willie. I must find out who was at the stables that morning.''

Belle nodded. ''And the other note?''

''The other note is for Patrick.'' Anne was fully aware of Belle's disapproval. ''He is my friend,'' Anne said. ''I need him now,'' she said simply.

''It's not right,'' Belle muttered. ''You should go to His Lordship.''

''Belle!'' Anne whirled. ''Don't you dare breathe a word of any of this to Dom. Do you hear me?''

Belle stared, pale and mute but not quite defiant.

''I will dismiss you,'' Anne said fiercely, almost meaning it. ''Don't you understand? He betrayed me.''

''Where did she go?''

''I don't know, my lord. Her Ladyship did not say,'' Bennet replied.

Dom was pacing the library, his expression grim. He could not get Anne's frozen white image out of his mind. Hadn't she heard him calling her? Why hadn't she stopped? And where the hell had she gone?

''This doesn't make sense,'' he finally said, raking a hand through his hair. ''She left at noon, and, dammit, it's almost midnight.'' It was as if she weren't coming back.

Dom was sick. But surely she hadn't left him. If

Anne wanted to end their alliance, she would have referred to their ugly pact—and asked him to leave.

"My lord, I am sure that Her Ladyship had an overnight visit planned, but forgot to mention it to you," Bennet said, but his face was set in lines of worry, too. Clearly he did not believe his own words.

"Anne is too efficient to forget to tell you or me or someone that she is going somewhere." Dom said harshly. "I don't like this, not one bit."

He paced. His fists clenched. "Dammit, Bennet—she isn't coming back."

Bennet met his gaze. Dom was so devastated by the thought of Anne's leaving him, that he looked away, his breathing shallow.

"My lord, sir," Bennet said.

Dom looked up, having recomposed his features. "Yes? Speak whatever is on your mind."

"Lady Anne is in love with you. She has been in love with you since she was a child and she first arrived at Hunting Way. She will return. She had to have had an engagement which she forgot to mention. I am sure of it."

Dom forced a smile. "Thank you, Bennet."

"Are you reassured?"

"Yes," Dom lied.

"Do you wish to take a late supper?"

"No. You may retire, Bennet, and tell Verig he may do the same."

"Good night, sir," Bennet said.

When he was gone, Dom sank in a chair. Something was terribly wrong.

A few moments later Bennet reappeared. Dom was startled. Then he saw the sealed envelope with the ducal crest in his butler's hand. Dom leapt to his feet.

"His Grace sent a messenger," Bennet began.

Dom did not wait for him to finish. He seized the envelope, tearing it open.

*Dom,*

> *Your wife is in residence at Rutherford House.*
> *Prepare yourself. She has learned all about the*
> *trust. I suggest you wait a day or two before*
> *arriving here to take her home.*

*Your Grandfather, Etc.*

Dom stared at the page he held in his hand until the letters blurred. A moment later he crumpled the note in his hand and turned and threw it with a violent motion into the fire in the hearth.

He should have known that this would happen. He should have confessed all while he had the chance.

"My lord," Bennet said, eyes wide, "is aught amiss with Her Ladyship?"

"No. Anne has misunderstood a certain matter, and is sulking in town," Dom growled. "Good night, Bennet."

He stared at the fire, fists clenched, his back to the room. When Bennet left, discreetly closing the door, Dom made a choked, furious sound. He swung around, but there was nothing to hit except the wall, and he did not feel like breaking his hand.

Even though a broken hand was the least that he deserved.

Anne hadn't misunderstood anything. She had learned the ugly, rotten truth.

Somehow she had learned about the trust and now she thought that he had seduced her in order to regain Waverly Hall. Even if he denied it, she would not believe him.

Nor could he blame her. How did someone inspire trust after four years?

Dom cursed, and this time, he did hit the wall with his fist.

Dom cantered the black hunter across the soggy meadow through a light morning mist. Effortlessly he guided his mount over a series of stone walls in a smooth ballet of motion. He was trying not to think about Anne, and what the future boded for them.

Dom leaned over his mount's neck, urging him into a gallop. They flew across the meadow, alongside a meandering dirt road. Dom had always loved speed. He let the horse have his head. Perhaps he could outrun his thoughts of Anne.

He was quite certain that he was not going to be able to let her go, and he was certain that she hated him now and wished to be free of him. He was also ill, imagining how she must be suffering.

"Dom! Wait!"

Dom cursed inwardly and slowed his mount, trying to hide his rising annoyance. Felicity called out again.

Dom turned the hunter about reluctantly. His eyes narrowed. On the road which ran parallel to the pasture, he could make out the small gig approaching. Felicity lashed her horse, whipping the reins, until she drew abreast of him. Then she pulled up abruptly. "Dom!" She waved a gloved hand vigorously, signaling him to come over.

Dom trotted his black gelding over to her. He made no effort to dismount, but settled deeper in the saddle. "Good morning, Felicity." His regard was probing. Felicity did not look like a woman capable of committing arson, administering poison, and hating Anne enough to want to hurt her badly or even kill her.

But no one had as much cause.

"Good morning," she gushed, her blue eyes warm, glowing. "I have been looking for you."

"Really?" He couldn't keep the faint hint of mockery out of his voice.

She ignored it. "Yes. I heard Anne has left Waverly Hall."

His jaw tightened. "That's correct."

She smiled. "Dom, you should be pleased. You never wanted her to begin with. Now you are free to do as you wish."

Dom stared. "Felicity, I thought I made myself clear the last time we spoke privately."

Her gaze widened with feigned innocence. "I cannot remember what we spoke about, Dom—other than the fact that you promised me a tour of your stable." She licked the curve of her lips—deliberately.

Dom thought of all the women he had taken to his bed over the past ten years, and the ways in which he had taken them, his body tensing with sudden, surprising revulsion. Felicity revolted him, too.

Felicity grinned slyly. "Do you have the time, now?"

"No, I do not," he said, far more crossly than was polite.

Her face fell. "But you promised."

"Isn't Blake still about? I imagine he will be glad to show you all that you wish to see."

Felicity stared. For a moment she did not speak. "Blake is a boor."

Dom smiled. "I have heard a rumor that he has escorted you everywhere this past week while Anne and I were in Scotland."

She flushed. "He escorted me nowhere. He has been *following* me everywhere!"

Dom had to laugh.

"It's hardly funny," Felicity said, "to be pursued by someone you are not interested in."

"*I* am in complete agreement," Dom said pointedly.

"Dom," Felicity began plaintively.

"No. Do not say anything that will embarrass you—or me."

Tears filled her eyes.

"Anne is my wife, and I intend to treat her with the respect she is due."

Felicity flushed.

"Now that we have reached that understanding, let us start a new topic." Dom leaned forward casually, one elbow on his thigh, his reins loose. But his gaze was piercing. "Someone is trying to hurt my wife. And I think, Felicity, that it is you."

Dom frowned, staring through the window of his bedroom at the mist-shrouded hills outside. He had never chased a woman in his life. But he was miserable. He wanted Anne. And not just in his bed. Now was not the time for pride, and he certainly owed her an explanation. But would it get him anywhere? He seriously doubted it.

However, he had to try.

Dom turned at the sound of a knock upon his door. His valet was packing his clothes into a trunk, and he answered it himself. "Come in, Mother." He forced a smile he did not feel.

Verig promptly disappeared and Clarisse entered the room. She stared at the open trunk half-full of clothing. "You are leaving?"

"Yes."

Clarisse met Dom's gaze. "Where are you going, Dom? To town?"

He nodded.

"You're going after Anne?"

Dom's stare hardened. "That's right."

"But she doesn't want you."

Dom flinched. "Yes. But what she wants is irrelevant, isn't it? She is my wife. What I want is at issue."

Clarisse's mouth trembled. She was pale. "And you want her?" There was the faintest note of incredulity in her tone.

"Yes," Dom said. "I do."

"She isn't good enough for you," Clarisse cried.

"I think I shall be the judge of that," Dom said stiffly. "And I believe that the opposite case is true— that I am not good enough for her."

"She has bewitched you, again!"

"That is enough, Mother," Dom said.

Clarisse walked away from Dom abruptly. She sat down on a red velvet chair and scooped up one of her cats, which had followed her into the room.

Dom stared at her. He could not help thinking about Philip's diary now, which he had done his best to forget about. He had enough problems; he did not need this one. Yet now that he had returned to Waverly Hall, he did not feel that he could avoid reality any longer. His temples throbbed. "Mother, there is something that I must speak with you about."

Clarisse met his gaze and quickly looked away.

"This is a very delicate, even awkward subject," Dom began. "My father . . ."

Clarisse did not respond.

Finally Dom said, "He hated me. He hated you. In fact, he hated this entire family."

"Yes."

"Why?"

Clarisse tried to smile and failed. "Haven't you guessed?"

"Yes, I have."

Clarisse hugged her cat harder. It meowed in protest. "Burn it, Dominick. It's all the ramblings of a weak, angry man."

"Mother." Dom paused. He wanted to ask, *Am I really his son?*

But Clarisse was standing, her mouth trembling, ready to burst into tears. Dom tamped the question down. It did not matter. It would never matter. He would burn the diary, immediately, and the world would never suspect that such a question had even existed.

Clarisse still stared at him, wide-eyed and frightened.

Dom knew he had to do it—in order to protect her. Abruptly he walked to the table beside his bed, opening a drawer and withdrawing the diary. A moment later he tossed it into the hearth. Flames licked the red leather binding immediately.

Clarisse watched as the pages caught fire, the diary—his one legacy—blackening, shriveling, disappearing.

When it was beyond recovery, Dom turned, relieved—and ill. He would never know the truth, but that was for the best.

"Thank you, Dominick," Clarisse whispered gratefully.

Dom forced a smile.

Dom was almost ready to leave for town. Soon it would be dusk, but he would travel at night. Impatience now ruled him, and he was eager to explain to Anne. If all went well, if he could overcome his pride and his hurt, in a few hours he might even be reconciled with Anne.

Outside, Dom crossed the graveled drive, leaving the house and the waiting carriage behind. The stables were dimly lit. Dom traversed a corridor, striding past a row of dozing horses. At the end of the hall was a set of stairs. He hurried up and knocked on the door atop the landing.

Willie opened it immediately. "My lord," he said, somewhat suprised.

"May I come in? This will only take a moment."

Willie had grown nervous. He backed up, admitting Dom. "Wh-what is it, my lord?"

"What have you found out?"

Willie relaxed, as if he had been expecting something else from Dom, perhaps a reprimand. Dom wondered what he was hiding. "My lord, the Widow Reed was not at the stables that morning."

Dom was grim. "You are sure?"

"If she had been at the stables, she would have been noticed. A woman like that could not have gone unremarked."

Willie was right. Unless she were disguised. But Felicity would not have had enough time to change her clothing twice in order to poison Anne's horse—and she would have needed help if she had somehow defied the element of time. "Who else was at the stables that morning?"

"The duke was riding that morning."

Dom waved his hand. His grandfather was not a suspect. His grandfather loved Anne. "Go on."

"And your mother also took an early morning ride."

Dom started. Instantly he recalled how thoroughly his mother disliked Anne.

"The dowager marchioness rides three mornings a week at eight o'clock," Willie said. "She claims it is good for her constitution. She has been riding on such a schedule for more years than I can remember."

Dom relaxed. Besides, his mother was incapable of malice intended to harm anyone, much less Anne.

"Someone else had to have been at the stables," Dom said flatly.

Willie looked him in the eye. "Yes, sir. Someone else was there that morning. Three grooms saw him."

Dom tensed. "Out with it, man."

"My lord, Patrick Collins was there as well."

# Chapter 21

*A*nne was exhausted. She had slept poorly her first night at Rutherford House, disturbed by her certainty that someone wished her harm and by her newfound knowledge of Dom's perfidy. She kept hearing prowlers and ghosts in every creak of the house and groan of the wind and trees. Her dreams had been as eventful— filled with people she did not know, people with harsh, menacing visages and maniacal, contorted expressions. Unfortunately, one of those mocking her and chasing her in her nightmares was Dom.

Belle had not returned yet, of course, for she had only left for Waverly Hall last night. But Caldwell himself had already brought her her morning hot chocolate and the day's newspaper. One of the housemaids was temporarily serving Anne, and she was laying out Anne's morning gown. Anne sipped her chocolate, still in bed, despondency settling over her like a cloak. Although she was determined to find a solicitor to represent her that morning, she had no enthusiasm for that task or any other.

She heard the door to her room open. Anne started as Dom said, "Hello, Anne."

Anne knocked over her cup, staining the white linen cloth. "Dom!"

He was not smiling. He stared. He stared at her as if he wished to read—and comprehend—her very soul.

Anne's heart felt as if it were ricocheting in her chest. Harsh, angry, desperate emotions flooded her. "What are you doing here?"

"Clearly I have chased you across half of England all the way to town." His tone was not mocking, but dead serious. "I wish to speak with you."

It was then that Anne realized that she was at a distinct disadvantage. She was still in bed, and hardly dressed. Flushing, Anne slipped to her feet. Ignoring Dom's stare, she slipped on a ratty robe, one which Belle had procured for her before departing. She belted it tightly before facing Dom. "Get out."

He ignored her. Turning to the slack-jawed maid, he said, "You are dismissed."

The maid began to flee.

"Stop," Anne commanded. The plump girl halted, her face ashen. "You are not dismissed, Lizzie." Anne softened her tone. "I need you to help me dress." She turned a deadly stare on Dom. "Get out."

An unpleasant smile formed on his handsome face. "Not until we have spoken—and reached an understanding." He glanced at Lizzie. "Leave. Now. If you wish to retain your employment at Rutherford House."

Lizzie ran out of the bedroom.

"That was uncalled for," Anne cried.

"No matter what I have done in the past, or what I do in the present, *never* countermand me, Anne."

Anne knew better than to argue, in spite of the answering fury filling her veins. "I have no wish to speak with you, Dom. Not now, not ever. So now I will ask you again. Please leave."

His response was to fold his arms, cross his ankles, and lean comfortably against the doorjamb. "Something happened between us in Scotland, Anne. Surely you cannot dismiss it—and me—as lightly as Lizzie?"

Anne lost all control. "Damn you!" She shouted, shaking her fist at him. "Scotland was a lie! A huge,

horrid lie. You used me, you cad. You used me ...
ruthlessly, coldly ... you are as blackhearted as they
say. Allowing me to love you again ..." She could
not continue. Anne choked on her own words.

Dom straightened and crossed the room rapidly. His
face was stark.

Anne realized now that she was crying—and that he
intended to embrace her, to comfort her. She ran around
to the other side of the bed. "Don't touch me. You
miserable heartless bastard!" It was the worst epithet
she could manage.

He paled, flinching. "I do not deserve your curses,
Anne. I have come here to explain."

"No." She shook her head. "I do not want your
explanation. I am not interested in anything you wish
to say. I have had enough of your lies." She brushed
her fist across her eyes, but the tears would not stop
flowing, like a dam suddenly opened. "I hate you,"
she said, lying, knowing it. "God, I hate you."

He was stiff, his face waxen, his eyes unreadable. "I
intend to explain, Anne, whether you wish me to do so
or not."

"Will you deny that you seduced me in order to give
me your child? So that you might regain Waverly
Hall?" Anne cried.

He was silent, grim. "Yes. I deny it."

Anne turned her back to him, fists clenched, panting
with anguish and rage.

A moment later he laid his hands on her shoulders,
gently, firmly. "Please don't cry. I know I have hardly
given you cause to trust me, but I am asking you to
trust me, now."

Anne whirled and struck him with all of her might
across the face. He rocked backward on his heels from
the sheer force of her blow. The sound of the slap
echoed in the cavernous room.

Anne stared, shocked by her own violence.

Dom wet his lips, touched his jaw. Anne suddenly noticed that the hand he had raised, his right, was heavily bandaged. His eyes had darkened with anger. "God damn it, Anne. You haven't even listened to a word I said."

"That's right," Anne said through her teeth. "Enough has been said. Leave before I lose all control and disgrace myself even further."

He stared into her eyes. "When Rutherford told me the terms to the trust, I was furious. My intention was to leave Waverly Hall—and you—immediatcly."

Anne stiffened. "But you didn't."

"No."

Their gazes locked.

"I couldn't," Dom said flatly. "I couldn't leave because of you, Anne."

"No," Anne said. "You didn't leave because you knew how easily you could seduce me and get an heir out of me for yourself and Rutherford."

"No!" Dom said sharply. "I didn't leave because I was so bloody intrigued by you—because I wanted you so damn much—because I was falling in love with you already and regretting the past."

Anne finally found her voice. "You have betrayed my trust for the very last time."

"You refuse to believe me in spite of the passion and happiness we shared at Tavalon."

"Yes."

Something bleak and hopeless flitted through his eyes. "So this is the end, then?"

"Yes."

He was silent. "Do you intend to divorce me?" he finally asked, his tone odd.

Anne could hardly speak. "No. I would never do such a thing."

Relief flooded his features. "Good, because I would not allow it."

Anne inhaled. "I am thinking of the family and not the fact that it is almost impossible for a woman to divorce her husband."

He stared until the silence grew uncomfortable. "No, Anne," he said. "I think that deep down you still care for me."

Anne swiped at her tears. "You are right, damn you. You are right. But that won't change anything."

He turned, and his broad shoulders seemed to sag slightly as he walked away.

Anne pressed her fist to her mouth, so she would not call him back.

At her door, Dom paused. His eyes seemed suspiciously moist. "I know you will not believe this, but I am in love with you, Anne."

Anne gasped, her fist against her mouth.

Dom stared into her eyes for another heartbeat—one which felt like an eternity. In it, she knew, he waited for her to change her mind.

But Anne was not going to trust him and take him back.

He turned and left.

"Wait up, St. Georges!"

Dom had been cantering one of Rutherford's finest hacks down a straightaway on one of Hyde Park's numerous riding trails. He had passed numerous members of the ton all morning, the ladies in their gigs and curricles, the gentlemen astride, but Dom had ignored everyone—when everyone was most eager to stop him and converse. His sudden reappearance in London and his wife's first appearance in town was cause for excitement and speculation. Dom, however, could not possibly make light social chitchat now. He did not bother to wonder about what the gossips were making of the event. Sooner or later the entire ton would know that he and Anne were still estranged.

But the caller shouted his name again. Dom slowed his chestnut mount, realizing that it was his best friend, Blake, calling him.

Blake cantered up to him on a frisky pitch-black gelding. In his black riding coat and tan breeches, he cut an impeccable and dashing figure. "I've been chasing you for ten minutes, old man." Then he got a good look at Dom's face. "What's wrong?"

"I need a drink," Dom said grimly.

"It's not yet noon."

"I don't really give a damn."

Blake nodded. In unison, they turned their mounts and trotted down a path that would lead them out of the park, both oblivious to the fashionable ladies who gazed openly after them. Blake shot a curious glance at Dom, but asked no questions. They rode up Oxford Street toward Pall Mall.

"I thought you were in the country," Dom finally said as they were dismounting in front of their club, a stately brick building four stories high with a temple front.

Blake grimaced. "I spent a sennight chasing the Widow Reed and now I am disgusted—and far randier than before."

Dom eyed him but could not smile. "You? Unsuccessful?"

"She is holding a torch for you, old man—and you know it."

"But my interest lies elsewhere," Dom said quietly as they climbed the short set of stone steps and were ushered inside by a liveried dooman. They paused in the wood-paneled foyer.

"Yes, that is obvious," Blake said.

Dom looked away from Blake's sympathetic gaze, afraid his grief was too apparent.

Blake laid a hand on his arm. "She is in love with you, too, Dom."

"No. Not anymore." Dom tried to smile and failed. "I have never felt this way before. If this is love, then it is quite terrible."

Blake had to smile. "I am sure you can charm her into forgiving you for whatever it is you have done."

"Not this time."

"So you will give up? And allow her to be snared by a snake like Pat Collins?"

Dom stiffened.

"He is in love with her, too. No, excuse me. He wants her—but I am not sure that he loves her."

"I am aware of that. He spent four years by her side after I left her."

"So they say. He is in town, you know. I saw him riding this morning, before I saw you."

Dom's expression grew dark. He could guess what had brought Patrick to town—and whom. "Dammit," he said angrily. He might have lost Anne, but he would never allow her to be comforted by another man. Never.

"That's better," Blake was affable. "I suggest you do something to interest your wife again. Perhaps you might make her jealous? She was very jealous of Felicity that night at Waverly Hall."

Dom hesitated.

"Dom," Blake said, with some urgency, "Collins is not to be trusted. Pull a rabbit out of your hat. And quickly."

Dom said nothing at first. Then thinking about Willie's revelation, he said, "I agree with you completely."

Anne pulled back from her bedroom window when she saw a hired hansom stop on the street in front of Rutherford House. She was angry with herself for watching for Dom. He had left hours ago, well before dinnertime, but it was teatime now and he had not yet returned. Anne, meanwhile, had found herself strangely apathetic. She had forced herself to meet with a single solicitor—one who had refused to deal with her once he realized what she wanted to do.

Rutherford's power was immense. Dom's was also formidable. Anne had realized then and there that it might be very difficult finding a solicitor to represent her in her conflict with the St. Georges family.

Anne was about to turn away from the window when she realized that it was Patrick who had alighted from the hansom. Relief flooded her. She opened the window, calling out, waving.

He looked up and smiled.

Anne turned and raced downstairs.

"I'm so glad you're here!" Anne cried, meeting Patrick in the foyer as Caldwell took his gloves, walking stick, and hat.

Patrick moved directly to her and Anne went into his arms. A public embrace was unseemly, but this was her dearest friend, and Anne found herself overwhelmed with her rioting and brutal emotions yet again.

"What happened? Why are you so upset?" Patrick asked, setting her apart from him so he could scrutinize her face. "Why did you leave Waverly Hall so abruptly—without seeing me?"

Anne was aware of Caldwell standing by a marble table, his face set in stone. Although he pretended not to have noticed their embrace, she felt that he was disapproving. "Caldwell, please bring tea into the drawing room," she said, careful not to take Patrick's hand. She hurried down the hall with Patrick following her.

Once inside the huge red-and-gold drawing room with its high, trompe l'oeil walls and frescoed ceiling, he took both of her hands in his. "Anne, dear, what is wrong!" he cried. "Your message frightened me."

"I'm so distraught," Anne blurted. "Oh, Patrick, I am such a fool."

Patrick studied her, then led her to the couch where

they sat down simultaneously, still gripping one another's hands. "That bastard has done it again, hasn't he?" Patrick said bitterly.

Anne looked down at her knees. "Yes. But I am as much to blame."

Patrick cursed, shocking Anne, who had never heard him curse before. He was on his feet, pacing, flushed an angry red. "You fell for it all, didn't you, Anne? His smooth, winning smile, his seductive words, his perfect polish, and his charm."

Anne looked up. "Yes," she whispered.

"He's used you again."

"Yes."

Patrick's face was contorted. "Dammit, Anne!"

"Please don't," Anne cried. "I feel terrible enough."

Patrick went to her immediately and sat down beside her and enfolded her in his arms. "When will you realize that I love you, that I would never abuse you, that I am here for you, always?" he asked huskily.

Anne started instantly, and pushed against his chest. But he did not budge. She was alarmed. "Patrick, we are the best of friends, but, no matter what has happened, I am married to Dom."

His jaw tightened. "I don't care about Dom, and if you still do, then you are hopeless, Anne."

Anne looked away. "No. I am finished," she said tersely. "But I am his wife."

"Divorce him," Patrick said.

Anne jerked. She could not believe what he had said, and she was afraid that, in his next breath, he would ask her to marry him. "I would never do that," she whispered unsteadily.

Patrick stood. "Because you still love him?"

"No." Anne was also standing. "Because I am a lady. And," she blushed, "because I might very well be pregnant."

Patrick watched her closely. A moment later he said, "When will you know?"

"In another week," she said, blushing furiously at his question.

He stared at her, clearly distressed.

"Patrick," Anne said softly, "I know that you care about me, but please, for everyone's sake, care for me as you would a dear and beloved sister."

His glance skewered her. He did not respond.

Anne felt more despondent than before. There was too much here to bear. She felt guilty, as if she were betraying Dom, which she was not. And she felt terribly sad for Patrick.

"Patrick, there is more," Anne said into the lengthening silence.

He looked at her wordlessly.

"Someone is trying to harm me. Maybe they are only trying to frighten me, but I do not think so."

She had Patrick's full attention now. "What are you saying?"

Anne told him everything. About the fire in her bedroom, the charred rose, about the riding accident being the result of poison—and finding a broken stirrup in her trunk. Now Patrick guided her back to a red brocade couch and urged her to sit down. Anne did, clasping her hands nervously. "I think someone followed me to Scotland," she said in a low voice.

"What?"

Anne told him about the rider on the heath, and the feeling she'd had of being watched several times—and the open window in her bedchamber at Tavalon Castle.

"Does Dom know about this?" Patrick demanded.

"He knows about the window—and the riding accident. But I have no idea what he is thinking."

"What do *you* think?"

Anne lowered her eyes, worrying the folds of her skirt. "I think that there are several people who do not like me,'' she said carefully, ''but it is absurd to even think that one of them might want to frighten me—or even want to hurt me.'' She glanced up and met Patrick's unwavering blue stare.

''Who?'' Patrick asked.

But Anne fell silent, for Caldwell wheeled a cart into the room, one containing silver and settings and their refreshments. Anne and Patrick waited for the butler to serve the tea and leave.

''Whom do you suspect?'' Patrick asked in a whisper.

Anne chose her words with great care. ''At first, I thought maybe Clarisse is behind everything.'' She had expected Patrick to scoff at the suggestion, but he did not. ''But she has not left Waverly Hall at all recently, so she could not have followed Dom and me to Scotland.''

''Perhaps you only imagined being watched in Scotland, and being followed—and dreamed of closing the window—as Dom said.''

''Perhaps,'' Anne said, not convinced.

''Do you suspect someone else?''

''Yes,'' Anne whispered uneasily, not meeting his gaze. She wet her lips, raised her eyes. ''Patrick, Felicity couldn't hate me so much to want me . . . harmed, could she?''

He jerked. ''Good God, no!'' His gaze was wide; it hardened. ''You also suspect my sister?''

Anne did not reply.

''Felicity is not mad, Anne.'' He seemed agitated.

''I don't know,'' Anne said uneasily. ''She hates me. Four years ago, she swore that she would get even with me.''

He was stiff. ''I'm not certain that she does hate you, Anne. Not anymore. She is very busy with the fortune she inherited from her husband, and she has made out as well as if she had married Dom. Right now she is in high demand—she is a wealthy widow with numerous suitors."

Anne did not respond.

"My sister certainly did not follow you to Scotland, Anne," Patrick said coldly. "She was in the country, and there are dozens of witnesses to prove it."

Anne chose not to remind Patrick of his own words—that she might have imagined all of the strange little happenings in Scotland. Felicity had been at Waverly Hall the morning of her riding accident and Anne was acutely aware of it. But could she have stolen into the house two nights before, and then into Anne's room, in order to overturn the candles and start a fire? And then again, the very next night, in order to leave a charred rose? That night Felicity had also been present, at the supper party. But how would she have put the broken stirrup leather into Anne's trunk? All in all, it was a stretch.

Patrick was watching her closely. "My sister is not capable of that kind of malice, Anne."

"It's hard for me to think that anyone is capable of that kind of malice," Anne said with a frown. "But there is proof. My horse was injected with a poison that is frequently used to overexcite racehorses. Someone purposefully wished to frighten or harm me."

Patrick stared, his gray eyes sympathetic.

Anne grew uneasy. "*You* suspect someone."

"Perhaps."

"Who?"

"Who knows more about racehorses than anyone?"

At first, Anne did not understand where Patrick was leading. Then her cheeks lost all of their color. Her chest began to feel tight and constricted. She stared, wide-eyed. "Not . . . Dom!"

Patrick stood. "Dom knows more about racehorses—and horses—than anyone, including you, me, Felicity, or even my father."

Anne was also standing. Her hands were becoming icy and cold. "This is ... preposterous. Dom is ... many things. But not ..." she broke off, unable to continue.

"Not a killer?" Patrick supplied.

"He is not capable of such malice!"

Patrick smiled grimly. "No? I think you are wrong, Anne. I think you have just realized it, too. I think no one has more to gain from hurting you—even from killing you—than your own husband."

Anne closed her eyes tightly. What Patrick was suggesting was impossible. Wasn't it?

# Chapter 22

$\mathcal{D}$om nodded to Caldwell, who had let him in. The butler said, "Good afternoon, my lord. The marchioness is in the drawing room."

Dom absorbed this bit of information, but headed toward the sweeping, curved staircase, carpeted in red.

"Mr. Collins is with Her Ladyship," Caldwell added.

Dom faltered. His knuckles, on the bronze banister, turned white. He stepped off of the stairs. "Oh, really?" His smile was not pleasant. "Thank you, Caldwell."

Abruptly Dom strode to the drawing room. He paused on the threshold. At the scene which greeted him, his pulse exploded.

Anne and Patrick sat on the same sofa, their knees almost touching. Their heads were bent together, and Patrick held one of Anne's hands. Patrick was doing a lot of talking, and Anne was absolutely silent, and very pale and drawn.

"What a pretty surprise," Dom drawled, sauntering into the room.

Immediately they drew apart, Anne reclaiming her hand. She stared at him as if she had never seen him before.

Her strange gaze made Dom a little uneasy. "Hello,

Anne.'' When she failed to respond, he stared coldly at Patrick. "I do hope I am not interrupting anything?"

Patrick now stood, slowly. "Hello, Dom. We were just discussing the Harding ball.''

Dom had the uncanny feeling that they had been discussing *him*. "Ah yes, the event of the Season." He stared at Anne. "Are we going, my dear?"

Anne jerked.

He stalked to her and towered over her. "Surely you wish to attend the biggest, most lavish, most extravagant ball of the Season?"

"If . . . I must.''

"But Patrick is undoubtedly attending, aren't you, Collins? The two of you can sneak off and share a private moment. No opportunity could be better.''

Anne did not even respond to him.

And Dom was furious, frustrated. He whirled. "You move very quickly, Collins.''

Patrick flushed. "I have no idea what you mean.''

"No? I think that you do." Dom smiled.

"My sister invited me to town,'' Patrick said.

"Oh, really?'' His fists were clenched at his sides. "And who invited you here, to my home?''

Patrick shifted. "There is nothing wrong with my calling upon your wife.''

"There most certainly is,'' Dom said.

Patrick paled. "Dom, isn't it about time that you grew up? Your jealousy is childish and uncalled for.''

"I think I am well within my rights being jealous now, Patrick.''

Patrick recoiled.

Dom had had enough. He turned his frost-filled stare on Anne. "I thought I had made myself clear weeks ago, Anne.''

Anne still stared at him. "And''—her voice was very low and almost inaudible—"I thought that I was as clear. I am allowed my friends.''

*"Not this one."*

To Dom's surprise, again Anne did not challenge him. She rose to her feet. "Patrick, perhaps you should leave."

Patrick turned a worried gaze upon her. "Will you be all right?"

Anne nodded, her mouth pursed, not looking at Dom.

And he did not like their private exchange, not one damn bit. Dom was no longer able to control his jealousy or his rage. He grabbed Anne's arm. "Enough, Anne. Say good-bye to Collins now."

"You're manhandling me," Anne gasped.

"Let her go," Patrick cried.

Dom released Anne and turned his fury on Patrick. *"Get out."*

Patrick drew himself up.

"I believe I threw you out of Waverly Hall, and now I am throwing you out of Rutherford House."

"Dom," Anne whispered. "Don't."

He ignored her. "Not only am I throwing you out of this house, I am forbidding you from ever entering here again."

"You can't stop me from seeing her!"

His hands itched to plow into Patrick's face. "Yes, I can. I am. I am forbidding it." He turned his livid gaze on Anne. "Did you hear me, Anne? I forbid your seeing Patrick."

She said not a word.

"Caldwell," he barked. The butler appeared immediately. "Escort Mr. Collins out."

"Yes, my lord," Caldwell said.

Patrick's expression was drawn. "Perhaps, Waverly, if your own behavior were more circumspect, your wife would not seek a friendship with me."

Anne was shocked at Patrick's bravado. She certainly had not given him any cause to hope.

Dom snarled, "You lay one hand on my wife—regardless of my behavior—and I'll see you at Guilford Crossing at dawn—your choice of weapons.''

Patrick was pale, but he marched from the room, Caldwell escorting him. Anne remained in her trance-like state.

Dom strode to the double doors and slammed each one closed. Then he turned and faced Anne. ''How convenient this is. You arrive in town—and so does Collins. It's too bad, isn't it, that I did not stay in the country? So the two of you could meet without my interference? Perhaps I failed to satisfy you in Scotland?'' He was purposefully crude. ''Is that why you need a lover, Anne?''

Anne flushed. ''I do not have to answer you.''

He eyed her. Was she in love with Patrick? Had she responded to him in Scotland out of animal passion— while her heart belonged to the other man? He could not stand the very idea. Fortunately, he did not really think it true. What he did think was that Anne was naive, allowing Patrick a genuine friendship, which he was manipulating to his own advantage.

In any case, Patrick could no longer be trusted. Dom ignored the small stabbing of hurt he felt at the comprehension. ''Stop seeing him.''

''No.''

Dom paced toward her. ''You may want separate beds now, Anne, but I am your husband in fact. Under the law, I can direct you as I will. I am forbidding the continuation of your relationship with Patrick.''

To his surprise, tears filled her eyes. ''Damn you.''

''I am probably destined for hell without your help.''

''Undoubtedly.'' She stood and walked away from him. Dom realized that she was leaving the room, just like that.

He strode after her. Before she could reach for the door, he had placed his hand on it, bracing it closed. ''We must talk, Anne.''

She did not look at him. To the door she said, "We have said all that there is to say."

Pain blossomed in his chest, very much the way it might if a bullet had struck him there. Silently, Dom wondered what Anne would do if he told her that he was miserable now, consumed with both love and longing.

"Anne, we must talk. We are man and wife, and we cannot continue to exist as such in a state of warfare like this. In any case, I don't want to fight with you."

"That's good, be-because I don't want to fight with you," she said, stammering slightly.

"Then let us begin anew," he heard himself say.

She laughed hoarsely. "For the third time? I think not."

He hadn't meant to press and plead, he would never beg, but her adamant refusal hurt him nonetheless. "Forgive my spontaneity," he muttered. "Let us discuss the future then, as we have no present prospects."

"We have no future."

"Anne, we may not agree and we may end up estranged, but we are married. We most definitely have a future—even if it is to grow old and gray whilst leading separate lives privately and publicly maintaining a facade."

She whimpered.

He felt a savage satisfaction that he was somehow wounding her, too. "There are certain rules which we both must conform to."

She closed her eyes briefly. "I am sure those rules will benefit you."

"Those rules will benefit us both," he said quietly. "One of them calls for civility. You and I must deal with one another regardless of your feelings for me."

Anne finally looked him in the eye, and as quickly, glanced away. "As you w-wish."

"Shall we start with the Harding ball?" he asked.

She started. "I really don't think—"

"What? That it is appropriate? Of course it is. Everyone will expect us to attend. My return to town is the talk of this Season, Anne. And you have never been to London. We have never appeared anywhere together since our marriage, and the ton is waiting to see us."

"How wonderful," Anne whispered.

"You need not worry," Dom said tersely. "I shall behave toward you as a devoted husband would."

She jerked and stared at him.

"I am going to make things up to you," Dom said.

"Don't!"

Their gazes clashed. And held. But again, for the umpteenth time, Anne quickly looked away. Something was wrong. Anne had been behaving oddly since he had first walked into the room. If he did not know better, he would think her afraid of him. "What is bothering you, Anne?"

"Nothing."

He studied here downturned, set face. There was another question he had to ask. "Is there any chance that you are pregnant?"

She looked at him furiously, her cheeks flushed.

He almost felt like blushing himself. "I am not trying to discomfit you, Anne. But I need to know. It is important to me."

"Of course it is—of course you need to know!" Anne cried angrily. "So you can plan on whether or not you shall regain Waverly Hall!"

He tensed. His temper flared. "That is not why I wish to know if you carry my child."

"I don't believe you." She tried to move past him.

Dom gripped her shoulder. Anne flinched, her breath escaping in a rush.

He stared at her. "Something is wrong. What?"

"Nothing."

"You almost act as if you are frightened of me."

She stared at him, her eyes huge, her face pale. "Why—why would you say that?"

Dom hesitated. Could Anne be frightened of him? "Anne, as unhappy as I am with the turn of circumstances, I would never hurt you. Surely you know that."

Anne lost the last of her color. It was quite clear she did not believe him. "H-how long are you staying here?"

He hesitated. "I have not decided."

"I . . . I want my own flat, Dom. Here in London."

"No." The word rang out, harsh, final. Dom did not have to think about it. "Absolutely not."

"Why?"

"I have numerous estates—you can go to any one of them. But I am not setting you up in your own flat."

"I see. And if I go elsewhere?"

"What do you mean? Speak plainly, Anne," he snapped.

"If I go to Highglow? Or Campton?"

His jaw flexed. His eyes darkened. "You would be uncomfortable, to say the least. They are old estates, with no modern conveniences."

She licked her lips. "But if I go to one of those places?"

His gaze narrowed. "I might decide to join you."

"I see." She backed up against the door. "You intend to live with me. No matter what my wishes are."

He hadn't, not until then. He had intended to be civil and allow her a separate residence—as most married couples resided apart. But he could not do it. He could not let her go. He could not give up. Not yet. Maybe not ever. "Yes."

"Even though I have said that I do not want you, that it is over, for . . . forever."

He stared very hard at her. "I could make you want me, Anne."

She pinkened. A slow silence unfolded between them. Dom was rewarded by the movement of her Adam's apple in her throat. "Yes," she said huskily. "I am sure that you could. But that would not change my feelings for you."

"*Touché*," he said bitterly.

She stared at him for a long time. When she spoke, he heard desperation in her tone. "What do I have to do to make you leave me alone?"

"Become someone else," he said. Dom reached for her. The urge to hold her, stroke her, comfort her, was overwhelming.

But Anne leapt away from him.

Dom was stunned. He reached for her again, and this time, he seized her wrist. She cried out. He was blunt. "You *are* afraid of me, and I don't like it."

"No—I am not!"

"I'm beginning to think that you have been frightened ever since I walked into the room." He stared at her. "Have I done something, Anne? Have I given you cause to be afraid?"

"No!" Anne appeared agitated. "No! I am not afraid, not of anything . . . not of you!"

This time, when she shoved past him, he let her go.

And Dom stared after her—long after she was gone.

Anne debated remaining in her room and decided against it. Dom was right. They did have appearances to keep up, even in front of the servants, who gossiped notoriously.

She allowed Belle to help her change for supper and she went downstairs.

She clung very tightly to the brass banister as she descended the steps. Her pulse raced. *It was not true.*

Someone was trying to hurt her, or frighten her, but it could not be Dom.

*The very idea was absurd.*

Dom had made love to her ceaselessly for an entire week. He could not have been biding his time, waiting for the perfect moment to do away with her. A moment that would make her death appear a fateful accident.

Patrick believed that Dom wanted to kill her and rid himself of an unwanted wife. He had pointed out to her that Dom would have nothing to gain by scaring her or merely hurting her. But he had everything to gain should she suffer a fatal accident. He would have his freedom; he would have Waverly Hall.

Anne was not convinced. She had spent the past dozen years worshiping Dom. She had loved him completely, even during the past four years—perhaps even now. It was terrible enough to admit that he was capable of seducing her in order to regain Waverly Hall, but she could not, would not, believe him capable of murder. No. Patrick was wrong.

But Anne's nerves were frayed. There was one other obvious fact that could not be ignored. No one had had better access to herself and her possessions than Dom St. Georges.

Anne entered the dark green-and-gold salon. She forced a smile as the duke greeted her, kissing her cheek. His own smile faded. "You seem pale, Anne. Are you ill?"

"No. I am fine." Anne's eyes found Dom. Her heart pounded with explosive force. His black dinner jacket and snowy white shirt made a marked contrast to his bronzed skin and gold-streaked hair. He was also wearing a blue-and-silver brocade vest with a darker cravat. A satin seam ran down the leg of his black wool trousers, and his patent evening shoes gleamed. He was tall, elegant, disturbingly handsome. And his gaze was upon her, as well. Steady, unwavering—seeking.

Anne looked away. He was capable of treachery, but not murder. She knew that in her heart.

"Anne?"

He was right beside her. "D-Dom. I did not hear you approach."

"But you were looking right at me. Had you but smiled, I would have thought you were issuing an invitation." His gaze slid lazily over her features, one by one, finally lingering on her mouth.

Anne realized that she had been staring at his mouth, too, and she yanked her gaze to the green marble mantel behind his shoulder.

"Whatever could you be thinking of to be so lost in thought?" Dom asked languidly.

Anne swallowed, could not force a smile. His tone was too smoky for comfort. But surely she was imagining it—surely he did not think to try to bed her after all that had happened. "It doesn't matter."

"I think that it does."

She met his bold yet somber gaze. "You would not wish to know."

"Ahh—then you are thinking about me."

"My thoughts are not flattering," Anne said with rising temper. "Dom, stop."

"I am not even allowed to flirt with you?"

She flushed. "No. You are not."

His eyes darkened. "But we agreed to be civil, did we not?"

Anne was at a loss. "Yes. We did."

"Then I shall flirt with you if the mood takes me, and perhaps, in time, you will even relax and enjoy it." He held out his arm. "May I?"

Anne inhaled. How was she going to survive this so very civil arrangement? Anne realized that she did not have a civil bone in her body. And that living together like this was going to be terribly painful.

His glance became speculative. "Anne?"

She tucked her hand on his arm. Trembling. Patrick's horrid claims flashed through her mind.

Dom pressed her close to his side. Her memory of

her recent conversation with Patrick died. As they left the salon, Anne was acutely aware of every hard lean inch of his body against hers. She could feel his muscles quivering with tension—a tension that answered her own.

Two maids cleared the dinner dishes. Caldwell poured both men brandies, then looked inquiringly at Anne. "A sherry, madam?"

"No, thank you." Anne sat as stiffly as a board. Supper had been a terse, silent affair. The duke had tried to make conversation, but Anne found herself incapable of responding to inane social chatter. He had then tried to talk to her about a poaching problem at Waverly Hall, but it hurt too much for Anne to talk about the estate she loved so much, but would never return to now.

The duke had then turned his efforts to Dom. But Dom responded to the duke's comments in monosyllables, and by the third course, he had given up.

Anne watched the maid serving brandied figs and crème brûlée. Anne knew now, after one interminable meal, that she and Dom could not have a civil understanding. It would never work.

As if he knew that she thought about him, his gaze connected with hers. He said to the maid, "No, thank you."

The maid tried to serve the duke, but he also declined.

Dom stared at Anne.

Anne stared back helplessly. His regard made her breathless, uneasy—unhappy.

Suddenly Dom shoved back his chair. "Well, as everyone appears to be finished, I will leave."

"Are you going somewhere?" the duke asked.

Dom was standing. Anne had tensed. He did not look

at her, only at his grandfather. "Yes. I am going to a soirée at Lord Heath's."

Anne was surprised. Dom was going out for the evening—and it was close to eleven o'clock. But she should have guessed by his formal evening wear. In the next instant, she felt dismayed, and, oddly, crushed.

The duke nodded, not raising a brow.

"Good night," Dom said. He looked at Anne.

Anne forced the words out. "Good night."

Dom turned and strode from the room, an impossibly attractive man.

Anne let him go.

Anne delayed going upstairs to her room. She read for a while in the library, but could not concentrate on the words in front of her, and she gave it up. She kept imagining Dom dancing with another woman. She couldn't help wondering if Felicity would be at the Heaths' tonight.

Anne walked upstairs slowly.

She had never been to Rutherford House before, but she did not notice the opulent furnishings, the gilded ceilings, the marble columns and trompe l'oeil walls, surroundings fit for kings. She was oblivious to the sculptures she passed, and the numerous works of art, many of them masterpieces. The huge house was terribly silent. Although the duke was in residence, along with fifty staff, the house felt starkly empty and Anne felt very alone.

She entered her suite of rooms, immediately going to the bellpull and ringing for Belle. She glanced at the gilded grandfather clock in the corner of the room. It was just past midnight. Dom would probably be out for hours and hours yet. Enjoying himself.

While she was utterly miserable.

Perhaps she should have gone with him. For appearances' sake, of course.

Belle was tardy. Anne entered her bedroom. And froze.

She recognized the red plaid blanket that covered her bed instantly. It was the same red plaid that had been draped at the foot of the bed she had shared with Dom in the master chamber at Tavalon Castle in Scotland. But it had been whole then. Now it was torn in two.

Anne stared, and slowly, she turned white.

# Chapter 23

"*B*elle!" The moment the maid appeared in Anne's private sitting room, Anne dragged her inside and slammed the door and bolted it.

"My lady! What is wrong?" Belle cried, paling.

Anne seized the little maid's arm and pulled her into the bedroom. When Belle saw the torn red plaid blanket on the beautiful amber silk bed, she was confused. "Now, who put that ugly thing there?" she muttered, whipping it off.

"Belle!" Anne cried. "Don't you understand? Don't you see?"

Belle looked at Anne.

"I did not imagine it! Someone was watching me in Scotland! And whoever it was, he wants me to know that he is here—in this very house!" Anne cried. "He wants me to know that he is watching me now!"

Belle gasped. She paled. Her knees buckled. It was Anne who guided her to a chair so that she could sit down.

Anne turned her back on the ripped plaid, which now lay on the floor. She was rigid with fright.

"Oh Lord," Belle whispered. "Who could do such a thing? Why is someone watching you? What does he want? Oh, mum! We need help! We must go to His Lordship!"

"No!" Anne shouted, whirling. She forced her tone down. "No."

Belle gaped, wide-eyed.

Anne took a deep breath. And stared at the torn plaid.

Someone was watching her. Following her. Someone had watched her in Scotland, following there from Waverly Hall—someone who was now here, at Rutherford House.

And whoever it was, he had access to her bedroom at Rutherford House.

And he also had access to her bedroom at Waverly House and Tavalon Castle.

It flashed through Anne's mind now that the rider who had followed her on the heath might have been Dom. She might have mistaken Dom's bay mount for a chestnut.

Anne's legs collapsed. This time it was Belle who caught her and moved her to a settee. Anne turned a tear-stained gaze on her French maid. "Belle, tell me the truth. Do you think Dom is the one trying to frighten me? Trying to hurt me?"

Belle did not answer.

Anne closed her eyes.


"Are you going to ask him to dance?"

Felicity turned, scowling. She had recognized Blake's deep, smooth voice the moment it sounded in her ear. "You! I did not even know you were here," she lied. She had noticed him the moment he first entered the Heath's Mayfair residence. "And I have no idea what you are talking about."

He smiled at her, amused. "Liar. You saw me an hour ago—just as I saw you." His gaze lingered on her very full lower lip.

Felicity shrugged dismissively and turned her back quite deliberately upon him. She stared at Dom. He was surrounded by couples, the women in boldly colored gowns and fabulous jewelry, the men in dress coats. He appeared somewhat bored, very sober and stiffly polite, but the men were eager to engage him in their conversation, and the ladies were casting looks at him from beneath their lashes. Felicity wondered where Anne was.

"You are drooling again, my dear," Blake murmured, his breath tickling her bare nape.

Felicity snapped the sticks of her fan together. In spite of how much she disliked him and his presumption toward her, his proximity made her flushed and warm. "You are the one who is drooling—over me."

He laughed, moving to stand beside her. He eyed her very bare, heaving bosom. "I do not deny it."

She glared. "Chase someone else, Lord Blake. I am not interested!"

He folded his arms, leaned his shoulder against the marble pillar they stood beside, and grinned. His blue eyes gleamed. "Who are you trying to convince? Me—or yourself?"

Felicity was furious. "I don't care what you choose to think—or believe. All I want is for you to stop following me everywhere."

"Come, darling, you like the chase as much as I do. In fact, I daresay you *love* being chased so intently."

"You arrogant jackass."

He laughed. "I'll bet you know how to curse as well as any man."

She hissed, "Bastard."

"That's a bit better."

Out of the corner of her eye, Felicity saw Dom leaving the group he had been cornered by—and he was coming in her direction. Immediately she straightened, thrusting out her bosom, smiling at him.

An instant later Blake seized her arm, jerking her against his hard hip. "Tell me one thing. What is it you really want? To seduce Dom—or hurt Anne?"

Felicity turned, intending to strike him. She forgot that they were in a very public place.

Blake caught her wrist, not gently. "I do believe that once was enough."

"How dare you speak to me in such a manner." Tears came to her eyes. Not tears of hurt, tears of anger.

"Your behavior calls for far worse," Blake ground out. "Why don't you leave him alone? He is in love with his wife, Felicity."

"In love with Anne?" She scoffed. "That is a joke!"

He tucked her arm in his. "Come with me." It was a command.

Felicity had no intention of obeying, though, and she cried out as he literally began dragging her with him—away from Dom. But she quickly thought better of struggling, for several people had noticed them already. Felicity could feel that she was very flushed, and her bodice had slipped quite indecently—she dared not make a scene. Giving up momentarily, Felicity hurried now to keep up with him, no easy task in her tiny, slim heels. Her pulse had quickened alarmingly.

He led her through the library, where a few couples were conversing, and outside onto a small balcony.

Felicity could guess exactly what he intended now. They were alone, and it was dark. She had not been able to forget his first and only kiss outside of Waverly Hall, either. She could not help anticipating the moment when his lips would seize hers. She met his gaze. His was knowing.

She scowled, and recalled the fact that Dom was in the ballroom—without Anne. "Let me go."

He released her.

"You're lucky I don't slap you again."

He eyed her, unperturbed by her words, leaning his hip against the wrought-iron railing. "You're lucky I don't turn you over my knee and spank you as you deserve."

Felicity's eyes widened. Any and all response escaped her.

Blake smiled. "But I'd bet you'd like that, wouldn't you?"

She found it hard to breathe. "No." Felicity wasn't sure if she lied or not. She had never been spanked, not even as a child. For some reason, she could not get the idea of Blake spanking her out of her mind.

Silence, heavy and intense, reigned between them.

Blake smiled. "I can arrange it." His eyes were dark, glittering. "Tonight, if you like."

She recovered her senses. "No. You are . . ."

"Impossible?" he supplied.

She wet her lips. Imagining his large, strong hand on her soft, full buttocks. "Your reputation . . . is well earned . . . I have no doubt."

He smiled at her. It was a devastating smile. But then, he was a devastating man. "Yes, it is."

"And you are so very proud of it!"

He shrugged. "Would you care to test me out? See if I am half as manly as it is claimed?"

Felicity could not help herself, she glanced down once, at his loins. Of course, he wore dark trousers, and it was well past midnight, so she could see nothing. But he saw, and he laughed, the sound smoky and rich and too damned amused.

Felicity hissed incoherently and tried to shove past him and leave. But as she did, her body brushed his. For one instant, her hand made contact with the startling length and breadth of his very definite arousal. Felicity faltered, glancing back over her shoulder. Their gazes clashed.

And he saluted her with one finger tipped to his temple, smiling.

Felicity shoved through the balcony doors as fast as she possibly could.

Anne heard him coming down the hall.

It was two in the morning. The Tiffany clock on the mantel over the fireplace had chimed twice not moments ago. Anne was not sleeping, and a kerosene lamp burned beside her bed. Belle slept on the daybed in her dressing room. Anne was taking no chances.

Anne tensed, curled up around her pillow, listening as his footsteps grew louder as he approached her room. Her heart felt as if it had stopped. She could not move, could not breathe. She had been awaiting his return for hours now.

But the footsteps did not stop or even pause beside her room. But she hadn't really thought that he would try to force her locked door open. Not for any purpose—not to hurt her.

The door down the hall opened, and closed. There was finality in the sound.

Anne lay in bed, perspiring, her body limp. She knew Dom was not a killer. Just as she knew, in her foolish, crazy heart, that he had to have had some real affection for her, or he could have never loved her as he had that week in Scotland. Tears streaked down her cheeks silently.

Belle crept into the room. "Mum? He's home. Are you all right?"

Anne sat up, nodding. "Fine." She gulped down some air. "It cannot be him."

But Belle was now convinced of Dom's treachery. "But mum, as *you* said to *me,* who else could have done all those things? Who else could have been in your private rooms? Who else would gain the way *he* would if you should die?"

It was a very good question. Anne did not have the answer. She shivered then, refusing to feel the cool fingers of doubt.


Dom came downstairs to breakfast late, missing Anne. According to Belle, who refused to hold his eye, Anne had gone riding in the park.

Dom gazed after the abigail, somewhat perplexed.

He had a mild headache from too much champagne. He had overimbibed last night, thinking to drown his sorrows, thinking to have an enjoyable time. It had proved impossible.

What was the meaning of the French maid's odd behavior? He couldn't help being suspicious. If Anne had gone riding in the park at this ungodly hour in order to meet Patrick, clandestinely, defying him, many heads were going to roll.

Caldwell interrupted his morning meal, which Dom had no appetite for anyway. The butler bore a silver platter, and on it was an engraved calling card. "My lord, Mr. Matthew Fairhaven is here to see you. He insists upon waiting for your response to his call."

Dom was instantly alert. All thoughts of Anne and last night were gone. He took the card, staring at the name and address. Matthew Fairhaven, his father's best friend, the recipient of most of his small fortune, had come calling. What did he want?

And not only did he want something, he was violating basic etiquette by remaining in the house, awaiting Dom. A proper caller would merely drop off his card—and wait for Dom to reciprocate the gesture.

"Escort him into the morning room."

Caldwell nodded and hurried out.

Abruptly Dom left the room. His strides were long and hard as he entered the large red-and-gold drawing room. Fairhaven was sitting in one delicate pink-and-white-striped bergère, but upon seeing Dom, he jumped to his feet. The two men stared at one another.

Dom was shocked. Fairhaven was a few years younger than himself, a very beautiful young man, dark-haired and dark-eyed but extraordinarily fair-skinned. But there were large circles around his eyes now; and his face was drawn in an expression of depression and grief.

Dom crossed the room, extending his hand, his tone polite. "Fairhaven."

Matthew shook his hand, but he stared wide-eyed at Dom. "My lord." He trembled. "I am sorry to intrude. I w-wished to offer my-my condolences." His voice broke, his face crumbled, and he turned away. He began blowing his nose noisily into a handkerchief.

Dom stared at his slim back. He was in shock. Clearly Fairhaven had been far more to Philip than a best friend. The younger man had been in love with his father. Had they been lovers?

If so, their affair had been secretly conducted and discreet. Homosexuality was a crime.

Finally Matthew faced him again. "Forgive me," he said softly, his eyes as swollen as they were red. "But I am afraid that my misery is hopeless."

Dom was stunned. He had expected almost anything but this. Cautiously, he said, "You loved my father."

"Yes. Very much." Fairhaven began to cry again.

Dom walked away, his pulse racing. Had Philip loved Fairhaven as deeply?

The liquor cabinet was locked, but Dom knew where the key was. He had soon poured the younger man a large whiskey, and he handed it to him. Matthew sipped it several times.

Dom gestured for him to sit. He obeyed at once, and Dom sat in an opposite chair. "What can I do for you?" he asked.

Matthew shook his head, briefly unable to speak. But his gaze lingered on Dom's face, studying him openly, making Dom uncomfortable. Finally Matthew set his glass down. "I merely wanted to commiserate with the family for such a terrible, tragic loss. Philip was far too young to die. . . ."

Dom crossed one booted ankle over one of his thighs, staring at the youth. "Was my father in love with you, as well?"

Matthew closed his eyes. "I think so. He was a discreet man. Not given to showing his feelings or expressing his thoughts. As you must know."

Dom nodded.

"He never told me that he loved me, but his actions led me to believe that he was sincerely fond of me. He knew that I loved him," Matthew said.

Dom felt sorry for him. "Well, he did leave you every penny that he had." But had Philip made such a gesture to comfort Fairhaven, or solely to mock him and Clarisse?

Matthew flushed. "I do not care for money."

Dom stared at him, deciding that Fairhaven lied. He had known about the will. Perhaps he had even demanded his share of Philip's small fortune. Matthew looked anywhere now but at Dom. The moment became uncomfortable.

Dom wondered again just what Fairhaven knew. He wondered if Fairhaven had come to Rutherford House to blackmail him.

"How is the dowager marchioness?" Matthew asked.

"As well as can be expected."

Matthew swallowed. "I am sorry. I have seen your mother, she is very beautiful and so very elegant, but I understand completely why Philip despised her. He certainly had every right."

Their gazes locked. Dom was tense. He forced a smile. "So now we come to the very heart of the matter."

Matthew shifted in his seat. "Did you read his journal?"

"No," Dom lied. "Did you?"

Fairhaven blanched. "Y-yes."

Dom gripped the arms of his chair, then launched himself out of it. "If you have something to say, Fairhaven, why do you not spit it out?"

Matthew also stood. "He said that you do not know, that you have no idea."

Dom forced himself to remain expressionless, but he thought his eyes gave him away, for he was so damn angry—and secretly, he was also frightened. "I have no idea what you are talking about."

Matthew stared at him. "Surely you know that he hated you—and that he hated Clarisse."

"Did he?"

Matthew wet his lips. "Where is the diary?"

"It's gone."

"Gone?"

"Burned," Dom said flatly.

Matthew's large eyes seemed uncomprehending.

"Just what is it that you want to tell me?" Dom asked coldly.

"I ... don't you want to know why Philip hated her—and you?"

"Not really," Dom lied. He felt a bead of sweat trickle down his left cheek.

"She ... she betrayed him. With another man," Matthew said. "He never forgave her."

"Surely my mother is not the first married woman to take a lover."

Matthew stared at him, as white as a freshly bleached sheet.

"Do you really think I'd give in to this blackmail?" Dom asked contemptuously. "Do you think the world cares about another instance of adultery in a society full of them?"

"It cares. It cares when there are repercussions," Matthew said hoarsely.

Dom tensed.

Matthew wet his lips. "It cares when issues of paternity—and heredity—are raised."

For one moment, as Dom stood there, his world went black. But when his vision cleared, he was still standing upright, and Fairhaven was cowering away from him. "Don't hit me," Fairhaven sobbed.

Dom realized that his expression was one of rage. "I am not paying you—not one single penny. *Is that clear?*"

Matthew's eyes widened. "Are you mad?"

"It would be your word—against mine. Against my mother's. Against the duke's."

Matthew Fairhaven was quaking. "But I have proof."

Dom froze.

"I have the letter Philip wrote to Clarisse after he learned the truth. He never sent it to her. But in it, he reveals everything—except for your real father's identity."

Dom felt his world crumbling beneath his feet. He felt his hopes and dreams shatter. He felt the past disappear, becoming meaningless. The future loomed, a void.

"Get out," he said.

His heart had been bothering him all day. His doctors had warned him repeatedly to slow down, to rest more, to do less, to give up the cigars and whiskey he was so fond of. He was seventy-four, and even he knew it was time to retire from his life as he had always known it. It was time to hand over most of his duties to his grandson. There was even temptation in the idea of passing along the dukedom to Dom before he actually died. Such a happenstance was rare, but it could be done if Rutherford truly wanted to step aside—to step down.

And in a way, he did. He was tired. Every inch of him. It was tiring walking, riding, and just being sometimes. He had come to dislike the numerous social events he had to attend. He always left early.

But he was not dead yet, and his mind was still vitally alive and as active as ever. He still loved the challenge of managing his ducal empire. He was not going to step aside for Dom while he was still alive, in spite of the temptation.

It was morbid to think of dying. But today he had been far shorter of breath than had been usual these past months. And he had been so tired that he could not keep the rest of his commitments for the day. He had sent a footman around town begging off. It was only dinnertime and he was going home—and looking forward to it.

A strange feeling swept the duke when he entered his home. "Caldwell, is something amiss?"

Caldwell had been employed for thirty-one years now, ever since the last family butler had died. He was pale and drawn. His eyes were grave. "I am afraid so, Your Grace."

Rutherford paused, aware of a small stabbing in his temples. And the air was still far too thick for comfort. His pulse picked up its shallow beat, adding to Rutherford's general feeling of not being well. "What has happened?"

"Matthew Fairhaven was here, sir, and he has sent the marquis into the library in a state which I have never quite witnessed before. I think it is shock, Your Grace."

Caldwell and Rutherford's eyes met. An unspoken comprehension passed between them. Caldwell had been employed by the duke at the time of his son's marriage to Clarisse.

Rutherford rubbed his chest, which ached. His hand trembled. *Fairhaven could not have known.* "Where is Lady Anne?"

"She left hours ago, Your Grace, and I must say, she looked unwell. And last night, her abigail slept in her rooms with her."

Now what? he thought with an inward moan. Several of his friends had already commented to him that day about Dom's surprising appearance—alone—at the Heath soirée last night. "I had better speak with Dom."

"Yes, Your Grace. A capital idea."

Rutherford hurried down the hall. He quickly grew out of breath. He finally had to stop before reaching the library to draw fresh oxygen into his lungs. It was hard to think clearly now, when he had never needed to be so razor-sharp. What had Fairhaven said? What had he wanted? *What had he known?*

Once, Rutherford had moved heaven and earth to bury the truth, forever. Then he had thought to protect everyone. But he was old now, his life was running out, and he wanted Dom to know. But he did not want him to discover half-truths and lies. Perhaps it was time for him to tell Dom himself.

As Rutherford opened the doors, Dom rose unsteadily to his feet, facing him. He had obviously been waiting for him. He said not a word, not even in greeting. Clearly he was angry.

Rutherford's heart sank. This was what he had always feared—Dom's enmity, his condemnation. "Dom. Caldwell has told me that you have had a caller. Fairhaven. What did he want?"

Dom's smile was brittle. "He wanted money. I refused."

Rutherford did not move. "I see."

"Do you?" Dom stared at him. "He told me the truth."

Rutherford stared. He said roughly, "What did he say? Precisely?"

"He told me that Philip is not my father, goddammit!" Suddenly Dom stood in front of Rutherford, nose to nose with him and furious. "Tell me the truth! You! Surely you know about this! *You* tell me the truth!"

Their gazes connected. Something powerful and timeless surged between them, deeper than love. And suddenly Rutherford was relieved. There was no going backward now. No way to close an open book. Now he had no choice but to tell Dom. And together they would share and keep this secret, avoiding recriminations, avoiding repercussions. Avoiding any and all scandal.

He opened his mouth to speak. But no words came forth. Instead, his body reeled. He could hardly breathe. A huge pressure was building in his head.

In fact, he could hardly stand upright. Rutherford was frightened—but determined, too. He gasped, "Dom, God . . ."

Dom stared at him searchingly.

And when Rutherford did not speak, he whirled, and strode from the room.

"Wait," Rutherford rasped. But Dom was gone.

Rutherford cried out then, consumed with a sudden explosion of pain. As he fell forward, clinging to the door, he realized that this was the end.

He crashed to the floor.

Blackness swirled about him. Death. It loomed over him, a pale and maniacal specter, skeletal arms and hands outstretched.

But Rutherford realized he could not die. Not yet. He hadn't told Dom the truth. And he had one last battle to wage.

He had his family to save.

## Chapter 24

$\mathcal{W}$hen Anne finally returned to Rutherford House, it was eerily quiet.

She herself was disturbed. She had spent the entire morning riding in circles around Hyde Park, oblivious to the curious stares of the other riders and drivers. In fact, she had been hard-pressed not to rudely rebuff a few ladies who had made friendly overtures to her. Anne was so distracted that she could not remember the names of the several women she had chatted with. All she did remember was that she had been urged to call and had been invited to several functions, the dates of which eluded her.

She could not manage a social life now.

She had not slept at all last night. She had finally wept, filled with grief because she had once, so recently, wanted Dom so desperately, because she had loved him so completely. Just a few days ago her dreams had seemed about to verge onto reality. But it had been a horrid deception. Dom had not been falling in love with her; he had not cared. And if Belle and Patrick were right, Dom was plotting to murder her in order to rid himself of an unwanted wife.

But they could not be right. Anne refused to entertain their suspicions.

And Anne tried to ignore her hurt and fear so that

she might be sensible. She must at least accept the fact that *someone* sought to hurt her or even kill her. It had to be Felicity, yet Anne could not fathom how her cousin had gained entry into her rooms so many times. But Felicity had been in the vicinity of each strange happenstance. And Anne had recently learned that she had come to London immediately after Anne had.

A small voice inside of Anne's head urged her to go to Dom and unburden herself. To seek comfort and safety in his arms. Like a centuries-old knight in shining armor, he would catch her would-be assailant, rescuing her from her jeopardy. Unless, of course, the assailant was really he.

Caldwell greeted her in the foyer. The silence felt heavy, threatening—different. Anne shifted uneasily. "Caldwell, is anyone home?"

"Yes, my lady. His Grace is in the library."

Anne had the urge to go to the duke and tell him everything. But he loved Dom deeply, and he would urge her to forgive him this latest betrayal. Surely, though, he would start an investigation immediately into the odd series of mishaps that had occurred. What if Dom was the culprit responsible for the strange events which had happened? What if, for some incomprehensible reason, he sought to frighten her but not harm her? But he had made love to her! No, her imagination was now running wild; she must not heed either Belle's or Patrick's warnings. "And . . . the marquis?"

"He left some time ago. He did not say when he would return."

Anne relaxed slightly. "Please send Belle to me," she said, turning to the stairs.

But Anne did not ascend the sweeping, red-carpeted staircase. She hesitated. Why could she not tell the duke half of the truth? That someone sought to harm her, and that it might very well be Felicity? Anne knew that she was not a good actress. He would immediately see that there was more to the subject than what she was relaying. But she would have to remain firm, deny it, and not breathe a single word of her uncertainty about Dom.

Anne paused before the closed library door. Clearly the duke did not wish to be disturbed.

Anne knocked lightly. When there was no response, Anne decided that he must be asleep. She was disappointed now that she had decided to take him into her confidence.

But Anne felt disturbed. She could not pinpoint why, but she did not like the silence coming from behind that library door. Yet Rutherford was only napping. Anne swiftly decided that she would check on him anyway.

She opened the door and a horrible sight spread out before her. The duke of Rutherford lay prone on his stomach on the floor. He appeared waxen and pale. He appeared lifeless.

But Rutherford was alive. He lay in his bed unmoving, covered in blankets, barely breathing. According to the doctor, he had been the victim of apoplexy.

Anne was holding back her tears with great effort. Caldwell wept silently as he tended the duke now—he had been weeping ever since he had rushed to Anne's side in the library. Belle hovered nearby, her cheeks tear-streaked. A housemaid was stoking a small fire.

"Tell me the truth, Dr. Mansley," Anne said brokenly. "What is the prognosis? Will His Grace live?"

The physician packed up his leather bag. "There is little hope, my lady. Apoplexy is often severe. Sometimes the victim never awakens, living just as you see His Grace now, until he or she wastes away. Other victims of apoplexy do eventually wake up, but cannot move or speak. In which case, recovery of speech and movement is an impossibility. However, these victims are fully conscious, capable of seeing, hearing, of thought, of feeling."

Anne glanced at the duke worriedly. "And?"

"In a very few cases, the victim will awaken and have some capability. He might have limited or distorted speech, and limited or distorted movement in all of his body, or just the upper half. It is very rare, but once in a great while the victim might recover all of his bodily functions, including speech."

"So there is some hope?" Anne said.

"There is very little hope, especially if the duke does not wake up within the next twenty-four hours," the physician said firmly.

Anne went and sat down beside the duke, groping for his hand. It was completely inert. "Thank you, Doctor."

"Do not thank me. I have not done a thing. But I have warned His Grace repeatedly to rest more and drink and smoke less." The doctor sighed. "If he awakens, send for me immediately. I will wish to examine him."

Anne nodded, staring at the duke's face, which seemed old and haggard now as he lay suspended between life and death. She gripped his hand more tightly. "Your Grace, we all need you, we do. Please, wake up, please fight for your life."

But he did not move. His eyelids did not even flutter.

"Your Grace," Anne swallowed, "I know that this is too bold, most brazen, really, but I have to tell you— I have come to love you in these past few years." Tears streaked Anne's cheeks. "You have been so good to me, Your Grace. I thank you for everything." She choked. "Please, please get well."

Caldwell came to stand beside her, his eyes puffy, his nose red, tears running down his face. "We are all praying that you recover, Your Grace," he said hoarsely. "Every single servant and all of the staff, sir.

We are all most fond of you, forgive my impertinence, Your Grace.''

But the Duke of Rutherford did not move. For all intents and purposes, he was dead.

''What happened?'' Dom cried.

Anne tensed as Dom charged into the room. He was unbelievably white as he stared down at his grandfather. ''He has had an apoplexy,'' Anne said harshly.

''Oh, God,'' Dom whispered, still as a stone.

Anne stood up, releasing the duke's hand. She had been chatting with him for more than an hour, hoping for some small response on his part—but there had been nothing. She thought she could feel him slipping away.

Now she moved to the foot of the bed, careful to not even brush Dom with her skirts. He did not look like a killer now.

He was crying. Silently, but the tears had begun running down his cheeks in an endless stream. He walked to his grandfather's side. If he realized Anne was even present now, he gave no sign. ''Grandfather, this is all my fault, I'm sorry!''

Rutherford lay still.

Dom sank down by his hip. He gently brushed a lock of lank white hair off the duke's forehead. ''Oh, God, I am so sorry!'' He choked on a sob. ''How could this be?'' he whispered. ''You are so powerful, so omnipotent—I think that I actually believed you immortal.''

Anne hugged herself, wanting to look away, but she could not. She was weeping silently again.

''I need you,'' Dom whispered. ''You can't leave us now.'' His voice broke.

He brushed his eyes with his sleeve. ''Grandfather, I did not mean to condemn you for deceiving me. I do not know why you did what you did—I assume it was for lack of another heir—but wouldn't a distant cousin have been preferable? Oh, God." He could not continue, choking, breathing harshly.

Anne almost forgot her own dilemma. She wanted to go to Dom and lay her hand upon his shoulder, comforting him. Instead, she remained frozen, gripping her own palms tightly.

"This is all my fault," Dom whispered to his grandfather in great anguish. "I upset you. I did not mean to. Damn Fairhaven!"

Anne wondered what he was talking about.

"I can only assume that you want me to continue this charade. I will, to the best of my ability. Even though I do not understand. Even though I think Fairhaven is dangerous. Perhaps I should have paid him. Perhaps Clarisse will be able to help me understand all of this." He forced a ragged smile. "I have already sent for her."

Rutherford appeared to be carved from stone.

"Perhaps," Dom cried, "nothing matters now!"

"Dom," Anne heard herself whisper.

But he did not hear her. He took his grandfather's cold hands in his. "I am so sorry. I am sorry for everything." Dom leaned forward and kissed his grandfather's forehead. "Don't die. Please don't die." Tears streamed down his face. "I love you very much, Grandfather, and I always have, I always will. Had it not been for you, my childhood would have been so empty and so lonely. You were more of a father to me than Philip ever was." He covered his face with his hands, his shoulders shaking.

Anne laid her palm on his shoulder, weeping.

"Is he any better?" Clarisse asked, standing in the open doorway of the duke's bedchamber.

It was later that night. Clarisse had just arrived. Dom stiffened. "No." He swiveled so he could see his mother, his expression stark. He had been sitting beside his grandfather for a dozen hours. It was black outside. Black and moonless, starless and cold.

Clarisse stared at the duke. "This is a terrible thing," she said slowly. "But he is an old man, Dominick."

Dom got to his feet. "You don't care, do you? I don't know why, I don't know what was between you, but you don't care. So don't pretend that you do!"

Clarisse began to cry. "Why are you speaking to me like this? What have I done? I didn't cause his apoplexy!"

Dom realized how right she was, and he fought for self-control. "I beg your pardon, Mother. Forgive me. I am very upset."

Clarisse nodded, her eyes watery, her mouth trembling. She went to him and cupped his cheek. "There is no reason for us to fight, Dominick. Especially not now."

He closed his eyes briefly. When he opened them he pulled away. "Matthew Fairhaven came here today to blackmail me."

Clarisse gasped. She gripped the bed's poster for support. "Oh, God!"

"You need to know everything," Dom said grimly, his back to the duke. "Fairhaven was far more to Philip than his best friend. He is a young, beautiful man, he appears to have been in love with him."

Clarisse did not move. Her eyes filled with caution. "I know."

"You knew." Dom was stunned, and then he was angry. "Don't you think I might have been told—so I could have been prepared for something like this?"

"I never expected Fairhaven to try to blackmail us."

"He wasn't trying to blackmail us over the issue of his affair with Philip—as that would bring criminal prosecution down on his own head should the authorities get wind of it."

Clarisse hesitated, having grown pale. "Then ... what?"

"He knows the truth," Dom said brutally. "He knows that Philip is not my father, and he has proof. Or"—Dom was grim—"so he claims."

Clarisse walked over to a heavy chair and sat down. "What proof?"

"A letter Philip wrote to you just after he discovered your betrayal." Dom watched her.

"I never received any letter." Clarisse looked up, pleading. "I didn't know that Philip realized. He never let on."

"Fairhaven swears he has this letter, and that it was never mailed." Dom shrugged. "What difference does it make? The will is a fact. The gossip, in conjunction with Fairhaven's share of Philip's fortune and his own-ership of Waverly House, will be enough to give the gossips a field day." He stared. He felt dead inside. "Besides," he said, "it is the truth, isn't it?"

Clarisse inhaled, glancing up, meeting his gaze.

"Mother," Dom said, "is there any chance that Philip is my father?"

She wet her lips. She did not answer.

"Mother?" Dom took a step forward. *"Please."*

Clarisse's eyes filled with tears. "No. He is not your father. When I married Philip, I was already three months pregnant."

"And he did not know?!"

"You came late, thank God. The doctor was told to say that you were early, not unusually so. Philip believed us."

"You paid the doctor to lie. *He* knew."

"No."

"Someone paid the physician off," Dom said harshly.

Clarisse refused to answer.

Dom glanced behind him, at the comatose duke. "Grandfather. I see."

"What do you see?" Clarisse asked anxiously.

"Grandfather paid the doctor for his silence—and his lie. In order to protect you—and Philip—from scandal. How generous he was. To accept me as his own flesh and blood. God." Dom sat down on the bed by the duke's feet and stared at him.

Clarisse also stared, but she was utterly silent.

Dom sighed heavily, then skewered Clarisse with his gaze. "Who is my father?"

Clarisse's eyes widened. "It is irrelevant."

"It is not irrelevant to me," Dom cried.

Clarisse's mouth was pinched, her nostrils flared. "It does not matter. Your real father is dead."

Dom closed his eyes. She was wrong. It did matter. It mattered so much. But what if his father was a groom or a gypsy? Or some notorious lecher? A criminal or a murderer? Perhaps he was better off not knowing.

"What are you going to do now?" Clarisse cried. "Fairhaven must not reveal what he knows!"

Dom looked at his mother. "Although I object on principle, I will meet with Fairhaven immediately, and I will pay him a small fortune to keep his mouth shut and leave the country."

"This will hang over our heads forever," Clarisse said. She was standing. "Dom, I am frightened. He will ask for more money eventually, and the threat of his disclosure will remain with us forever. If this gets out, you and I will both be ruined!"

"If this gets out, then you and I will hold our heads very high and weather the storm," Dom said flatly.

Clarisse stared at him as if he were insane. "*I* will be ruined," she whispered.

Dom stood. "Please, Mother, tears will not help us. Don't cry. You are not ruined yet."

She accepted the handkerchief he offered. She blew her nose gently.

"In any case, there is one bright side to this mess. Fairhaven is a coward, and frightened of what he is doing. I am not sure he will talk, ever," Dom said. "But when I meet with him tomorrow, I will feel him out very carefully."

Clarisse closed her fist around the handkerchief. "If only Fairhaven were dead."

"You do not mean that, Mother."

"Yes, I do. I wish he were dead."

A silence fell between them. "You are very over-wrought and you do not know what you are saying," Dom finally said very firmly. But he was shaken.

Clarisse glanced up at him, dabbing her eyes with the handkerchief. "How can you be so calm when we are going to lose everything?"

Dom was grim. "I am hardly composed."

Clarisse continued as if she had not heard him. "I will never be welcome in society again. And you shall lose the entire dukedom to some fat, stupid, greedy distant cousin."

"That is certainly possible," Dom said without inflection. "If Fairhaven does reveal what he knows."

"I am going to my room," Clarisse said, drying her eyes again. "I need to think."

Dom watched her leave. He sank down on the foot of his grandfather's bed, covering his face with his hands. He realized that he ached for his mother far more than he did for himself. If worst came to worst, he would survive, but he was not sure about Clarisse. However, he would protect her to the best of his ability.

And he did not see Rutherford's fingers twitch, or his eyelids flicker. He did not hear his soft, desperate moan.

Clarisse did not hesitate, even though it was the supper hour. There was far too much at stake.

She ordered the carriage brought around. Within twenty minutes, she was alighting on the pavement in front of Waverly House.

She marched up the wide stone front steps of the limestone mansion, feeling ill. This house had been Philip's. Now it should belong to Dom. Instead, it belonged to Matthew Fairhaven. He deserved to die.

He had kept on the regular staff, Clarisse realized when the butler opened the heavy front door. He failed to hide his surprise, then he bowed. "My lady," he said.

Clarisse wanted to cry. But the tears she could turn on and off so easily were not needed now. "Hendricks, I am here to see Fairhaven. Is he in?"

"Yes, he is about to dine." Hendricks took her calling card and ushered her into the salon. He did not blink an eye at Clarisse's odd and untimely call.

Clarisse shuddered. She had not been inside this house in at least ten years. She had preferred the country, and Philip had stayed in London when he was not traveling abroad. The salon had been redone. She wondered if Philip had made the ghastly changes, or his young man. In any case, she thought the red fabrics too purple, the golds too bright. The carpets were too vibrant, too new. And she wondered where the money had come from for all the beautiful paintings and sculptures. Bitterness flooded her. Clearly, while Philip lived, he and Fairhaven had spent a great deal of time and money on this house and their life together.

Fairhaven paused on the threshold. "Lady St. Georges," he said politely.

She stiffened with revulsion at the sight of him. How beautiful he was. How young. How perfect. And even though he was a man, he made Clarisse feel every single one of her years. He made her feel unwanted and old. Their gazes locked.

Clarisse smiled at him, hating him, even though she

had not ever wanted Philip herself. "At last, we meet. Forgive me for not being overjoyed."

Fairhaven's mask slid away. His face contorted, becoming angry. "Forgive me, madam, for not offering you refreshments or a seat." His eyes blazed.

"I do not want your hospitality," Clarisse shot back.

"I did not think so," he said. "What *do* you want?"

Clarisse stared coldly, although her hands were shaking. "No. The real question is, what do you want? And what do you intend to do?"

"Frightened?"

"Yes," Clarisse admitted, "I am frightened—and angry—and very, very desperate."

"You deserve to suffer."

"What have I ever done to you? I turned my back on your tawdry affair with my husband—ignoring it!" Clarisse exclaimed.

Tears filled Fairhaven's eyes. "You made him miserable. You betrayed him, and Philip hated you. He told me so again and again. I hate you, too."

"And I hated Philip," Clarisse cried. "I had no choice but to marry him—I didn't know what he was and I hated him even then!"

A deadly silence fell between them.

Clarisse forced a smile. "It doesn't matter. He is dead. And I, for one, am glad."

"You bitch," Fairhaven cried, turning white.

Clarisse almost laughed. When she recovered, she said stiffly. "Name your price. I will see that Dominick meets it. "

"There is no price."

Clarisse faltered. "That is hardly funny."

"It was not meant to be funny," Fairhaven said. He was white and his hands were shaking. "You see, I loved Philip. Money is not the issue."

"What is the issue, then?"

Fairhaven wet his lips. "Justice." He swallowed, but held her gaze. "I only want justice."

Clarisse was frozen. "This is absurd."

Fairhaven shook his head. "No. Philip hated you, and he hated Dom. He hated the lie. So I have exposed it."

Clarisse thought that she had misheard. She had to have misheard.

"You see, I have but one ambition, and that is telling the world the truth about you and your son."

# Chapter 25

$\mathcal{A}$nne ate supper alone. Clarisse did not appear, and Anne assumed that she supped in her rooms. Dom remained in the duke's bedchamber as he had all afternoon.

Anne had no appetite, and she quickly finished and retired to her room. Although she desperately wanted to check on Rutherford before bed, knowing Dom was with him prevented her from doing so. But Belle dutifully reported to her as Anne asked her to. According to the maid, there was no change. Rutherford remained unconscious, and Dom had fallen asleep while sitting in the chair he had pulled up beside the bed.

Anne paced her bedroom, clad in a silk nightgown and matching peignoir, her hair in a single long braid. She was so worried about the duke. Already she was grieving as if he had died.

And Dom was worried and grieving, too. But Anne must not think about what he was suffering—she must not.

"Anne, I wish to speak to you."

Anne whirled as Dom walked unannounced and uninvited into her room. "Is the duke . . . ?" She could not continue.

"There has been no change." Dom paused, staring at her grimly. Anne gripped the poster of her bed. What did he want? Apprehension filled Anne. She was acutely aware of the tension cracking in the air between them. Anne tried to compose herself. But it was impossible.

Not when Dom stood just a few feet away from her, staring at her, his gaze closed and unreadable. But he was disheveled, and clearly he had just woken up. His hair was mussed, he was still clad in his riding breeches and muddy boots as he had been earlier, but now he had discarded his jacket and vest and wore only a shirt that was terribly wrinkled and more unbuttoned than closed. Anne was careful not to look at his tanned, hard chest.

And she was instantly, painfully aware of the fact that the peignoir she wore was designed to reveal the gown beneath, for it was closed only by two ribbons. "Perhaps you might have knocked," Anne finally managed, flushed. What did he want? Patrick's and Belle's suspicions flashed through her mind.

He ignored her objection. "Fairhaven came to see me today. He was not just Philip's friend, he was far more. He came to blackmail me."

Anne gaped. She forgot all about her nightclothes. Her mind raced. "He came to blackmail you?" she echoed.

"Yes." Dom spoke as if he were reciting lines he had memorized. "He says that he has proof that I am not Philip's son."

Anne's grip on the poster tightened. "Wh-what! That is absurd!"

Dom's expression did not change. It was carved in stone. "Actually, I have suspected that Philip was not my father for some time now. It is the truth. Clarisse has admitted it."

Anne had to sit down. She chose a chair that was even farther away from Dom than the bed. She did not realize that she was hugging herself. When she lifted her shocked gaze to Dom's, she noticed how tense the muscles in his face were. How strange the light in his eyes. "Who is your father?"

"I do not know. I do not care to know."

Anne was still suspended in a state of disbelief. His words only vaguely penetrated through her shock.

"In any case, I thought you should know of the day's events, as you are my wife, even if you choose not to live with me," Dom said.

Anne jerked, her gaze flying to his, wondering if she had detected a note of bitterness in his tone. But his gaze was hooded. Yet surely he was devastated by this turn of events. Anne herself was close to being devastated. Good God! The ramifications of what Dom was saying began to dawn upon her. He could lose everything. His name, his titles, his wealth, position, and estates. Her pulse raced now with fear. Fear for Dom. Anne did not think of herself.

"You will pay off Fairhaven?"

"Yes. First thing tomorrow."

If Fairhaven were paid off, he would remain silent. Relief swept Anne. Even though she should not be moved by Dom's plight.

He continued to stare at her. Although his eyes were on her face, Anne grew uneasy. She pulled her peignoir closed at the throat and held it that way. His gaze immediately dropped to her white knuckles, making her regret her modesty.

She was aware of being flushed. When his gaze connected with hers again, she saw the knowing light in his eyes. Her stomach lurched. Did he guess that she still found him attractive? Or did he guess something else?

Could he be a killer? No, it was impossible, absurd, despite the fact that he had more motivation than anyone else. What if he knew what she was thinking now—and Patrick and Belle *were* right?

She licked her terribly dry lips. No, he could not know, he could not guess. Her imagination and fear were running away with her again, because it was late and they were alone together. Anne forced a smile to her lips.

Dom's stare became distinctly cold. He did not return her smile.

Anne slowly rose to her feet. She was breathless and far too warm, uncomfortable. Not looking at Dom, knowing he stared at her, she went to the window and tried to open it. It was a moment before she realized that it was locked. Finally, she shoved it open and took a deep breath of cool night air. She could feel Dom's eyes boring holes in her back. Why didn't he leave?

Anne reminded herself that, if Dom truly wanted to kill her, he could have done so long ago. Again it crossed her mind that perhaps he was the culprit, but his intention was only to frighten her. Anne's heart raced. Perhaps he wanted to drive her away from Waverly Hall?

Anne turned to look at him. As she had thought, he was staring at her. What if he were innocent? What if his gravest crime was seducing her without affection? If that were the case, then it was Anne's moral duty to stand by him now, as his entire life crumbled around him.

The silence lengthened and thickened between them. Anne forced herself to speak. "Is there something else?"

"Yes," Dom said flatly. "There is."

Anne suddenly understood.

His gaze moved lower, searing now, past her hand—she still clutched the throat of her peignoir. Anne's nipples were hard and erect and she knew now that he had noticed.

Dom's jaw flexed. Their gazes locked.

Anne's heart beat far too swiftly now. "It is time for you to leave."

"Why?"

Anne lost all of her composure. "What are you thinking! What do you want! You are mad!" she cried.

"Maybe." His mouth curled. "Can't you guess what I want, Anne? What I need?"

"No." It was a refusal, not an answer.

"Come, Anne." His voice turned smoky and seductive. He walked to her. Anne could not move. His hand closed on her fist.

"I w-want you to leave."

His brow lifted. "Really? I think otherwise."

"You think wrongly," Anne gasped.

Their gazes held. "I want to know if you are sorry."

Anne wet her lips. She did not even bother to try to remove her hand from his. But she was trembling—and he stood so close to her that her thigh brushed his knee. "Of course I am sorry."

His smile was twisted. "How sorry?"

She stared. "I beg your pardon?"

His gaze slid down her body. "How sorry are you, Anne? Sorry enough to regret the fact that we are estranged? Sorry enough to change your mind? To comfort me? To invite me to your bed?"

Now Anne tried to jerk her hand free of his, but she only succeeded in making him tighten his grip. His hold on her was almost brutal, and it was uncompromising— she was not going anywhere. And suddenly she was afraid.

He leaned forward; her breasts brushed his bare chest though her silk gown. "Are you sorry enough to offer me the comfort of your body?" he asked, low.

Anne inhaled. The sensation of his skin against her silk-draped nipples, and the sound of his warm, husky tone, sent ripples of shock and excitement through her body. She was a traitor to herself. She was molten, swollen, ready. "Is—is that why you came to my room?" Anne whispered.

His eyes darkened. "No. Yes."

Anne could not speak. He slid his other arm around her waist, drawing her up against him tightly, and holding her there as if his arm were an iron vise.

Anne gasped.

"I want to make love to you, now," Dom said bluntly.

"Don't," Anne whispered. But she was acutely aware of his body, which was hard and aroused and wedged against hers. "Don't." She wasn't at all sure that she meant it.

And he sensed her indecision. His gaze darkened, grew bolder. "One kiss, then," he whispered roughly.

Anne tried to protest, she tried to think. But his mouth took hers abruptly, hungrily. Anne stiffened, overwhelmed by an onslaught of sensation, all engendered by his mouth and body. Yet in the back of her mind there was a soft dangerous, mocking voice: What if it was Dom? What if Dom was the one trying to frighten her—trying to kill her?

He tore his mouth from hers, panting. Anne was panting too. Her lips felt ravished, bruised. Their gazes locked.

"Don't fight me," he said. "I *need* you, Anne."

And suddenly his eyes weren't cold at all, they were hot, naked, and filled with torment. Before Anne could respond, he captured her chin in his hand and fused his mouth roughly to hers a second time.

Anne stood absolutely still. In the back of her mind, the protest sounded, but already it was fading, distant, dying. His desperation was contagious, a conflagration consuming them both. His mouth opened hers. Anne gasped as he shoved his tongue inside, against her gums, her throat. Her hands lifted of their own volition and pressed against his chest—but she did not push him away.

He sensed his victory. Crying out, he slid one palm up, lifting her breast out of its bodice. Dom choked, bending, claiming the distended tip. Anne gasped as he sucked hard, growing dizzy with pleasure and need.

His hands gripped her buttocks through the thin silk gown. Abruptly he pulled her up high and hard against his arousal, so that Anne felt all of him. Every single quivering inch. She whimpered, but the sound was cut off by his frenzied kiss.

And while he kissed her, he pulled up the back of her nightgown, cupping her bare buttocks. Anne gasped. Tears spilled down her cheeks. She slid her hands inside his open shirt, across his chest, then down his flat, tensely drawn stomach. She heard the material rip. Anne did not care, her fingertips delving inside the tight waistband of his breeches. One of her fingers suddenly brushed the ripe tip of his penis.

Dom groaned. His hand clamped on hers, pressing it lower, and he filled her palm.

Anne shook with excitement, maddened by it.

He tore his mouth from hers with a muffled exclamation. Their gazes locked.

An instant later he had lifted her into his arms and was striding to the bed. As Anne's spine touched down, he moved on top of her, parting her thighs. Their chests touched, bare flesh to bare flesh, and their mouths fused hungrily.

Anne gripped his broad shoulders as tightly as she could. A second later he began tugging at his shirt; Anne rained kisses on his jaw and throat, his chest and abdomen as he swiftly tore it from his pants and threw it to the floor. He choked, his hands moving to the fly of his breeches. Anne kissed his navel. "Anne," Dom gasped, his manhood springing free.

Anne dared to touch him again.

Immediately he pushed her down on her back, prodding her thighs apart, his face strained. Anne gasped as he drove himself into her.

His penetration almost sent her crashing into the headboard of the bed. But Anne did not care. Eyes closed, she clung to him, arching wildly to meet him, allowing him to drive deep and deeper still, again and again. Their bodies slapped, slick and wet. The bed bumped the wall. He gripped her buttocks, raising her up. Plunging even more deeply. Anne's nails raked down his back. A wild, animal sound came from deep inside her chest. And then Anne cried out as a huge wave of almost painful pleasure crashed over her, pounding into her.

He cried out as well, his mouth against her throat, buried deep inside of her, convulsing there and spewing wet heat inside her womb.

They lay with limbs entwined, recovering their breaths. And suddenly Anne was capable of thought. Suddenly Anne tensed, shocked, agonizingly aware of the man lying beside her, one leg over both of hers, holding her loosely in the circle of his arms.

"Anne?" Dom whispered.

Anne sat up, shoving free of his embrace. She stared down at him out of wide eyes.

And her horror must have showed. Dom's relaxed, tender expression changed immediately. He also sat up, his golden eyes wary, evasive.

Anne immediately looked away, fumbling with her bodice, which had somehow become torn, pulling it up, holding it together. Her hands were beginning to shake. Oh, God. *What had she done?*

"Anne," he said tersely. And he touched her back.

"Don't!" Anne cried, leaping off of the bed. She backed away from it, staring at him, repulsed with herself, with what she had done. How could she have made love to him now, after all that had happened, after he had deceived her again? How?

Dom's jaw tightened. "I see."

"No." She swallowed, breathing heavily again. This man had used her, betraying her. Yet she had allowed him to use her again. And he might even harbor malice toward her. . . . Oh, God.

But Anne could not calm herself. Her breathing was harsh and loud. Her heart was trying to wing its way right out of her chest.

Dom levered himself off of the bed. "Having second thoughts?" he mocked. His tone was nasty, a tone she had never heard him use before. Anne stared. Facing her, his eyes holding hers, he yanked his breeches closed and buttoned them.

Anne looked away, coloring in spite of what they had just done.

Dom bent and reached for his torn shirt, then held it loosely in his hand. There were flecks of blood on it. Anne's eyes widened. Had she done that? She glanced at her fingernails, trembling.

His smile was tight, angry. "That's right, Anne. My blood, your hands."

Anne swallowed a cry of distress. Their gazes connected suddenly, and Anne did not have the power to look away.

His mouth curled into what might have been a leer. "Play the prude with the world if you will, but we both know the truth, don't we?"

She inhaled. His words were meant to hurt, and they did.

"But don't *ever* play the prude with me."

Anne paled.

He was openly furious. He started toward her. Anne flinched, and that made him even angrier. Abruptly, he turned and stormed out of the room.

\*       \*       \*

Dom was still angry the following morning. He had never been angrier. And he was far more furious with Anne than he was with anyone or anything else. For some stupid, insane reason, he felt that if Anne were loyal to him now, he could withstand anything.

But she wasn't loyal to him, and never mind that he had abused her in the past. She wanted his body, that was very clear, but did not give a damn for all he was suffering now. He needed her, and not just physically, although that would have to do. Damn her.

Dom ignored the vast breakfast that had been laid out on the table before him by his staff in an effort to cheer or entice him. Caldwell hovered nearby, only leaving to answer the front door. Sipping steaming black tea, Dom was informed that Lord Blake was calling. Dom shoved the porcelain cup aside. "Send him in," he said curtly.

A moment later Blake appeared, immaculate in pale trousers and a dark morning coat, his blue eyes filled with worry. "Dom, good morning. No, don't get up."

Dom sank back down in his chair at the head of the gleaming oak breakfast table. "Have a bite, Blake."

"I've already eaten." Blake sat down beside Dom. "You're up late today."

Dom did not reply. He had not slept a wink all night, in spite of the explosion of passion with Anne—or because of it. But he had finally fallen asleep after the sunrise. He was exhausted. And his first waking action had been to look in on the duke.

Still dazed and unfocused, Dom had been deluded into thinking that the duke was actually trying to open his eyes. But once he had fully awoken, he had realized that there was no change at all in his grandfather's condition.

"How is the duke?" Blake asked with real concern, as if reading his thoughts. But by now word of the duke's apoplexy was all over town.

"There has been no change."

"I am sorry," Blake said somberly. "Very sorry."

Dom managed to meet his friend's gaze. "So am I."

Blake hesitated. "Dom, I hate to bring up an unpleasant topic when you are in this situation. But there is something you must know."

Dom tensed. He knew what was coming. But he could not brace himself adequately.

Blake took his silence as encouragement to proceed. "There is a ghastly rumor flying about town."

Dom poured himself another cup of tea. Waiting. Caldwell immediately appeared at his elbow. "My lord, please, let me!"

Dom relinquished the silver teapot to the butler. "Go on," he said grimly.

"I don't know who started such nasty gossip, but I hope you wring his neck," Blake said. His smile was forced. "If you do not, I certainly shall."

Dom said nothing, staring at his hands.

"The gossip is that you are not Philip St. Georges's son," Blake said, "and therefore not the real heir to the dukedom."

"It's true."

Blake was accepting a cup of tea from Caldwell. He started, tea splashing everywhere, but if it burned his strong, tanned hand, he did not appear to notice. Eyes wide, face white, he said, "What?"

"It's true."

Blake stared in absolute shock.

Dom rose to his feet. "It's no rumor, Blake. I am not a St. Georges. Of course"—his smile was bitter—"I have only learned this astonishing fact recently myself."

"Oh my God," was all Blake could manage.

"Unfortunately, I do not think He gives a damn." Dom paced the huge arched window which looked out on the rioting gardens behind Rutherford House, gardens planted by a woman he had thought to be his grandmother, the Duchess Sarah.

Blake also stood up. "Dom, are you positive about this? There is no mistake?"

"None."

"But surely you will refute this?" Blake finally said to Dom's back.

Dom turned. "If Fairhaven truly has proof, which he claims, my refuting this would be costly and pointless."

"Dom, you will lose everything if you do not fight this," he warned.

"I am not a very good liar. In fact, I am a damned poor one." Dom managed a shrug. "I have an appointment with a solicitor. One of the best in town. Let me see what he says, before I decide upon any course of action."

Their gazes locked. "Christ," Blake said.

"Yes," Dom agreed.

Blake raked a hand though his curly dark hair. "Well, you will not lose my friendship."

Dom forced a smile. "Thank you. But I did not think that I would."

Blake smiled back. Then his eyes brightened. "I just realized something. You won't lose everything. You won't lose Waverly Hall."

Dom's gaze locked with his. "No. I won't lose the Hall. Thank God for Rutherford's trust," he said flatly. A moment later, he added, with open bitterness, "Thank God for Anne."

Anne had no intention of going downstairs for breakfast. She remained in bed, trying not to think, unable to avoid her own thoughts, filled with self-recrimination. To make matters worse, she could not rid herself of Dom's image as he had last appeared before he had left her room so furiously. He had been both angry and mocking, and somehow that was both hurtful and distressing to Anne.

It was as if she were the one behaving wrongfully, Anne thought, when that was not at all true.

Anne had taken a small breakfast in bed. Finally she could avoid the day no longer. Anne slid from the bed, ringing for Belle. She was wearing a flannel nightgown which buttoned up to her chin; nevertheless, just in case Dom decided to pay her another unwelcome visit, she donned a matching flannel robe, one as modest and as ugly.

Belle entered the room. "Mum?" She was smiling and cheerful. Belle had always had a pleasing disposition, but Anne thought that she was far happier these past few weeks than before.

"Will you draw my bath, Belle?" Anne asked. As Belle complied, Anne followed her at a leisurely pace, crossing her bedchamber. She was about to enter her dressing room, when Belle raced out of it. Her face was white, and tears were spilling down her cheeks.

Anne paused. Dread swept through her. "Belle, what is wrong? What has happened?"

"Don't go in there, mum—do not!" Belle choked.

Anne pushed past the little abigail, and shoved open her boudoir door. She gasped.

The nightgown and peignoir she had worn last night while making love to Dom lay in a pile on the carpeted floor—ripped into shreds.

## Chapter 26

*A*nne continued to stare at the pile of her shredded clothing. No! Surely Dom had not crept into her room last night, while she slept, and violated her belongings this way. For if he had, then he was insane. If he had, then he hated her viciously—murderously. If he had, Belle and Patrick were right.

"My lady?" Belle asked fearfully.

Anne tried to think. But she was too frightened to think of anything except that when Dom had left her last night he had been furious at her for her open rejection of him and her revulsion at what had happened. But had he been furious enough to do this?

And if he had, was this a single, isolated incident?

"What are you going to do?" Belle cried.

Anne jerked out of her frightened reverie. "It can't be Dom, Belle, oh God, it can't!" Anyone but Dom, she found herself praying. Anyone else!

"My lady, you said *yourself* that all the evidence points to him!"

But Anne had been parroting Patrick. Patrick! She had not seen him in days—she needed to see him now. God, she did!

"Help me dress," Anne snapped. "I will bathe later." It wasn't really necessary anyway, because Anne had bathed last night.

Belle rushed to produce Anne's underclothes. "You are going to Lord Collins?" she asked as Anne shimmied into her drawers.

Anne pulled on a thin chemise and a whalebone corset and turned so Belle could lace her up. "Yes."

"If His Lordship finds out, he will be enraged," Belle warned, yanking on the corset strings.

Anne gasped. "That's too tight." As Belle loosened the stays, Anne realized that she must be very cautious, for Belle was right. Anne did not want to do anything now to attract Dom's attention. "I must make certain, then, that he does not find out," Anne said grimly. And strangely enough, she felt guilty for planning to meet Patrick. But Patrick was her cousin and her friend, and she was hardly betraying Dom by going to Patrick now—even though Dom had forbidden her any contact with her cousin.

Belle held up a dark green gown. "Will this do?"

Anne nodded, then saw that the gown was very fashionable. "No, get me the black bombazine."

"Again?" Belle shook her head, but returned to the closet.

"Your maid has far better taste than you."

Anne whirled, aghast.

Dom leaned against the doorjamb of her boudoir, staring at her. His gaze dropped to the full swell of her breasts, pushed up and out by her corset, then lower, to her lace-trimmed drawers.

Anne turned, grabbed the first thing she saw hanging in the closet, and pressed the dress to her bosom. "This is insufferable," she ground out, flaming now. "Last night you failed to knock and—"

"I knocked. I knocked several times. But the two of you were so caught up in your conversation that neither one of you heard me," Dom said flatly.

Anne became still. Her breathing was shallow and

harsh. And dammit, her corset was too tight—she was feeling dizzy and faint. How much had he heard?

Anne lost all of her color again. She darted a fast glance down, but the pile of shredded nightclothes was mostly out of sight, behind her and partially concealed by the low ottoman in front of her dressing table. Anne shifted so that she blocked Dom's view of the evidence entirely.

Her wide gaze lifted, met Dom's.

"What are you up to, Anne?"

"Nothing."

"Then what are you hiding? You look as guilty as all sin."

Anne shifted nervously. "I have nothing to hide." She managed a stiff smile. But her gaze, of its own accord, dropped to the pile of ruined clothes.

Dom's eyes followed hers. Suddenly he stepped forward, forcing her backward. He stared at her shredded nightgown.

Anne's heart was palpitating dangerously. He looked up. Their gazes met.

Anne forced the words out hoarsely. "Did ... did you do that?"

He studied her for an endless amount of time. "No. I most certainly did not," he ground out.

Anne wanted to believe him. But who else could have possibly done such a thing?

Dom turned to Belle, who stood motionless behind Anne. "I wish to speak with my wife privately."

Belle did not move to leave. She turned and glanced at Anne.

Anne's heart skipped a beat. "Whatever you wish to say, you may say it in front of Belle," she croaked.

Dom's eyes darkened. "But I don't want to speak in front of your maid, Anne."

Anne could not think of a suitable reply.

"What's wrong? Afraid to be alone with me? Don't

you trust yourself?'' His regard was frankly insulting. ''Or don't you believe me when I said I didn't do that.''

Anne followed his gaze to the torn nightgown. She did not want to provoke him, even though he was trying to provoke her. ''Belle, go.'' When Belle hesitated, she added softly, ''It is all right.''

When Belle had left, Dom exploded. He turned, slammed her boudoir door shut, trapping them together in the small, lushly appointed space of her dressing room. Anne was panting. He stalked forward and towered over her. ''What the hell is going on?'' he roared.

She cringed.

''The two of you act like you are scared witless of me!''

Anne managed to shake her head.

''Anne!'' he barked. ''Because of that?'' He gestured at the shredded nightclothes.

She jerked. To her horror, a tear slipped from her eyes. She dared not respond.

''Oh, God,'' Dom said. He reached out and caught the tear on the pad of his thumb in an incredibly tender gesture. Then his hand wrapped around her neck.

Anne froze.

Dom bent toward her and brushed her mouth with his.

Anne remained rigid.

Dom's eyes darkened and he released her. ''Damn you!''

Anne backed away, her heart banging so hard that it was hurtful. Sweat drenched her bare skin beneath her underclothes. If only she could read this man's mind.

Dom cursed again, his eyes glued to hers. ''Just what is it that you think I'm going to do, Anne? You act like you think I'm going to hurt you. I had nothing to do with those clothes.''

She shook her head. She could not speak. Her knees

were buckling. Somehow she remained standing upright.

Dom reached angrily inside the breast pocket of his jacket. Anne's eyes widened at the long, flat velvet jeweler's box he extended toward her. "Take it," he snapped.

A hundred thoughts raced around in Anne's head. Oh, God. Was she wrong? Had he come to apologize for last night, and to give her a gift—a token of his love? Instead of coming to harm her? But one look at Dom's dark, angry countenance chased all such fanciful thoughts away. Apprehensively, Anne took the box, but she did not open it. "What is this?"

"Something for you to wear tonight. Open it."

"Tonight? Where are we going tonight?" she asked, both incredulous and fearful at once.

"To the Harding ball."

Anne gasped. "Dom! Are you mad? Your grandfather is ill!"

"On the contrary, I am perfectly sane, and well aware of Rutherford's condition. Circumstances dictate that we must attend. Please open the box." It was hardly a suggestion.

Horrified that he would insist that she attend the ball with him, Anne obeyed. She stared dismally down at a triple-tiered necklace of rubies and diamonds. The small fortune lay heavily in her palm.

"Do you like it?" He asked quietly.

She lifted moist eyes to his. And found herself incapable of lying. "No. Under different circumstances, perhaps." She could not continue.

"But you have created these circumstances, Anne," he said smoothly.

"No." Anne shook her head.

"You insist on estrangement, not I."

She stared at him. "You betrayed me."

"Once again, I tell you I did not seduce you in order to regain Waverly Hall," he snapped.

Anne almost hesitated. Instead, she pushed out her hand. "I don't want this."

"But it is yours. You are the marchioness of Waverly, and you have appearances to keep." He reached inside his breast pocket, producing another, smaller version of the same jeweler's box. "Matching earrings. Wear your hair up." He turned to go, then paused. "You do have something appropriate to wear?"

She was becoming angry. "You mean an evening gown, I presume?"

"Yes. I mean an evening gown. That is to say, I mean something fashionable and elegant—and not black," he snapped.

"I do not want to go to the ball," Anne said.

"But I did not ask you what you wanted, Anne," Dom returned coldly.

"Why are you doing this?" Annie cried.

"Why am I doing what? Why am I giving you a king's ransom in jewels? Why am I insisting that you wear them—and attend the most important ball of the Season with me?" His gaze bored into her. "Four years ago, I gave you my name. For better or worse. Well, now it's worse. Be ready at nine."

Anne stared at his cold, handsome face, clutching the necklace so tightly that the stones cut her palm. "As you wish," she finally said.

He stared, some of his anger dying, his gaze enigmatic. Then he wheeled and started away, only to pause in the center of her bedroom. "I suggest that you prepare yourself," he warned.

"I . . . I do not understand."

"Fairhaven has told the world that I am an illegitimate bastard."

Anne stared.

"They will try to cut me to pieces—and perhaps you as well." Dom turned and crossed the room.

Anne stared after him. Anguish rose up, flooding her. Too well, she recalled the cruelty of the gossips, but this time, Dom would be their target, not herself. This time, her heart went out to him, achingly, as if her suspicions and his betrayal had never existed. "Don't do this," she whispered. But now she understood why they both had to attend the ball.

He was at the door. Not facing her, he said, low, "I have no choice."

"Is this a matter of pride?"

"Yes," he said. And he looked over his rigid shoulder at her with his piercing golden eyes. "For that is all that I have left."

Taking no chances, Anne left her driver and brougham on Oxford Street, ostensibly to shop at a milliner's. Instead, she slipped out of the back door, leaving Belle inside to cover for her. She quickly hailed a hansom. Ten minutes later the hired conveyance was rolling through Hyde Park.

Anne knocked smartly on the door. "Halt, driver."

The coach stopped.

Anne opened the door. Outside, the sky was an azure blue, and it was a merry day. She watched two fashionably dressed ladies riding sidesaddle past her halted hansom, their grooms behind them, chatting happily with one another. She could hear the rumble of an approaching carriage, the cheerful chirping of a blue jay somewhere above her, and the laughter of children not far away.

Anne was wearing a black hat with an opaque veil so that no one could see her face and identify her no matter how they might try. Anxiously, she scanned the visible length of the riding trail, and the parkland beyond it. A pair of riders were approaching at a rapid trot. Relief made Anne slump. A moment later she waved furiously.

And Patrick was waiting, as had been arranged. He slid off his hack, leaving the reins with the groom he had been riding with, and rushed to her cab and stepped inside. Anne slammed the door closed behind him.

Patrick sat on the seat opposite her. "Anne?" He asked, his expression very grave.

Anne blinked to recover her composure. She began removing the pins from her hat. Carefully she took it off and laid it on the seat beside her. She lifted her blue eyes to his.

"What has happened?" he asked anxiously, reaching for her gloved hands.

"I am frightened, Patrick," Anne said unsteadily. "Oh, God!"

He pulled her forward, off the seat and into his arms.

Anne allowed him to embrace her, laying her cheek against his red silk cravat. He stroked his hand over her hair. Anne closed her eyes.

But she was not comforted by his embrace, as she had expected to be. Instead, she felt guilty for allowing him such a form of intimacy, and oddly enough, she was somewhat uneasy being alone with him now.

Patrick slid his hand around to her face. He tilted it upward. Anne started.

"Let me help you, Anne," he whispered.

Shocked, Anne saw the fierce light in his eyes—and realized he was about to kiss her. She had not come to the park for that. She tried to draw away, opened her mouth to protest, but Patrick's grip was unyielding, and his mouth swallowed her words.

It was not a chaste kiss. His lips molded hers, then swiftly forced her mouth open. Anne choked when his tongue touched hers.

Dom had kissed her much the same way, and even more thoroughly, more times than she could ever count, but with Dom, she had found it infinitely exciting, and his kisses had sent her body into instant and feverish frenzy. She felt no such attraction for Patrick. In fact, his kiss was rather repulsive. She loved him, but as she would a brother.

Anne finally managed to push him away. Immediately she slid back to her own seat, across from him. She was panting, one gloved hand on her breast. "What are you doing!" she exclaimed.

He stared at her. Anne watched anger fill his eyes. "You let him kiss you, don't you?"

Anne became very uneasy. "Patrick, Dom is my husband."

"Dom is a fraud."

Anne stared.

"He is an impostor, a nobody," Patrick said harshly.

"And does that please you?" Anne asked.

"You defend him now?" Patrick cried. "He betrayed you terribly, not once but twice. And still you let him kiss you. Before, perhaps, I could understand. But now that the truth is out, I do not understand at all!"

Anger flared in her own breast. "The fact that Philip was not Dom's father changes very little—in my eyes. And what Dom and I do privately is not your affair."

He stared, and Anne watched the play of conflicting emotions on his face, in his eyes. His tone softened. "I'm sorry. I only want to help you. Anne, by now you know that I—"

"No!" She held up both hands, forced a smile. She was beginning to feel sick inside. "I am married to Dom. It is not a good marriage, but divorce is out of the question, and I will be married to him until one of us dies." The moment she finished, she paled, regretting her choice of words.

Patrick stared. "Until someone dies," he echoed softly.

Anne started. Suddenly the hansom felt far too small, the air stuffy and too warm. But Anne did not feel capable of reaching across the interior space to shove open a window.

"Is he still trying to hurt you?" Patrick asked.

"No!" She swallowed. "I'm not sure." She wet her lips. "Oh, God, I do not know what to think."

"Tell me what is happening, Anne," Patrick said urgently.

Anne complied. She told Patrick about her torn night-clothes, careful to omit the significance, though, of those clothes and that night.

"Anne, you cannot go back to Rutherford House," Patrick said flatly.

"I must."

"Are you mad?"

"No. I asked for a separate residence, but Dom refused. He insists that we live together." She looked away. His gaze was far too piercing.

"And what else does he insist upon?" Patrick asked harshly.

Anne jerked, meeting Patrick's angry gaze. She knew she did not have to answer him, but she did, carefully. "Patrick, I am doing my very best to withstand a very difficult situation. I am only one woman, one hardly perfect. What is it you want of me?"

"I don't want you hurt by him again. He is not good enough for you, Anne, he was never good enough for you, and now that we know that he is a bastard—"

"I came here for help, not accusations and recriminations," Anne said far more sharply than she intended, cutting him off.

He reached out and took her hands again. Anne wanted to withdraw them, but one look at his rigid face decided her against it. Yet she was frightened now, dismayed ... and sad. What had happened? For four aching years, Patrick had been her very best friend, her dear and cherished friend, her sole confidant. But suddenly that had changed. Suddenly Anne was filled with wariness. And how was it that she had never noticed his animosity toward Dom before? "Patrick, you are my best friend," she said. "I need you now. I have no one else to talk to."

"And I am here for you, Anne, always," Patrick said earnestly. Then, "You must leave Rutherford House. No matter what Dom says. You owe him nothing, Anne. I will help you run away."

On the surface, Patrick was right and Anne knew it. She owed Dom little after all that he had done. "I cannot run away like some common woman," Anne said softly. "I just cannot do that."

Patrick was silent. Then, "What will you do when Dom loses his name, his titles, his estates?"

"What are you suggesting? Nothing will change. Not for me. Until he gives me permission to live separately, I will go wherever he goes."

"Christ," Patrick flared. "That man is a fraud. He is a goddamned bastard! Perhaps the spawn of a stable boy, Anne! And still you will stay with him?"

Anne yanked her hands from his. "I do not have a choice." But she was shaking with anger now. "You know, Patrick, you are being very small-minded. I do not care who Dom's father is. If Dom had not betrayed me in Scotland—if he were innocent of my suspicions—I would forgive him those four years."

Patrick gaped. "One would almost think that you are still in love with him."

"No. That is ridiculous."

"Tell me something, Anne. What if you discovered that Dom's real father was a thief—or a murderer?"

Anne's eyes widened. "That . . . is unlikely."

"Is it?" Patrick was openly mocking. "Given all that is happening, is it really so unlikely?"

Anne opened her mouth—and shut it. She was sweating.

"And who knows what a man of such birth is capable of?" He paused dramatically. "So you will stay, warm his bed—and allow him to choose when, where, and how he kills you?"

Anne cried out.

"Will you sleep with him tonight, Anne?" Patrick accused. "And what if he grows tired of this cat-and-mouse game? What if, while he is loving you, he decides to be done with it? It would be very easy for a man to place his hands around his lover's neck, while she is consumed with passion, and squeeze . . . and squeeze . . . and squeeze."

Anne could not move. She was so sickened by his graphic words—words which described the most horrifying, the most terrifying, possibility—that when she could move, she turned and rammed the window open.

"Anne, you must face it. Dom is no highborn aristocrat. He is not the heir to Rutherford. He is a common lowly bastard, a total fraud, and he never wanted you in the first place. He does not want you now. Except, of course, the way all men want any woman."

Anne was so stricken with hurt that she clapped her hands over her ears.

But Patrick pulled them off. "He has been using you since he returned home, and he will continue to use you as long as it pleases him." His frightfully fierce blue gaze held hers. "And then, when the time is right, he will do away with you, Anne. Face it. You may love Dom, but he doesn't love you. *He wants you dead.*"

## Chapter 27

*T*hey had to wait their turn to drive up to the front steps of Harding House and alight.

Dozens of carriages snaked around the block, also awaiting their turns. The night was foggy and that peculiar shade of yellow which can only be caused by London streetlights. Inside the Waverly coach, Anne sat stiffly beside Dom, careful that her taffeta skirts did not touch his legs or any other portion of his body. She pretended to be preoccupied with watching one group of guests after another tromping up the pale limestone steps guarded by two ferocious stone lions and entering though the open, oversize front doors of the earl's stately mansion.

Dom was also silent.

Their turn finally came. The Waverly coach inched up to the broad staircase. The two liveried footmen leapt off the back of the coach and swiftly opened the carriage doors. Anne rose, accepted one of the footmen's hands, and stepped down onto the sidewalk. A moment later Dom stood beside her in his long black tailcoat and black trousers. "We will leave early, at midnight," he instructed.

He turned to Anne, his gaze totally shuttered, and, very formally, he extended his arm. Anne took it, daring to stare openly up at him. He was far more than handsome in his evening clothes. He exuded power and he exuded masculinity. He was the epitome of elegance. No one, looking at him, would ever think him anything but an exalted aristocrat. Until now.

Anne shut off her thoughts. They climbed the stone steps briskly, Anne's navy skirts trailing after her. Not for the first time, she raised one gloved hand to her throat and fingered the rubies and diamonds there.

They were ushered into a spacious foyer. White marble floors slid away to gold-painted walls, and a high-domed ceiling was above their heads. Anne was divested of her wrap, a white boa. She was rigid with tension, and acutely aware of it. Coming to the Harding ball, given all the circumstances of their life, was sheer madness.

She realized that Dom was staring at her, and that she was fingering the necklace again. She dropped her hand.

Dom still stared. She could not decipher his gaze. But she began to flush. Secluded as she had been in the country her entire life, she had never worn an evening gown like this before. The navy taffeta was iridescent. It was almost purple in color, the effect at once dramatic and flattering, contrasting sharply with Anne's pale, porcelain skin, yet complementing her blue-black hair. The bodice was not only tightly fitted; Belle had insisted on taking an entire extra inch off of Anne's waist when tying the stays of her corset. A dozen ivory bones held the bodice up, for the sleeves were for effect only, being two mere scraps of blue taffeta that hung low on Anne's upper arms. The gown was exceedingly low-cut. Horizontal panels of taffeta covered her bosom tightly, showcasing her breasts, vividly contrasting the smooth, seamless bodice beneath.

Anne's skirts were full. Wider horizontal panels of navy chiffon alternated with the taffeta. The gown's hem was flounced.

Anne was also wearing ivory satin gloves, which

covered her entire forearms and her elbows. Her evening shoes were also ivory satin, but buckled with gold.

Anne stood absolutely motionless while Dom stared at her. His gaze moved over her face, the necklace, her décolletage, to her narrow, nipped-in waist, and then the nearly sheer panels of chiffon. He stared a moment longer and she shifted nervously, wondering if he was mistaking the ivory satin petticoat she wore for a glimpse of her own flesh. The ivory tone matched her skin's color more precisely than she would have liked.

Anne felt her cheeks burning. Worse, she was afraid to breathe, afraid she might breathe herself right out of her bodice. And mostly she was dismayed because the woman inside of herself still craved Dom's admiration.

His gaze lifted to hers. "I approve," was all he said.

Anne swallowed, her pulse racing. There had been a wealth of meaning in those three simple words, and she dared not dwell upon it.

Anne allowed him to lead her through the foyer and to the ballroom. He guided her with his fingertips at her waist. Anne was acutely aware of his touch, as light as it was.

He was the most fascinating man she knew, but did she really know him? She would be a fool if she allowed her heart to rule her head. Especially tonight. Tonight, when they were surrounded by five hundred curious guests, he needed her support, and Anne was morally obligated to give it. But she was afraid of the intimacy such support would engender—she wasn't really afraid of him—she was afraid of herself. Anne's steps faltered; she tripped.

He caught her instantly. His arm locked around her waist. For the span of several heartbeats, Anne was pressed helplessly to his side. The contact was like a match being struck to tinder. Anne's blood raced. Her body tightened. Midnight memories assaulted her. Anne's gaze riveted to his.

"Don't be so frightened," he said, and his tone was no longer cold or remote. "It is me they wish to chew up and expectorate, not you."

Anne stared at his face, thinking that Belle and Patrick were wrong. And surely he hadn't shredded her nightclothes. Her gaze searched his. "It doesn't matter what they think," she finally said.

"No? That is easy for you to say. You have spent your entire life in the country. I have business in town, but soon we shall see if anyone wishes to traffick with me." He hesitated.

"What is it?" Anne asked.

His palm tightened on her waist. "Thus far, three distant cousins have come forth to claim the *throne*. Their claims are far more legitimate than mine. My solicitor is convinced that I will be able to retain several small, ignominious estates, which will barely sustain us. But the bulk of the Rutherford holdings are now up for grabs, and there is nothing I can do to prevent one of the claimants from eventually taking it all."

Reality slipped away. It was just her and Dom now, and the horrible fact that Philip was not his biological father. She stared into his eyes, aching for him. She almost touched his cheek. "It doesn't matter." She was vehement.

"No?" He lifted a brow, his tone was mocking.

There was so much that she wanted to say. She wanted to say that, if he loved her, she would go anywhere with him—and be anything. Anne managed to tear her gaze from his. She was very close to giving in to her heart, to giving in to him. She could not continue like this for much longer. Frightened, hurt, desperate, so in love—so terribly torn.

Anne wet her lips, took a deep breath, than regretted it. But a quick glance assured her that she was intact. Lifting her eyes, she saw Dom smiling at her—really smiling, amused. She began to blush.

"We may be estranged, but you are still beautiful, and your naïveté is adorable," he said, and before Anne could object, he bent and kissed her in the small sensitive spot where her jaw joined her ear. He pulled away. Anne shivered, a delicious tingling sensation flooding her, weakening her limbs.

He held out his arm. "Shall we join the wolves?"

Anne nodded, tucking her gloved hand in his elbow.

They walked down three short marble steps into the ballroom, which was half-full already. Heads swiveled, turning. Voices stopped. Then the whispers began.

Anne looked around and saw one wide-eyed face after another, staring at her and Dom. Male and female, young and old. Then, embarrassed, the lords and their ladies quickly looked away. Hot color stained Anne's cheeks.

She stole a glance at Dom. His face was impassive, his head high. The sapphire studs on his shirtfront caught the light from the numerous chandeliers overhead. He halted and stole two flutes of champagne off a tray held by a passing waiter. "Cheerio," he murmured.

Anne forced herself to take a sip. But her gaze wandered. She had never been to a ball before. Never had she seen so many beautifully dressed women. Never had she seen so much fabulous jewelry. She barely looked at the men. And the ballroom itself was so impressive. Huge, potted palms were in all the corners of the room. Where the orchestra played, more palms had been erected, and numerous ferns. The walls of the room were covered in a soft gold fabric. Oversize portraits and landscapes adorned them, and a hundred red velvet chairs were lined up beneath them.

The ceiling was high, vaulted. Two dozen plaster pillars appeared to support it. The base of each pillar featured a biblical story with small carved figurines and objects. Anne smiled at the sight of Noah's ark. The top of each pillar was graced by trumpet-blowing angels.

Anne shifted her gaze to the crowd. Everyone seemed to know everyone else. Greetings rang out, as did laughter and raucous conversation. But no one approached her and Dom. People still remarked them, though, and stared. Her gaze turned to his. He was staring at the crowd, too.

Anne had caught him unaware. In spite of his unreadable expression, there were two faint spots of pink high up on his cheekbones.

He was as humiliated as she. Anne's heart broke.

His gaze whipped to hers. And remained that way.

"They are all horrid. Their conduct is unforgivable."

"Is it?"

"Of course it is!"

"Once, you told me that my conduct was unforgivable." His gaze was searching.

Anne gripped her flute more tightly. "Yes, I did."

"If you cannot forgive me the error of my ways, why should you expect others to forgive me the equally atrocious error of fraud?"

Anne wet her lips. She scrambled for an answer. "You were responsible for what you did to me—but you are not responsible now for the fact of your parentage."

He refused to release her gaze. "I want your forgiveness, Anne. I want your forgiveness for *everything*."

Anne could not speak. Quickly she sipped her champagne. When she glanced at him again, his golden gaze was very frank and very male. "You have the prettiest pink blush," he murmured.

"Don't," she heard herself say.

"Why?" He challenged.

Anne tried to think. Tonight felt like a magical fairy tale, and Anne recognized the jeopardy that she was in. Forgetting, forgiveness, both were far too dangerous.

She could not allow passion to rule her again. "We cannot go backward," she said huskily.

"Why not? You expect others to be generous with me. But you are my wife. I want *your* generosity, Anne. To hell with everyone else." His eyes flashed.

Anne wanted to plug up her ears, to run away. "You are making me feel as if I was the one who wronged you."

"Good."

Their gazes locked. Anne could not look away.

Dom was grim. "Anne, I am sorry. I am sorry for everything. What do I have to do to earn your forgiveness?"

Anne found it difficult to breathe. Her pulse pounded in her ears. "It is not my forgiveness which you must earn, Dom. It is my trust."

He stared.

Anne looked around, and saw numerous faces staring at them. A silence built between them. She stole a glance at Dom and saw how tight his jaw was, how dark his eyes. Again, she felt as if she were wronging him, which was insane.

"Very well, Anne," Dom finally said.

She exhaled, their gazes meeting. When he did not speak, she glanced around at the onlookers half-turned their way with barely disguised curiosity. She said, low, "Is *anyone* going to speak with us?"

"I doubt it. Being a bastard while parading as a ducal heir is quite unforgivable."

"So what shall we do?"

"Ignore them. Pretend we do not care." His tone dropped seductively. "Pretend that we are madly in love."

Anne froze. Dom's gaze bored into hers. "I . . . I do not think that is such a good idea."

"Why not?" He took her glass from her hand and

gave it and his to a passing waiter. "Dance with me," he said. It was not a question.

Nor was Anne given a chance to respond, either. Dom led her to the dance floor and took her into his arms. The orchestra was playing the waltz, which had recently been approved by the queen. And suddenly Anne was gliding across the parquet floor, and she felt as if she were dancing on air.

Anne was dazed. Dom's arms were strong, his steps sure. She had only danced one or two times in her life, and it had never been like this. In an incredible ballroom, dressed and bejeweled like a princess, in the strong, capable arms of a man like Dom.

Dom smiled down at her. His eyes were warm. Anne's heart skipped a beat. And he whisked her around and around. He was a superb dancer. Lightfooted, graceful, confident. Anne did not have to know the steps of the waltz, or do anything other than allow him to guide her as he willed. They floated. They whirled. Her chiffon and taffeta skirts ballooned about them both. The crowd of dancers around them blurred and faded. The music softened. The lights dimmed. There was only Dom. In sharp, bold relief.

He held her more closely now. "Anne."

Her mouth parted. Yearning overwhelmed her. Anne recognized the desire pooling in her loins. It was strong and timeless, and she was no longer shocked.

He pressed her even closer, as oblivious as she to the crowd, and their bodies fused. Her heart beat against his. Her legs moved with his. Their bodies melded. Heat against heat, hardness to softness. They danced now as one.

And then the music changed. A lively garish beat replaced the romantic strains of the waltz. Dom halted, one arm around her waist. He did not smile at her.

His eyes were wide, fierce, smoking. Anne understood.

If they were in Tavalon Castle right now, Anne knew she would be leading him upstairs to their bedchamber.

Her heart pounded.

But they were not in Tavalon Castle. They were in Harding House, in London. Dom led her off the dance floor.

Faces appeared. A redheaded lady stared openly at them, with distaste. A pudgy bald man talked behind his hand to another gentleman. A pretty blond was pouting at Dom, and eyeing Anne with malevolence. Anne avoided them all. The crowd parted for them. People moved out of their way. No one, not one single man or woman, dared to approach and greet Dom St. Georges.

Anne despised them all.

And then she stiffened. They approached one person who did not back away. He was staring intensely at them both. And he was angry. It was Patrick.

And something in his expression caused Anne to falter—and reach out blindly to grip Dom's hand.


"Hello, Anne," Patrick said. He was actually blocking their path, as if confronting them.

Anne was aware of Dom holding her tightly to his side, his arm possesively around her waist. "Patrick."

Patrick turned to Dom. "Hello, St. Georges."

Dom nodded.

"Or is it St. Georges? Do you still use that name? Or is there another name you might prefer me to address you by?"

"I was baptized St. Georges," Dom said tersely.

"Lucky for you," Patrick said.

"Patrick, stop it, please," Anne said urgently.

Patrick looked at her. "Are you enjoying yourself tonight, Anne? You certainly seem to be having an excellent time."

Anne knew that she should not anger him; he was

already angry enough. But she was livid. She ignored the firm, warning pressure of Dom's fingers on her waist. "Yes. Or rather, I was enjoying myself. Until you behaved so rudely."

Patrick's eyes widened. He stared at her with a thunderous expression. Then he shot Dom a furious look, and turned and stalked away.

Dom said softly, "Good show, Anne."

But Anne did not smile. She pulled free of his arm. What was she doing, allowing herself to be seduced by him again? Only this time, she might very well be wooed into a fatal attraction. Her life was not a fairy tale. This opulent, dreamy night was an illusion. There was no romance in her life, only hard, cold, ugly reality. To enjoy herself with Dom, to fall under his spell again, was ultimately dangerous. He would break her heart again, Anne had no doubt. "Dom, I would like to go home."

He stiffened. "That is not possible."

"Of course it is. I do not mind waiting for the carriage to come around," Anne pleaded.

"I need you, Anne," Dom said. "I need you here with me."

Anne froze.

"Please stay."

She met his eyes. "Don't leave me," he said.

Felicity smiled at her reflection in the mirror above the white marble vanity, then pouted prettily. When she had finished posturing, she opened her beaded reticule and took out a small pot of rouge. She dabbed it on her full lower lip, stared at herself, then dabbed it again on both of her cheeks. She smiled, liking what she saw, and smoothed down the dark pink satin of her bodice. She loved the feeling of the sensuous fabric beneath her fingertips, so she smoothed the fabric again. Her nipples tightened.

Felicity stared at herself. Her bodice was very fitted, without a flounce or seam. Her large nipples were visible to her eyes, hard and pointed and clearly erect. She had declined to wear a chemise.

Her eyes narrowed, she adjusted the bodice so that it was lower. She wondered what Blake would think if he saw her tonight. Surely he would be here at his father's ball.

Not that he mattered, of course. Dom was the one who mattered.

Felicity had heard the rumors, of course, but she did not believe them. And even if it was true, she still owed Anne.

"I think you could pull it down another fraction of an inch and still lay claim to some decency," Blake murmured.

Felicity jerked, her gaze arrowing to his reflection in the mirror. She gasped. Blake stood well behind her, leaning casually against the bathing room door, smiling at her. His eyes gleamed with appreciation.

"Don't you?" he queried.

Felicity turned, her buttocks pressing into the hard edge of the marble vanity. "What are you doing in here."

His dimples formed. "Well, the truth is I followed you, darling, and I did intend to make my presence known sooner, but I have always had a weakness for females at their toilette," he said, his white teeth flashing. "And then, of course, it became *very* interesting." His gaze lowered. He made no attempt to hide the fact that he stared at her breasts.

"You are far too bold," Felicity said with less assertiveness than she wished.

"But that is what you like about me."

"I don't like anything about you."

He laughed and pushed himself off the wall and proceeded to walk slowly toward her.

Felicity stiffened. She knew what he intended—this game had gone too far for too long. Her pulse accelerated, careening, her body tightened, swelling. "What if someone tries to use this room?" she heard herself say hoarsely.

He paused in front of her. Carelessly he toyed with one of her blond curls. "The door is locked. They will either be very discouraged and leave, or, if astute, they will be fascinated."

Felicity swallowed. "You wouldn't care if someone knew what we were doing in here?"

He shrugged, releasing her hair. "Not really. Would you?"

Felicity could not answer. Excitement filled her veins. "You are reprehensible," she whispered.

"Mmmm," he said. His hand dropped. His fingertips grazed her collarbone. His eyes remained glued to her face. "I am very reprehensible. As reprehensible as you wish me to be."

"I . . . don't wish . . . anything," Felicity said weakly.

"Liar." He grinned, trailing his forefinger down her bare chest. Felicity's bosom heaved. Goose bumps formed in his wake. He stroked the pad of his finger over the mound of her breast, in the gentlest of caresses, then paused at the edge of her bodice.

"I think," Blake said softly, "that you wish for me to do this . . . and this." His gaze searing, he tugged her bodice down. Her nipples popped out. Blake touched his finger to one large point.

Felicity moaned.

Blake smiled. "Am I right?" he asked, lifting his long lashes and looking into her eyes.

Felicity stared at his finger, just barely touching her nipple. "Please," she heard herself say.

"At your command, madam," he said, bending and sucking the tip into his mouth.

Felicity gripped his head, her knees buckling. She could not prevent herself from moaning. Blake supported her with one arm while torturing her expertly. Licking, tugging, sucking, kissing her.

He raised his head and stared into her eyes.

"Blake," Felicity cried, her fingertips digging into his neck.

"Turn around," he ordered.

Felicity only hesitated an instant before obeying. She faced herself in the mirror. She had never seen herself this way before, flushed with excitement, her eyes dazed, her breasts bare, yet dressed in a lavish evening gown and opulent pearl jewelry. And Blake, staring at her in the mirror, dark and devastating, his blue eyes glittering. But there was something ruthless about the tight line of his mouth.

Her loins hurt her now. She clutched the marble countertop, wondering what Blake was going to do to her. Slowly, he began pulling up the back of her pink satin skirt and the black silk petticoat beneath it.

She could hardly breathe. His hands were on her crinoline. And he was pulling the flexible hoop down. "Step out of this goddamned cage," he said.

Felicity obeyed.

He tossed it behind them. It rolled, collapsed, bounced back.

Their gazes met in the mirror. And then Felicity felt him sliding her silk drawers down her thighs. As he did his hands brushed her sex very briefly. She whimpered.

"Step out."

She did.

His hands slid over her naked buttocks, then between her legs. Felicity clawed the marble counter. From behind, his long fingers reached up, stroking between slick, thick folds. She closed her eyes, arching her back like a cat.

He kissed her neck, still fondling her. Only now Felicity felt his manhood rearing up between her buttocks. Her eyes flew open. He nipped the skin on her collarbone, massaging himself against her. He felt huge, impossibly hard.

And then he touched her clitoris very gently.

Felicity cried out, falling onto the sink, climaxing wildly. Blake gripped her hips. "Hold on," he said.

"Yes," she wept, her cheek against the cold marble, still convulsing.

His sudden entry pushed her up against the mirror. And caused her to weep with pleasure again.

"My," he murmured, pausing when he was fully embedded inside of her. "Has it been a while, dear?"

"Yes, damn you, Blake, don't stop!" Felicity shouted.

"As I said, at your command." He began to move powerfully, yet with restraint. Felicity opened her eyes, their gazes met in the mirror. His handsome face was strained. His hands lifted, covering her breasts, squeezing. His thrusting rhythm increased.

And then he was palming her sweaty sex again. Felicity peaked. Her wild cries filled the small bathing chamber.

Blake pulled her off the sink. Felicity was only vaguely aware of his laying her down on the rug on the floor. She could not move. She floated, as if drugged. Until she heard him murmuring her name.

Felicity forced herself to open her eyes. He was kneeling over her, between her legs, which were spread widely apart. Her gaze became transfixed. His fully erect penis stabbed the air.

"Can you take some more?" he murmured, smiling slightly. "I'm afraid I have only just begun."

Felicity lifted wide, astonished eyes to his.

His dimples formed and he laughed. "Surely you are woman enough for a man like me?" he challenged.

Felicity managed to speak despite the red-hot haze

of anticipation. "The question is—are you man enough for me?"

He grinned. Shifting his hips, he slid deeply, slowly into her. And then, as slowly, he pulled out. "I think so. But if you insist, I will just have to prove it."

Anne heard church bells tolling the midnight hour. She was terribly relieved. The ball had been interminable. They had not danced again; Anne would have refused had Dom suggested it, which he did not. They had stood and watched the dancers and the other guests, strolled once in the gardens, and tried to eat some of the buffet dinner. But Anne had no appetite, and neither did Dom. However, five gentlemen, including their host, Lord Harding, had defied the rest of society to speak with Dom, offering him condolences for the duke's illness, and were introduced to Anne. And Blake had chatted with them for almost an hour. Patrick had disappeared.

"Dom, let's go," Anne urged when the church bells fell silent.

"I have had enough," Dom agreed. He took her arm. They worked their way through the crowd, and up the three steps into the foyer. Suddenly Dom faltered.

Two constables were standing at the front doors, while another gentlemen, short and portly, clad in a badly made suit, stood speaking with the earl, Harding's butler at his side. When Anne and Dom appeared on the threshold, everyone looked up, falling silent.

Then the earl, a tall, silver-haired man, separated himself from the group and strode to them. Anne's eyes widened, her grip increased on Dom's arm. It suddenly occurred to her that the police had come because of Dom, that Belle and Patrick were right after all. But that made no sense, none at all, because the police could not suspect Dom of wanting to murder her. No one knew other than Belle and Patrick.

But why was Harding coming this way? She turned a frightened gaze upon Dom. And slowly dropped her hand from his arm.

"Dom," the earl said gravely. "I am afraid there is a matter that must be settled."

Dom stared past the earl, his gaze meeting the portly gentleman in the ill-fitting suit.

"Inspector Hopper," the earl said.

Hopper came forward, his cheeks turning red. "My lord," he addressed Dom, "I am very sorry, and please, let me express my condolences over your . . . er . . . the duke's ill health, but I must ask you to come with me."

"What is this about?" Dom asked.

Anne felt faint.

Hopper and Harding shared a glance. The inspector cleared his throat. "Matthew Fairhaven is dead," he said.

Anne gasped, shooting Dom a stunned look. He also appeared shocked.

"And you are under arrest for his murder," the Inspector added.

# Chapter 28

*D*om did not even flinch.

Anne, however, cried out.

Hopper coughed again. His cheeks were redder than before. "My lord, er, sir. Please, come with me."

Dom did not move. His jaw flexed. His eyes had turned dark and dangerous.

Anne stared at him, becoming aghast. Surely Dom had not murdered Matthew Fairhaven! Surely not!

Dom must have felt her staring, because he abruptly looked down at her. Anne knew her horror showed. He grimaced, his expression darkening further.

Hopper spoke to everyone present. "It was murder," he announced. "He died this afternoon. His body was found at Covent Garden. The coroner has determined his cause of death to be a blow to the head."

Anne felt very faint. Was Dom a killer after all? Was this the final, conclusive proof? She licked her dry lips. "My husband ... my husband did not do this," she managed, without conviction.

Dom turned away from her, staring at Hopper. "But I, of course, am the most likely suspect. After all, who had the most reason to silence Fairhaven?"

"Dom, don't," Anne whispered.

He continued to ignore her.

"Dom," Harding said. "I suggest you remain silent

until you have had a chance to speak with your solicitor.''

"I did not kill him," Dom said flatly.

"Sir," Hopper said, "a citizen has reported seeing you engaged in an argument with Fairhaven this afternoon.''

Anne's eyes widened.

"That's a lie," Dom said tersely.

"Did you argue with Fairhaven?" Hopper asked.

"Yes," Dom snapped. "But this morning, not this afternoon, and at his home, privately, not at Covent Garden. I did not strike him.''

"I am sorry, sir. You understand the law, I presume. The law is clear. The coroner has determined murder to be the cause of death, and a subject has come forth to indict you. Besides, this was found in Fairhaven's hand. It is yours, is it not?" Hopper reached into his pocket, then held up his hand.

Anne gasped. A sapphire cuff link lay on the inspector's palm. And it matched the studs on Dom's shirt-front exactly.

"Sir?" Hopper asked.

"Yes," Dom ground out, "that is mine.''

Anne returned to Rutherford House alone. Dom had been taken by the police to the Central Criminal Court at the Old Bailey to be formally charged with Matthew Fairhaven's murder.

She was frightened. It was difficult to think clearly. But there was evidence against Dom, and a citizen's indictment. Had he murdered Fairhaven? Was it possible? If so, then surely he was capable of cold-bloodedly murdering her!

Anne did not know what to think. Her heart screamed wildly in protest. That none of this could be true. Anne felt that she was living a nightmare.

Anne had not come home directly. Before Dom had

been taken away, guests had begun to gather around them, the shocking news of Fairhaven's murder and Dom's arrest spreading amongst them like wildfire. Blake had offered to see Anne home. Instead, Anne had insisted that he help her find the family solicitor—and a barrister as well. Canfield had already left for the courts.

It was two o'clock in the morning now. Anne was exhausted, but too distraught to sleep. Belle, who should have been waiting for her to help her disrobe, was nowhere to be found. Caldwell, looking unusually tense, sent a chambermaid to aid her. Anne had told Caldwell what had transpired, seeing no reason to hide the cause of Dom's absence.

Anne knew she would never be able to sleep. She decided to sit with the duke. A fire blazed in the hearth in his room, but Anne lit candles until the room was bathed in a cheery light that belied the awful night.

She pulled a chair up to his bed. He lay stiff and waxen, but his cheeks were slightly flushed. Anne reached for his hands—and thought she saw a muscle in his face move.

She remained motionless, staring. But she had been mistaken. The duke remained unconscious.

"We need your help," she began. She wanted desperately to unburden herself. But what if he could hear her? She did not want to shock him, perhaps even causing his death. On the other hand, what if she shocked him into consciousness? It was a terrible risk. "Oh, Your Grace, please, we are in so much trouble!" Anne cried.

And she poured out her heart to him.


"But you said you fought with Fairhaven."

"No. I said we spoke privately, at his home, early yesterday morning," Dom said flatly.

He was in a small, square room, one dully lit with

kerosene lamps. Two burly constables were with him, as were Inspector Hopkins and another inspector, Gatling, who was as tall and gaunt and pale as Hopper was short and fat and flushed. Dom had removed his jacket and tie. His sleeves were rolled up, the collar of his shirt open. They had been interrogating him for two full hours. It was three in the morning, but Dom was not tired. He was angry.

He was not a murderer. He had not murdered Fairhaven. He had no idea who had. But no one believed him. Not even Anne.

He was sickened, recalling her white, horrified expression.

"He's lying," Gatling said. His eyes were almost black, and filled with the capacity for cruelty. "He followed Fairhaven to the Gardens, fought with him, killed him. How else did Fairhaven get his hands on that cuff link?" Gatling smiled and it was ugly.

"I lost those cuff links weeks ago. I have not worn them since I was in Scotland."

"But someone saw you with Fairhaven," Gatling sneered.

"Who?" Dom demanded. "Tell me who the liar is." He started to rise out of his chair.

"Sit down," Gatling ordered, and one of the bobbies stuck out his huge, hamlike hand and shoved Dom down.

Dom inhaled, fighting to control his temper. He knew Gatling wanted him to lose it. Gatling wanted to set the two thugs on him. Gatling would enjoy seeing him beaten to within an inch of his life. He would probably even participate.

"Sir," Hopper said, "a confession might make things a bit easier on you."

Dom lifted a brow. "Really? Has the penalty for murder changed? Last I heard it was hanging."

Hopper flushed. "We are all tired, sir. If you confess,

we can end this session now and get some rest. You will be able to speak with your solicitor in the morning.''

Dom stared at him coldly.

Hopper cringed.

"Look at 'im,'' Gatling spit. "He still thinks he's a big man! But he ain't, now is he? He's nothing but some puny bastard. You ain't the duke's grandson anymore,'' Gatling taunted. "You ain't no lord. You're nobody, boy.''

"But at least my mother was not a fishmonger's whore,'' Dom said coolly.

Gatling's face contorted. His fist lashed out. Dom had already noticed the iron knuckles. He leapt aside as that fist landed on his jaw. But dear God, those iron knuckles were meant to break bones, and it felt as if Gatling had cracked open his jaw. Dom fell back against the wall. He had to fight himself to remain standing upright.

And then a heavy wooden stick smashed down on his shoulder.

Dom gasped in pain, falling to the floor, clutching his shoulder. He managed to think through the haze of blazing pain.

"Stop it!'' Hopper cried. "There's no need for that.''

"Shut up,'' Gatling said. He towered over Dom. His fist—and the iron knuckles—punched the air. "Confess.''

Dom stared up at him. Sweat beaded his brow, trickled into one eye. It burned. "No,'' he said.

Anne finally slept. Having told the duke everything, even though he could not hear or respond, had been cathartic. She was so tired afterward that she could hardly walk to her bedroom—she could hardly stand up. It was half past four in the morning. The chambermaid who had been assigned to aid her in Belle's absence was as bleary-eyed, but somehow Anne was divested of her evening gown, clad in her nightclothes, and helped into bed. Instantly she was asleep.

Anne heard the pounding on her door. But she did not want to awaken. She burrowed under her pillow. In her subconscious mind, she knew no good could come from a new day. The pounding increased.

Anne moaned, opening one eye. She was facing the windows and the draperies had not been properly drawn. A gray, misty dawn greeted her. And the damned pounding on her door. "Go away," she whispered, and then she remembered everything.

Dom's betrayal in Scotland, her fleeing Waverly Hall. The Harding ball, Fairhaven's murder, and Dom's arrest.

"My lady," Caldwell shouted, banging again, apparently with his fist. "Please, please, wake up!"

Anne sat up, her grogginess miraculously disappearing, replaced with dread. She slipped to her feet, donning a dressing gown, and opened the door. She was pale. Caldwell stood there, absolutely disheveled, his black suit wrinkled, his cravat askew, his hair standing up in tufts. "What is it?" Anne asked anxiously.

But Caldwell burst into wild laughter. He gripped her by both shoulders, shaking her in excitement. "The duke is awake!"

Anne gasped.

"He is awake. I believe he is trying to speak!"

Anne studied his happy face for a moment. And then she threw herself at Caldwell, hugging him fiercely. "Oh, thank God!" She wasn't sure she could have withstood another tragedy. But this miracle was so very welcome.

"Thank God," Caldwell echoed. They beamed at one another.

"I am coming right down," Anne decided. Then it occurred to her how she must look. Probably worse than poor Caldwell. "Where is Belle?" She grew uneasy, recalling Belle's absence last night.

"I don't know where she is, my lady." Caldwell's smile faded.

Anne hesitated. Something was wrong. Belle was very reliable. Then she forced herself to the present. She had so much to worry about—she could not worry about Belle's strange disappearance now, no matter how fond of her abigail she was. "Caldwell, I think you had better mount a search," she said, starting down the hall.

"I already have," he said, on her heels. "No one saw her leave the house. I do not understand."

How could this be happening? Anne prayed that Belle was all right. And as she hurried down the hall, she thought she heard the low rumble of a man's voice.

Anne slowed.

Caldwell almost careened into her, halting behind. "My lady?"

"Did you hear that?"

"No."

Anne turned to stare at him, her brow furrowed. Surely she had not imagined the sound of someone speaking. She gazed at the closest door. "Do we have guests?"

"No."

"Then who is in that room?" Anne asked.

"There is no one in that room," Caldwell began.

But Anne heard something again. Not a voice, but the sound of an object scraping the floor.

Anne moved to the door, hesitating, unsure of what she would find if she opened it now. Her pulse was racing uncomfortably. Anne gripped the knob. And then she heard a woman's laughter.

Eyes wide, Anne swung the door open.

Belle cried out, clutching her black dress, which she was clearly in the act of donning, to her breasts.

Anne gaped at her maid, clad only in her under-clothes. Then her gaze swung to the man sitting on the bed. She gasped.

Patrick stared at her, clad only in his black evening trousers—the very same pants he had worn to the Harding ball.

Anne stared, dumbfounded.

Belle rushed forward, holding the dress up like a shield, her long red hair streaming wildly about her face. "My lady! Oh please! Please, I am sorry!"

Anne stared at her maid.

Belle dropped to her knees, crying. "Mum, I didn't mean any harm. Oh, God!"

Anne managed to breathe. She looked at Patrick again. He was standing, reaching for his white shirt. He did not appear in the least perturbed to have been discovered in an indiscretion with Anne's maid.

"How could you?" Anne finally whispered, not to Belle, but to her cousin.

He shrugged. "I am a man, Anne."

"Mum!" Belle was still on her knees on the floor. She clutched Anne's skirts. She was weeping. "I know that this is wrong, terribly wrong, and I am so sorry—oh please forgive me!"

Caldwell moved to stand beside Anne. His voice darkly furious, he said, "Get up. Do not touch Her Ladyship. You are dismissed. I will see that you receive any monies due you."

Belle cried out.

"No!" Anne took a deep breath, met Patrick's steady, almost satisfied gaze. "How long has this been going on?"

Patrick smiled, shrugging again.

"Not long!" Belle shrieked. "Just a few weeks. Since the funeral, that is all."

Since Philip's funeral—since Dom's return home.

Anne felt sorry for Belle. "Did he promise you marriage?"

"Oh, no," Belle said. "And even if he had, I'm no fool to believe a lord would ever lower himself to marry me."

"Then why, Belle?" Anne asked plaintively. She loved Belle. She could not understand this.

Belle started to cry again. "I was lonely, mum."

Anne wanted to weep, too. She took Belle's hand and lifted her to her feet. "Belle, you are not losing your employment with me, you mean far too much to me. But this was very wrong. It is wrong to give yourself outside of marriage to any man, and it is wrong to dally with a gentleman in *my* house."

"I know! Oh, thank you!" Belle looked as if she wanted to embrace Anne. Anne smiled and hugged her gently. Belle clung a moment.

Anne looked at Patrick. "I don't understand you, either."

"No, you do not." He slipped on his shirt. "You rejected me, Anne. And you would deny me the comfort another woman could provide?"

"Belle is my maid." Anne was furious. "You used her. You have hurt her. You could have cost her her job."

"But I did not, now did I?"

They stared at one another, Anne openly furious. Anne finally whirled. At the door she paused. "When you are dressed, you may leave."

"You would throw me out of this house?" Patrick asked, amazed.

Anne hesitated. She recalled Dom ordering Patrick to leave, not once, but twice. She recalled the friendship they had once had. "No. I am merely asking you to leave. There are family matters that must be settled."

Patrick's face tightened. He strode to her. "I am also family, Anne. You cannot throw me out."

"I do not want to fight with you." She turned her back on him. "When you are dressed, Belle, you may attend me as usual. I am going to the duke." She left the room, feeling horrible.

Patrick was a cad. She did not know him at all.

The duke had been propped up on pillows by Caldwell. His amber eyes were open, and they were pleading. Anne rushed to him, took his hands, and was rewarded when she felt him squeeze her hands very slightly. "Your Grace! Thank God you have come to your senses!"

But the duke did not speak. He stared at her, the light in his eyes wild, beseeching. Anne quickly realized that he could not speak—but that he wanted to speak to her.

Dismay chased away much of her joy. She had somehow expected him to be perfectly restored to health. She sat down at his hip. "Your Grace, can you move at all?"

He stared at her. How agonized he was.

Anne forced a small smile, keeping her tone light. "Your Grace, if you can move your fingers, please do so for me," Anne said.

She stared at his hand. It was immobile, lying limply on the gold coverlet. And then Anne saw one of his fingers twitch. She forced another smile. "That is wonderful. I think that you are well on your way to recovery, Your Grace."

He stared at her out of wide eyes. Anne had no idea if she spoke the truth or not. The duke was awake, and cognizant, but he was mostly paralyzed. And she had no idea just how much he could comprehend. She turned, careful to guard her expression so that it was cheerful. "Caldwell, please send for Dr. Fanderidge."

Caldwell nodded, quickly leaving.

Revealing that Patrick stood behind him.

Anne stared. He stared back. Anne could not believe

the man's audacity, but she did not want to distress the
duke now by starting a fight with Patrick. She turned
back to Rutherford. "Your Grace, if you understand
me, you must blink your eyes once."

The duke blinked.

Anne was terribly relieved. She smiled brightly.
"Wonderful! And when you do not understand me, you
blink twice, all right? That way we can communicate."

The duke blinked once.

Anne nodded. "Good. I don't know what to do. So
much is happening. Dom is in trouble, Your Grace.
Fairhaven has told everyone that he is not Philip's son,
and yesterday Fairhaven was murdered. Last night they
arrested Dom."

The duke's eyes widened. Although his facial expression did not change, the light in his eyes did. It was
shocked.

And from the doorway, Patrick gasped.

He strode forward. "What?" he exclaimed. "Dom
has been arrested for Fairhaven's murder?"

"Yes," Anne said coldly. She turned her back on
him. The duke was gazing past her with open determination. Anne followed his glance. He was looking at
the bedside table. "What is it?" she asked gently.

He kept shifting his eyes from her to the table, trying
to tell her something.

Anne looked at the table and saw a feather quill.
Excitement filled her. "Can you write?"

He blinked twice.

Anne slumped.

"I don't know what you expect from Rutherford,"
Patrick said, "but he is clearly incapable of helping
Dom now."

Anne stiffened.

The duke shot a dark glance at Patrick, and stared
again at the quill.

An idea formed in Anne's mind. "Your Grace," she

said, bubbling now, "if I write a letter, you can blink when it is correct, and that way we can spell words and you can dictate whatever it is you wish to say to me!" she cried.

The duke blinked once. He seemed excited too.

Anne laughed, rising. Within moments she was seated at his hip with a sheaf of paper and a quill and inkwell. Patrick stood by the bed beside her. Anne had decided to ignore him.

It was a laborious process. But twenty minutes later, Anne had written down ten letters: papersdesk.

"Papers!" she shouted, on her feet. "In the desk!"

The duke blinked.

Anne kissed him. And whispered, "I pray that this will save Dom!"

An hour later, at seven o'clock in the morning, Anne was so discouraged that she was ready to give up. She, Caldwell, and Belle had gone through every single paper in the duke's desk, and there had been dozens of files and folders and hundreds of notes, letters, missives, and contracts. But nothing seemed relevant to the crisis at hand. And Patrick, who had refused to leave, had even grudgingly helped.

"Maybe he does not understand the way that I think he does," Anne said, dejected. She was sitting on the floor, surrounded by open files and masses of papers.

Caldwell and Belle were also seated on the floor, papers up to their knees. "Perhaps we missed something," he said despondently.

Patrick stood, one hip against the massive seventeenth century desk. His attempts to help had been half-hearted and he had been openly skeptical of their efforts. Anne had hoped that he would grow tired and leave, but he hadn't. Now he said, "You are all mad. And so is Rutherford. I am going home."

Belle had pointedly ignored him, and now she turned

to Anne with timidity that was not characteristic of her. "My lady, don't all the big lords have hidden drawers in their desks?"

Anne straightened. Caldwell jerked. In unison, they exclaimed, "A hidden drawer!"

Anne jumped to her feet.

Caldwell rose more slowly. Belle bounced up.

And Patrick stiffened, instead of leaving.

"Let's look for a hidden drawer," Anne said.

Drawers were pulled out and turned over. Every seam was inspected. Bottoms were tapped. Sides were scrutinized. Anne was in a state of disbelief. There did not seem to be any hidden drawer anywhere.

"Let's have breakfast, my lady," Caldwell suggested.

"No," Anne said. "Maybe what we need to look for is a hidden compartment." She turned and stared at the massive rosewood desk. It had been in the family for more than two hundred years, and with its inlaid top and gilded feet, it was truly beautiful; Anne felt regret. "Get an ax," she said.

Caldwell gaped. "I beg your pardon?"

"Get an ax and our biggest footman."

Caldwell nodded and disappeared.

"You are crazy, Anne," Patrick remarked. "You aren't going to find anything."

"You don't want to help Dom, do you?" Anne asked, sickened by her own words.

"And why should I?" he flashed. "Why should you, for that matter—when he is a murderer?"

Anne swallowed. She had been consumed with her quest. She had not had the leisure to dwell on her suspicions and fears—or her heart's determination to believe the best instead of the worst. "Dom has not been convicted yet. Until that happens, I am his wife, and he needs my help."

"Christ! You are too noble to be true!" Patrick spat.

Before Anne could reply, a footman standing six-foot-four and weighing at least fifteen stone hurried into the room with Caldwell, carrying a huge ax. "Smash open the desk," Anne ordered.

The footman did not hesitate. He lifted the ax and crashed it down and split the desk in two. He raised the ax again; Anne called, "Stop!" For she could already see a large sheet of paper caught in the desk's middle section. Clearly there had been a hidden compartment after all.

Anne extracted several papers. Her hands were shaking. She saw that the first and last paper were stamped with a legal seal.

"What is that?" Patrick asked suspiciously.

"I don't know. These are legal documents. I cannot skim them." Anne moved to Rutherford's chair, sat down, and began reading.

And when she was finished, she was both saddened and joyous. She looked up at the circle of faces peering down at her.

"Well?" Patrick demanded.

"This is proof that Dom is not Philip's son, as Fairhaven said," Anne said quietly.

Patrick started to smile.

"But," Anne said, cutting him off, "Philip adopted Dom on his first birthday. Philip also made him his sole and legal heir."

# Chapter 29

𝒜nne was finishing her morning toilette when she heard a commotion on the street below, outside her open window. She heard a carriage stopping, a driver calling to his horses, their impatient snorts, and two other male voices.

Impossibly, one of them sounded like Dom's.

Anne raced to her bedroom window. Half-hanging out so she could see clearly, she spied the black-and gold Harding coach at the curb. And Blake and Dom stood there, shaking hands and exchanging words.

Anne was flooded with relief. She turned and, lifting her blue skirts, ran from her room and downstairs. She raced into the entry hall as Dom came through the front doors. A moist-eyed Caldwell was beaming at him. "My lord, sir! Thank God you are home!" For a moment Anne thought the butler was going to embrace Dom.

Dom nodded. "Thank you, Caldwell."

Anne clung to the newel post of the banister. Her pulse was racing wildly.

"My lord," Verig cried, skidding into the foyer. "Please, sir, let me!" The valet took Dom's dress coat immediately. "Where are your hat and gloves, my lord?"

Dom said without reflection, "I have lost them."

Verig nodded eagerly. "Shall I draw you a hot, scented bath and bring you your breakfast upstairs?"

Dom nodded, his gaze meeting Anne's.

And Anne was now noticing his appearance. He had been carrying his black dress coat over one arm. He was not wearing his necktie and his shirt was open almost to his chest. It was terribly rumpled, his pants as wrinkled. His hair was mussed, a lock hanging in one eye, and his face was drawn and haggard. There was a huge purple bruise on his left jaw.

How terrible he looked. "Dom," she said hoarsely.

"Hello, Anne." He did not move to her.

"What happened?"

"Blake came forward and swore that we spent the afternoon together." His gaze was steady. "At a brothel."

Anne paled. She looked into his eyes and saw his utter exhaustion. "Thank God for Blake."

"Yes, he is a damnably good liar." Their gazes met.

Anne could not help being relieved. "Did they drop the charges?"

"For now. But I am under certain restrictions. I am not allowed to leave London. Not until this investigation is closed."

Anne nodded.

And Dom sighed. "I am tired, Anne. I am going upstairs to wash and rest."

Anne did not move aside to let him pass. She asked, "Dom, what happened to your jaw?"

His gaze was piercing. "Why, I fell down."

"Do you need a doctor?"

"Probably." He moved stiffly toward her, and Anne gasped. He was limping.

"Dom, have you had an accident?" Anne cried.

Dom's smile was brief and sardonic. "Only if you will call a bully and his two bobbies an accident. Why then, yes, I have."

"What did they do to you?!" Anne was outraged.

"I will survive. Now, if you will excuse me, I am going upstairs."

Anne was noticing now that his right arm seemed to hang quite woodenly by his side. He had not used it once. She shot Caldwell a look and said, "Get Fanderidge." Then she faced Dom. "What can I do?"

"Ring up Canfield and Hirsch Newman, another well-known solicitor. Tell them I will see them both at three o'clock this afternoon."

"It's not over, is it?" she asked fearfully.

"No. It is not over until they find Fairhaven's real killer."

Anne wet her lips nervously. Dom could not have killed Fairhaven, she knew it with all of her heart. But who had? And why had someone claimed to have seen Dom arguing with Fairhaven that afternoon? What if he *had* been with Fairhaven that afternoon?

His gaze darkened. "What's wrong, Anne? You haven't had a change of heart? You still believe me capable of murder?"

Anne swallowed. "No. I . . . don't." Anne met his gaze cautiously. Fairhaven's murder was a terrible coincidence. It had to be.

His expression was grim, angry. He turned his back on her abruptly. His movements stiff, he started up the stairs, his limp more pronounced.

"Dom, I do have some good news," Anne said quickly to his back.

He paused, glancing down at her dispassionately.

Anne almost flinched. "Rutherford awoke at dawn. Although he cannot speak and he cannot move, we managed to communicate with a writing tablet and some sign language. Doctor Fandcridge was here. He says this is a vast improvement. But he warned us not to expect much more." She forced a bright smile.

"Still, this *is* an improvement, and he is fully cognizant, Dom."

Dom's eyes brightened; he smiled slightly. "That is the best damn news I've had all day. I'll go see Grandfather first."

"He is asleep," Anne said. "I fear I exhausted him. But there is more."

He waited.

"We found several legal papers. Not only did Philip adopt you on your first birthday, he also made you his sole legal heir."

Dom stared. If he felt at all triumphant, or relieved, he gave no sign of it.

"Dom? Don't you see? Legally you are Philip's heir. Legally you are a St. Georges. I am not a solicitor, but I feel certain that you will still inherit the dukedom," Anne said in a rush.

"If I don't hang," Dom said brusquely.

"There's something else, isn't there?" Anne whispered.

Dom stared past her. At first Anne thought he was staring blindly at the wall behind her, but as he continued to stare, she turned and looked and was faced with an immense portrait of the man they had believed to be his great-great-great-great-grandfather, the fourth duke of Rutherford. Anne inhaled.

"I have one question," Dom said flatly. "If I am not Dom St. Georges, then who the hell am I?"

He was so tired.

Eyes closed, Rutherford drifted, vaguely aware of the morning sunlight streaming through his bedroom windows and shining warmly on his face, of the fresh air blowing gently on him as well, and of a bird singing cheerfully from just outside the windowsill. Otherwise, his bedchamber was absolutely still and silent. He knew he was going to die.

But he wasn't afraid. For he knew that death wasn't final, that there was some kind of life after death. Because *she* was waiting for him.

And he had been waiting for her for most of his lifetime.

But he wasn't ready to die yet. Not yet, dammit.

*She hovered over him. He could see her so clearly, and her presence calmed him, comforted him—thrilled him. Luminous ivory skin, startling blue eyes, and shocks of midnight black hair. And her warm, genuine smile. Yes, she was waiting for him now, in death, although she had not waited for him in life.*

*How he loved her. How he missed her.*

*But she was patient. She had waited so many years, she could wait a little while longer.*

The duke sighed, silently communicating with her, asking her not to distract him. He had affairs to attend to. Dom was in trouble. The duke had no intention of dying until Dom's name was cleared regarding Fairhaven's murder, and until Dom's future as the ninth duke of Rutherford was assured.

God, how had this crisis occurred? The duke decided that it was mostly his fault. Years ago he should have spoken with Dom frankly. But Philip had made it abundantly clear when he had adopted Dom, making him his sole heir, that the truth must never be revealed to anyone or he would disown Dom and scandalize the world. Rutherford had allowed him his threat and his pride, but at what cost?

Had Anne found the papers? Frustration filled the duke, not for the first time. His mind shouted at him to get up, walk to the door, go downstairs and, with a few sharp commands, set all that was awry right.

Get up.

The duke stared furiously, helplessly at the door, willing himself to rise, having never wanted anything more—but he could not move a single muscle. Damn it and bloody hell!

The duke was exhausted now from trying to move, but after a few moments, he willed himself to rise again. He fought his body with his mind. Sweat streaked his cheeks. And this time, his fingertips twitched.

He cursed and cursed, wanting to weep, and felt *her* hand on his brow.

*"Be calm, my dearest,"* she said. *"It will end well, trust me."*

The duke's heart, which had accelerated dangerously, slowed. And although his mouth could not form a smile, his heart could, and did.

Anne was so much like *her*.

Anne, whom he loved as he would his own daughter—had he been blessed with one.

Where was she now? Still in the library, searching for the adoption papers? She had not waited for him to finish his thoughts. But the next time she came to visit him, he would communicate the truth to her. It was a vow.

He wanted to tell her now. Anne! He shouted silently. Anne! He commanded inwardly. Come back! Come back!

But his door remained closed. No one could hear him, and he grew agitated. In his mind, he shouted more loudly. Anne!

*"Hush,"* she whispered in his ear. *"She will come."*

The duke did not have to open his eyes to see her, the one and only love of his lifetime. He smiled with his heart. Janice smiled back.

She was hiding.

Clarisse paced her room at the Cavendish Hotel. She did not know what to do.

Fairhaven had destroyed her socially—Clarisse could

not show her face in town, or anywhere else, and she would never be able to do so again. She knew exactly how cruel the ton was from experience. In town, they had never really accepted her, and now there would not be any invitations for a weekend in the country, or a dinner party or a ball. And in the country not one of her friends would even speak to her should they pass in the village or on the road by pure chance—she would be cut directly, fatally. In fact, people would look past her if she approached *them*, and if she tried to converse, or even explain herself, they would would pretend that she did not exist.

In fact, to both worlds, the one she had been born into and the one she had married into, she did not exist, not anymore—she was as good as dead.

Oh, God! This time Clarisse's tears were real. Clarisse was frightened. What kind of future awaited her now? And even if she told the truth about her lover, she would not be redeemed in society's eyes. In fact, Clarisse imagined that the ton would be appalled, and the wagging tongues would quickly make the truth far worse than it was.

Clarisse knew she was finished.

And what about Dom? She stared out the window down onto the heavy traffic of Claridge Street. Had Dom killed Fairhaven? Was her son a murderer? Oh, how the gossips must be enjoying the scandal about Dom and herself, and even they must be tearing Dom apart like a pack of wolves would a downed deer!

She clenched her fists. Surely Dom was innocent, and surely a man of his means would not go to prison or be hanged even if guilty. And if Dom had resorted to murder, Clarisse would forgive him. Fairhaven had deserved to die. It was only too bad he had not died *before* telling the world what he knew.

Clarisse wanted to scream and hurl furious accusations at Rutherford. *This was all his fault.*

But Clarisse had a plan. A plan of ultimate revenge.

This was Clarisse's last chance to hurt the duke as much as he had hurt her.

He lay dying. Finally, he had been made powerless. Clarisse couldn't smile. But she was glad. Fiercely glad. And although he was already defeated, she would be the one to deliver the final, fatal blow.

It was time to visit the duke of Rutherford and reveal her intention.

Anne was informed that Dom would not be taking his supper downstairs.

She had no wish to eat, especially not alone. Anne decided to take tea and toast in her rooms. But she had no appetite, she could only stare at her food, while wondering and worrying about Dom and the future.

Twice that afternoon she had gone downstairs to see the duke, wanting to tell him that they had found the adoption papers, so that he would be reassured. But on both occasions he had been soundly asleep, so soundly, in fact, that Anne's first reaction had been one of alarm. She had thought him either unconscious again, or dead. But he had been breathing, and Caldwell told her that he had awoken once briefly around noon.

According to Fanderidge, the duke desperately needed his sleep in order to restore his health.

Anne had not yet undressed for bed. She sat before the fire in her bedroom, clenching and unclenching her hands. Fanderidge had examined Dom, too. Anne's chest grew tight every time she thought about what had been done to him in the prison cell. According to Fanderidge, he had been beaten.

His shoulder had nearly been dislocated. His jaw was badly bruised, as were his ribs. Two of his toes on his left foot had been broken, the cause of his limp. He had other bruises as well, sustained from physical blows with a solid, heavy object.

Anne massaged her throbbing temples. It was such a terrible coincidence that Fairhaven had been murdered after revealing the truth about Dom's paternity. Immediately she forced her thoughts to stop. She did not dare speculate on who had killed him or why.

Anne stiffened, hearing slow, offbeat footsteps. They were awkward—she recognized them instantly. Dom was limping down the hall toward her room.

Anne stood up, her pulse racing. As quickly, she sat back down. She laid a palm on her speeding heart, hoping to quiet it. She could not find any calm. She grew still when Dom knocked sharply on her door. "Anne?"

She stood, breathing a bit too rapidly. What did he want? Although she was worried about him, she had not thought to see him again until the morrow, after a sorely needed night of sleep. "Come in," she said, hoping her tone sounded normal.

He shoved open the door and she met his golden, opaque eyes. He was wearing a loosely belted smoking jacket with velvet lapels over a pair of fine black trousers. His feet were bare except for the bandage on his toes.

"Come in," Anne repeated, tearing her gaze from his and wringing her hands. She did not trust herself. The urge to go to him and comfort him was overwhelming.

His gaze dipped to her hands.

Anne relaxed, cursing herself for betraying her own tension so openly. She forced a smile. "This is unexpected."

He limped into her room and kicked the door closed with the heel of his undamaged foot. "But not a pleasant surprise?" he challenged.

She did not like his tone. It was frightening. "I am glad you are up and about."

His face darkened. "Really?" he snorted. "What's wrong, Anne?" It was another challenge.

Anne was much tenser now. He was so angry, and she could not blame him. "I'm sorry, Dom. I'm sorry about everything."

"Are you? Are you really sorry . . . about everything?"

It was a moment before she could respond. "It's been a difficult day," she began, not wanting to continue the discussion, afraid of where it would go.

"I can vouch for that." His stare was hostile. "You appear upset. Frightened."

She had never seen him in this kind of mood before. Alarmed, she shook her head.

"You're frightened. Are you frightened of me?"

"No, of course not." She paled. "Dom, surely you don't think that I believe you guilty of murder?"

"I don't know what to think, Anne. You're my wife. I need you now. But you don't trust me and you have made that very clear." He paused, staring.

Anne wet her lips. "I . . . I don't know what to say. I *know* you didn't kill Matthew Fairhaven!"

Still he stared. Finally he said, "So you've changed your mind since last night."

Anne flushed. "That's not fair. Last night I was taken by surprise. You can't blame me for that."

"But I do."

Anne became motionless. "What are you blaming me for?"

He took a single, aggressive step toward her. Instinctively Anne backed up. "I'm blaming you for doubting my innocence. Confess. Last night you thought me a murderer."

"That's not fair," Anne cried.

"Not much of life is fair, is it?" Dom asked with heavy sarcasm.

"I'm sorry," Anne said again, desperately, meaning it.

"I don't want your pity!" he erupted furiously. "Damn you, Anne! Damn you! I want your trust ... your love!"

Anne was frozen. Tears filled her eyes. "You are distraught. Understandably so. Don't do this, Dom. We need more time."

"Damn right I'm distraught!" he shouted. "Don't do what? Don't demand my rights as a human being? As a man? As a husband?" He shook one fist, which was clenched so tightly that the knuckles were starkly white. "Maybe I don't *have* time."

"I can't," Anne choked.

His chest heaved. "You can't trust me, love me ... or you won't?"

"Dom, it has been a long, grueling day. Please!"

"But you're my wife. My *loyal* wife." His eyes glittered brightly, unnaturally; his face was flushed. He shoved himself off her door and, despite his limp, stalked toward her.

Anne did not back away. Her shoulders squared, stiffened, her breath got stuck in her chest. He towered over her. "You *are* my loyal wife, aren't you?"

Anne managed a slight nod. His mouth was very close to hers, far too close for comfort. The memory of what his mouth felt like, tasted like, was forever imprinted on her mind. But the look in his eyes made her recoil. "Why are you doing this?"

He gripped her arms and dragged her body up against his. "Maybe I can't make you love me, but I can make you want me."

"No," Anne cried. "Dom, stop, not this way!"

Too late. He ground his mouth down on hers. He had been talking about trust and love, but he was furious and she knew that he wanted to punish her and his kiss was punishing. Anne whimpered. She knew he wanted to hurt her.

Anne struggled, tearing her mouth from his, crying out. A sob was lodged in her throat.

Dom lifted his head. "Damn you," he whispered. "Damn you for doubting me—damn you for doing this to us."

Anne gazed up at him out of wide, frightened eyes.

He paled as if finally realizing what he had done. Swearing savagely, he released her.

The moment he did, Anne ran past him, out of the room. She fled mindlessly down the hall. She heard Dom calling her, but she ignored his cries, which sounded anguished now, instead of angry.

In the entry hall she collapsed.

She could not continue this way. Loving Dom so, hurting so, and still harboring doubts over his sincerity. She could not.

Anne decided then and there that she would return to Waverly Hall. There, at least, she would have space to breathe, and time to think.

For there she must decide what to do. Clearly a civil separation would not work, not for her and Dom. Passion ran too deeply for the both of them. Either she must return to him wholeheartedly as his wife, or she must abandon him now, as he had once abandoned her.

# Chapter 30

$\mathcal{A}$nne arrived at Waverly Hall the next day. Dom had watched her, through the windows of the front parlor, depart with Belle and her bags that morning, saying not a single word, his expression impossible to read. If he was sorry for his harsh words and loss of temper the night before, he gave no indication.

Anne had felt guilty, and she still did, as if she were abandoning him without just cause. But he had pushed her to this point.

She had no plans. She wanted to stay as far away from Dom as possible, so that she could think clearly and make the right decision about her marriage and her future.

But she was worried. She was anxious about leaving Dom now, during both the murder investigation and the scandal of his illegitimacy.

She refused an afternoon meal. Clad in her custom-made black riding habit, an ensemble which allowed her to ride astride, she ordered Blaze brought around. Willie assured her that the red gelding was just fine.

Anne stroked his velvety muzzle, feeding him a carrot and blinking back tears. Perhaps fleeing to Waverly Hall was a mistake. She loved it so here. But there were so many memories, all bittersweet. Everywhere she looked she was reminded of Dom.

Taking a deep breath, Anne mounted Blaze with Willie's help. The chestnut had not been tacked up with a sidesaddle, as Anne had requested. She intended to ride like the wind. As if she could outrace her sorrows and her troubles and the decision she must make.

Blaze snorted, eager to go. Anne cantered down the crushed shell drive, away from the Hall.

She took several low jumps as they entered the parkland. Blaze increased his pace. They galloped down a riding trail Anne knew by heart. She ducked several low-lying branches, noticing that the leaves were turning red and gold. The summer had passed so quickly. Anne felt choked; she swallowed a sob. How could she abandon Dom when she herself knew exactly what it was like to be left bereft and alone?

Anne slowed Blaze as they came to the edge of the blue-black lake in the center of the woods. The ruins of the keep, made of pale beige stone, shimmered in the sunlight, set on a knoll in the tiny island's midst. Several swans floated by the rotting dock there. Anne almost smiled at the sight. As a child she had often rowed over there with Patrick, to wander about and play. After her marriage to Dom, she had gone there as frequently, somehow, foolishly, still filled with hope.

Anne had to confront her feelings. They were impossible to deny. She still loved Dom. She always had. She would die loving him. But did she dare return to him now?

Her heart shouted yes!

Caution warred with life's most profound emotion.

Blaze lifted his head from the water, droplets clinging to his muzzle, snorting.

Anne was in no mood for a casual passerby. "What is it, boy?" Anne whispered, stroking his neck with her gloved hand.

Blaze was listening intently. He turned his head toward the trail and snorted again.

Anne looked at the woods behind them, but she saw nothing. Just a thick stand of shimmering birch trees. If someone was out there, she would make it clear that no trespassing was allowed on Waverly land.

She turned to the horse. "There's no one there, boy," she said, tightening her hold on Blaze's reins. The horse seemed anxious. Anne's unease increased.

"Hello, Anne," Dom said.

Anne gasped as Dom rode slowly out of the woods on a black hunter. She could not believe her eyes.

His expression was grim. "We must speak, Anne."

Anne managed to find her voice. "Dom, I left town purposely. I returned to Waverly Hall in order to clear my head. I came here because I wanted to be alone."

His tone was somber. "I know why you came here, Anne. You came here to decide about us."

Anne jerked.

He wet his lips. "After last night, I could not let you leave. I cannot let you make a unilateral decision, Anne." His stare was level, unwavering. "I'm not letting you leave me, Anne. I won't allow it."

Anne knew that she should be angry with his autocratic intention, but she felt no anger. Inwardly, elation bubbled. Anne tamped it down with the caution that had become first nature to her.

"Anne?"

"You cannot force a decision from me, Dom. I need time in which to think. But ... I am glad you are here. You are right. We should reach a decision on our future together."

He appeared relieved. "Thank you, Anne." Nudging his horse closer to hers, he said, his gaze fastened to hers, "I also wish to apologize. For my abominable behavior last night."

Anne smiled a small but heartfelt smile. "You do not have to apologize. I understand."

Their gazes held. Dom finally tightened his reins.

"I'll return to the house so you can ride alone and think. Why don't we plan to take tea together at five?" He swallowed, flushing slightly. "Casually, of course. We need not rush a decision."

Anne's heart felt as if it were soaring. She was aware that she blushed like a bride. "That would be nice."

He nodded, his gaze intent, and turned his black away.

"Dom," Anne called out. She smiled briefly. "Thank you."

His eyes, holding hers, warmed. And then he trotted his mount away, into the woods.

Anne watched the trees close behind him as he disappeared into their midst. There was no mistaking the joy in her heart. She had felt bad about fleeing from Dom; she was glad he had come after her.

Anne urged Blaze into a gentle trot. The afternoon now seemed sunnier and brighter; she was going to enjoy the outing.

But a few moments later she heard someone calling her name. Anne had taken Blaze on a different path through the woods. She looked over her shoulder, but saw only damp earth and swaying trees. Then her eyes widened as Patrick came riding around the bend.

An image of him with Belle flashed through her mind.

Patrick cantered up to her. His smile was brief and strained. "Hello, Anne."

"I don't understand," she said. "What are you doing here? I thought you were in London?"

"I followed you."

Anne's stomach lurched. "You . . . followed me?"

"I was at Rutherford House last evening when you fought with Dom," Patrick said. "And I watched you leaving town this morning."

Her confused mind tried to comprehend what he was saying. "You followed me from Rutherford House to the country?'' she whispered. Thinking about Patrick and Belle.

His smile flashed, it was fierce. ''Dom followed you, too. Have you left him, Anne?''

Anne blinked at Patrick. Her pulse was pounding. It was clicking in her mind that Patrick had been at Rutherford House very frequently. And if he had been seeing Belle since the funeral, he had been at Waverly Hall as often.

He had been seeing Belle since Dom's return home.

And since then, someone had been frightening her, trying to harm her—perhaps even trying to kill her.

Suddenly Anne was frightened. She was assailed with doubt, incredulity, confusion. Images chased one another through her mind, images of Dom, at once passionate and loving—and images of Patrick.

''Anne, you are staring at me as if I am a monster.'' He smiled at her. ''Darling, I have come to rescue you from the monster who is your husband, or are you forgetting that?''

Anne stiffened. Her heart pounded rapidly. Her imagination was running wild again. Because Patrick had no cause to want her dead. *It could not be Patrick.*

Yet the alarm bells continued to shriek inside of her head.

''Anne? Let's go. I will take you to Hunting Way. You will be safe there. He won't be able to hurt you.'' Patrick smiled at her oddly.

Anne hesitated. ''Patrick, Dom is not a killer. I believe that he loves me.'' Too late, as Patrick's eyes widened, Anne realized that she had said the wrong thing. Her words came out in a rush. ''I don't want to go to Hunting Way! I must return to Waverly Hall!'' She knew her forced smile was sickly.

''No.'' The word was boomed cannonlike. And Patrick reached for her bridle.

Anne did not have to decide what to do. She whipped

Blaze's head around so sharply that Patrick failed to seize her reins, while lashing his flank with her crop. The horse shot off.

"Anne!" Patrick shouted.

Anne did not respond. She leaned forward, whipping the gelding again. His strides lengthened. They tore down the trail. Trees approached and were passed at a dizzying speed, but Blaze weaved between them, staying on the path. Branches scratched Anne's cheek. Blaze's hooves ripped up huge chunks of dirt and sent them flying behind them.

And then Anne heard Patrick shouting her name again—only he was not far behind her.

Anne cried out, glancing over her shoulder, and saw Patrick a few lengths behind her, his expression thunderous. His mount was galloping all out—and gaining on Blaze.

Anne choked on fear and panic. She sawed on Blaze's reins—and sent him off the trail, crashing down a thickly wooded slope.

"Anne, stop, you'll kill yourself!" Patrick shouted. "Stop! I won't hurt you!"

Anne lashed Blaze with her crop again.

And then there was nothing but Blaze's heavy, labored breathing, mingled with her own. The sound of his muffled, drumming hoofbeats, and her own wild, pounding heart.

Branches whipped Anne's face and body. Dead leaves and earth flew up around them, churned by Blaze's big hooves. Blaze stumbled. Anne was thrown abruptly over his head.

She landed hard on her shoulder and rolled onto her back. For a moment she lay still, the wind knocked out of her. And then, when she could breathe, when her vision cleared, she heard someone crashing through the undergrowth on the ridge above. Patrick was calling her name.

Anne sat up, her heart sinking like a rock. The abrupt movement caused Blaze, who was standing a few yards away, to shy nervously. Anne bit her lip, not daring to call out to the nervous horse, afraid of sending him galloping away.

She got to her knees slowly. Her heart was beating like a drum. She could still hear Patrick and his horse descending the ridge which she had taken at such breakneck speed.

Blaze's eyes were rolling, his sides heaving. As Anne stood, he snorted, prancing away. Anne wanted to weep with despair. She did not dare even whisper his name to calm him and get him to stay.

She shot a glance behind her, but all she saw was sunlight filtering through the birch, poplar, and fir trees. But Patrick was up there, looking for her. She could still hear him, but clearly he was walking his mount now as he searched for her.

Periodically he would call her name. He sounded worried. He must realize that she knew the truth about him. His determination to catch her—and do away with her—had probably never been higher. But why? Oh, God, why?

Panic bubbling in her chest, Anne reached for Blaze's reins.

But a bird took flight above their heads at the exact same moment and Blaze snorted and darted away.

Anne muffled a gasp with her hand, watching the horse disappear through the trees in the direction of Waverly Hall. And then she heard Patrick shouting again, but this time he sounded far too close for comfort. Anne crouched, holding her breath, her knees knocking together in fear.

"Dammit, Anne," she heard Patrick cry. And then, miraculously, she heard him heading away, back up the ridge. He was following her runaway horse!

Anne sank to her buttocks in the leaves and dirt,

covering her face with her hands, choking on a sob. She felt so ill she thought she might vomit. Finally she managed to take a few big lungfuls of air.

Slowly she stood. Would Patrick eventually catch her horse, and discover that she was not riding him? Or would Blaze make it back to Waverly Hall? Hope leapt in Anne's breast. Dom was there. If only she could return safely to the Hall, to Dom.

Anne suddenly realized that she wasn't exactly certain where she was.

Oh, God, was she lost? She had taken so many twists and turns in her terrified flight. She decided she must continue in the direction she was going—which was opposite the direction in which Blaze had fled.

The going was difficult. The ridge had become very steep. Angling across was hardly better. The undergrowth was thicker now, growth of new trees and bushes coming past her knees and even to her thighs at times. The woods were denser now, and darker. Looking up, Anne could see but a small patch of the sky. She was very frightened.

She tripped on her skirts. Her gloves were in shreds. And then Anne became aware of an odd, disturbing sensation, one which caused her neck to prickle with unease. And it occurred to her that she was no longer alone.

Anne froze, holding her breath. Patrick was watching her now—she was certain of it. He was stalking her on foot.

Anne's steps quickened. She stumbled more often, tearing the hem of her skirts. Tiny branches cut and stung her face. Anne slapped them away impatiently, her breathing harsh and loud. She saw no sign of her cousin, but she sensed he was out there.

Anne began to run. Branches ripped her skirt. Stones stubbed her toes, rocks bruised her legs. Anne did not stop, gasping for air, sobbing. She fell against an oak tree, caught herself, clung to the thick trunk, panting, tears streaking her cheeks.

And she tried to listen to the silent surrounding woods, through the loud, disturbing cacophony of her harsh panting and frantic heartbeat.

She thought she could detect a bird singing, somewhere far above, and much closer, the faintest rustle of leaves.

There was no wind.

Anne gasped, shoving herself off the oak, running, mindless now.

She hurled around another ancient oak tree, stumbling over one of its serpentine roots. Anne levered herself upward—right into another thick solid wall.

Anne looked up, not at a tree, but at Patrick.

She screamed.

# Chapter 31

*A*nne looked into Patrick's eyes and knew he was the one trying to kill her.

Terror immobilized her. She could not move, she could not breathe.

Her mind began to function. "Why?" she whispered. "Why, Patrick?"

"Why what, Anne?"

She was so terribly dry. "Why did you do all those things to frighten me? It was you, wasn't it? You are the one who has been stalking me, frightening me, trying to kill me!"

Patrick's gaze was unreadable. "I would never hurt you, Anne. You have to believe that."

Anne was shaking. "I could have died if the fire in my bedroom got out of hand, Patrick! I could have broken my neck when Blaze ran away! You must despise me, Patrick, but dear God, why?"

"I don't hate you," he cried fiercely. "I didn't do those things." He glanced around, as if afraid of an intruder. "Now let's go." His tone was harsh, uncompromising. His grip tightened and suddenly he was striding toward the path where his horse nibbled grass.

Anne balked. "No. Where are you taking me? What are you going to do?"

He whirled, facing her. "Why don't you believe me?

I would never hurt you!'' He shouted at her. ''I love you, Anne.''

She shook her head. Her heart was pumping in huge, frightened bursts. ''This is not love, Patrick. You must hate me greatly to want me dead.''

He shook her once, hard. ''I don't want you dead. Your husband is the murderer, Anne, not I.''

Anne almost argued with him. But he must be insane; she should not protest. But what should she do? She was terrified; despite what Patrick insisted, she knew that her life was in jeopardy.

''Let's go, Anne,'' Patrick said firmly.

But before he could pull her toward his mount something suddenly crashed through the bushes and undergrowth above them. Anne cried out as Dom appeared on foot, vaulting down the slope. ''Anne!'' he shouted.

Anne froze. Her heartbeat accelerated. Dom skidded and slipped the rest of the way to its foot.

Patrick moved in front of her. ''Go away, St. Georges,'' he said almost conversationally. ''She doesn't want you. She knows you for what you are— a lowly bastard and a foul murderer. Anne is staying with me.''

Anne made one attempt to pull free of Patrick and ceased struggling. Then her gaze met Dom's and she saw the warning in his eyes. He wanted her to stay still, he wanted to handle Patrick himself.

But Patrick saw their silent exchange and his eyes brightened with anger. ''God, I can't believe it! You still love him? After all he has done—after what he has been proved to be?''

Anne bit off an affirmation.

''Patrick, why don't you let Anne go. You don't want to hurt her; she is your friend.''

''No!'' His fists were clenched. ''You had your chance, Dom, and now you have lost her. Finally, once in your life, things have not gone your way—they have gone mine."

Dom did not move. He stood with his legs braced in a wide, wary stance, his eyes unwaveringly upon Patrick. "Many things have not gone my way, Patrick," he said in a soothing tone. "As you have pointed out, I have recently become some lowly bastard, and I am accused of murder."

Patrick was panting. "Yes, but even so, you are still Rutherford's heir. It is unbelievable. I thought that finally, this time, you might not come out on top! But once again, like a damned cat with nine lives, you land on all fours."

Anne was breathing harshly. She glanced from Patrick's furious face to Dom's implacable one. If only Patrick could be distracted, then she might break free of him and run to Dom.

"You cannot force Anne to go with you against her will," Dom said softly. "Let her go." It was a command, spoken softly, but unmistakable. He turned a penetrating gaze upon Anne. "Come here, Anne."

Anne hesitated. Then Patrick's grip tightened and he jerked her against his side.

"Anne is staying with me. I have waited four long years for this day, Dom." Patrick was fierce. "I have waited four years for Anne to leave you, for Anne to choose me over you."

Anne did not move. Neither did Dom.

"I want her to divorce you," Patrick said.

"I will never give her a divorce," Dom said quietly. "Patrick, I do not blame you for falling in love with my wife. Now, why don't you give me the gun that is hidden in your jacket."

Anne gasped.

"No." Patrick glanced at Anne, suddenly holding a small pistol. "Will you love him when he is nothing but a ghost, Anne? When are you going to give me a chance? A real chance? When are you going to see me as a man? A real man!"

"No, don't," Anne whispered, terrified for Dom. "No, I . . . I do not love him, really, I do not, and . . . I will leave him, Patrick, I will! Please give Dom the gun!" Her voice quaked.

"You're lying," Patrick cried. "Damn you, Anne, you still love him and you are lying." Patrick suddenly pointed the gun at Dom.

"No!" Anne screamed.

Dom stared. "Don't do this. We are friends. I saved your life when we were at Cambridge," he added softly. "You do remember the boating accident, don't you?"

"We are not friends! Not now, not anymore, not since Anne! And I don't give a damn that you saved my life!" Patrick erupted.

"Put the gun down," Dom said.

"Please put the gun down," Anne whispered.

"Will you marry me?" Patrick turned to her. "We can run away together, Anne. In a foreign country it won't matter if you aren't divorced. No one will know the truth. Will you leave him and marry me?"

Anne knew she had to agree. Patrick was unhinged. She looked at Dom, saw the silent encouragement in his eyes. Slowly she nodded.

"Yes," Anne whispered.

But Patrick saw and understood their exchange. "Damn you!" he cried, turning toward Anne. His abrupt movement caused the pistol to point directly at her chest.

Anne gasped.

And Dom leapt at Patrick from behind.

Patrick whirled, the pistol blasting. Dom landed on Patrick, knocking him over backward. The two men struggled, Patrick pushing Dom onto his back. Anne glimpsed blood but could not tell whose it was. The pistol went off again, and Dom slumped lifelessly, his head lolling.

Anne froze, horror-stricken, as Patrick slowly got to his feet. He had splotches of blood everywhere, but Anne could only stare at Dom, blood blossoming on his chest.

She ran forward, dropping to her knees, clutching his face. It was warm. His lids fluttered. "Dom! God, no!"

She bent and laid her cheek to his chest, and was rewarded by the sound of his evenly racing heart. Anne realized that the wound was between his collarbone and his armpit. She inhaled, shaking, and looked up at Patrick. She had to fight to keep the rage from her face.

And his expression was one of shock.

Hope surged in Anne's breast. "He needs a doctor. Patrick, go get a doctor."

But Patrick did not move, staring down at Dom, his face draining of all color. "Oh, my God," Patrick said, eyes wide. "Oh, my God. Is he dying?"

"We need a doctor!" Anne cried. She removed her riding jacket, her movements fast and furious, and pressed the wadded coat on top of Dom's wound. "Patrick, Dom is going to die. He may be dying right now." Tears formed helplessly. *"Please go and get a doctor."*

Suddenly Patrick was on his knees beside Dom, whose lashes were fluttering. "Oh, God," he whispered again, his eyes filling with tears, "what have I done?"

"Dom, Dom," Anne cried, pushing down harder on her coat, not daring to remove the material to see how badly he was bleeding. "Can you hear me? Dom, darling, you will be fine."

Dom moaned. His eyes opened slowly. His irises were huge, unfocused.

"You will not die," Anne said fiercely. "Go get the doctor, Patrick, and servants, *now!*"

Suddenly Patrick leapt to his feet. He was as white

as any sheet. Without a word, giving no indication that he had heard her or even understood her or what he intended to do, he ran to his horse, dropping the pistol as he did so. He mounted and spurred the bay into a gallop and disappeared, leaving Anne and Dom alone.

Anne's heart raced with fright. Panic threatened to consume her. She took a deep, steadying breath. What if Patrick were running away?

"Anne."

She looked down at Dom, who was a ghastly shade of gray. But his eyes were focused now. "You are going to be fine." She forced a smile.

"How badly am I hurt?"

She licked her lips. "I don't know. There was a lot of blood. But the wound seemed closer to your shoulder than your heart." She could hardly speak. If Dom died, she would die, for she would never be able to bear it.

Sweat had beaded on his temples. "I'll hold your coat to the wound. Take off your petticoat and rip it into strips for bandages." By the time he had finished the sentences, he was out of breath, his voice barely audible.

"Don't speak. Save your strength." Anne placed Dom's hand on her coat, pressing it down. It made her sick to see him stanching the flow of his own blood. "I don't know if Patrick went for the doctor or not."

He did not respond. He was eerily white now, sweating profusely, his eyes closed. But he was holding her coat to his wound.

Anne stood, divesting herself of her petticoat. Ripping the material should not have been an easy task, but she was consumed with superhuman strength. She glanced at Dom and saw that he was watching her. "Don't worry. I won't die." His voice was somewhat stronger now.

Anne managed a weak smile.

"Help me sit up."

Anne dropped to her knees. Dom's face was set in hard lines of determination as she helped him sit. Clearly he refused to groan. She removed the coat. The wound began to bleed freshly all over again. As quickly as she could, while Dom panted out nearly inaudible instructions, Anne bandaged him. Then she helped him lie down, using her coat as a pillow.

His eyes were closed, he was grayer than before, covered with sweat.

Anne stroked his brow. Tears of helplessness and fear filled her eyes. Where was Patrick? She prayed that he had gone for help, any help.

The shadows lengthened. Anne tried to decide how long she had been waiting there with Dom, praying that he was not dying, but she could not determine if it had been a quarter of an hour or a full hour. Anxiety made each minute seem like an eternity. And Dom had lapsed into unconsciousness.

The bandage had turned bright red.

Anne heard a rider. No, riders. She jumped to her feet. Patrick's bay galloped down the path, followed by two other horses. She heard more riders approaching in the distance. "Thank God!" she cried, recognizing Bennet and Verig.

"Grooms are following with a litter," Bennet said, dismounting. "And a groom went for the doctor."

Anne almost fainted with relief. Then she turned and saw Patrick kneeling beside Dom. He was weeping.

"Don't die," he whispered. "I never meant to kill you. Dom . . . I love you more than my own brothers; God, please, don't die."

Anne could no longer control her fear, and the doctor brusquely sent her from Dom's chamber. Outside she paced, holding a wadded handkerchief to her eyes, praying for her husband, and regretting every single moment of conflict, misunderstanding, and estrangement. Patrick sat on a settee, his head hanging.

And despite what he had done, Anne felt sorry for him.

He sensed her regard and looked up for the first time in the past half hour. "I must have gone mad."

"Yes."

"I would have never hurt you, Anne. I only wanted to marry you. To steal you away from Dom."

Anne did not remind him that his actions might have hurt her badly, or even killed her. She had no doubt, despite his denials, that he had set the fire in her bedroom and poisoned her horse. "Is it Dom you hate, Patrick? I thought the two of you were friends from boyhood."

"I don't hate Dom." A tear rolled down his cheek. "All of my life I have lived in Dom's shadow. You can't possibly understand what it was like. When I saw the two of you together in Scotland, something snapped. I know that now. But if he dies, I do not think I could live. I will kill myself."

"You will do no such thing," Anne snapped. Never before had she realized how weak Patrick was. "And Dom is not going to die."

"Why is the doctor taking so long?" Patrick asked.

Anne was wondering the exact same thing. A moment later the door to the bedroom opened and Bennet appeared. He looked exhausted. "Doctor Cobb says you can come in now, my lady. And His Lordship is awake."

Her heart leaping, Anne ran past Bennet into the bedroom. She did not see Verig hovering over the bed, or the doctor, who was gathering up his bandages and equipment. She saw only Dom. He was sitting up, the covers pulled up to his waist, bare-chested. A snowy white bandage covered his wound, and he was no longer a ghastly shade of gray.

Anne hurried forward, and it seemed that her feet trod the air. "Dom."

His gaze fastened on hers. "Are you all right?"

Tears filled her eyes. "Me?" She laughed, a shaky sound, and sat by his hip. Suddenly they were clasping hands. "You are the one who was shot, darling."

His eyes darkened. "I like that endearment, Anne."

She moistened her lips. "Dom, if you had died . . ." She was so overcome with emotion that she could not continue.

Dom cupped her face with one strong hand. "Are you trying to tell me that you love me, Anne?"

She nodded, still incapable of speech.

His own gaze became suspiciously moist. "When I realized that Patrick was carrying on with Belle—Caldwell informed me last night—I also realized he was the one stalking you. My fear for you, Anne, brought me here. I have never been so afraid in my life as when I found out that Patrick had also come to the country." Suddenly he had her hands in his. "I don't understand what happened to Patrick," he said, and his voice broke.

Anne's heart twisted. She recalled how Patrick and Dom had ridden about the countryside together as boisterous young men when she was a moonstruck child of eleven. They had both been handsome and cocky, and all the single ladies had been agog over the two of them. She remembered Patrick's stories of the pranks they had pulled together at Cambridge. At that age, Patrick and Dom had seemed inseparable. "I can't understand either," Anne finally admitted.

They exchanged a long look. Anne hurt for Dom, sharing his sorrow for this painful betrayal.

Then Anne rose, ushering the doctor and Verig out of the room. "How is my husband?" she asked Cobb quietly.

He nodded, saying, "You have nothing to worry

about, Lady Anne. Your husband is young and strong and will be up and about in a day or two. Until then, though, bed rest. I will return tomorrow to check on his condition."

"Thank you," Anne said, wringing his hand. She returned to Dom.

"Patrick is not evil," Dom told her with a flash of anger.

Before Anne could comment, and agree, Patrick said from the open doorway, "I never meant to hurt Anne, Dom. Please believe me. I only wanted her to think that you were doing those things, to scare her away from you."

Dom stared at Patrick, his expression one openly heartbroken. "It doesn't matter, Patrick. I forgive you."

Patrick seemed about to burst into tears. "It's just never been fair," he whispered. "But I am sorry, so sorry."

"Patrick, what do you plan to do?" Dom asked gravely.

Anne suddenly looked from her husband to her cousin, horrified by a sudden comprehension. "Patrick, do you know who killed Matthew Fairhaven?"

He hesitated.

Dom stared, tensing. "Patrick—no!"

Patrick flushed. "It was an accident. I didn't mean to do it. I wanted to know what was in that diary. He refused to tell me and I grew angry and we fought. But afterward it seemed so perfect—to lay the blame on Dom. I'm the one who went to the police."

Anne was sick, almost violently so. She returned to the bed and reached for Dom's hand. He gripped hers, hard. A silence fell upon the room.

Dom finally spoke, quietly, authoritatively. But his eyes were filled with grief. "Patrick, you must go to the police and tell them what you have just told us."

"No! They would lock me up." Patrick turned and

went to the door. There he paused. "It was an accident. I don't want to hang."

"Were there any witnesses?" Dom asked.

"No."

He hesitated. "How did you get my sapphire stud?"

"I followed you and Anne to Scotland," Patrick said. "Anne knows. I stole into the castle several times." His chest heaved. "Dom, I am sorry."

"So am I," Dom said sadly. "Patrick, if you do not go to the authorities, I am afraid I will have to go myself."

Patrick's gaze was wrenching. Without another word, he fled the room.

Anne sat down beside Dom; he pulled her against his side. She looked at him, sharing his grief.

"We have to tell the police what we know, Anne," he said.

"I know," she said, laying her head carefully upon his good shoulder.

He held her tightly, then shifted so their gazes could connect. "But there is no law that says we must go to the police immediately."

Anne's heart raced. Despite what Patrick had done, she did not want to see him imprisoned or hanged. "Yes. After all, you are ill. Perhaps in a few days, or next week, we shall tell the inspector everything."

Dom's gaze was piercing. He said softly, "I hope Patrick is smart enough to recognize that he must flee the country."

Anne hoped so, too.

# Chapter 32

*Rutherford House*

"I am here to see His Grace," Clarisse announced.

Caldwell nodded without expression. "He has just awoken from his nap."

"His nap." Clarisse felt quite jubilant. How infantile he had become. She was no longer afraid of him. "So there is no real improvement?"

Caldwell was leading her not upstairs, but to the library. "No, madam, to the contrary. He speaks a few words now, although he has yet to regain the use of his lower body."

Briefly Clarisse was dismayed. She had imagined him to be completely paralyzed. But then she consoled herself with the fact that he was still bedridden, could hardly speak, and would soon, undoubtedly, die.

But not before she came to tell him what she had come to tell him, not before she had her revenge.

Caldwell announced her at the massive double doors. The duke was sitting up in a chaise, draped in a light gold cashmere throw. A fire burned cheerfully in the hearth. The *London Times* was open at his hip. For a moment, Clarisse was taken aback. His expression as he regarded her was so patrician and so daunting that she thought Caldwell had lied, that the duke had recovered completely. For a moment, Clarisse lost her nerve.

But then he spoke. He rasped, "Wh-what?"

Clarisse's pulse was racing now. She could not smile. She had waited so long for this. Nervous tension beset her, making her voice husky when she spoke. "Hello, Your Grace. I have come to call upon you."

His nostrils flared. "D-D-Dom?"

Her gaze narrowed. "Are you worried about Dom? Well, he is certainly in trouble, is he not? And I do not speak of the murder he is accused of, I am speaking about the fact that the entire world now knows him to be illegitimate." She felt almost faint. Then Clarisse realized with a start that Caldwell remained. "We don't need you, Caldwell, you may go."

Caldwell turned and looked at the duke.

"G-go," he said, a command.

Clarisse felt savagely satisfied.

Caldwell left, appearing strangely reluctant, closing the door behind him.

Clarisse smiled now and came to stand beside the duke. "You do know, don't you, that I still hate you, and that I have not forgiven you for what you have done?"

His answer was a cool smile. His eyes were alarmingly sharp.

Clarisse felt a brief frisson of fear then, as though he were still powerful enough to control her, to master her, but she dismissed it. "Yes, I know, you hate me, too. But you have no reason to!" She cried. "You hurt me—not the other way around!"

The duke's expression remained set and implacable.

Clarisse stared down at him. "You hurt me! You almost destroyed me! And why? Why? Because you loved your precious Janice!"

The duke started. His eyes were wide. He had paled.

"Do you think me a fool? I know you never loved Sarah, not that way. I guessed the truth a very long time ago. When I was nine years old, I saw you looking at her. I had accompanied my father when he came to call on you. I was hiding in the bushes while Sarah and Janice sat in the garden with my father, waiting for you to return. You were coming back from riding and you thought you were alone. To this day, I have never forgotten the way you looked at her.''

Rutherford appeared aghast. His fists gripped the coverlet. He was trying desperately to speak. ''Wh—wh—what?''

Clarisse's throat was suddenly tight with tears. ''Never, never did you look at me that way.''

''Wh-what!'' the duke almost shouted. ''What you do!''

''You are afraid, aren't you, that I will tell the entire world that you were in love with your sister-in-law?'' Her expression hardened. ''That's why Janice ran away after her debut—the debut you gave her. Damn her! Damn you!'' Clarisse was close to weeping.

Rutherford was turning red. ''Wh  what,'' he said with great difficulty, ''you . . . w-want!'' It was a furious exclamation, not a question.

''I want my revenge,'' Clarisse hissed. She swiped at her tears and stood over him, shaking. ''Listen well, old man. You will soon die. And the truth—*our* truth—will die with you.''

Rutherford gasped, ''N-nooo.''

But Clarisse ignored him. ''I am never going to reveal the fact that Dom is our son—that he is *your* son. *Never!*''


Blake couldn't help but be pleased. His mood was very primitive and very male. In fact, he felt quite smug. Although he was worried about his best friend Dom, he had a woman on his mind, one who had given him quite the chase. But he had already seen Felicity twice since his father's ball. When it came to sensuality and passion, Felicity seemed to be his match exactly.

He wasn't in love with her, of course. He had only loved once, and it had been a heartbreaking experience. He knew, without a doubt, that he would never love any woman that way again. Still, he was twenty-eight, and perhaps it was time to marry. He was considering making Felicity his wife.

His open brougham rumbled around the block and drew abreast of Harold Reed's stone mansion. Immediately Blake saw the Reed coach being readied for travel. Two footmen were loading up baggage. Felicity's maid stood on the curb, carrying a small bag that must belong to her mistress, a light cloak on her shoulders. Suddenly Felicity emerged from the house.

Her voice rang out as she spoke to her butler. "I have no idea when I shall be back. You may keep the house prepared for my return."

He bowed obediently.

Blake's good humor vanished. A bad feeling replaced it. He stepped down from the brougham; his driver did not have to be told to wait. Felicity was coming down the wide front steps, and upon seeing him, she faltered.

Blake strolled toward her. "Hello, darling."

She did not smile and her chin lifted. "Hello, Blake."

He eyed her traveling cape. "Where are you off to now, Felicity?"

She had halted and she hesitated before replying. "I am in need of some country air."

"Oh, really?" he was mocking. "Let me guess. You are off to Hunting Way."

"That's right." She leveled a cool stare on him.

He stepped closer to her, gripping her arm. "My, how affectionate you are this afternoon, darling. It's hard to believe that you are the same woman I left at dawn."

She jerked her arm free. "Go away, Blake. I am busy and in a rush, in case you haven't noticed."

"I have noticed," he drawled, but he was angry; worse, he was dismayed. "You have learned that Dom is at Waverly Hall and that is why you are returning home."

"Of course not," she said, clearly lying.

He wanted to shake her until she came to her senses and forgot about his best friend. "Damn it! He doesn't want you, Felicity. He is in love with his wife."

"Anne?" Felicity scoffed. "That's impossible."

"When are you going to give up?"

She faced him, flushing. About to protest.

"Don't," he said, lifting one hand. "Don't deny it."

"All right, I won't." She shoved past him and hurried to her coach, her green skirts lifted to her ankles.

Blake stared after her, aware of a rising tide of hurt. It was distinctly unpleasant. Then he followed her. "Don't go."

Felicity was being helped inside the coach by a footman. He slammed the door closed. She settled herself on the plush seat and faced Blake through the window. She said not a word, her jaw squared with determination.

Blake recognized the fact that he was an utter fool. "Goodbye, Felicity." It was hard to get the words out clearly; his voice was thick. "Have a pleasant trip."

Suddenly she paled. "I *will* see you when I get back," she said, finally smiling. "I won't stay in the country long."

"No," Blake said. "Under the circumstances, that would be impossible."

Felicity's eyes widened.

Blake knocked on the side of the coach. "Off with you, sir," he commanded.

The coachman released the brakes, slapped the reins, and the coach rolled forward.

"Blake!" Felicity cried, straining now to see him.

Blake turned his back on her and walked away.

\*      \*      \*

Two days had passed since the accidental shooting. Dom was in bed, not happily. Although Doctor Cobb had been there that morning, and was pleased with Dom's recovery, he wanted Dom to rest for another day. A tray of food was by Dom's right hip; Anne sat by his left side.

"Why won't you eat?" she scolded.

"Good God, I've eaten enough to feed an army." His arm went around her waist and suddenly Anne found herself on her back on the bed beside him—with Dom leaning over her with unconcealed intent. "There is only one way I am going to remain in this bed another day, darling," he said in a very seductive tone of voice.

"You are ill!" Anne squeaked, her heart fluttering.

"Hardly," he growled, and then, to prove it, he kissed her.

It was not a chaste kiss. Anne gave up all resistance quickly. His mouth opened hers, languidly, expertly, his tongue stroked hers. When he raised his head, his golden eyes were bright and Anne was breathless and filled with yearning.

"Dom, it is the middle of the day."

"I thought I cured you of all ladylike inclinations in Scotland?" His tone was teasing.

Anne relaxed, reaching up to stroke his beloved face. "But we were alone there. Here we are in a house full of servants—all of whom are justifiably concerned for your welfare, and as you well know, Bennet and Verig peek in on you repeatedly."

"There's a damn good lock on the door," Dom said. Then his smile faded. Suddenly he flopped on his back on the bed. "But we weren't alone in Scotland, Anne."

Anne sat up. "I know." She reached for his hand. "The good news is that Patrick has disappeared."

"Yes." Dom stared at the ceiling. "He should be well out of the country by now."

Anne wished she could ease his sorrow. "Let's try to forget him, Dom. Please. We must try to forget all of the past."

His gaze roamed her face. "Do you finally forgive me, Anne? For being an utter coward and an utter fool?"

"Do you forgive me for thinking, even for a moment, that you were the one trying to frighten me—that you had murdered Matthew Fairhaven?" Anne replied.

"Yes, I do. What matters is that we have somehow overcome a terrible misunderstanding, and a terrible mistrust of one another."

Tears filled Anne's eyes. She laid her head on his chest. "I love you so, Dom."

He reached up to touch her cheek, cupping it. "What matters now is that we put the past behind us, completely, and forge a wonderful future together, you and I."

Anne nodded. "If only you could know just how I have dreamed of this kind of moment happening between us. I have dreamed of this since I was a child, Dom."

"I hurt you so badly, Anne." Dom sat up, pulling her against him. "How can you really forgive me?"

"Not only do I forgive you," Anne said without hesitation, "I think I understand why you did what you did."

"If you understand, then you are smarter than I," Dom said with a short laugh.

Anne smiled at him tenderly, stroking his brow. "We were too well suited, I believe, and meant to be, and that terrified you. You grew up a lonely, forsaken child. Your parents set a frightening example of what marriage can be. You were afraid to love a woman."

"I was afraid to love you," Dom said simply. "I had

learned to be self-reliant for so long, and instinctively I knew you were my destiny—but it quite scared me to death.''

Their gazes met, held. Their smiles faded. Anne gripped Dom's hands more tightly and leaned forward, touching his mouth with hers. "Neither one of us will ever be lonely again."

Dom wrapped his hand around her neck, a primitive and proprietary gesture Anne now recognized, and kissed her deeply. When he was through, she was flushed. He grinned mischievously at her. "Did Doctor Cobb say we *can't* make love?"

Anne gasped. "As if I would ask him such a thing!"

Dom laughed. "When did the doctor say I can travel?"

"At the end of the week."

Dom frowned. "I want to return to Rutherford House tomorrow."

"Tomorrow!" Anne gasped. "You most certainly cannot—will not—travel tomorrow."

"Anne, I am worried about my grandfather. I am certainly well enough to travel."

Anne sobered. "There is nothing you yourself can do to help the duke. We receive reports from Caldwell every day and your grandfather is holding his own now. But I agree, as soon as you are better, we must return to town."

Dom nodded, but stared into space. His brow was furrowed.

"Dom, what is it?"

He met her gaze, but quickly looked away. "Nothing. I am suddenly tired, that is all, and worried about my grandfather's health."

"There's more, isn't there?"

He glanced at her. "Yes."

Anne lifted his hands and clasped them to her breast. "Dom, I have loved you since I first laid eyes upon

you when I was a little girl. I know what is bothering
you. I have always loved you, I will always love you,
and it doesn't matter to me that Philip wasn't your
father. It doesn't matter to me who your father is.''

Dom was silent. He finally said, ''It matters to me.
A great deal.''

''You must not dwell upon it. You are Philip's legal
heir, forget the rest.''

He met her searching eyes. ''I would forget if I
could. But it is a haunting question, and I will be
haunted by it for the rest of my life.''

''Don't do this to yourself, please.'' Anne laid her
head on his chest. ''It truly doesn't matter. I would
love you whether you were a duke or a pauper.''

Dom kissed the top of her head. ''And I love you,
Anne,'' he said. ''I love you so much that sometimes
it hurts.''

Anne and Dom were taking tea in the sitting room
of the master suite when Inspector Hopper's arrival
was announced.

Anne jumped guiltily to her feet. She was pale. ''You
weren't supposed to leave town,'' she said to Dom.

Dom sat on the chintz chaise, having bullied Anne
into allowing him to leave his bed. ''Relax. I am innocent. Or have you forgotten?'' He turned to Bennet,
who stood in the doorway, as agitated as Anne. ''Bennet, ask the inspector if he wishes to come upstairs and
take tea with me and my wife.''

''Yes, my lord,'' Bennet bowed and left.

Silence fell across the room. Anne began to pace.
Dom lifted the delicate Wedgwood teacup and sipped
from it. Anne spun around. ''How can you drink tea at
a time like this?''

''This is the perfect time to take tea, Anne. Come sit
and drink with me.'' He was issuing a mild command.
Her face mirroring her anxiety, Anne obeyed, re-

turning to the bergère she had vacated. She managed to force a swallow of the warm brew down. Then there was a knock on the door. Anne jumped up, knocking her teacup over. The dark liquid spilled over the pristine white tablecloth.

"Anne," Dom said firmly. "Bennet, you may enter."

"Inspector Hopper, Your Lordship," Bennet said, ushering the plump inspector inside.

Hopper paused in the center of the room, his baggy suit disheveled from his journey, a flush creeping up his neck to his face. "My lord, my lady, forgive me for interrupting."

Dom smiled. "All is forgiven, Inspector. Come, sit, join us."

Hopper came forward, gingerly sitting on a red velvet chair with clawed arms and feet. He waved off Anne's attempt to serve him tea. And although Dom wore a dressing gown, Hopper was shrewd and he said, "Have you hurt yourself, my lord?"

"I was accidentally shot," Dom said casually, as if this kind of event happened every day. "Are you here to berate me for leaving town?"

"No, to the contrary," Hopper began.

Anne jerked, eyes wide.

"I have come with the pleasure of informing you that you are no longer a suspect in Fairhaven's murder."

"What?" Anne cried, on her feet.

Dom smiled. "That is very good news. What have you discovered?"

"A witness has come forward, a very impeccable personage, I assure you. The witness saw the entire struggle, including Fairhaven's fall, which caused his death."

Anne and Dom exchanged looks. "I see," said Dom. "You have learned the murderer's identity?"

"No. She was heavily veiled."

"She?" Anne echoed, looking at Dom again.

"Yes, apparently Fairhaven struggled with a woman. Amazing, isn't it? Had he not lost his balance at the precise moment she pushed him, he would still be alive today. We have no clue as to the woman's identity, though. Not only was she veiled, she traveled in a hired hansom. But we have several leads." He beamed.

"Well," Dom said, sitting up straighter. "This is indeed good news. Thank you for bringing it to me and my wife personally and promptly, Inspector. We are very grateful."

Hopper stood. "It truly was my pleasure, my lord. I, personally, am thrilled you are innocent. Now, I do not wish to intrude, so I must be off."

"Nonsense," Anne came forward and clasped his hands. She was smiling widely. "You cannot go back to London tonight. You will stay here. We dine at eight. Please, Inspector. We would love to have you."

His eyes were wide. He glanced around the high-ceilinged room with its magnificent furnishings. "Why, I have never spent the night in such a palace before, thank you, my lady!"

A few moments later he was escorted by a servant to a guest room. Anne faced Dom. They stared at one another in stunned silence. Outside, twilight was falling, and shadows crept into the sitting room.

Anne wet her lips. "Dom, Patrick denied setting the fire in my bedroom. He denied poisoning my horse. He swore he never wanted to hurt me. He only admitted to following us to Scotland." She was hoarse. "Why would Patrick lie about Fairhaven?"

"I can think of only one reason." Dom's jaw flexed. "To protect Felicity."

## Chapter 33

*A*nne knew that Dom was not as fully healed as he claimed when he lay down after Hopper left and promptly fell asleep. Anne would use the moment to change into her supper gown, but before doing that, she would ask Bennet to ice a bottle of champagne. Dom was now a free man, and tonight they would celebrate that fact and the beginning of the wondrous future they would share.

But as Anne went downstairs, she was very disturbed by what she and Dom had learned.

Had Felicity set the fire in her bedroom? Had she poisoned Blaze? Felicity had once sworn revenge. Was she capable of murder?

Who else could it be? Surely not Clarisse, Dom's very own mother.

Anne shoved her terrible forebodings—and dread—aside. "Bennet?" she called, hurrying down the hall. The salon doors were open, and, catching a movement inside the room, she turned, expecting to find Bennet inside.

"Hello, Anne," Felicity smiled at her.

Anne froze.

Felicity's brows rose. "Anne, you are as white as a sheet. Is something wrong?"

Anne tried to think. But it was impossible. She was

stunned and terribly afraid. Where was Bennet? Where
was everyone? "I ... I wasn't aware that you were
here, Felicity," she managed.

"The front door was open. As we are family, I decided to forgo formalities and just come in."

Anne's heart thundered in her ears. "I see. Do you
wish to speak with me?"

"Actually, I came to see Dom." Her smile faded.
"How is he?"

Anne's scrambled wits began to function. If Felicity
knew about Dom's wound, then she had spoken with
Patrick before he fled the country. Patrick—who was
protecting her.

"Dom is recovering nicely, thank you." Anne looked
over her shoulder again, hoping to espy a footman or
a maid. The hall outside the salon was silent, empty.
"Dom is sleeping now," Anne added. "Perhaps you
might return tomorrow?"

"I don't think so," Felicity said. "You do know
why I am really here, don't you, Anne?"

Anne stiffened. The word "no" was on the tip of
her tongue. Slowly, she nodded. Perspiring. "You are
the one, aren't you, Felicity? You set the fire, you poisoned my horse. You are the one who wants me dead."

"Yes!" Felicity snarled. "Yes! Yes! I should have
been the duchess of Rutherford, not you! Do you understand me?" She was livid. She spit her words with
venom, with hatred. "I can never forgive you for taking
that away from me! And now the duke lies near death.
Dom will soon be the ninth duke of Rutherford. Do
you really think I would allow you to be his duchess?
The title, the wealth, the power, it all belongs to me!"
she cried.

Anne did not hesitate. She whirled to leave the room.
Her pulse roared in her ears. She was tense with dread,
expecting the worst, perhaps even a knife in her back.

"Stop!" Felicity shrieked.

Anne halted in midstride, turned, and saw the small pearl-handled revolver in Felicity's gloved hand. "Don't."

"Why not?" Felicity smiled coldly, pointing the gun at Anne's heart. "I am an expert shot. I have been practicing for years. For four long years, to be exact. Will you beg me to spare you, Anne?"

Anne felt the sweat trickling down her face, between her breasts. Dom was upstairs sleeping, Hopper in the far west wing, and no staff was present. With utter clarity, she realized that no one could help her now, she must save herself—if she wished to live.

And Anne did wish to live. With Dom, the prince of all of her dreams.

"Yes, I will beg," Anne said, gauging the distance between them. A dozen steps separated Anne from her cousin, no more.

Felicity smiled, and it reminded Anne of a cat's cunning expression before pouncing on—and killing—a mouse.

Suddenly Anne looked past Felicity with a gasp. "Patrick!"

Felicity whirled.

Anne ran forward, barreling into her cousin and knocking her down. The derringer flew from her hand, bouncing across the floor. As it did so, it went off, exploding loudly in the salon. The glass dome on one of the lamps burst loudly, shattering everywhere. Patrick, of course, was not behind Felicity.

Felicity howled, trying to claw Anne's face. Anne managed to keep the plumper woman beneath her, and finally gripped her wrists hard, pinning her cousin to the floor. Both women were panting harshly. Anne narrowly avoided being kneed in the groin.

Bennet and several footmen exploded into the room. "My God, Your Ladyship, what happened! Are you all right? Are you hurt?'' Bennet cried, skidding to a stop beside them. His face was starkly white.

"Someone get Mr. Hopper,'' Anne said, suddenly overwhelmed with an intensely savage satisfaction. She continued to straddle Felicity, pressing her wrists into the Persian rug, while her cousin stared up at her with unadulterated hatred.

Anne almost smiled. Felicity had succeeded in terrorizing her, had intended to hurt her, to murder her. But Anne had defended herself—Anne had won.

"Anne,'' Dom shouted, rushing into the room. He halted beside the two women, wide-eyed with shock. An instant later he recovered. "Jacobs, the gun!'' he snapped. As the footman raced to retrieve it, Dom reached down to help his wife up.

Anne rose, moving into Dom's arms. Felicity sat up, but did not try to rise from the floor. She stared at Dom and Anne, her eyes filling with tears. "Dom, please, listen to me,'' she cried. "I love you—''

"Be silent,'' he ordered, not even looking at her. He only had eyes for Anne. "Are you hurt?'' he asked urgently.

"No,'' Anne said, laying her head on his chest and wrapping her arms around him. How good he felt. How good it felt to be alive. "No, I have never been better.''

Dom's arms tightened around her. He held her solidly, close.

Felicity wept.

A few moments later Inspector Hopper took Felicity to the village, where the constable promptly jailed her for the night.

Dom was helped out of the Waverly coach by both footmen, Anne having preceded him to the sidewalk. He shrugged off further assistance, earning a reproving glance from Anne. It was the next day and close to dusk. "I am much better," Dom insisted, as they slowly ascended the stairs to Rutherford House.

"That is clearly true, but it was a long trip, and you should not be too proud to accept some assistance from your staff under these circumstances," Anne harped.

"Shrew," Dom murmured affectionately.

Anne smiled, holding his arm tightly.

At the door, Caldwell appeared instantly. "My lord, my lady," he almost cried, smiling.

"How is my grandfather?" Dom asked as they entered the foyer.

"He is vastly improved," Caldwell beamed. "Today he stood up!"

"That is wonderful!" Anne exclaimed.

Dom was thrilled.

"My lord," Caldwell continued, "the duke is most anxious to speak with you."

"And I with him," Dom said. "Where is His Grace?"

"In the library, my lord."

Dom hurried down the hall, Anne on his heels. The double doors had been left wide open. Dom halted when he saw his grandfather sitting in his favorite leather armchair, a newspaper open on his lap. The duke looked up, saw him, and smiled. "Dom."

"Grandfather!" Dom rushed into the room and gripped his grandfather's hand. He wanted to embrace him. His voice, when he spoke, was rough with tears. "Thank God you are recovering," he choked.

"S-son," the duke said as roughly.

Dom smiled, gestured to Anne. "I know this will make you very happy, Grandfather. Anne and I have reconciled."

The duke smiled as Anne came forward. She bent and kissed his cheek, then moved into Dom's embrace. "We have more than reconciled, Your Grace," she said softly. She turned a potent look on Dom.

"Yes," Dom said. "I admit I have been an utter fool. I am madly in love with my wife."

"Good," the duke approved. "S-sit down."

Dom pulled up a chair for Anne and an ottoman for himself. "Do not tire yourself on our account," he began

"D-dom." It was a bark. "You . . . are . . . my . . . s-son."

Dom stared. "I beg your pardon?" he finally said, certain that he had not heard his grandfather correctly.

"You! Son!" the duke quite shouted. "You! My son!"

Dom stared, blanching.

Anne stood. "Your Grace?" She gasped. "Are you saying that Dom is your son? That you and Clarisse . . . ?" She trailed off, bewildered, stunned. Unsure of whether to be horrified or thrilled.

"Yes. Caldwell!"

Caldwell appeared instantly. "My lord," he said to Dom, "the duke wishes me to explain."

Dom was staring at his grandfather—at his father? He hardly heard Caldwell. This was impossible! He was shocked, disbelieving—Clarisse had betrayed Philip with Rutherford? "I don't understand," he whispered to the duke.

"Caldwell!" the duke commanded.

Caldwell cleared his throat. Dom turned to him, dazed. "Your mother had a liaison with His Grace before she ever met Philip. She became pregnant during that time. The duke had no interest in marrying, not her or anyone, and he did not especially believe her to be with child when she went to him and pressed him to marry her. He thought it a ploy to trap him into marriage. It was a ploy he had already encountered twice since Sarah's death."

Dom began to understand. He began to tremble. He

looked at the duke—his father. "Oh, God," he whispered.

"Clarisse was furious with the duke's rejection. She eloped with Philip almost immediately. Philip did not realize the truth until you, my lord, were a year old. He was sworn to secrecy. You were legally adopted and made Philip's heir. Clarisse knew none of this, it was between the duke and the marquis."

Dom was staring at his grandfather though a haze of tears. He wet his lips. "Grand ... Father. You never told me. I ... I am overwhelmed."

The duke was crying. "I love you," he said very clearly.

Tears streaked down Dom's cheeks. "And I love you ... Father." He was suddenly kneeling at the duke's side. At his father's side. He gripped his hands, holding them against his heart. "This explains everything," he whispered.

"Please," the duke said. "Forgive ... me?"

"God, yes!" Dom cried.

"Public!" the duke cried.

Dom wiped his eyes. "Public?"

"W-world! To know!" the duke shouted. "W-won't ... die! Yet!"

Dom stood and embraced his father. The duke's arms moved slightly enough to close around Dom's back gently.

Anne wept. Caldwell was also crying. He offered her his handkerchief, then he left the room in order to find another one.

"Mother," Dom said, his tone urgent, his gaze intense. His mother had, according to Caldwell, locked herself in the bedroom since the day before. He stood on the threshold now. Although she had not come out since an interview with the duke yesterday, she had opened it for him.

Clarisse stood at the window, gazing out onto the bustling street below. The trees were brilliantly orange and yellow. She did not look at him.

Dom entered the room, closing the door. "I know. He told me. My father told me everything."

Clarisse was pale, red-eyed. She glanced at Dom. "I hate him." Tears trickled from her eyes.

"Don't speak that way," Dom cried, moving swiftly to her. He took her by the arms. "Why didn't you tell me? How could you let me suffer so? Didn't you care? The scandal would have destroyed me. I was going to lose everything."

She looked at him. "I cared, Dominick. But not as much as I cared about revenge against your father."

"Because he rejected you?" Dom asked, puzzled, aching.

She nodded. "Because he loved someone else."

"Sarah."

"No. He loved Anne's mother, Janice."

Dom started. "Surely—"

"He loved Janice Stanhope Stewart," Clarisse cried, "and that is one of the reasons why he loves Anne so, why he wanted to see you and Anne together. But it doesn't matter anymore. He has won. God, he has won, again."

"I am sorry he hurt you. Very sorry. But you should have told the truth when Fairhaven broke the scandal."

Clarisse did not respond.

"Mother," Dom said hoarsely, "I do want you to know that I am trying very hard to understand your motivations, and that this doesn't change anything. You are still my mother. My feelings for you remain the same. I will protect you from any scandal."

"I don't think you can protect me, Dominick." Her mouth trembled. "What should I do, now?"

"I think that you should retire to the country."

"Yes." Clarisse closed her eyes briefly, resigned.

"The duke and I intend to make the truth public. He has placed a notice in tomorrow's *Times*. He has already adjusted his will, adding a clause proclaiming the truth. There will be an uproar for a while. It would be best if you remained in the country for a while. I am Rutherford's son and I will be forgiven all, immediately. In time, because of my position and power, you will be able to reenter society, I promise you that, Mother."

Clarisse nodded.

Dom hesitated, then kissed her cheek. He turned and crossed the room. When he was at the door, Clarisse called out. "Dominick."

He paused.

"You know, this has been a very painful secret. It has caused a great deal of anguish to everyone. I think I am relieved now that the lies are finally over, now that the truth is finally out."

Their gazes met.

"Perhaps I should have done things differently," Clarisse said. "I am sorry, Dominick, if I have hurt you."

"Thank you, Mother," he said.

It was a mild autumn day. The sky was brightly blue, the trees in the park behind Waverly Hall were resplendently red and gold, and the gardens where Anne waited were filled with the last roses of summer. Red and white and gold, the roses crept up the terrace walls, and meandered about the limestone fountain.

Anne smiled to herself, then glanced down at the note she held in her hand. How reminiscent it was! The note was from Dom, suggesting a rendezvous. *Meet me in the garden behind the ballroom,* it read. It was signed, *Dom.* Anne held the ivory vellum to her breast. Four years ago she had received just such a note that night of Dom's engagement to Felicity.

Anne sobered. She and Dom had decided not to press charges against Felicity for her malicious efforts against Anne. But Felicity had been tried for Fairhaven's accidental murder. Felicity had tearfully pleaded her innocence, and the verdict had been not guilty. These days, Felicity was residing in Paris.

Meanwhile, all of England had recovered from the shock of learning that Dom was actually the duke's son. Anne and Dom had retired to Waverly Hall immediately after the public announcement in the newspapers, but from that moment on they had been deluged with invitations to teas and balls; in fact, Anne had hired another secretary to handle the endless correspondence. It was quite clear to her that when they returned to London they would find precious little private time to spend together, alone.

Not that it mattered. Anne was so terribly in love that she rarely walked on the ground. And Dom was so happy, as well.

Clarisse continued to reside in the country at Highglow, a small estate Dom owned in the south. Dom intended to bring her to London for the Little Season, during the Christmas holidays. Anne did not doubt that he would have her fully accepted by everyone.

Blake was still a bachelor about town. Most of the ton's eligible ladies were madly in love with him, but he seemed oblivious, and showed no intention of settling down. Rumor held that his latest mistress was a very young Russian princess who had fallen upon bad times.

And there was no word from Patrick. But last week Anne had received a small paper-wrapped parcel from Belgium. There had been no sender's address on the package, and no correspondence with it. But inside she had found a delicate porcelain pillbox, shaped like a heart. She had not needed a sender's address or a letter

then to know who had sent her the gift. It had saddened her.

"A penny for your thoughts, Anne," Dom said in
her ear.

Anne was startled, but then Dom's arms went around
her and she melted against him, accepting his leisurely
kiss. Their mouths fused. Anne cupped Dom's head,
threading her fingers through his thick gold hair. When
they finally parted, they were smiling into one another's
eyes and absolutely breathless.

"You are no gentleman, Dom," Anne scolded. "Is
this why you sent me a note? Did you intend an illicit
rendezvous with your very proper wife?"

His dimples were deep, but he protested immediately.
"Whoa, Anne! You mean, your note to me, of course.
Clearly it is you who wishes an illicit rendezvous with
your dashing husband." He pulled her closer and began
to kiss and nibble her throat. "And I do protest, darling,
your use of the word *proper*."

Fiery sensation flooded Anne as she blushed. Her
knees buckled, her pulse quickened. Anne managed to
press against Dom's chest, stalling him. "You are a
dangerous man."

"Ummm." He bent and kissed her mouth quickly,
lightly. "But not half as dangerous as you, my dear."

Anne couldn't help but like that. "Am I a tempt-
ress, then?"

"Absolutely," he said, sliding his hands down her
hips. He was smiling and trying to kiss her mouth.

But Anne dodged. "Dom, I did not send you a
note."

He was nuzzling her cheek; he straightened.
"Really?"

Their glances met.

An inkling occurred to Anne. "Dom, darling, did
you not just send me a note suggesting that we meet
in this garden?"

He regarded her thoughtfully. "No, Anne, I did not. I received a note from you."

Anne eyes widened. "Darling, I did not send you a note."

His amber eyes were searching. "Anne, that night four years ago," he began.

"Yes," Anne said, "The night of your engagement to Felicity . . ."

"I received a note . . ."

"So did I . . ."

"I never wrote you a note that night," Dom said slowly.

"I never wrote you a note either," Anne said, as reflectively.

"And you did not send me this note now?" Dom pulled a piece of parchment out of his pocket.

"No, I did not. My handwriting is far more graceful than that!" Anne cried. She pulled the note she had just received out of her shirtwaist. "This looks like your handwriting, Dom," she stated.

He studied the note. "The signature is a good copy, but it is not mine," he finally said. Their gazes locked, held.

And suddenly he looked over his shoulder at the house.

Anne followed his gaze.

Across the terrace, they could clearly see the duke of Rutherford standing in one of the windows of the ballroom, gazing out at them.

Anne and Dom looked at one another. "My God," Dom said. "That cagey old man."

"Oh, Dom, to think that he arranged it all—that he brought us together!" Anne was overwhelmed. She pressed closer to Dom. "How I love him," she whispered.

Dom was also overcome. "If he hadn't tricked us into a rendezvous that night, I might now be married to Felicity," Dom whispered. He kissed the top of Anne's head. "Bless his clever soul."

Anne lifted her face to look up at him. "We owe him a great debt, Dom. Shall we go inside and tell him the wonderful news?"

Dom froze. "Anne?"

She smiled, tears of joy coming to her eyes. "It is confirmed. I saw Doctor Cobb today. I am with child, Dom. In fact, the doctor suspects I may be with twins."

Dom whooped, lifted Anne in his arms, and spun her around and around, her skirts whirling about them, until they were both laughing and crying and dizzy.

From inside the house, standing with a cane in the huge and silent ballroom where he had once reluctantly announced Dom's engagement to Felicity, the duke smiled at Dom and Anne.

He watched them hugging. Their love was so strong that it formed a visible and shining white halo around them. Tears of joy filled the duke's own eyes.

"All's well that ends well," the duke thought with a silent sigh. He was very pleased this day. And so, he knew, was Janice. He had never felt her presence more strongly than he did now, not even when he had been at Death's door. "Darling," he said aloud, "have a little more patience. I have a grandchild to greet. And then I will come to you."

Her loving touch was featherlight on his cheek. He thought he heard her whisper *"yes."*

The duke turned to leave the ballroom, eager to compose the announcement of his grandson's birth, even though it would be many months now before it could be printed. As he did so, he glimpsed Dom leading Anne farther into the garden, his arm around her, their hips brushing. The duke could not remember ever being happier.

Love had prevailed—on all fronts.